PENGUIN MODER

COLLECTED STORIES

Isaac Babel was born in Odessa in 1894, the son of
a Jewish tradesman. He published his first stories
in 1916. During the First World War he fought
with the Tsarist army and in 1917 went over to
the Bolsheviks. He served with the *Cheka* and later
with Budyonny's cavalry in Poland. He disappeared
in the purges of the 1930s and was rehabilitated in
1957. His fame rest mainly on his sketches of his
experiences in Poland and of the Jewish and
criminal communities in Odessa.

COLLECTED STORIES

ISAAC BABEL

—

Translated or revised by
Walter Morison
with an introduction by
Lionel Trilling

PENGUIN BOOKS

Penguin Books Ltd, Harmondsworth, Middlesex, England
Penguin Books, 625 Madison Avenue, New York, New York 10022, U.S.A.
Penguin Books Australia Ltd, Ringwood, Victoria, Australia
Penguin Books Canada Ltd, 2801 John Street, Markham, Ontario, Canada L3R 1B4
Penguin Books (N.Z.) Ltd, 182–190 Wairau Road, Auckland 10, New Zealand

—

First published by Criterion Books
Published in Great Britain by Methuen 1957
Published in Penguin Books 1961
Reissued in Penguin Modern Classics 1974
Reprinted 1983

—

—

Made and printed in Singapore by
Richard Clay (S.E.Asia) Pte Ltd
Set in Monotype Bembo

—

The stories in the section entitled Red Cavalry, *with the exception of 'Argamak',
were originally published in America in Nadia Helstein's translation and in
Great Britain in John Harland's translation by Alfred A. Knopf Inc., in 1929;
they have been revised by Walter Morison for this edition. 'The Sin of Jesus'
was translated by Mirra Ginsburg; 'First Love' by Esther and Joseph Riwkin;
and 'Guy de Maupassant' by Raymond Rosenthal and Waclaw Solski. All the
other stories have been translated by Walter Morison.*

*Acknowledgement is made to the following for their kind permission to reprint:
Alfred A. Knopf Inc., for the* Red Cavalry *stories; to Sylvan Press Ltd,
London, for 'The King'; to* Partisan Review *for 'The Sin of Jesus' and 'Guy
de Maupassant'; and to* Commentary *for 'First Love'.*

Contents

Contents

TALES OF ODESSA

STORIES

Contents

Introduction

A GOOD many years ago, in 1929, I chanced to read a book which disturbed me in a way I can still remember. The book was called *Red Cavalry;* it was a collection of stories about Soviet regiments of horse operating in Poland. I had never heard of the author, Isaac Babel – or I. Babel as he signed himself – and nobody had anything to tell me about him, and part of my disturbance was the natural shock we feel when, suddenly and without warning, we confront a new talent of great energy and boldness. But the book was disturbing for other reasons as well.

In those days one still spoke of the 'Russian experiment' and might still believe that the light of dawn glowed on the test-tubes and crucibles of human destiny. And it was still possible to have very strange expectations of the new culture that would arise from the Revolution. I do not remember what my own particular expectations were, except that they involved a desire for an art that would have as little ambiguity as a proposition in logic. Why I wanted this I don't wholly understand. It was as if I had hoped that the literature of the Revolution would realize some simple, inadequate notion of the 'classical' which I had picked up at college; and perhaps I was drawn to this notion of the classical because I was afraid of the literature of modern Europe, because I was scared of its terrible intensities, ironies, and ambiguities. If this is what I really felt, I can't say that I am now wholly ashamed of my cowardice. If we stop to think of the museum knowingness about art which we are likely to acquire with maturity, of our consumer's pride in buying only the very best spiritual commodities, the ones which are sure to give satisfaction, there may possibly be a grace in those moments when we lack the courage to confront, or the strength to endure, some particular work of art or kind of art. At any rate, here was Babel's book and I found it disturbing. It was obviously the most remarkable work of fiction that had yet come out of revolutionary Russia, the only work, indeed, that I knew of as having upon it the mark of exceptional talent, even of genius. Yet for me it was all too heavily charged with the intensity, irony, and ambiguousness from which I wished to escape.

There was anomaly at the very heart of the book, for the Red cavalry of the title were Cossack regiments, and why were Cossacks fighting for the Revolution, they who were the instrument and symbol of Tsarist repression? The author, who represented himself in the stories, was a Jew; and a Jew in a Cossack regiment was more than an anomaly, it was a joke, for between Cossack and Jew there existed not merely hatred but a polar opposition. Yet here was a Jew riding as a Cossack and trying to come to terms with the Cossack ethos. At that first reading it seemed to me – although it does not now – that the stories were touched with cruelty. They were about violence of the most extreme kind, yet they were composed with a striking elegance and precision of objectivity, and also with a kind of lyric *joy*, so that one could not at once know just how the author was responding to the brutality he recorded, whether he thought it good or bad, justified or not justified. Nor was this the only thing to be in doubt about. It was not really clear how the author felt about, say, Jews; or about religion; or about the goodness of man. He had – or perhaps, for the sake of some artistic effect, he pretended to have – a secret. This alienated and disturbed me. It was impossible not to be overcome by admiration for *Red Cavalry*, but it was not at all the sort of book that I had wanted the culture of the Revolution to give me.

And, as it soon turned out, it was not at all the sort of book that the Revolution wanted to give anyone. No event in the history of Soviet culture is more significant than the career, or, rather, the end of the career, of Isaac Babel. He had been a protégé of Gorky, and he had begun his career under the aegis of Trotsky's superb contempt for the pieties of the conventional 'proletarian' aesthetics. In the last years of the decade of the twenties and in the early thirties he was regarded as one of the most notable talents of Soviet literature. This judgement was, however, by no means an official one. From the beginning of his career, Babel had been under the attack of the literary bureaucracy. But in 1932 the Party abolished RAPP – the Russian Association of Proletarian Writers – and it seemed that a new period of freedom had been inaugurated. In point of fact, the reactionary elements of Soviet culture were established in full ascendancy, and the purge trials of 1937 were to demonstrate how absolute their power was. But in the five intervening years the Party chose to exercise its authority in a lenient manner. It was in this atmosphere of seeming liberality that the first Writer's Congress was held in 1934. Babel was one of the speakers at the Congress. He spoke with considerable jauntiness, yet he spoke as a penitent – the stories he had written since *Red Cavalry* had been published in a volume at the end of 1932 and since that time he had written nothing, he had disappointed expectation.

His speech was a strange performance.* It undertook to be humorous; the published report is punctuated by the indication of laughter. It made the avowals of loyalty that were by then routine, yet we cannot take it for granted that Babel was insincere when he spoke of his devotion to the Revolution, to the Government, and to the State, or when he said that in a bourgeois country it would inevitably have been his fate to go without recognition and livelihood. He may have been

---

* I am indebted to Professor Rufus Mathewson for the oral translation of Babel's speech which he made for me. Professor Mathewson was kindness itself in helping me to information about Babel; he is, of course, not accountable for any inaccuracy or awkwardness that may appear in my use of the facts.

sincere even when he praised Stalin's literary style, speaking of the sentences 'forged' as if of steel, of the necessity of learning to work in language as Stalin did. Yet beneath the orthodoxy of this speech there lies some hidden intention. One feels this in the sad vestiges of the humanistic mode that wryly manifest themselves. It is as if the humour, which is often of a whimsical kind, as if the irony and the studied self-depreciation, were forlorn affirmations of freedom and self-hood; it is as if Babel were addressing his fellow-writers in a dead language, or in some slang of their student days, which a few of them might perhaps remember.

Everything, he said at one point in his speech, is given to us by the Party and the Government; we are deprived of only one right, the right to write badly. 'Comrades,' he said, 'let us not fool ourselves: this is a very important right, and to take it away from us is no small thing.' And he said, 'Let us give up this right, and may God help us. And if there is no God, let us help ourselves. . . .'

The right to write badly – how precious it seems when once there has been the need to conceive of it! Upon the right to write badly depends the right to write at all. There must have been many in the audience who understood how serious and how terrible Babel's joke was. And there must have been some who had felt a chill at their hearts at another joke that Babel had made earlier in his address, when he spoke of himself as practising a new literary genre. This was the genre of silence – he was, he said, 'the master of the genre of silence'.

Thus he incriminated himself for his inability to work. He made reference to the doctrine that the writer must have respect for the reader, and he said that it was a correct doctrine. He himself, he said, had a very highly developed respect for the reader; so much so, indeed, that it might be said of him that he suffered from a hypertrophy of the faculty of respect – 'I have so much respect for the reader that I am dumb.' But now he takes a step beyond irony; he ventures to interpret, and by his interpretation to challenge, the official doctrines of 'respect for the reader'. The reader, he says, asks for bread, and he must indeed be given what he asks for – but not in the way he expects it; he ought to be surprised by what he gets; he ought not be given what he can easily recognize as 'a certified true copy' of life – the essence of art is unexpectedness.

The silence for which Babel apologized was not broken. In 1937 he was arrested. He died in a concentration camp in 1939 or 1940. It is not known for certain whether he was shot or died of typhus. Both accounts of the manner of his death have been given by people who were inmates of the camp at the time. Nor is it known for what specific reason he was arrested. Raymond Rosenthal, in an admirable essay on Babel published in *Commentary* in 1947, says, on good authority, that Babel did not undergo a purge but was arrested for having made a politically indiscreet remark. It has been said that he was arrested when Yagoda was purged, because he was having a love-affair with Yagoda's sister. It has also been said that he was accused of Trotskyism, which does indeed seem possible, especially if we think of Trotsky as not only a political but a cultural figure.

But no reason for the last stage of the extinction of Isaac Babel is needed beyond that which is provided by his stories, by their method and style. If ever we want to remind ourselves of the nature and power of art, we have only to think of how accurate reactionary governments are in their awareness of that nature and that power. It is not merely the content of art that they fear, not merely explicit doctrine, but whatever of energy and autonomy is implied by the aesthetic qualities a work may have. Intensity, irony, and ambiguousness, for example, constitute a clear threat to the impassivity of the State. They constitute a *secret*.

Babel was not a political man except as every man of

intelligence was political at the time of the Revolution. Except, too, as every man of talent or genius is political who makes his heart a battleground for conflicting tendencies of culture. In Babel's heart there was a kind of fighting – he was captivated by the vision of two ways of being, the way of violence and the way of peace, and he was torn between them. The conflict between the two ways of being was an essential element of his mode of thought. And when Soviet culture was brought under full discipline, the fighting in Babel's heart could not be permitted to endure. It was a subversion of discipline. It implied that there was more than one way of being. It hinted that one might live in doubt, that one might live by means of a question.

It is with some surprise that we become aware of the centrality of the cultural, the moral, the *personal* issue in Babel's work, for what strikes us first is the intensity of his specifically aesthetic preoccupation. In his schooldays Babel was passionate in his study of French literature; for several years he wrote his youthful stories in French, his chief masters being Flaubert and Maupassant. When, in an autobiographical sketch, he means to tell us that he began his mature work in 1923, he puts it that in that year he began to express his thoughts 'clearly, and not at great length'. This delight in brevity became his peculiar mark. When Eisenstein spoke of what it was that literature might teach the cinema, he said that 'Isaac Babel will speak of the extreme laconicism of literature's expressive means – Babel, who, perhaps, knows in practice better than anyone else that great secret, "that there is no iron that can enter the human heart with such stupefying effect, as a period placed at just the right moment."'* Babel's love of the laconic implies certain other elements of his aesthetic, his

* Eisenstein quotes from Babel's story, 'Guy de Maupassant'. The reference to Babel occurs in the essay of 1932, 'A Course in Treatment', in the volume *Film Form: Essays in Film Theory*, edited and translated by Jay Leyda, New York, 1949.

commitment (it is sometimes excessive) to *le mot juste*, to
the search for the word or phrase that will do its work with
a ruthless speed, and his remarkable powers of significant
distortion, the rapid foreshortening, the striking displacement
of interest and shift of emphasis – in general his pulling all
awry the arrangement of things as they appear in the 'certified
true copy'.

Babel's preoccupation with form, with the aesthetic surface,
is, we soon see, entirely at the service of his moral concern.
James Joyce has taught us the word *epiphany*, a showing forth
– Joyce had the 'theory' that suddenly, almost miraculously,
by a phrase or a gesture, a life would thrust itself through the
veil of things and for an instant show itself forth, startling us
by its existence. In itself the conception of the epiphany makes
a large statement about the nature of human life; it suggests
that the human fact does not dominate the scene of our
existence – for something to 'show forth' it must first be
hidden, and the human fact is submerged in and subordinated
to a world of circumstance, the world of things; it is known
only in glimpses, emerging from the danger or the sordidness
in which it is implicated. Those writers who by their practice
subscribe to the theory of the epiphany are drawn to a particular aesthetic. In the stories of Maupassant, as in those of
Stephen Crane, and Hemingway, and the Joyce of *Dubliners*,
as in those of Babel himself, we perceive the writer's intention
to create a form which shall in itself be shapely and auto-
nomous and at the same time unusually responsible to the
truth of external reality, the truth of things and events. To
this end he concerns himself with the given moment, and,
seeming almost hostile to the continuity of time, he presents
the past only as it can be figured in the present. In his commitment to event he affects to be indifferent to 'meanings' and
'values'; he seems to be saying that although he can tell us
with unusual accuracy what is going on, he does not presume
to interpret it, scarcely to understand it, certainly not to judge

it. He arranges that the story shall tell itself, as it were; or he tells it by means of a narrator who somehow makes it clear that he has no personal concern with the outcome of events – what I have called Babel's lyric joy in the midst of violence is in effect one of his devices for achieving the tone of detachment. We are not, of course, for very long deceived by the elaborate apparatus contrived to suggest the almost affectless detachment of the writer. We soon enough see what he is up to. His intense concern with the hard aesthetic surface of the story, his preoccupation with things and events, are, we begin to perceive, cognate with the universe, representative of its nature, of the unyielding circumstance in which the human fact exists; they make the condition for the epiphany, the showing forth; and the apparent denial of immediate pathos is a condition of the ultimate pathos the writer conceives.

All this, as I say, is soon enough apparent in Babel's stories. And yet, even when we have become aware of his pathos, we are, I think, surprised by the kind of moral issue that lies beneath the brilliant surface of the stories, beneath the lyric and ironic elegance – we are surprised by its elemental simplicity. We are surprised, too, by its passionate subjectivity, the intensity of the author's personal involvement, his defenceless commitment of himself to the issue.

The stories of *Red Cavalry* have as their principle of coherence what I have called the anomaly, or the joke of a Jew who is a member of a Cossack regiment – Babel was a supply officer under General Budyonny in the campaign of 1920. Traditionally the Cossack was the feared and hated enemy of the Jew. But he was more than that. The principle of his existence stood in total antithesis to the principle of the Jew's existence. The Jew conceived his own ideal character to consist in his being intellectual, pacific, humane. The Cossack was physical, violent, without mind or manners. When a Jew of Eastern Europe wanted to say what we mean by 'a bull in a china shop', he said 'a Cossack in a *succah*' – in, that is, one of the fragile decorated booths or tabernacles in which the meals of the harvest festival of *Succoth* are eaten: he intended an image of animal violence, of aimless destructiveness. And if the Jew was political, if he thought beyond his own ethnic and religious group, he knew that the Cossack was the enemy not only of the Jew – although that in special – but the enemy also of all men who thought of liberty; he was the natural and appropriate instrument of ruthless oppression.

There was, of course, another possible view of the Cossack, one that had its appeal for many Russian intellectuals, although it was not likely to win the assent of the Jew. Tolstoy had represented the Cossack as having a primitive energy, passion, and virtue. He was the man as yet untrammelled by civilization, direct, immediate, fierce. He was the man of enviable simplicity, the man of the body – and of the horse, the man who moved with speed and grace. We have devised an image of our lost freedom which we mock in the very phrase by which we name it: the noble savage. No doubt the mockery is justified, yet our fantasy of the noble savage represents a reality of our existence, it stands for our sense of something unhappily surrendered, the truth of the body, the truth of full sexuality, the truth of open aggressiveness. Something, we know, must inevitably be surrendered for the sake of civilization; but the 'discontent' of civilization which Freud describes is our self-recrimination at having surrendered too much. Babel's view of the Cossack was more consonant with that of Tolstoy than with the traditional view of his own people. For him the Cossack was indeed the noble savage, all too savage, not often noble, yet having in his savagery some quality that might raise strange questions in a Jewish mind.

I have seen three pictures of Babel, and it is a puzzle to know how he was supposed to look. The most convincing of the pictures is a photograph, to which the two official portrait sketches bear but little resemblance. The sketch which serves as the frontispiece to Babel's volume of stories of 1932 makes the author look like a Chinese merchant – his face is round, impassive, and priggish; his nose is low and flat; he stares through rimless glasses with immovable gaze. The sketch in the *Literary Encyclopedia* lengthens his face and gives him horn-rimmed spectacles and an air of amused and knowing assurance: a well-educated and successful Hollywood writer who has made the intelligent decision not to apologize for his profession except by his smile. But in the photograph the face is very long and thin, charged with emotion and internality; bitter, intense, very sensitive, touched with humour, full of consciousness and contradiction. It is 'typically' an intellectual's face, a scholar's face, and it has great charm. I should not want to speak of it as a Jewish face, but it is a kind of face which many Jews used to aspire to have, or hoped their sons would have. It was surely this face, or one much like it, that Babel took with him when he went among the Cossacks.

We can only marvel over the vagary of the military mind by which Isaac Babel came to be assigned as a supply officer to a Cossack regiment. He was a Jew of the ghetto. As a boy – so he tells us in his autobiographical stories – he had been of stunted growth, physically inept, subject to nervous disorders. He was an intellectual, a writer – a man, as he puts it in striking phrase, with spectacles on his nose and autumn in his heart. The orders that sent him to General Budyonny's command were drawn either by a conscious and ironical Destiny with a literary bent – or at his own personal request. For the reasons that made it bizarre that he should have been attached to a Cossack regiment are the reasons why he was there. He was there to be submitted to a test, he was there to be initiated. He was there because of the dreams of his boyhood. Babel's talent, like that of many modern writers, is rooted in the memory of boyhood, and Babel's boyhood was more than usually dominated by the idea of the test and the initiation. We might put it that Babel rode with a Cossack regiment because, when he was nine years old, he had seen his father kneeling before a Cossack captain who wore lemon-coloured chamois gloves and looked ahead with the gaze of one who rides through a mountain pass.

Isaac Babel was born in Odessa, in 1894. The years follow-ing the accession of Nicholas II were dark years indeed for the Jews of Russia. It was the time of the bitterest official anti-Semitism, of the Pale, of the Beilis trial, of the Black Hundreds and the planned pogroms. And yet in Odessa the Jewish community may be said to have flourished. Odessa was the great port of the Black Sea, an eastern Marseille or Naples, and in such cities the transient, heterogeneous popula-tion dilutes the force of law and tradition, for good as well as for bad. The Jews of Odessa were in some degree free to take part in the general life of the city. They were, to be sure, debarred from the schools, with but few exceptions. And they were sufficiently isolated when the passions of a pogrom swept the city. Yet all classes of the Jewish community seem to have been marked by a singular robustness and vitality, by a sense of the world, and of themselves in the world. The upper classes lived in affluence, sometimes in luxury, and it was possible for them to make their way into a Gentile society in which prejudice had been attenuated by cosmopolitanism. The intellectual life was of a particular energy, producing writers, scholars, and journalists of very notable gifts; it is in Odessa that modern Hebrew poetry takes its rise with Bialyk and Tchernokovsky. As for the lower classes, Babel himself represents them as living freely and heartily. In their ghetto, the Moldavanka, they were far more conditioned by their economic circumstances than by their religious ties; they were not at all like the poor Jews of the *shtetln*, the little towns of Poland, whom Babel was later to see. He represents them as characters of a Breughel-like bulk and brawn; they have large, coarse, elaborate nicknames; they are draymen and dairy-farmers; they are gangsters – the Jewish gangs of the Moldavanka were famous; they made upon the young Babel an ineradicable impression and to them he devoted a remarkable group of comic stories.

It was not Odessa, then, it was not even Odessa's ghetto, that forced upon Babel the image of the Jew as a man not in the actual world, a man of no body, a man of intellect, or wits, passive before his secular fate. Not even his image of the Jewish intellectual was substantiated by the Odessa actuality – Bialyk and Tchnernokovsky were anything but men with spectacles on their noses and autumn in their hearts, and no one who ever encountered in America the striking figure of Dr Chaim Tchernowitz, the great scholar of the Talmud and formerly the Chief Rabbi of Odessa, a man of Jovian port and large, free mind, would be inclined to conclude that there was but a single season of the heart available to a Jew of Odessa.

But Babel had seen his father on his knees before a Cossack captain on a horse, who said, 'At your service,' and touched his fur cap with his yellow-gloved hand and politely paid no heed to the mob looting the Babel store. Such an experience, or even a far milder analogue of it, is determinative in the life of a boy. Freud speaks of the effect upon him when, at twelve, his father told of having accepted in a pacific way the insult of having his new fur cap knocked into the mud by a Gentile who shouted at him, 'Jew, get off the pavement.' It is clear that Babel's relation with his father defined his relation to his Jewishness. Benya Krik, the greatest of the gangsters, he who was called King, was a Jew of Odessa, but he did not wear glasses and he did not have autumn in his heart – it is in writing about Benya that Babel uses the phrase that sets so far apart the intellectual and the man of action. The exploration of Benya's pre-eminence among gangsters does indeed take account of his personal endowment – Benya was a 'lion', a 'tiger', a 'cat'; he 'could spend the night with a Russian woman and satisfy her'. But what really made his fate was his having had Mendel Krik, the drayman, for his father. 'What does such a father think about? He thinks about drinking a good glass of vodka, of smashing somebody in the face, of his horses – and nothing more. You want to live and he makes you die twenty times a day. What would you have done in Benya Krik's place? You would have done nothing. But *he* did something. . . .' But Babel's father did not think about vodka, and smashing somebody in the face, and horses; he thought about large and serious things, among them respectability and fame. He was a shopkeeper, not well to do, a serious man, a failure. The sons of such men have much to prove, much to test themselves for, and, if they are Jewish, their Jewishness is ineluctably involved in the test.

Babel, in the brief autobiographical sketch to which I have referred, speaks with bitterness of the terrible discipline of his Jewish education. He thought of the Talmud Torah as a prison shutting him off from all desirable life, from reality itself. One of the stories he tells – conceivably the incident was invented to stand for his feelings about his Jewish schooling – is about his father's having fallen prey to the Messianic delusion which beset the Jewish families of Odessa, the belief that any one of them might produce a prodigy of the violin, a little genius who could be sent to be processed by Professor Auer in Petersburg, who would play before crowned heads in a velvet suit, and support his family in honour and comfort. Such miracles had occurred in Odessa, whence had come Elman, Zimbalist, Gabrilowitsch, and Heifetz. Babel's father hoped for wealth, but he would have foregone wealth if he could have been sure, at a minimum, of fame. Being small, the young Babel at fourteen might pass for eight and a prodigy. In point of fact, Babel had not even talent, and certainly no vocation. He was repelled by the idea of becoming a musical 'dwarf', one of the 'big-headed freckled children with necks as thin as flower stalks and an epilectic flush on their cheeks'. This was a Jewish fate and he fled from it, escaping to the port and the beaches of Odessa. Here he tried to learn to swim and could not: 'the hydrophobia of my ancestors – Spanish rabbis and Frankfurt money-changers – dragged me to the bottom.' But a kindly proof-reader, an elderly man who loved nature and children, took pity on him. 'How d'you mean, the water won't hold you? Why shouldn't it hold you?' – his specific gravity was no different from anybody else's and the good Yefim Nikitich Smolich taught him to swim. 'I came to love that man,' Babel says in one of the very few of his sentences over which no slightest irony plays, 'with the love that only a boy suffering from hysteria and headaches can feel for a real man.'

The story is called 'Awakening' and it commemorates the boy's first effort of creation. It is to Nikitich that he shows the tragedy he has composed and it is the old man who observes that the boy has talent but no knowledge of nature and undertakes to teach him how to tell one tree or one plant from another. This ignorance of the natural world – Babel refers to it again in his autobiographical sketch – was a Jewish handicap to be overcome. It was not an extravagance of Jewish self-consciousness that led him to make the generalization – Maurice Samuel remarks in *The World of Sholom Aleichem* that in the Yiddish vocabulary of the Jews of eastern Europe there are but two flower names (rose, violet) and no names for wild birds.

When it was possible to do so, Babel left his family and Odessa to live the precarious life, especially precarious for a Jew, of a Russian artist and intellectual. He went to Kiev and then, in 1915, he ventured to St Petersburg without a residence certificate. He was twenty-one. He lived in a cellar on Pushkin Street, and wrote stories which were everywhere refused until Gorky took him up and in 1916 published in his magazine two of Babel's stories. To Gorky, Babel said, he was indebted for everything. But Gorky became of the opinion that Babel's first stories were successful only by accident; he advised the young man to abandon the career of literature and to go 'among the people'. Babel served in the Tsar's army on the Rumanian front; after the Revolution he was for a time a member of the Cheka; he went on grain-collecting expeditions in 1918; he fought with the northern army against Yudenich. In 1920 he was with Budyonny in Poland, twenty-six years old, having seen much, having endured much, yet demanding initiation, submitting himself to the test.

The test, it is important to note, is not that of courage. Babel's affinity with Stephen Crane and Hemingway is close in many respects, of which not the least important is his feeling for his boyhood and for the drama of the boy's initiation into manhood. But the question that Babel puts to himself is not that which means so much to the two American writers; he does not ask whether he will be able to meet danger with honour. This he seems to know he can do. Rather, the test is of his power of direct and immediate, and violent, action – not whether he can endure being killed but whether he can endure killing. In the story 'After the Battle' a Cossack comrade is enraged against him not because, in the recent engagement, he had hung back, but because he had ridden with an unloaded revolver. The story ends with the narrator imploring fate to 'grant me the simplest of proficiencies – the ability to kill my fellow-men.'

The necessity for submitting to the test is very deeply rooted in Babel's psychic life. This becomes readily apparent when we read the whole of Babel's canon and perceive the manifest connexion between certain of the incidents of *Red Cavalry* and those of the stories of the Odessa boyhood. In the story 'My First Goose' the newcomer to the brigade is snubbed by the brilliant Cossack commander because he is a man with spectacles on his nose, an intellectual. 'Not a life

for the brainy type here,' says the quartermaster who carries
his trunk to his billet. 'But you go and mess up a lady, and a
good lady too, and you'll have the boys patting you on the
back. . . .' The five new comrades in the billet make it quite
clear that he is an outsider and unwanted, they begin at once
to bully and haze him. Yet by one action he overcomes their
hostility to him and his spectacles. He asks the old landlady for
food and she puts him off; whereupon he kills the woman's
goose in a particularly brutal manner, and, picking it up on
the point of a sword, thrusts it at the woman and orders her
to cook it. Now the crisis is passed; the price of community
has been paid. The group of five reforms itself to become a
group of six. All is decent and composed in the conduct of
the men. There is a general political discussion, then sleep.
'We slept, all six of us, beneath a wooden roof that let in the
stars, warming one another, our legs intermingled. I dreamed:
and in my dreams I saw women. But my heart, stained with
bloodshed, grated and brimmed over.' We inevitably read
this story in the light of Babel's two connected stories of the
1905 pogrom, 'The Story of My Dovecot' and 'First Love',
recalling the scene in which the crippled cigarette vendor,
whom all the children loved, crushes the boy's newly-bought
and long-desired pigeon and flings it in his face. Later the
pigeon's blood and entrails are washed from the boy's cheek
by the young Russian woman who is sheltering the Babel
family and whom the boy adores. It is after her caress that the
boy sees his father on his knees before the Cossack captain;
the story ends with his capitulation to nervous illness. And
now again a bird has been brutally killed, now again the
killing is linked with sexuality, but now it is not his bird but
another's, now he is not passive but active.

Yet no amount of understanding of the psychological
genesis of the act of killing the goose makes it easy for us to
judge it as anything more than a very ugly brutality. It is not
easy for us – and it is not easy for Babel. Not easy, but we must

make the effort to comprehend that for Babel it is not violence in itself that is at issue in his relation to the Cossacks, but something else, some quality with which violence does indeed go along, but which is not in itself merely violent. This quality, whatever it is to be called, is of the greatest importance in Babel's conception of himself as an intellectual and an artist, in his conception of himself as a Jew.

It is, after all, not violence and brutality that make the Cossacks what they are. This is not the first violence and brutality that Babel has known – when it comes to violence and brutality a Western reader can scarcely have, unless he sets himself to acquire it, an adequate idea of their place in the life of Eastern Europe. The impulse to violence, as we have learned, seems indigenous in all mankind. Among certain groups the impulse is far more freely licensed than among others. Americans are aware and ashamed of the actuality or potentiality of violence in their own culture, but it is nothing to that of the East of Europe; the people for whom the mass impalings and the knout are part of their memory of the exercise of authority over them have their own appropriate ways of expressing their rage. As compared with what the knife, or the home-made pike, or the boot can do, the revolver is an instrument of delicate amenity and tender mercy – this, indeed, is the point of one of Babel's stories. Godfrey Blunden's description of the method of execution used by the Ukrainian peasant bands is scarcely to be read. Nor is it only in combat that the tradition of ferocious violence appears, as is suggested by the long Russian concern with wife-beating as a national problem.

The point I would make is that the Cossacks were not exceptional for their violence. It was not their violence in itself that evoked Tolstoy's admiration. Nor is it what fascinated Babel. Rather he is drawn by what the violence goes along with, the boldness, the passionateness, the simplicity and directness – and the grace. Thus the story 'My First

Goose' opens with a description of the masculine charm of
the brigade commander Savitsky. His male grace is celebrated in a shower of epithet – we hear of the 'beauty of his
giant's body', of the decorated chest 'cleaving the hut as a
standard cleaves the sky', of 'the iron and flower of that
youthfulness', of his long legs, which were 'like girls sheathed
to the neck in shining riding boots'. Only the openness of
the admiration and envy – which consitutes, also, a qualifying
irony – keeps the description from seeming sexually perverse.
It is remarkably *not* perverse; it is as 'healthy' as a boy's love
of his hero of the moment. And Savitsky's grace is a real
thing. Babel is not ready to destroy it by any of the means
that are so ready to the hand of the intellectual confronted by
this kind of power and charm; he does not diminish the glory
he perceives by confronting it with the pathos of human
creatures less physically glorious, having more, or a higher,
moral appeal because they are weaker and because they suffer.
The possibility of this grace is part of what Babel saw in the
Cossacks.

It is much the same thing that D. H. Lawrence was drawn
by in his imagination of archaic cultures and personalities
and of the ruthlessness, even the cruelty, that attended their
grace. It is what Yeats had in mind in his love of 'the old
disturbed exalted life, the old splendour'. It is what even the
gentle Forster represents in the brilliant scene in *Where Angels
Fear to Tread* in which Gino, the embodiment of male grace,
tortures Stephen by twisting his broken arm. This fantasy of
personal, animal grace, this glory of conscienceless self-
assertion, of sensual freedom, haunts our culture. It speaks to
something in us that we fear, and rightly fear, yet it speaks
to us.

Babel never for a moment forgets what the actualities of
this savage glory are. In the story 'The Brigade Commander'
he speaks of the triumph of a young man in his first command.
Kolesnikov in his moment of victory had the 'masterful

indifference of a Tartar Khan', and Babel, observing him with genuine pleasure, goes on to say that he was conscious of the training of other famous leaders of horse, and mentions 'the captivating Savitsky' and 'the headstrong Pavlichenko'. The captivating Savitsky we have met. The headstrong Pavlichenko appears in a story of his own; this story is his own account of his peasant origin, of the insults received from his aristocratic landlord, of how when the Revolution came, he had wiped out the insult. 'Then I stamped on my master Nikitinsky; trampled on him for an hour or maybe more. And in that time I got to know life through and through. With shooting . . . you only get rid of a chap. Shooting's letting him off, and too damn easy for yourself. With shooting you'll never get at the soul, to where it is in a fellow and how it shows itself. But I don't spare myself, and I've more than once trampled an enemy for over an hour. You see, I want to get to know what life really is. . . .' This is all too *raffiné* – we are inclined, I think, to forget Pavlichenko and to be a little revolted by Babel. Let us suppose, however, that he is setting down the truth as he heard it; let us suppose too that he has it in mind not to spare himself – this is part, and a terrible part, of the actuality of the Cossack directness and immediacy, this is what goes along with the grace and charm.*

In our effort to understand Babel's complex involvement with the Cossack ethos we must be aware of the powerful and obsessive significance that violence has for the intellectual. Violence is, of course, the contradiction of the intellectual's characteristic enterprise of rationality. Yet at the same time

* The celebration of the Cossack ethos gave no satisfaction to General Budyonny, who, when some of Babel's *Red Cavalry* stories appeared in a magazine before their publication in a volume, attacked Babel furiously and with a large display of literary pretentiousness, for the cultural corruption and political ignorance which, he claimed, the stories displayed. Budyonny conceived the stories to constitute a slander on the Cossacks.

it is the very image of that enterprise. This may seem a strange thing to say. Since Plato we have set violence and reason over against each other in reciprocal negation. Yet it is Plato who can tell us why there is affinity between violence and the intellectual life. In the most famous of the Platonic myths, the men of the Cave are seated facing the interior wall of the Cave, and they are chained by their necks so that it is impossible for them to turn their heads. They can face in but one direction, they can see nothing but the shadows that are cast on the wall by the fire behind them. A man comes to them who has somehow freed himself and gone into the world outside the Cave. He brings them news of the light of the sun; he tells them that there are things to be seen which are real, that what they see on the wall is but shadows. Plato says that the men chained in the Cave will not believe this news. They will insist that it is not possible, that the shadows are the only reality. But suppose they do believe the news! Then how violent they will become against their chains as they struggle to free themselves so that they may perceive what they believe is there to be perceived. They will think of violence as part of their bitter effort to know what is real. To grasp, to seize – to *apprehend*, as we say – reality from out of the deep dark cave of the mind – this is indeed a very violent action.

The artist in our time is perhaps more overtly concerned with the apprehension of reality than the philosopher is, and the image of violence seems often an appropriate way of representing the nature of his creation. 'The language of poetry naturally falls in with the language of power,' says Hazlitt in his lecture on *Coriolanus* and goes on to speak in several brilliant passages of 'the logic of the imagination and the passions' which makes them partisan with representations of proud strength. Hazlitt carries his generalization beyond the warrant of literary fact, yet all that he says is pertinent to Babel, who almost always speaks of art in the language of force. The unexpectedness which he takes to be the essence of art is that of a surprise attack. He speaks of the manoeuvres of prose, of 'the army of words, . . . the army in which all kinds of weapons may be brought into play.' In one of his most remarkable stories, 'Di Grasso', he describes the performance of a banal play given by an Italian troupe in Odessa; all is dreariness until in the third act the hero sees his betrothed in converse with the villainous seducer, and, leaping miraculously, with the power of levitation of a Nijinsky or a panther, he soars across the stage, falls upon the villain and tears out his enemy's throat with his teeth. This leap makes the fortune of the Italian company with the exigent Odessa audience; this leap, we are given to understand, is art. And as the story continues, Babel is explicit – if also ironic – in what he demonstrates of the moral effect that may be produced by this virtuosity and power, of what it implies of human pride and freedom.

The spectacles on his nose were for Babel of the first importance in his conception of himself. He was a man to whom the perception of the world outside the Cave came late and had to be apprehended, by strength and speed, against the parental or cultural interdiction, the Jewish interdiction; it was as if every beautiful violent phrase that was to spring upon reality was a protest against his childhood. The violence of the Revolution, its sudden leap, was cognate with this feral passion for perception – to an artist the Revolution might well have seemed the rending not only of the social but of the perceptual chains, those that held men's gaze upon the shadows on the wall; it may have seemed the rush of men from the darkness of the cave into the light of reality. Something of this is suggested in a finely wrought story 'Line and Colour' – like other stories of the time of Babel's sojourn in France in the early thirties, it was written in French – in which Kerensky is represented as defending his myopia, refusing to wear glasses, because, as he argues very charmingly, there is so much that myopia protects him from seeing, and imagination and benign illusion are thus given a larger licence. But at a great meeting in the first days of the Revolution he cannot perceive the disposition of the crowd and the story ends with Trotsky coming to the rostrum and saying in his implacable voice, 'Comrades!'

But when we have followed Babel into the depths of his experience of violence, when we have imagined something of what is meant in his psychic life and in the developing conception of his art, we must be no less aware of his experience of the principle that stands opposed to the Cossack principle.

We can scarcely fail to see that when in the stories of *Red Cavalry* Babel submits the ethos of the intellectual to the criticism of the Cossack ethos, he intends a criticism of his own ethos not merely as an intellectual but as a Jew. It is always as an intellectual, never as a Jew, that he is denounced by his Cossack comrades, but we know that he has either suppressed, for political reasons, the denunciations of him as a Jew that were actually made, or, if none were actually made, that he has in his heart supposed that they were made. These criticisms of the Jewish ethos, as he embodies it, Babel believes to have no small weight. When he implores fate to grant him the simplest of proficiencies, the ability to kill his fellow-man, we are likely to take this as nothing but an irony, and as an ironic assertion of the superiority of his moral instincts. But it is only in part an irony. There comes a moment when he should kill a fellow-man. In 'The Death of Dolgushov', a comrade lies propped against a tree; he cannot be moved, inevitably he must die, for his entrails are hanging out; he must be left behind and he asks for a bullet in his head so that the Poles will not 'play their dirty tricks' on him. It is the narrator whom he asks for the *coup de grâce*, but the narrator flees and sends a friend, who, when he has done what had to be done, turns on the 'sensitive' man in a fury of rage and disgust: 'You bastards in spectacles have about as much pity for us as a cat has for a mouse.' Or again, the narrator has incurred the enmity of a comrade through no actual fault – no moral fault – of his own, merely through having been assigned a mount that the other man passionately loved, and riding it badly so that it developed saddle galls. Now the horse has been returned, but the man does not forgive him, and the narrator asks a superior officer to compound the quarrel. He is rebuffed. 'You're trying to live without enemies,' he is told. 'That's all you think about, not having enemies.' It comes at us with momentous force. This time we are not misled into supposing that Babel intends irony and a covert praise of his pacific soul; we know that in this epiphany of his refusal to accept enmity he means to speak adversely of himself in his Jewish character.

But his Jewish character is not the same as the Jewish character of the Jews of Poland. To these Jews he comes with all the presuppositions of an acculturated Jew of Russia, which were not much different from the suppositions of an acculturated Jew of Germany. He is repelled by the conditions of their life; he sees them as physically uncouth and warped; many of them seem to him to move 'monkey-fashion'. Sometimes he affects a wondering alienation from them, as when he speaks of 'the occult crockery that the Jews use only once a year at Eastertime'. His complexity and irony being what they are, the Jews of Poland are made to justify the rejection of the Jews among whom he was reared and the wealthy assimilated Jews of Petersburg. 'The image of the stout and jovial Jews of the South, bubbling like cheap wine, takes shape in my memory, in sharp contrast to the bitter scorn inherent in these long bony backs, these tragic yellow beards.' Yet the Jews of Poland are more than a stick with which Babel beats his own Jewish past. They come to exist for him as a spiritual fact of consummate value.

Almost in the degree that Babel is concerned with violence

in the stories of *Red Cavalry*, he is concerned with spirituality. It is not only Jewish sprituality that draws him. A considerable number of the stories have to do with churches, and although they do indeed often express the anticlerical feeling expectable in the revolutionary circumstances, the play of Babel's irony permits him to respond in a positive way to the aura of religion. 'The breath of an invisible order of things,' he says in one story, 'glimmered beneath the crumbling ruin of the priest's house, and its soothing seduction unmanned me.' He is captivated by the ecclesiastical painter Pan Apolek, he who created ecclesiastical scandals by using the publicans and sinners of the little towns as the models for his saints and virgins. Yet it is chiefly the Jews who speak to him of the life beyond violence, and even Pan Apolek's 'heretical and intoxicating brush' had achieved its masterpiece in his Christ of the Berestechko church, 'the most extraordinary image of God I had ever seen in my life,' a curly-headed Jew, a bearded figure in a Polish great-coat of orange, barefooted with torn and bleeding mouth, running from an angry mob with a hand raised to ward off a blow.

Hazlitt, in the passage to which I have referred, speaking of the 'logic of the imagination and the passions', says that we are naturally drawn to the representation of what is strong and proud and feral. Actually that is not so: we are, rather, drawn to the representation of what is real. It was reality that Babel found in the Jews of the Polish provinces. 'In these passionate, anguish-chiselled features there is no fat, no warm pulsing of blood. The Jews of Volhynia and Galicia move jerkily, in an uncontrolled and uncouth way; but their capacity for suffering is full of a sombre greatness, and their unvoiced contempt for the Polish gentry unbounded.'

Here was the counter-image to the captivating Savitsky, the image of the denial of the pride of the glory of the flesh to which, early or late, every artist comes, to which he cannot come in full sincerity unless he can also make full affirmation of the glory. Here too is the image of art that is counter to Di Grasso's leap, to the language in arms – the image of the artist's suffering, patience, uncouthness, and scorn.

If Babel's experience with the Cossacks may be understood as having reference to the boy's relation to his father, his experience of the Jews of Poland has, we cannot but feel, a maternal reference. To the one Babel responds as a boy, to the other as a child. In the story 'Gedali' he speaks with open sentimentality of his melancholy on the eve of Sabbaths – 'On those evenings my child's heart was rocked like a little ship upon enchanted waves. O the rotted Talmuds of my childhood! O the dense melancholy of memories.' And when he has found a Jew, it is one who speaks to him in this fashion: '. . . All is mortal. Only the mother is destined to immortality. And when the mother is no longer living, she leaves a memory which none yet has dared to sully. The memory of the mother nourishes in us a compassion that is like the ocean, and the measureless ocean feeds the rivers that dissect the universe.'

He has sought Gedali in his gutted curiosity-shop ('Where was your kindly shade that evening, Dickens?') to ask for 'a Jewish glass of tea, and a little of that pensioned-off God in a glass of tea'. He does not, that evening, get what he asks for; what he does get is a discourse on revolution, on the impossibility of a revolution made in blood, on the International that is never to be realized, the International of the good.

It was no doubt the easier for Babel to respond to the spiritual life of the Jews of Poland because it was a life coming to its end and having about it the terrible strong pathos of its death. He makes no pretence that it could ever claim him for its own. But it established itself in his heart as an image, beside the image of the other life that also could not claim him, the Cossack life. The opposition of these two images made his art – but it was not a dialectic that his Russia could permit.

LIONEL TRILLING

RED CAVALRY

The stories in Red Cavalry *are based on Babel's experiences during the Russo-Polish Campaign of 1920 when he served in Budyonny's cavalry. They describe the Cossack cavalry and the towns of eastern Poland during the short-lived Russian occupation of that territory.*

Crossing into Poland

THE Commander of the VI Division reported: Novograd-Volynsk was taken at dawn today. The Staff had left Krapivno and our baggage train was spread out in a noisy rearguard over the highroad from Brest to Warsaw built by Nicholas I upon the bones of peasants.

Fields flowered around us, crimson with poppies; a noontide breeze played in the yellowing rye; on the horizon virginal buckwheat rose like the wall of a distant monastery. The Volyn's peaceful stream moved away from us in sinuous curves and was lost in the pearly haze of the birch-groves; crawling between flowery slopes, it wound weary arms through a wilderness of hops. The orange sun rolled down the sky like a lopped-off head, and mild light glowed from the cloud-gorges. The standards of the sunset flew above our heads. Into the cool of evening dripped the smell of yesterday's blood, of slaughtered horses. The blackened Zbruch roared, twisting itself into foamy knots at the falls. The bridges were down, and we waded across the river. On the waves rested a majestic moon. The horses were in to the cruppers, and the noisy torrent gurgled among hundreds of horses' legs. Somebody sank, loudly defaming the Mother of God. The river was dotted with the square black patches of the wagons, and was full of confused sounds, of whistling and singing that rose above the gleaming hollows, the serpentine trails of the moon.

Far on in the night we reached Novograd. In the house where I was billeted I found a pregnant woman and two red-haired, scraggy-necked Jews. A third, huddled to the wall with his head covered up, was already asleep. In the room I was given I discovered turned-out wardrobes, scraps of women's fur coats on the floor, human filth, fragments of the occult crockery the Jews use only once a year, at Eastertime.

'Clear this up,' I said to the woman. 'What a filthy way to live!' The two Jews rose from their places and, hopping on their felt soles, cleared the mess from the floor. They skipped about noiselessly, monkey-fashion, like Japs in a circus act, their necks swelling and twisting. They put down for me a feather bed that had been disembowelled, and I lay down by the wall next to the third Jew, the one who was asleep. Faint-hearted poverty closed in over my couch.

Silence overcame all. Only the moon, clasping in her blue hands her round, bright, carefree face, wandered like a vagrant outside the window.

I kneaded my numbed legs and, lying on the ripped-open mattress, fell asleep. And in my sleep the Commander of the VI Division appeared to me; he was pursuing the Brigade Commander on a heavy stallion, fired at him twice between the eyes. The bullets pierced the Brigade Commander's head, and both his eyes dropped to the ground. 'Why did you turn back the brigade?' shouted Savitsky, the Divisional Commander, to the wounded man – and here I woke up, for the pregnant woman was groping over my face with her fingers.

'Good sir,' she said, 'you're calling out in your sleep and you're tossing to and fro. I'll make you a bed in another corner, for you're pushing my father about.'

She raised her thin legs and rounded belly from the floor and removed the blanket from the sleeper. Lying on his back was an old man, a dead old man. His throat had been torn out and his face cleft in two; in his beard blue blood was clotted like a lump of lead.

'Good sir,' said the Jewess, shaking up the feather bed, 'the Poles cut his throat, and he begging them: "Kill me in the yard so that my daughter shan't see me die." But they did as suited them. He passed away in this room, thinking of me. – And now I should wish to know,' cried the woman with sudden and terrible violence, 'I should wish to know where in the whole world you could find another father like my father?'

The Church at Novograd

I SET out yesterday to report to the Army Commissar, who had set up shop in the house of a fugitive Catholic priest. In the kitchen I was met by Pani* Eliza, the Jesuit's housekeeper, who set before me amber-coloured tea and spongecakes. Those sponges of hers had an odour of crucifixes. A subtle juice was in them, together with the aromatic fierceness of the Vatican.

Pulled by some distraught ringer, bells yelled in the church next to the house. It was an evening filled with July stars. Shaking her grey head and all attention, Pani Eliza kept filling my plate with pastries, and I enjoyed the food of Jesuits.

The old Polish woman addressed me as 'Pan': in the doorway grey-headed old men with ossified ears stood as if on parade, and somewhere in the snaky twilight a monk's cassock flitted. The priest had fled, but he had left behind his assistant, Pan Romuald.

This Romuald, a eunuch with a giant's body and a nasal twang, honoured us with the title of 'comrades'. He drew a yellow finger over the map, tracing the circles of the Polish débâcle; seized with a hoarse enthusiasm, he enumerated his country's wounds. May mild oblivion swallow up the memory of Romuald, of him who betrayed us without pity and fell to an incidental shot. But that evening his narrow cassock stirred at every door-hanging, swept tumultuously

* Polish for 'madame, lady'; feminine of *Pan*, 'sir, gentlemen, master, Mr'.

along every passage, smiling at all who wished to drink vodka. That evening the monk's shadow followed me about persistently. He would have become a bishop, this Pan Romuald, had he not been a spy.

I drank rum with him. The breath of an invisible order of things glimmered beneath the crumbling ruin of the priest's house, and its soothing seduction unmanned me. O crucifixes, tiny as the talismans of light ladies; parchment of Papal Bulls; satin of feminine letters rotting in the blue silk of waistcoats!

I can see you now, faithless monk, in your mauve cassock, with your plump hands and your soul as gentle and pitiless as the soul of a cat; I can see the wounds of your god oozing seed, a fragrant poison to intoxicate virgins.

We drank rum, expecting the Commissar, but still he did not return from the Staff. Romuald dropped in a corner and fell asleep. He started fitfully in his sleep, while beyond the window the garden path shimmered beneath a black and passionate sky. Thirsty roses swayed in the darkness. Flashes of green lightning blazed amid the cupolas. A corpse bereft of clothing lay huddled down the slope. Moonbeams slanted over thin legs thrust wide apart.

Here is Poland, here is the proud distress of the *Res Publica*! And I, a violent intruder, spread out a lousy mattress in a church abandoned by its priest, and placed beneath my head folios in which were printed hosannas to the Most Excellent and Illustrious Head of State, Joseph Pilsudski.

Hordes of paupers roll toward your ancient cities, O Poland, and above them thunders the serfs' chant of union. Woe unto you, *Res Publica*; woe unto you, Prince Radziwill, and unto you, Prince Sapieha, risen for the space of an hour!

Still my Commissar did not appear. I looked for him at the Staff, in the garden, in the church. The church gates were open; I entered, and to meet me two silvery skulls gleamed on the lid of a broken coffin. Frightened, I dashed down into the crypt. An oak staircase led thence to the altar. And I saw a multitude of lights darting about, high up in the very dome. I saw the Commissar, the Chief of the Special Section, Cossacks with candles in their hands. They answered my feeble cry and led me up out of the basement.

The skulls, proving to be carvings on a catafalque, no longer alarmed me; and all together we continued the search – for search it was – begun after the discovery of piles of army outfits in the priest's house.

Flashing the horses's heads embroidered on our cuffs, whispering to one another, and clanging our spurs, we went around and around the echoing temple, guttering tapers in our hands. Many a Virgin Mary studded with precious stones followed us on our way with pupils pink like the eyes of mice. The flames fluttered in our fingers, and rectangular shadows writhed on the statues of St Paul, St Francis, St Vincent, on their little rosy cheeks, their curly beards touched up with carmine.

We went around and around, searching. Bone buttons sprang beneath our fingers, icons split down the middle and opened out, revealing subterranean passages and mildewed caverns. The temple was an ancient one, and full of secrets. In its glossy walls lay hidden passages, niches, doors that moved noiselessly aside.

O foolish priest, to hang the bodices of your parishioners upon the nails in the Saviour's cross! In the Holy of Holies we found a trunk with gold coins, a morocco-leather bag with banknotes, Parisian jewellers' cases filled with emerald rings.

Later on in the Commissar's room we counted the money. Piles of gold, carpets of paper money, a gusty wind blowing upon the candles, the birdlike bewilderment in Pani Eliza's eyes, Romuald's thundering guffaws, and the incessant yelling of the bells set pealing by Pan Robacki, the crazed bell-ringer.

'Away!' I said to myself. 'Away from these ogling Madonnas deceived by common soldiers!'

A Letter

HERE is a letter home that was dictated to me by Kurdyukov, a lad in our special group. It does not deserve to be forgotten. I have copied it out without improving on anything, and give it word for word exactly as it read:

Dear Mother, Evdokia Fyodorovna,
    In the first lines of this letter I hasten to let you know that, thanks to the Lord, I am alive and well which I would like to hear the same from you. And also I bow very humbly to you all. (Here follows an enumeration of relatives, godparents and the like. Let's leave that out and go on to the second paragraph.)
    Dear Mother, Evdokia Fyodorovna Kurdyukova, I hasten to write to you that I am in Comrade Budyonny's Red Cavalry Army, and here also is your gossip Nikon Vasilyich who is at the present moment a Red Hero. They took me into the Political Section, where we distribute literature and news-papers – the *Izvestia* of the Moscow Central Executive Com-mittee, the Moscow *Pravda*, and our own merciless paper the *Red Trooper*, which every fighting-man in the front lines wants to read, and after that with heroic spirit he hews down the Poles, and I am living with Nikon Vasilyich in magnificent style.
    Dear Mother, Evdokia Fyodorovna, send me whatever you can possibly manage. I beg you to kill the little speckled boar and send me a hamper to Comrade Budyonny's Political Section to the name Vasily Kurdyukov. Every day I lie down to rest without having eaten and without spare clothing, so that it's pretty cold. Write me a letter about my Steve, to say if he's living or not. I beg you to look after him and write me

about him, does he stumble still or has he stopped now? And also about the mange on his forelegs; has he been shod or not? I beg you, Dear Mother, wash without fail his forelegs with the soap I left behind the holy images, and if Dad has used up the soap then buy some more in Krasnodar and God won't ever abandon you. I can also write to you that the country hereabouts is quite poor, the peasants hide themselves from our Red eagles with their horses in the woods, there isn't much wheat about and what there is is pretty poor, it makes us laugh. They sow rye and also oats. Hops grow on sticks here so that it comes out very even. They make home-brewed vodka with them.

In the second lines of this letter I hasten to describe to you about Dad, that he killed my brother Theodore a year ago. Our Red brigade was advancing under Comrade Pavlichenko on the town of Rostov when treason took place in our ranks. Dad was then with General Denikin, commanding a company. Them as saw him said he wore medals on him like under the old régime. And they took us all prisoners because of that treason and my brother Theodore came to Dad's notice. And Dad began cutting him about, saying: 'Brute, Red cur, son of a bitch,' and all sorts of other things, and went on cutting him about until it grew dark and Theodore passed away. I wrote you a letter at the time how your Theo lies without a cross to mark his grave. But Dad caught me with the letter and said: 'You, your mother's children, you of her root, the slut, I got her with child and I'll go on getting her with child, my life is done for, I'll wipe out my seed for the sake of justice,' and various other things. I bore suffering from him like the Saviour Jesus Christ. Only I soon ran away from Dad and managed to get to my unit under Comrade Pavlichenko. And our brigade was ordered to the town of Voronezh to have its numbers made up, and we got reinforcements there, also horses, knapsacks, revolvers, and all we ought to have. About Voronezh I can write to you, Dear Mother, that the

43

town is a jolly fine one, a bit bigger than Krasnodar. The people in it are very good-looking, the river is all right for bathing. They gave us two pounds of bread a day, half a pound of meat, and the right quantity of sugar so that we drank tea with sugar when we got up and the same in the evening and forgot about hunger, but for dinner I used to go to brother Simon's place to eat pancakes or goose and after that I used to lie down and rest. At that time the whole regiment wanted to have Simon as commander because of his boldness, and an order to this effect came from Comrade Budyonny, and he got two horses, decent clothes, and a wagon to himself for his gear and the order of the Red Banner, and I counted as his brother when I was with him. So now if a neighbour starts giving you trouble, brother Simon is quite equal to settling his hash. Then we began to pursue General Denikin, and killed thousands of them, and drove them into the Black Sea. Only Dad was nowhere to be seen and Simon looked everywhere for him because he missed brother Theo very much. Only, Dear Mother, you know Dad and his pig-headed character, so what d'you think he did? He dyed his beard shamelessly from red to black and was staying in the town of Maykop in civvies so that none of the inhabitants knew that he was the same as was a cop under the old régime. But the truth will out, your gossip Nikon Vasilyich happened to see him in the house of one of the inhabitants and wrote a letter to Simon. We got on our horses and did two hundred versts – I, brother Simon, and the fellows from our settlement who wanted to come along too.

And what did we see in the town of Maykop? We saw there that the rear was not of the same mind as the front and that everywhere was treachery and full of dirty Yids like under the old régime, and Simon gave the dirty Yids a rough time of it for not handing Dad over but putting him under lock and key in prison, saying as an order had come from

A Letter

Comrade Trotsky not to kill prisoners and saying we'll judge him ourselves, don't you worry, he'll get what he deserves. Only Simon took what was his due and proved that he was in command of a regiment and had got from Comrade Budyonny all the orders of the Red Banner and threatened to kill them all as made a fuss about Dad's person and wouldn't give him up, and the boys from the settlement threatened too. But Simon got Dad all right and he began to whip Dad and lined up all the fighting-men in the yard according to army custom. Then Simon dashed water over Dad's beard, and asked him:

'You all right, Dad, in my hands?'

'No,' says Dad, 'not all right.'

Then Simon said: 'And Theo, was he all right in your hands when you killed him?'

'No,' says Dad. 'Things went badly for Theo.'

Then Simon asked: 'And did you think, Dad, that things would go badly for you?'

'No,' says Dad, 'I didn't think things would go badly for me.'

Then Simon turned to us all and said: 'And what I think is that if I got caught by his boys, there wouldn't be no quarter for me. – And now, Dad, we're going to finish you off . . .'

And Dad started to swear shamelessly at Simon, bringing in the Mother of God, and beating Simon about the face, and Simon sent me away so that I can't describe to you, Dear Mother, how they finished off Dad, because I was sent off.

After that we were quartered in the town of Novorossiisk. About that town it can be said that there isn't any dry land on the other side of it but only water, the Black Sea, and we stayed there right on till May, when we left for the Polish front, and now we're making the *pans* shake in their shoes.

I remain your loving son
Vasily Timofeyich Kurdyukov

45

Mum, do look after Steve and God won't ever abandon you.

Such is Kurdyukov's letter, not a single word having been altered. When I had finished it he took the written sheet and put it away in his breast, against his bare skin.

'Kurdyukov,' I questioned the boy, 'was your father a bad man?'

'My father was a dog,' was his surly reply.

'And your mother – better?'

'Mother's all right. If you'd like to see, here's our family.'

He handed me a broken photograph. It depicted Timofey Kurdyukov, a broad-shouldered rural policeman sporting a uniform cap and a beard parted in the middle – an inert figure with prominent cheekbones and the bright stare of vacant and colourless eyes. Next to him, in a little bamboo armchair and wearing a loose jacket, sat a tiny peasant woman with clear, timid, and emaciated features. And against the wall, against that wretched provincial photographer's background of flowers and doves, stiff as on the parade-ground towered two lads, the two monstruously tall, dull, broad-faced, goggle-eyed Kurdyukov brothers, Theodore and Simon.

The Remount Officer

THERE was a moaning in the village. The cavalry, trampling the crops, was changing horses. In exchange for their tired hacks, the troopers were confiscating draught-horses. Nobody was to blame. There can be no army without horses.

But that knowledge did not make things any easier for the peasants. They crowded importunately around the Staff building, pulling after them their nags that stumbled with exhaustion and dragged at the ropes.

Deprived of their breadwinners, feeling well up in them a courage born of bitterness which they knew could not last long, the peasants hastened to cry out hopelessly against the authorities, against God and their own wretched lot.

Zh—, the chief Staff Officer, in full uniform, stood at the top of the steps in front of the building. Shielding his inflamed eyelids, he listened with obvious attention to the peasants' complaints. But this obvious attention was nothing but a way he had. Like every experienced and overstrained worker, he knew how to stop all brainwork during the idle moments of existence. During those rare moments of blissful vacancy our Staff Commander wound up his worn-out mechanism.

So it was then, with the peasants.

To the soothing accompaniment of their incoherent and despairing clamour Zh—, aloof, took note of the gentle pulsing in his brain which foreboded clearness and energy of thought. Feeling at length the right beat, he snatched the last peasant tear-drop, snarled at them in the true commander's way, and went back to Headquarters to work.

This time there was no need to snarl. Up to the very steps galloped Dyakov on his fiery Anglo-Arabian – Dyakov, who had formerly been an athlete in a circus and was now a red-faced, grey-moustached remount officer with a black cloak and silver stripes down his wide red trousers.

'The Father Superior's blessing upon all honest black-guards!' he shouted, pulling his mount up at full gallop.

At that moment there rolled over beneath his stirrup a wretched-looking jade, one of those that had been given in exchange by the Cossacks.

'There, comrade commander,' wailed a peasant, clapping himself on his trousers, 'there, that's what you fellows give folk like us. You see what they give us? You try working with her.'

'For that mount, though,' Dyakov began, very distinctly and weightily, 'for that mount, my honourable friend, you are fully entitled to receive fifteen thousand roubles from the remount authorities, and if that mount were a little friskier, you would receive twenty thousand from the remount authorities. As for the mount falling – that's not a fact. If a mount falls and gets up again, then it's a mount. If, to put it the other way round, if it don't well then it isn't. But this nice little filly, you'll see, will get up for me.'

'O Lord, merciful mother of mine!' And the peasant waved his arms about. 'How's the poor orphan to get up? She'll go and die, the poor orphan!'

'You're insulting the mount,' replied Dyakov with profound conviction. 'As good as blaspheming, that's what you're doing, my lad.' And he swung his well-proportioned athlete's body skilfully out of the saddle. Straightening his perfect legs, caught at the knee with a small strap, he went with circus agility over to the moribund animal.

It fixed wide, deep eyes on Dyakov and licked from his ruddy palm a sort of imperceptible injunction. Immediately the exhausted beast felt a dexterous strength flowing from the bald and vigorous Romeo in the prime of life. Straightening its head and slithering on its staggering legs at the impatient and imperious flicking of the whip on its belly, the jade got up, slowly and warily.

Then we saw a delicate wrist in a wide, flowing sleeve patting the dirty mane, and perceived how the whip cracked whining against the bloodstained flanks. Her whole body trembling, the jade stood on her legs, her doglike eyes, filled with love and fear, never for an instant leaving Dyakov's face.

'That means she's a mount,' said Dyakov to the peasants, adding gently: 'And you were complaining, old friend.'

Throwing the bridle to his orderly, the Remount Officer took four steps at a bound and, swinging his opera-cloak, disappeared into the Staff building.

Belyov, July 1920

Pan Apolek

THE wise and beautiful life of Pan Apolek went to my head like an old wine. In Novograd-Volynsk, among the ruins of a town swiftly brought to confusion, fate threw at my feet a gospel that had lain concealed from the world. Haloed with ingenuousness, I then made a vow to follow Pan Apolek's example. And the sweetness of meditated rancour, the bitter scorn I felt for the curs and swine of mankind, the fire of silent and intoxicating revenge – all this I sacrificed to my new vow.

In the house of the fugitive Novograd priest an icon hung high up on the wall, bearing the inscription 'Death of John the Baptist'. I had no difficulty in recognizing in that John the likeness of a man I had seen some time or other.

I remember: the spiderweb stillness of a summer morning hung between the straight bright walls, and the base of the image was struck by a shaft of sunlight in which swarmed luminous dust-motes. The lanky figure of John was coming straight down to me from out of the blue depths of the niche. A black cloak hung regally about that implacable, that repulsively emaciated body. Drops of blood flashed on the round clasps of the cloak. John's head had not been cut off straight, and the neck was jagged. The head lay upon an earthenware dish gripped tight between the large yellow fingers of a warrior. The dead man's face seemed familiar to me. I scented a mystery. The dead head that lay on the earthenware dish had been painted from that of Pan Romuald, the fugitive priest's assistant. Out of the mouth with bared teeth looped the tiny body of a snake, scaly and glittering. The small, lively head of a delicate pink powerfully set off the dark background of the cloak.

I wondered at the painter's art, and at his sombre fancy. All the more astonishing was the discovery on the following day of a rosy-cheeked Virgin Mary that hung above the double bed of Pani Eliza, the old priest's housekeeper. Both canvases bore the marks of the same brush. The full face of the Virgin Mary was the portrait of Pani Eliza. And at this point I was close to solving the riddle of the Novograd icons. My guess led me into Pani Eliza's kitchen, where on fragrant evenings the shades of old feudal Poland assembled, the crazy painter presiding over them. But was he crazy, this Pan Apolek who had peopled with angels the outskirts of the town and raised the lame convert Yanek to sainthood?

He had come here on a depressing summer's day with blind Gottfried, thirty years ago. The companions – Apolek and Gottfried – went up to Schmerel's tavern that stands on the Rovno highroad two miles beyond the town limits. In his right hand Apolek carried a paintbox, and with his left he guided the blind accordion-player. The singing steps of their nailed German boots rang out with peace and hope. From Apolek's thin neck dangled a canary-coloured scarf. Three little chocolate-coloured feathers fluttered on the blind man's Tyrolean hat.

The newcomers spread out paints and accordion upon the tavern windowsill. The painter unwound his scarf, endless as the ribbon of a wandering juggler at a fair. Then he went out into the yard, undressed from head to foot, and poured cold water over his rosy, slight, and puny body. Schmerel's wife brought the guests raisin vodka and a dish of fragrant rissoles. When he had eaten his fill, Gottfried laid his accordion on his sharp-pointed knees. He sighed, threw back his head, and moved his thin fingers up and down. The songs of Heidelberg echoed around the walls of the Jewish pothouse. Apolek rendered a muted accompaniment in his tremulous voice. It all looked as though the organ had been brought to Schmerel's from St Indeghilda's, and as though the Muses had settled at the organ side by side in bright, wadded scarves and hobnailed German boots.

The guests sang on till dusk; then they stowed the accordion and the paints in linen bags, and Pan Apolek, bowing low, handed a sheet of paper to Brayna the landlord's wife.

'Gracious Pani Brayna,' he said, 'accept this your portrait from an itinerant painter christened with the name of Apollinarius, as a token of our most humble gratitude and witness to the magnificence of your hospitality. If the Lord Jesus prolongs my days and strengthens my art, I shall return to copy this portrait in colours. Pearls would be right for your hair, and we shall add an emerald necklace to your breast.'

On the small sheet of paper, in red pencil – red and soft, like clay – was portrayed the laughing face of Pani Brayna, encircled with coppery curls.

'My money!' cried Schmerel, perceiving the portrait of his wife. He seized a stick and dashed in pursuit of his lodgers. But on the way Schmerel remembered Apolek's rosy body streaming with water, the sunshine in his little yard, the low hum of the accordion. The tavern-keeper's mind was troubled; dropping his stick, he returned home.

Next morning Apolek presented his Munich Academy diploma to the Novograd priest and spread out before him twelve pictures of Biblical subjects. These were painted in oils on thin sheets of cypress-wood. The priest saw on his table the blazing purple of mantles, the brilliance of emerald fields and the flowery veils cast over the plains of Palestine.

Pan Apolek's saints – all that assembly of exultant and simple-minded elders, grey-bearded and rosy-cheeked – were pressed into flowing silks and the strong hues of evening.

That very day Apolek received an order to decorate the new church. And over their benedictine the priest said to the painter:

'Holy Mother of God!' he said, 'from what wonderful sphere have you brought down upon us so radiant a blessing, dear Pan Apollinarius?'

Apolek worked zealously, and at the end of a month the new church was filled with the bleating of flocks, the hazy gold of sunsets, and the straw-coloured udders of cows. Buffaloes with threadbare hides plodded beneath the yoke, dogs with pink noses ran before the flock, and plump babes swung in cradles suspended from the upright trunks of palm trees. The brown rags of Franciscan monks surrounded a cradle. The crowd of Wise Men was gashed with bald heads, with wrinkles blood-red like wounds. Among this crowd glimmered the guilefully smiling, little old face of Leo XIII; and the Novograd priest himself, fingering in one hand a Chinese-carved rosary, was blessing with his other hand the newborn Jesus.

For five months Apolek, confined in his wooden seat, crept along the walls, around the dome and the choir.

'You are partial to familiar faces, dear Pan Apolek,' said the priest one day, recognizing himself in one of the Magi and Pan Romuald in the decapitated head of John the Baptist. He smiled, the old priest, and sent a goblet of cognac to the painter at work beneath the dome.

Afterward Apolek completed the Lord's Supper and the Lapidation of Mary Magdalene. One Sunday he unveiled his frescoes. The eminent citizens who had been invited by the priest recognized Yanek, the lame convert, in St Paul, and in Mary Magdalene a Jewish girl named Elka, daughter of unknown parents and mother of numerous waifs and strays. The eminent citizens ordered the sacrilegious portraits to be covered up. The priest hurled threats upon the blasphemer. But Apolek did not hide his frescoes from sight.

Thus began a prodigious warfare between the all-powerful body of the Catholic Church on the one hand and the carefree painter of holy images on the other. For three decades it dragged on, and chance nearly made of the humble vagabond the founder of a new heresy. He would then have been the wittiest and most facetious combatant of all those with whom the Roman Church has had to deal in her seditious and evasive history; a combatant roaming the wide world over in a state of blissful intoxication, with two white mice in his bosom and in his pocket a collection of the finest brushes.

'Fifteen zlotys for a Virgin Mary, twenty-five for a Holy Family, and fifty zlotys for the Lord's Supper with the portraits of all the customer's relatives. The customer's enemy may be painted as Judas Iscariot, and that comes to ten zlotys extra,' was Apolek's announcement to the peasants of the neighbourhood after he had been driven away from the church in course of construction.

He knew no scarcity of orders. And when the commission summoned by the Novograd priest's raging messages arrived a year later from the Bishop of Zhitomir, it found these monstrous family-portraits, sacrilegious, ingenuous, and picturesque, in the most poverty-stricken and stench-filled huts. Grey-haired Josephs with partings down the middle, pomaded Jesuses, village Marys with knees apart, mothers already of many children; all these icons hung in the corners reserved for the holy images, festooned with paper flowers.

'He has made saints of you in your lifetime,' cried the Vicar of Dubno and Novokonstantinov in answer to the crowd's defence of Apolek. 'He has surrounded you with the ineffable attributes of holiness, you who have thrice fallen into the sin of disobedience, distillers of brandy in secret, merciless usurers, makers of false weights, and dealers in your own daughters' innocence.'

'Your Holiness,' then said the limping Vitold, buyer-up of stolen goods and keeper of the cemetery, 'who is to tell the ignorant folk about the things in which the all-merciful Pan God sees truth? And isn't there more truth in the pictures of Pan Apolek, who satisfies our pride, than in your words so full of blame and aristocratic wrath?'

The cries of the multitude put the Vicar to flight. The general feeling in the outskirts threatened the safety of the

Church's servants. The painter who had been appointed in Apolek's stead could not bring himself to paint over Elka and lame Yanek. They can still be seen today, in one of the side chapels of the Novograd church: Yanek as St Paul, a timid-looking lame man with the bushy black beard of a village apostate; and she, the loose woman from Magdala, with puny, contorted body, vacant expression, and sunken cheeks.

The struggle against the priest dragged on for three decades. Then the Cossack flood drove the old monk from his aromatic nest of stone, and Apolek – O freak of fortune! – took up his abode in Pani Eliza's kitchen. And here am I, the guest of an hour, drinking of an evening the wine of his words.

What about? About the romantic age of the Polish nobility, about the fierce fanaticism of the women of the people, about the painter Luca della Robbia, and about the family of the Bethlehem carpenter.

'I have something to tell the Pan writer,' Apolek announces to me before supper with an air of secrecy.

'Yes,' I reply. 'Yes, Apolek, I'm listening.'

But the church beadle, the stern and grey, bony and big-eared Pan Robacki is sitting too close. He hangs before us the faded linen of silence and enmity.

'I must tell you, Pan,' whispers Apolek, and leads me aside, 'that Jesus son of Mary was married to Deborah, a Jerusalem maid of obscure birth.'

'Oh, that fellow!' cries Robacki in despairing Polish, 'that fellow won't die in his bed. People will tear him limb from limb.'

'After supper,' rustles Apolek's voice, lower still, 'after supper, if it suits you, Pan writer . . .'

It does. My interest whetted by the opening of Apolek's story, I stride up and down the kitchen awaiting the appointed hour. Beyond the window, night stands like a black column; there too the live dark garden has grown still. Beneath the moon the road to the church flows in a milky, luminous stream. A shadowy radiance lies on the earth, and hanging from the bushes are necklaces of gleaming fruit. The scent of lilies is strong and clean, like that of raw spirits. This fresh poison is sucked up into the fat and gusty snorting of the cooking-stove, overpowering the resinous exhalation of the fir logs strewn about the kitchen floor.

Wearing a pink bow and threadbare pink trousers, Apolek stirs in his corner like some gentle and graceful animal. His table is smudged with paints and glue. The old man works with short, rapid movements, and a subdued and melodious humming comes from his corner. Old Gottfried is beating out the tune with his shaky fingers. The blind man sits motionless in the yellow, oily patch of lamplight. Bowing his bald head, he listens to the endless music of his blindness and the whisperings of Apolek his eternal friend.

'And what the priests and St Mark and St Matthew tell you, sir, isn't the truth. But the truth may be revealed to you, Pan writer, of whom for fifty marks I will paint a portrait in the image of the Blessed Francis, on a background of verdure and sky. He was quite a simple saint, Pan Francis. And if you, Pan writer, have a fiancée in Russia, women love the Blessed Francis; though not indeed all women, Pan.'

Thus began in the corner smelling of fir trees the story of the marriage of Jesus and Deborah. According to Apolek, this maid had a betrothed, a young Israelite who traded in elephant tusks. But Deborah's bridal night ended in misunderstanding and tears. The woman was overcome by fear when she perceived her husband approaching her couch. A hiccough distended her throat, and she vomited forth all she had eaten at the wedding feast. Shame fell on Deborah, on her father, her mother, and all her kin. Her bridegroom left her, mocking, and summoned all the guests. Then Jesus, seeing the anguish of the woman who thirsted for her husband and at the same time feared him, placed upon Himself the bridegroom's apparel and, full of compassion, was joined with

Deborah, who lay in her vomit. Then she went forth to the guests, noisily triumphant, like a woman who prides herself on her fall. And only Jesus stood aloof. A deathly perspiration had broken out on His body; the bee of sorrow had stung His heart. Observed by none, He departed from the banqueting-hall and made His way to the wilderness eastward of Judaea, where John awaited Him. And Deborah bore her first child. . . .'

'Where is he?' I cried.

'He was hidden by the priests,' said Apolek importantly, and put his light and chilly finger on his drunkard's nose.

'Pan artist,' clamoured Robacki, suddenly emerging from the shadows, his grey ears a-twitch, 'what are you saying? What you say is unthinkable.'

'Yes, yes,' Apolek hunched himself up, grabbing Gottfried, 'yes, yes, Pan . . .'

He dragged the blind man toward the door, but on the threshold he slowed down and beckoned me to approach.

'Blessed Francis,' he whispered, winking, 'with a bird on his sleeve – a dove or a goldfinch, just as the Pan writer chooses.' And he vanished with the blind man, his eternal friend.

'Oh, folly!' then cried Robacki the beadle. 'That fellow won't die in his bed.'

Pan Robacki opened his mouth wide and yawned like a cat. I said good-bye to all, and left to spend the night at home with my plundered Jews.

Over the town roamed the homeless moon. I went along with her, warming up in my heart impracticable dreams and discordant songs.

Italian Sunshine

YESTERDAY I sat once more in Pani Eliza's quarters, beneath the heated garland of green fir-twigs. I sat awhile beside the hot, live, muttering stove, and afterward returned home through the depths of night. Below, in the ravine, the noiseless Zbruch rolled its dark and glassy waters.

The scorched town – broken columns and, dug into the earth, the hooks of the little malevolent fingers of old women – seemed to me raised aloft in the air, as snug and chimerical as a dream. The crude brightness of the moon flowed down on it with inexhaustible force. The damp mould of the ruins flowered like the marble of opera seats. And I waited, disturbed in spirit, for Romeo to appear from the clouds, a satin-clad Romeo singing of love, while a dismal electrician in the wings keeps a finger on the moon-extinguisher.

Blue roads flowed past me like streams of milk spurting from many breasts. On my way home I dreaded meeting Sidorov, my neighbour, who nightly brought down upon me the hairy paw of his spleen. Happily that night, rent by the milky moonbeams, Sidorov did not utter a word. Surrounding himself with books, he wrote. On the table smoked a humpbacked candle, ill-omened beacon of dreamers. And I sat apart, dozing, dreams leaping about me like kittens. And not till late at night was I roused by an orderly coming to summon Sidorov to the Staff. They went off together. Then I hurried over to the table at which Sidorov had been writing, and turned the pages of his books. These consisted of a handbook of Italian, a picture of the Forum, and a map of Rome. The map was covered with little crosses and dots. I bent over a closely-written sheet; wringing my fingers and with fainting heart I read another man's letter. Sidorov, that anguished killer of men, tore into shreds the pink wadding of my imagination, and dragged me into the corridors of his own common-sense madness. The letter started with the second page; I dared not look for the beginning.

'. . . his lung is pierced and he has gone a little queer in the top storey. As Serge puts it, he has flown off his rocker; after all, he's not the sort of idiot simply to *go* off it. However, tail to the side and joking apart, let us return to the agenda, my dear Victoria.

'I have been through the three-months' campaign with Makhno – a tiresome swindle and nothing more. And only Volin is still with him. Volin dons sacerdotal vestments and clambers from anarchy to the Lenin level. Awful. And Old Man Makhno listens to him, strokes his dust-sprinkled wiry locks, and emits from between decaying teeth his moujik sneer. And now I don't know if there isn't in all that the weedy seed of anarchy and if we shall be able to pull your successful noses, you homespun members of the homespun Central Committee "made in" Kharkov, that homespun capital. Your stout fellows don't like to recall nowadays the sins of their Anarchist youth, and laugh at them from the height of their statesmen's wisdom – devil take them!

'Then I landed in Moscow. How did I get there? The boys offended someone or other in the matter of requisitioning and what not. I butted in like the dithering idiot I am, and came in for a proper dressing-down – serve me right too. The wound was a mere scratch, but in Moscow, oh dear, in Moscow, Victoria, I nearly went dumb with misery. Every day the nurses brought me gruel. Bridled with awe, they would lug it to me on a big tray, and I came to loathe that shock-brigade gruel, those supplies in addition to the plan, that Moscow according to plan. Afterward I came across a handful of Anarchists in the Soviet. They are either foppish young duds or senile dotards. I pushed into the Kremlin with a plan of real work. They patted me on the head and promised me the post of chief assistant if I reformed. I didn't reform. What happened next? The front, the Cavalry Army, the troops reeking of fresh blood and of human dust and ashes.

'Save me, Victoria. The wisdom of statesmen is driving me crazy. I am drunk with boredom. If you don't help, I shall pass out quite planlessly, and who would want to see a worker kicking the bucket in so unorganized a way. Anyhow, not you, Victoria, fiancée who will never be wife. Now I am getting sentimental – oh hell!

'Now to the point. I'm bored in the Army. I cannot ride because of my wound: that means I cannot fight. Do use your influence, Victoria, and get them to send me to Italy. I am learning the lingo, and in two months I shall be able to speak it. The earth is smouldering in Italy. Lots of things are all set there. It only needs a couple of shots, and one of them will be mine. The King must be sent to join his forbears. That is highly important. Their King is a nice old fellow who plays to the gallery and gets himself photographed along with tame Socialists for the family magazines.

'Don't mention Kings and shootings to the Central Committee or at the Foreign Office. They will only pat you on the head and mumble: "A romantic." Say simply: "He's ill, fed-up, drunk with depression. He wants Italian sunshine and bananas." I've surely deserved it; or haven't I? Just to get well again, that's all . . . But if not, then let them send me to the Cheka in Odessa. They're very sensible there, and . . .

'How stupidly – stupidly and undeservedly – I'm writing to you, dear Victoria. . . .

'Italy has got into my heart and is luring me on. The thought of that country I have never seen is as sweet to me as a woman's name – as your name, Victoria. . . .'

I read the letter to the end and began to dispose myself on my battered and unclean couch, but sleep would not come.

On the other side of the wall the pregnant Jewess was crying her heart out, and her long-bodied husband was muttering moaning replies. They were remembering their stolen possessions and bickering over their ill fortune.

Then, before dawn, Sidorov returned. The candle was flickering out on the table. Sidorov took another candle-end from a boot and, unusually deep in thought, crushed the guttering wick with it. Our room was dark and gloomy; everything in it breathed the dank odour of night; and only the window, overflowing with moonlight, shone forth like a deliverance.

He came, my depressing neighbour, and put away the letter. Stooping, he sat down at the table and opened an album of Roman views. The magnificent gilt-edged volume lay before his expressionless olive face. Over his rounded back gleamed the sharp-pointed ruins of the Capitol and the Colosseum lit up by the sunset. A photograph of the royal family was inserted between the large glossy pages. A scrap of paper that had been torn from a calendar pictured the amiable, puny King Victor Emmanuel with his black-haired wife, Prince Umberto his heir, and a whole brood of princesses.

And it was night, full of the distant and wearisome ringing of bells. In the damp gloom a square patch of light; and in it, an inanimate mask, Sidorov's deathly face, brooding above the yellow flame of the candle.

Gedali

ON Sabbath eves I am oppressed by the dense melancholy of memories. In bygone days on these occasions my grandfather would stroke the volumes of Ibn Ezra with his yellow beard. His old woman in her lace cap would trace fortunes with her knotty fingers over the Sabbath candles, and sob softly to herself. On those evenings my child's heart was rocked like a little ship upon enchanted waves. O the rotted Talmuds of my childhood! O the dense melancholy of memories!

I roam through Zhitomir in search of a shy star. By the ancient synagogue, by its yellow and indifferent walls, old Jews with prophets' beards and passionate rags on their sunken chests sell chalk and wicks and blueing.

Here before me is the market, and the death of the market. Gone is the fat soul of plenty. Dumb padlocks hang upon the booths, and the granite paving is as clean as a skull. My shy star blinks, and fades from sight.

Success came to me later on; success came just before sunset. Gedali's little shop was hidden away in a row of others, all hermetically closed. Where was your kindly shade that evening, Dickens? In that little old curiosity shop you would have seen gilt slippers, ship's cables, an ancient compass, a stuffed eagle, a Winchester with the date 1810 engraved upon it, a broken saucepan.

Old Gedali, the little proprietor in smoked glasses and a green frock-coat down to the ground, meandered around his treasures in the roseate void of evening. He rubbed his small white hands, plucked at his little grey beard, and listened, head bent, to the mysterious voices wafting down to him.

The shop was like the box of an important and knowledge-loving little boy who will grow up to be a professor of botany. There were buttons in it, and a dead butterfly, and its small owner went by the name of Gedali. All had abandoned the market; but Gedali had remained. He wound in and out of a labyrinth of globes, skulls, and dead flowers, waving a bright feather duster of cock's plumes and blowing dust from the dead flowers.

And so we sat upon small beer-barrels, Gedali twisting and untwisting his narrow beard. Like a little black tower, his hat swayed above us. Warm air flowed past. The sky changed colour. Blood, delicate-hued, poured down from an over-turned bottle up there, and a vague odour of corruption enfolded me.

'The Revolution – we will say "yes" to it, but are we to say "no" to the Sabbath?' began Gedali, winding about me the straps of his smoke-hidden eyes. 'Yes, I cry to the Revolution. Yes, I cry to it, but it hides its face from Gedali and sends out in front nought but shooting . . .'

'The sunlight doesn't enter eyes that are closed,' I answered the old man. 'But we will cut open those closed eyes . . .'

'A Pole closed my eyes,' whispered the old man, in a voice that was barely audible. 'The Poles are bad-tempered dogs. They take the Jew and pluck out his beard, the curs! And now they are being beaten, the bad-tempered dogs. That is splen-did, that is the Revolution. And then those who have beaten the Poles say to me: "Hand your gramophone over to the State, Gedali . . ." "I am fond of music, Pani," I say to the Revolution. "You don't know what you are fond of, Gedali. I'll shoot you and then you'll know. I cannot do without shooting, because I am the Revolution."'

'She cannot do without shooting, Gedali,' I told the old man, 'because she is the Revolution.'

'But the Poles, kind sir, shot because they were the Counter-Revolution. You shoot because you are the Revolution. But surely the Revolution means joy. And joy does not like orphans in the house. Good men do good deeds. The Revolu-tion is the good deed of good men. But good men do not kill. So it is bad people that are making the Revolution. But the Poles are bad people too. Then how is Gedali to tell which is Revolution and which is Counter-Revolution? I used to study the Talmud; I love Rashi's Commentaries and the books of Maimonides. And there are yet other understanding folk in Zhitomir. And here we are, all of us learned people, falling on our faces and crying out in a loud voice: "Woe unto us, where is the joy-giving Revolution?"'

The old man fell silent. And we saw the first star pierce through the Milky Way.

'The Sabbath has begun,' Gedali stated solemnly; 'Jews should be going to the synagogue. Pan comrade,' he said, rising, his top-hat like a little black tower swaying on his head, 'bring a few good people to Zhitomir. Oh, there's a scarcity of good people in our town. Oh, what a scarcity! Bring them along and we will hand over all our gramophones to them. We are not ignoramuses. The International – we know what the International is. And I want an International of good people. I would like every soul to be listed and given first-category rations. There, soul, please eat and enjoy life's pleasures. Pan comrade, you don't know what the International is eaten with . . .'

'It is eaten with gunpowder,' I answered the old man 'and spiced with best-quality blood.'

And then, from out of the blue gloom, the young Sabbath came to take her seat of honour.

'Gedali,' I said, 'today is Friday, and it's already evening. Where are Jewish biscuits to be got, and a Jewish glass of tea, and a little of that pensioned-off God in a glass of tea?'

'Not to be had,' Gedali replied, hanging the padlock on his little booth. 'Not to be had. Next door is a tavern, and they were good people who served in it; but nobody eats there now, people weep there.'

He buttoned his green frock-coat on three bone buttons, flicked himself with the cock's feathers, sprinkled a little water on his soft palms, and departed, a tiny, lonely visionary in a black top-hat, carrying a big prayerbook under his arm.

The Sabbath is coming. Gedali, the founder of an impossible International, has gone to the synagogue to pray.

My First Goose

SAVITSKY, Commander of the VI Division, rose when he saw me, and I wondered at the beauty of his giant's body. He rose, the purple of his riding-breeches and the crimson of his little tilted cap and the decorations stuck on his chest cleaving the hut as a standard cleaves the sky. A smell of scent and the sickly sweet freshness of soap emanated from him. His long legs were like girls sheathed to the neck in shining riding-boots.

He smiled at me, struck his riding-whip on the table, and drew toward him an order that the Chief of Staff had just finished dictating. It was an order for Ivan Chesnokov to advance on Chugunov-Dobryvodka with the regiment entrusted to him, to make contact with the enemy and destroy the same.

'For which destruction,' the Commander began to write, smearing the whole sheet, 'I make this same Chesnokov entirely responsible, up to and including the supreme penalty, and will if necessary strike him down on the spot; which you, Chesnokov, who have been working with me at the front for some months now, cannot doubt.'

The Commander signed the order with a flourish, tossed it to his orderlies, and turned upon me grey eyes that danced with merriment.

I handed him a paper with my appointment to the Staff of the Division.

'Put it down in the Order of the Day,' said the Commander. 'Put him down for every satisfaction save the front one. Can you read and write?'

'Yes, I can read and write,' I replied, envying the flower and iron of that youthfulness. 'I graduated in law from St Petersburg University.'

'Oh, are you one of those grinds?' he laughed. 'Specs on your nose, too! What a nasty little object! They've sent you along without making any inquiries; and this is a hot place for specs. Think you'll get on with us?'

'I'll get on all right,' I answered, and went off to the village with the quartermaster to find a billet for the night.

The quartermaster carried my trunk on his shoulder. Before us stretched the village street. The dying sun, round and yellow as a pumpkin, was giving up its roseate ghost to the skies.

We went up to a hut painted over with garlands. The quartermaster stopped, and said suddenly, with a guilty smile:

'Nuisance with specs. Can't do anything to stop it, either. Not a life for the brainy type here. But you go and mess up a lady, and a good lady too, and you'll have the boys patting you on the back.'

He hesitated, my little trunk on his shoulder; then he came quite close to me, only to dart away again despairingly and run to the nearest yard. Cossacks were sitting there, shaving one another.

'Here, you soldiers,' said the quartermaster, setting my little trunk down on the ground. 'Comrade Savitsky's orders are that you're to take this chap in your billets, so no nonsense about it, because the chap's been through a lot in the learning line.'

The quartermaster, purple in the face, left us without looking back. I raised my hand to my cap and saluted the Cossacks. A lad with long straight flaxen hair and the handsome face of the Ryazan Cossacks went over to my little trunk and tossed it out at the gate. Then he turned his back on me and with remarkable skill emitted a series of shameful noises.

'To your guns – number double-zero!' an older Cossack shouted at him, and burst out laughing. 'Running fire!'

His guileless art exhausted, the lad made off. Then, crawling over the ground, I began to gather together the manuscripts and tattered garments that had fallen out of the trunk. I gathered them up and carried them to the other end of the yard. Near the hut, on a brick stove, stood a cauldron in which pork was cooking. The steam that rose from it was like the far-off smoke of home in the village, and it mingled hunger with desperate loneliness in my head. Then I covered my little broken trunk with hay, turning it into a pillow, and lay down on the ground to read in *Pravda* Lenin's speech at the Second Congress of the Comintern. The sun fell upon me from behind the toothed hillocks, the Cossacks trod on my feet, the lad made fun of me untiringly, the beloved lines came toward me along a thorny path and could not reach me. Then I put aside the paper and went out to the landlady, who was spinning on the porch.

'Landlady,' I said, 'I've got to eat.'

The old woman raised to me the diffused whites of her purblind eyes and lowered them again.

'Comrade,' she said, after a pause, 'what with all this going on, I want to go and hang myself.'

'Christ!' I muttered, and pushed the old woman in the chest with my fist. 'You don't suppose I'm going to go into explanations with you, do you?'

And turning around I saw somebody's sword lying within reach. A severe-looking goose was waddling about the yard, inoffensively preening its feathers. I overtook it and pressed it to the ground. Its head cracked beneath my boot, cracked and emptied itself. The white neck lay stretched out in the dung, the wings twitched.

'Christ!' I said, digging into the goose with my sword. 'Go and cook it for me, landlady.'

Her blind eyes and glasses glistening, the old woman picked up the slaughtered bird, wrapped it in her apron, and started to bear it off toward the kitchen.

'Comrade,' she said to me, after a while. 'I want to go and hang myself.' And she closed the door behind her.

My First Goose

The Cossacks in the yard were already sitting around their cauldron. They sat motionless, stiff as heathen priests at a sacrifice, and had not looked at the goose.

'The lad's all right,' one of them said, winking and scooping up the cabbage soup with his spoon.

The Cossacks commenced their supper with all the elegance and restraint of peasants who respect one another. And I wiped the sword with sand, went out at the gate, and came in again, depressed. Already the moon hung above the yard like a cheap ear-ring.

'Hey, you,' suddenly said Surovkov, an older Cossack. 'Sit down and feed with us till your goose is done.'

He produced a spare spoon from his boot and handed it to me. We supped up the cabbage soup they had made, and ate the pork.

'What's in the newspaper?' asked the flaxen-haired lad, making room for me.

'Lenin writes in the paper,' I said, pulling out *Pravda*. 'Lenin writes that there's a shortage of everything.'

And loudly, like a triumphant man hard of hearing, I read Lenin's speech out to the Cossacks.

Evening wrapped about me the quickening moisture of its twilight sheets; evening laid a mother's hand upon my burning forehead. I read on and rejoiced, spying out exultingly the secret curve of Lenin's straight line.

'Truth tickles everyone's nostrils,' said Surovkov, when I had come to the end. 'The question is, how's it to be pulled from the heap. But he goes and strikes at it straight off like a hen pecking at a grain!'

This remark about Lenin was made by Surovkov, platoon commander of the Staff Squadron; after which we lay down to sleep in the hayloft. We slept, all six of us, beneath a wooden roof that let in the stars, warming one another, our legs intermingled. I dreamed: and in my dreams saw women. But my heart, stained with bloodshed, grated and brimmed over.

The Rabbi

'ALL is mortal. Only the mother is destined to immortality. And when the mother is no longer among the living, she leaves a memory which none yet has dared to sully. The memory of the mother nourishes in us a compassion that is like the ocean, and the measureless ocean feeds the rivers that dissect the universe.'

Such were Gedali's words. He uttered them with great solemnity. The dying evening surrounded him with the rose-tinted haze of its sadness.

The old man said: 'The passionate edifice of Hasidism has had its doors and windows burst open, but it is as immortal as the soul of the mother. With oozing orbits Hasidism still stands at the crossroads of the turbulent winds of history.'

Thus spoke Gedali. And having come to the end of his prayers in the synagogue he took me to Rabbi Motale, the last of the Chernobyl dynasty.

We went up the main street, Gedali and I. White churches gleamed in the distance like fields of buckwheat. The wheel of a gun-carriage groaned on a corner. A couple of pregnant Ukrainian women came out of a gateway, jingling their coin necklaces, and sat down on a bench. In the orange strife of the sunset a timid star lit up, and peace – Sabbath peace – rested upon the crazy roofs of the Zhitomir ghetto.

'Here,' whispered Gedali, and pointed out a tall building with a broken frontal.

We entered a room, stony and empty, like a morgue. Rabbi Motale was sitting at a table surrounded by the liars and the possessed. He wore a white dressing-gown drawn around him with a cord, and a sable cap was on his head. The Rabbi sat with closed eyes, digging his thin fingers into the yellow down of his beard.

'Whence comes the Jew?' he asked, raising his eyelids.

'From Odessa,' I answered.

'A God-fearing town,' said the Rabbi, 'the star of our exile, the involuntary well of our distress. What is the Jew's occupation?'

'I am putting into verse the adventures of Hersch of Ostropol.'

'A great task,' murmured the Rabbi, and closed his eyelids. 'The jackal whines when he is hungry, every fool has folly enough for despondency, and only the wise man can tear the veil of being with his laughter. What has the Jew studied?'

'The Bible.'

'What is the Jew seeking?'

'Merriment.'

'Reb Mordecai,' said the saddik, and shook his beard, 'let the young man sit down at the table; let him eat with all the other Jews this Sabbath eve, let him rejoice that he is alive and not dead, let him clap his hands when his neighbours dance, let him drink wine if he is given any.'

And to me darted Mordecai, a jester of old – a hunch-backed old man with turned-out eyelids, not taller than a boy of ten.

'Oh, my dear and so very young man,' said the ragged Reb Mordecai, winking at me, 'Oh, how many rich fools I used to know in Odessa! And how many penniless wise men I used to know in Odessa! Do sit down at the table, young man, and drink the wine you won't be given!'

We all of us seated ourselves side by side – possessed, liars, and idlers. In a corner some broad-shouldered Jews who resembled fishermen and apostles were moaning over their prayerbooks. Gedali, in his green frock-coat down to the ground, was dozing by the wall like a little bright bird. And suddenly I caught sight of a youth behind him, a youth with the face of Spinoza, with Spinoza's powerful brow and the wan face of a nun. He was smoking, shuddering like a re-captured prisoner brought back to his cell. The ragged Reb

Mordecai crept up to him from behind, snatched the cigarette from his mouth, and ran away to me.

'That's Elijah, the Rabbi's son,' he declared hoarsely, bringing his bloodshot eyelids close to my face. 'That's the cursed son, the last son, the unruly son.'

And Mordecai shook his fist at the youth and spat in his face.

'Blessed is the Lord,' rang out the voice of Rabbi Motale, and he proceeded to break bread with his monkish fingers. 'Blessed is the Lord God of Israel Who hath chosen us from amongst all the nations of the earth.'

The Rabbi blessed the food and we sat down at the table. Beyond the window horses were neighing, Cossacks were shouting. Beyond the window yawned the wilderness of war. In the midst of the silence and prayers the Rabbi's son went on smoking one cigarette after another. When the supper came to an end, I was the first to rise.

'My dear and so very young man,' muttered Mordecai after me, pulling me by my belt, 'if there were no one in the world besides the evil rich and the needy vagabonds, how would the holy ones live?'

I gave the old man some money and went out into the street. I took leave of Gedali and made my way to the station. At the station, in the propaganda train of the First Cavalry Army, there awaited me the flare of innumerable lights, the magical brilliance of the wireless station, the stubborn coursing of the printing presses, and my unfinished article for the *Red Trooper*.

The Road to Brody

I FELT sorry about the bees. The fighting armies treated them most brutally. There were no bees left in Volhynia.

We defiled the hives. We destroyed them with sulphur and blew them up with gunpowder. The smell of singed rags reeked in the sacred republic of the bees. Dying, they flew around slowly, humming so that you could hardly hear. And we who had no bread extracted the honey with our swords ... There were no bees left in Volhynia.

The chronicle of our workaday offences oppressed me without respite, like an ailing heart.

Yesterday was the first day of slaughter at Brody. Having lost our way on the blue earth, we had no inkling of it, neither I nor Afonka Bida, my friend. The horses had been fed oats in the morning. The rye was tall, the sun resplendent; and the soul, all undeserving of these blazing, winged skies, longed for drawn-out tortures.

'The womenfolk of the Cossack settlements tell all sorts of tales about the bee and its good qualities,' began the platoon commander, my friend. 'Whether folk offended Christ or didn't offend Him, that we'll get to know in good time. But the womenfolk of the settlements say that Christ was suffering upon the Cross, and all kinds of midges flew up to Christ to worry Him. And He looked at them and lost heart. But the multitude of midges didn't see His eyes. And a bee was flying round Christ too. "Strike at Him," cry the midges to the bee. "Strike at Him, and we'll be responsible." "Can't," says the bee, and raises its wings above Christ's head. "Can't. He's a carpenter like us." Got to understand the bee,' concluded Afonka, my platoon commander. 'Well, and the bee's got to stick it now; it's for them too that we're messing about here.'

And waving his arms Afonka struck up a song. It was a song about a light bay stallion. The eight Cossacks – Afonka's platoon – joined in.

'The light bay stallion, Djigit by name, belonged to a subaltern who drank himself tipsy with vodka the day his head was chopped off.' Thus sang Afonka, dragging his voice like the string of a musical instrument, and dozing in the saddle. 'Djigit was a faithful steed, and on holidays the subaltern's desires knew no bounds. The day his head was chopped off he had in all five bottles. After the fourth, the subaltern mounted his steed and started for the heavens. The ascent was slow, but Djigit was a faithful steed. They arrived in the heavens, and there he suddenly bethought himself of the fifth bottle. But the fifth bottle had been left behind on earth. Then he wept over the vanity of all his strivings. He wept, and Djigit flicked his ears and watched him.'

Thus sang Afonka, carolling and drowsing. The song floated away like smoke. And we were moving towards the sunset, whose foaming rivers flowed along the embroidered napkins of peasant fields. The stillness grew roseate. Like a cat's back the earth lay overgrown with the gleaming fur of crops. On the slope crouched the little mud-walled village of Klekotov. Awaiting us beyond the hilltop was the view over Brody, jagged and deathlike. But at Klekotov a shot rang out loudly before our very faces. Two Polish officers peered from behind a hut. Their horses were tethered to posts. Already the enemy's light battery was being briskly driven up the slope. Bullets were spinning out like threads along the road.

'Run for it,' cried Afonka.

And we fled.

O Brody! The mummies of your crushed passions breathed upon me their irremediable poison. I could already sense the deathly chill of orbits suffused with tears grown cold. And here am I being borne away at a jolting gallop, far from the dented stones of your synagogues.

Brody, August 1920

Discourse on the Tachanka

A DRIVER, or as it is customary among us to say, a 'wagoner', has been sent me from the Staff. His surname is Grishchuk, and he is thirty-nine years old.

Discourse on the Tachanka

For five years Grishchuk was in a German prison-camp.
A few months ago he escaped, crossed Lithuania and North-
west Russia, reached Volhynia, and in Belyov was caught by
the most brainless mobilization commission in the world and
set down to do military service. It was only fifteen versts more
to Grishchuk's native district of Kremenets. There dwelt his
wife and children. He had not been home for five years and
two months. The mobilization commission made him my
wagoner, and I ceased to be a pariah among the Cossacks.

I – master of the sort of little cart we call a *tachanka* and a
driver to boot! A tachanka! Upon that word had been erected
a triangle epitomizing our ways: massacre, tachanka, blood . . .

Through a caprice of our internecine dissensions, what had
been the common-or-garden *brichka*, in which priests and
officials drive about, came into prominence and grew to be a
mobile and formidable instrument of warfare. It created a
new strategy and new tactics, altered the usual aspect of war,
gave birth to the heroes and geniuses of the tachanka. Among
these was Makhno, the anarchist guerrilla, for whom the
tachanka was the axis of a mysterious and wily strategy.
Makhno had done away with infantry, artillery, and even
cavalry, and had replaced these cumbersome masses by three
hundred machine-guns screwed on to brichkas. Makhno, as
Protean as Nature herself. Haycarts disposed in battle array
take towns, a wedding procession approaching the Headquarters of a District Executive opens a concentrated fire, and
a meagre little priest, waving above him the black flag of
Anarchy, orders the authorities to serve up the bourgeois, the
proletariat, wine, and music.

An army of tachankas possesses undreamed-of possibilities
of manoeuvre.

Budyonny proved it no less than Makhno. To attack such
an army is difficult; to attempt to take it by surprise, absurd.
When the machine-gun is hidden in a haystack and the
tachanka stowed away in a peasant's shed, they cease to be

battle units. These concealed points – items surmised but imperceptible – form a whole analogous to the Ukrainian village of not long ago – savage, rebellious, and grasping. An army like this, with ammunition stuck in every corner, Makhno was able to get into battle order within the space of an hour. It took him even less time to demobilize it.

In our own force, in Budyonny's regular cavalry, the tachanka does not play such a predominant part. Nevertheless, all our machine-gun units are conveyed on brichkas only. The inventive mind of the Cossack differentiates between two types of tachanka: the colonist type and the official type. And it is no mere inventiveness either, for the distinction is a genuine one.

On the official brichka, that ramshackle vehicle made without care or imagination, government officials used to jolt about the wheat-steppes of the Kuban – wretched, red-nosed people suffering from lack of sleep, hastening to investigate crimes and conduct post-mortems. The colonist type of tachanka, on the other hand, came to us from the Ural and Samara, the Volga, the fertile territories of the German colonies. The broad oak of the colonists' tachanka was decorated with homely paintings – bulging garlands of pink flowers of the kind dear to the heart of Germans. The solid bottom was strengthened with bands of iron. One was borne along upon unforgettable springs; in these springs, now jolting over the churned-up roads of Volhynia, I could sense the warmth of many generations.

I knew then the rapture of first possession. Every day after dinner we harnessed up. Grishchuk lead the horses out of the stable. They were improving daily, and it was with pride and pleasure that I already noted a dull sheen on their groomed flanks. We rubbed down their swollen legs, trimmed their manes, threw over their backs the Cossack trappings – a tangled, dried-up network of fine straps – and drove out at a trot. Grishchuk sat sideways on the box. My own seat was padded with flowery tow, with hay that smelled of scent and restfulness. The tall wheels grated in the white sandgrains. Poppies brightened the earth in patches, the ruins of churches gleamed on the hillocks. High above the road, in a niche that a shell had smashed, stood the statue of St Ursula with plump bare arms. And the ancient, cramped lettering was linked in an uneven chain upon the blackened gilt of the pediment: AD MAI. GLORIAM IESV DIVAEQUE MATRIS EIVS.

Crouching at the feet of nobles' estates were lifeless little Jewish towns. On a brick wall shimmered a prophetic peacock – dispassionate apparition against the blue expanse of space. Hidden away behind scattered huts, a synagogue squatted upon the barren soil – sightless, dented, round as a Hasidic hat. Narrow-chested Jews hung mournfully about the crossways. The image of the stout and jovial Jews of the South, bubbling like cheap wine, took shape in my memory, in sharp contrast to the bitter scorn inherent in these long bony backs, these tragic yellow beards. In these passionate, anguish-chiselled features there was no fat, no warm pulsing of blood. The Jews of Volhynia and Galicia moved jerkily, in an uncontrolled and uncouth way, but their capacity for suffering was full of a sombre greatness, and their unvoiced contempt for the Polish gentry unbounded. Watching them, I understood the poignant history of this region: the stories of Talmudists renting taverns, of Rabbis carrying on usury, of young girls raped by Polish troopers and over whom Polish magnates fought pistol duels.

The Death of Dolgushov

THE curtains of battle were drawing toward the town. At noon Korochayev, wrapped in a black cloak, flashed past us – Korochayev, the disgraced Commander of the IV Division who fought single-handed, seeking death. He shouted to me as he rode past: 'Our communications are down – Radzi-willów and Brody are in flames!'

His cloak floating about him, he galloped away – black from head to foot, his pupils like live coals.

The brigades were reforming on the board-flat plain. The sun was travelling through purple haze. In ditches wounded men were taking a bite. Lying about on the grass were nurses, singing softly. Afonka's scouts were beating the fields in search of dead and equipment. Afonka himself rode past within two feet of me, and said, not turning his head:

'We've been getting it in the neck, sure as two and two makes four. I've an idea that Divisional Commander will get canned. The men aren't easy.'

The Poles had reached the forest about three versts from us, and posted their machine-guns somewhere in our neigh-bourhood. Bullets began to whine and wail, their lament growing unbearably. Bullets struck the earth and fumbled in it, quivering with impatience. Vytyagaychenko, the regi-mental commander, who was snoring in the sunshine, cried out in his sleep and woke up. He got into the saddle and rode off toward the vanguard squadron. His face was crumpled, lined with red streaks from his uncomfortable snooze, and his pockets were full of plums.

'Damned son of a bitch!' he cried angrily, and spat a plumstone out of his mouth. 'What a hell of a mess! Get out the standard, Timoshka!'

'Going to get moving, eh?' asked Timoshka, disengaging the staff from his stirrup and unrolling the ensign bearing a star and some lettering concerning the Third International.

'We'll see what's up over there,' said Vytyagaychenko, and suddenly yelled wildly: 'To horse, you girls! Squadron commanders, get your men together!'

The buglers sounded the alarm. The squadrons formed up in a column. Out of a ditch crawled a wounded man who said to Vytyagaychenko, covering himself with his palm:

'Taras Grigoryevich, I'm a delegate. Looks as if we're going to be left behind . . .'

'You'll look after yourselves,' muttered Vytyagaychenko, making his horse rear.

'Got a sort of feeling we can't look after ourselves, Taras Grigoryevich,' said the wounded man after him.

Vytyagaychenko turned:

'Stop whining. I'm not likely to leave you behind.' And he ordered the troopers to make ready.

At once there rang out my friend Afonka's whimpering, womanish voice: 'What d'you want to go and rush it for, Taras Grigoryevich? There's five versts to do. How the hell are you going to fight if the horses are fagged out? There's time and enough to spare, damn it!'

'Walking-pace!' commanded Vytyagaychenko without raising his eyes. And the regiment rode off.

'If my notion about the Divisional Commander's right,' whispered Afonka, lingering for a moment, 'if he gets canned, things are going to be a sight different. And that's that.'

Tears started to his eyes and brimmed over. I stared at him in utter amazement. Then he spun around like a top, caught at his cap, snorted, uttered the Cossack war-whoop, and tore off at full speed.

Grishchuk with his idiotic cart and I stayed on till evening, hanging about between two walls of fire. The Division's Staff had vanished, and other units would have none of us. The regiments entered Brody and were driven out again by a counter-attack. We drove up to the city cemetery, and from behind a tombstone there started up a Polish scout, who shouldered his rifle and opened fire on us. Grishchuk turned back, all four wheels of his tachanka squealing.

'Grishchuk!' I cried through the whistling and the wind.

'What a lark!' he answered mournfully.

'It's the end of us,' I shouted, seized with mortal frenzy. 'It's the end of us, old boy!'

'Whatever do women go and give themselves such trouble for?' he asked still more mournfully. 'Whatever do they want engagements and marriages for, and pals to make merry at the wedding?'

A pink trail lit up in the sky and died out again. The Milky Way appeared among the stars.

'Makes me laugh,' said Grishchuk sadly, pointing his whip at a man sitting by the roadside. 'Makes me laugh, what women want to go and give themselves such trouble for . . .'

The man sitting by the roadside was Dolgushov, a tele-phonist. He sat staring at us, his legs straddled.

'I've had it,' he said when we had driven over to him. 'Get me?'

'Yes,' said Grishchuk, pulling up the horses.

'You'll have to waste a cartridge on me,' said Dolgushov.

He was leaning up against a tree, his boots thrust out apart. Without lowering his eyes from mine he warily rolled back his shirt. His belly had been torn out. The entrails hung over his knees, and the heartbeats were visible.

'The Poles'll turn up and play their dirty tricks. Here are my papers. You'll write and tell my mother how things were.'

'No,' I answered, and spurred my horse.

Dolgushov laid his blue palms out upon the earth and gazed at them mistrustfully.

'Sneaking off, eh?' he muttered, sliding down. 'Well, sneak off then, you swine.'

Sweat trickled down my body. The machine-guns were rapping away with hysterical insistence, faster and faster. Framed in the nimbus of the sunset, Afonka Bida came galloping up to us.

'We're giving it to them good and strong!' he cried gaily. 'Hullo, what's all the fuss about here?'

I pointed Dolgushov out to him, and rode on a little way.

They spoke briefly; no words reached me. Dolgushov held his papers out to the platoon commander, and Afonka hid them away in his boot and shot Dolgushov in the mouth.

'Afonka,' I said with a wry smile, and rode over to the Cossack. 'I couldn't, you see.'

'Get out of my sight,' he said, growing pale, 'or I'll kill you. You guys in specs have about as much pity for chaps like us as a cat has for a mouse.'

And he cocked his rifle.

I rode away slowly, not turning around, feeling the chill of death in my back.

'Eh, you!' shouted Grishchuk behind me. 'Stop fooling about!' And he seized Afonka by the arm.

'The bloody swine!' cried Afonka. 'He isn't going to get off like that!'

Grishchuk caught me up at a bend in the road. Afonka was nowhere to be seen; he had ridden off in another direction.

'There, you see, Grishchuk,' I said; 'today I've lost Afonka, my closest friend.'

Grishchuk produced a shrivelled apple from his driving seat.

'Eat it,' he said to me. 'Do please eat it.'

Brody, August 1920

The Brigade Commander

BUDYONNY, in silver-striped red trousers, stood beside a tree. The Commander of the 2nd Brigade had just been killed, and the Army Commander had promoted Kolesnikov in his stead.

An hour ago, Kolesnikov had been in command of a regiment. A week ago, Kolesnikov had been in command of a squadron.

The new Brigade Commander was summoned to Budyonny. The Army Commander waited for him standing
beside the tree. Kolesnikov arrived with Almazov, his Commissar.

'We're being pretty hard pressed by those blackguards,'
said the Army Commander with one of his flashing smiles.
'We're going to beat 'em, or die for it. There's no other way
out. Understand?'

'I understand,' replied Kolesnikov, wide-eyed.

'You just try running away, and I'll shoot you,' the Army
Commander said. He smiled and turned his eyes to the Chief
of the Special Section.

'Right,' said the Chief of the Special Section.

'Roll on, Wheel!' one of the Cossack bystanders cried out
cheerily, punning on the Brigade Commander's name.

Budyonny turned sharply on his heel and saluted the new
Commander. The latter spread out five red, youthful fingers
by the peak of his cap, broke into a sweat, and went off along
the path between two fields. Horses awaited him two hundred
yards off. He walked head down, his long crooked legs picking
their way laboriously, bathed in the crimson haze of a sunset
that seemed as unreal as oncoming death.

And suddenly, on the earth stretching away far into the
distance, on the furrowed, yellow nakedness of the fields, we
could see nothing but Kolesnikov's narrow back, his dangling
arms, his sunken, grey-capped head.

An orderly led up a mount.

He leaped into the saddle and without turning around
galloped off to his brigade. The squadrons were waiting for
him on the main road, on the Brody highroad.

Rent by the wind, a groaning 'hurrah' reached us.

I focused my field-glasses and saw the Brigade Commander
twirling on his horse in pillars of thick dust.

'Kolesnikov has led his brigade off,' said an observer who
was sitting in the tree above our heads.

'Right,' answered Budyonny and lit a cigarette, and closed his eyes.

The hurrah died away. The cannonade petered out. Pointless shrapnel burst over the wood, and we heard the great noiselessness of a cavalry charge.

'Got some guts, that kid,' said the Army Commander. 'He's out for glory. Expect he'll get it, too.'

And calling for horses he rode away to the scene of action. The Staff moved after him.

I chanced to see Kolesnikov again that very evening, only an hour after the wiping-out of the Poles. He was riding on a dun stallion at the head of his brigade, alone and dreaming. His right arm hung in a sling. Three yards behind him a Cossack cavalryman bore the unfurled banner. The first squadron was lazily singing ribald couplets. Dusty, endless, the brigade stretched out like a line of peasant carts on the way to a fair. At the tail-end panted the weary bands.

In Kolesnikov's quarters that night I beheld the masterful indifference of a Tartar Khan and was conscious of the training of the famous Kniga, the headstrong Pavlichenko, and the captivating Savitsky.

Brody, August 1920

Sandy the Christ

SANDY was his name. He was called The Christ on account of his mildness. He was the communal herdsman in a Cossack settlement, and he had done no heavy work since about the age of fourteen, when he caught an evil disease. It all came about like this:

Tarakanych, Sandy's stepfather, had gone to spend the winter in Grozny and had there joined up with an association for group-work scratched together by Ryazan peasants.

Tarakanych did carpentering for them, and found the work profitable. As he was unable to keep up with it all, he wrote home for the boy to come and help him out. The settlement could manage quite well through the winter without Sandy. The lad worked with his stepfather for a week. Then came Saturday; they put their work away and sat down to drink tea. It was then October, but the air was light. They opened the window and kindled a second samovar. Under the window a beggarwoman was loitering. She knocked on the window-frame, saying:

'Good day, peasants from another town. Will you kindly consider my position?'

'What position?' asked Tarakanych. 'Come in, little cripple.'

The beggarwoman scrabbled about outside and then jumped into the room. She came over to the table and bowed low from the waist. Tarakanych seized her by the kerchief, pulled it off, and dug his fingers in her hair. The beggar-woman's hair was grey, white, matted, full of dust.

'Get away! Rough, ain't you, peasant! Think yourself handsome!' she said. 'With you it's like being at the circus. – Now don't scorn an old woman like me,' she whispered hurriedly as she clambered up on to the bench.

Tarakanych lay down with her. The beggarwoman kept tossing her head to one side and laughing.

'Rain on parched soil,' she laughed. 'What a crop I'll give!'

As she spoke she caught sight of Sandy, who was drinking tea at the table without raising his eyes.

'Your boy?' she asked Tarakanych.

'Mine, in a manner of speaking,' answered Tarakanych. 'The wife's.'

'What eyes the child's making,' said the peasant woman. 'Come over here, now.'

Sandy went over to her – and caught an evil disease. But there was no thought then of evil diseases. Tarakanych gave the beggarwoman some bones left over from dinner, and a bright silver five-copeck piece.

'Clean it with sand, you God-fearing woman,' said Tarakanych, 'and it will look finer still. If you lend it to the Lord on a dark night it'll shine instead of the moon.'

The beggarwoman wound her scarf round her head, took up the bones, and departed. And at the end of a fortnight it all became clear to the peasants. They suffered considerably from the evil disease and dragged on through the winter, curing themselves with herbs. When spring came they returned to the settlement, back to their work in the fields.

The settlement was nine versts from the railway. Tarakanych and Sandy went by the fields. The soil lay in its April dampness. In the black hollows emeralds shone, and green shoots embroidered the earth in complicated back-stitching. From the ground rose an acrid smell, as from a soldier's wife at dawn. The first herds were flowing down from the hillocks, foals were gambolling in the blue expanses of the horizon.

Tarakanych and Sandy followed paths that were barely perceptible.

'Let me go and be the village herdsman, Tarakanych,' said Sandy.

'What for?'

'I can't rid myself of the thought that the herdsmen have such a fine time.'

'You'll not have my consent.'

'For the love of God, let me go, Tarakanych,' begged Sandy. 'All the Saints used to be shepherds and herdsmen.'

'Sandy – a Saint!' guffawed the stepfather. 'Went and caught you know what.'

They passed the bend at the Red Bridge, crossed the copse, the pastureland, and came in sight of the cross on the settlement church.

The womenfolk were still busy in the kitchen-gardens, while the Cossacks, sitting among the lilac bushes, drank vodka and sang songs. Tarakanych's hut was still half a verst away.

'Pray the Lord it will be all right,' he said, crossing himself.

They went up to the hut and peered in at the little window. There was no one inside. Sandy's mother was in the shed milking the cow. The peasants stole up noiselessly. Tarakanych started laughing and shouting behind the woman's back:

'Motya, Your Highness, get some supper for your visitors!'

The woman turned, shuddered, ran out of the shed, and twisted about the yard like a top. Then she came back, cast herself on Tarakanych's chest, and threw a fit.

'You're a nice one! Not very inviting, are you?' said Tarakanych, gently disengaging her. 'Show us the children.'

'They've gone out,' said the woman, very white; and again she dashed about the yard and fell down on the ground. 'Oh, Alyosha,' she cried wildly, 'our kiddies went out feet foremost.'

Tarakanych waved a despairing hand and went off to see the neighbours. They told him that the week before God had taken his little boy and girl after typhus. Motya had written to him, but no doubt he had not received the letter. Tarakanych returned to the hut. His wife was lighting the stove.

'You've gone and done it all right, Motya,' he said. 'Ought to give you what for.'

He sat down at the table and grieved – grieved on till bedtime, ate meat and drank vodka, and did not go about his work. He snored at the table, would wake up, then start snoring again. Motya spread the bed for herself and her husband, and Sandy's bed was apart. Then she blew out the lamp and lay down with her husband.

Sandy stirred on the hay in his corner, his eyes wide open. He could not sleep, and as though in a dream he saw the room, a star in the window, the edge of the table, and the horse-collars beneath his mother's bed. The enforced vision held him spellbound, and rejoicing in his daydream he gave himself up to reverie. His fancy showed him two silver bands of coarse twisted thread suspended from the sky, and attached to them a cradle – a cradle of rosewood with a floral pattern. It swung high above the earth and far from the skies, and the bands swayed and sparkled; Sandy himself lay in the cradle, and the air was fanning him. The air, full of sound like music, came from the fields, and a rainbow blossomed over the unripe corn.

Sandy took delight in his daydream, and kept closing his eyes so as not to see the horse-collars beneath his mother's bed. Then he heard a wheezing from Motya's couch, and considered the fact that Tarakanych was tumbling his mother.

'Tarakanych,' he said, raising his voice, 'there's a matter I must talk to you about.'

'What matter, at this time of night?' Tarakanych returned angrily. 'Go to sleep, you fool!'

'I swear by the Cross that there really is something,' said Sandy. 'Come out into the yard.'

And in the yard, beneath a steadfast star, Sandy said to his stepfather:

'Don't worry mother, Tarakanych. You're tainted.'

'You know my nature, don't you?' said Tarakanych.

'I know your nature all right but did you see the body mother has? Her feet are clean, and her breast is clean. Don't wrong her, Tarakanych. We're tainted.'

'Young fellow,' said the stepfather, 'keep clear of my nature, keep clear of blood-letting. Here, take this twenty-copeck piece. Sleep the night through and sober up.'

'Twenty copecks are no good to me,' muttered Sandy. 'Let me go and be the village herdsman.'

'That I won't agree to.'

'Let me go and be the village herdsman, or I'll tell mother the sort of folk we are. Why should she suffer, with that body?'

Tarakanych turned away, went into the shed, and brought out a hatchet.

'You saint,' he whispered, 'I'm going to make a quick job of it. Going to chop you up, I am.'

'You won't do me in for a woman's sake,' said the boy, so low he could hardly be heard; and he bowed down before his stepfather. 'You have a fondness for me. Let me go and be herdsman.'

'Go to the devil!' cried Tarakanych, and threw down the hatchet. 'All right, go and be herdsman.'

He returned to the hut, and passed the night with his wife.

That morning Sandy went to offer his services to the Cossacks, and from that day on he led the life of the village herdsman. He became renowned through all the neighbourhood for his good nature and simplicity, and was called by the Cossacks Sandy the Christ. He served as herdsman right on till conscription came. Foolish old peasants would come to the pasture to wag their tongues with him, women would run to Sandy to recover from the everyday brutality of the peasants, and because of his love and because of his illness they were never angry with him.

The first year of the war Sandy was mobilized. He fought for four years, and returned to the settlement at a time when the Whites were lording it over the place. He was urged to go to the Platov settlement, where a detachment was being formed against the Whites. Simon Budyonny, the former sergeant-major, was in command of the detachment, and with him were his three brothers. Sandy went to the Platov settlement, and there his fate was decided. He served in Budyonny's regiment, in his brigade, in his division, and in the First Cavalry Army. He marched to free heroic Tsaritsyn; joined up with the X Army under Voroshilov; fought at Voronezh, at Kastornaya, and at the General's Bridge on the Donets. During the Polish campaign he served on the transport wagons because he had been wounded and pronounced unfit for active service.

This was how it all came about. It was only recently that

I got to know Sandy the Christ, and shifted my little trunk over to his cart. Since then we have often met the dawn and seen the sun set together. And whenever the capricious chance of war has brought us together, we have sat down of an evening on the bench outside a hut, or made tea in the woods in a sooty kettle, or slept side by side in the new-mown fields, the hungry horses tied to his foot or mine.

The Life and Adventures of Matthew Pavlichenko

COMRADES, countrymen, my own dear brethren! In the name of all mankind learn the story of the Red General, Matthew Pavlichenko. He used to be a herdsman, that general did – the herdsman on the Lidino estate, working for Nikitin-sky the master and looking after the master's pigs till life brought stripes to his shoulder straps; and with those stripes, Mat began to look after the horned cattle. And who knows, if this Mat of ours had been born in Australia he might have risen to elephants, he'd have come to grazing elephants; only the trouble is, I don't know where they'd be found in our Stavropol district. I'll tell you straight, there isn't an animal bigger than the buffalo in the whole of our wide region. And a poor lad wouldn't get no comfort out of buffaloes: it isn't any fun for a Russian fellow just getting a laugh out of buffaloes! Give us poor orphans something in the way of a horse for keeps – a horse, so as its mind and ribs can work themselves out at the far end of the fields.

And so I look after my horned cattle, with cows all around me, soaked in milk and stinking of it like a sliced udder. Young bulls walk around me – mouse-grey young bulls. Open space around me in the fields, the grass rustling through all the world, the sky above my head like an accordion with lots of keyboards – and the skies in the Stavropol district are very blue, boys. Well, I looked after my cattle like this, and as there was nothing to do, I used to play with the winds on reeds, till an old gaffer says to me:

'Matthew,' says he, 'go and see Nastasya.'

'Why?' says I. 'Or maybe you're kidding me.'

'Go,' he says, 'she wants you.'

And so I goes.

'Nastasya,' I says, and blush black in the face. 'Nastasya,' I says; 'or maybe you're kidding me.'

She won't hear me out, though, but runs off from me and goes on running till she can run no more; and I runs along with her till we get to the common, dead-beat and red and puffed.

'Matthew,' says Nastasya to me then, 'three Sundays ago, when the spring fishing was on and the fishermen were going down to the river, you too went with them, and hung your head. Why did you hang your head, Matthew, or was it some notion or other that was heavy on your heart? Tell me.'

And I answer her:

'Nastasya,' I says, 'I've nothing to tell you. My head isn't a rifle and there ain't no sight on it nor no backsight neither. As for my heart – you know what it's like, Nastasya; there isn't nothing in it, it's just milky, I dare say. It's terrible how I smell of milk.'

But Nastasya, I see, is fair tickled at my words.

'I'll swear by the Cross,' she says, and bursts out laughing with all her might over the whole steppe, just as if she was beating the drum, 'I'll swear by the Cross that you make eyes at the young ladies.'

And when we'd talked a lot of nonsense for a while we soon got married, and Nastasya and I started living together for all we was worth, and that was a good deal. We was hot all night; we was hot in winter, and all night long we went naked, rubbing our raw hides. We lived damn well, right on till up comes the old 'un to me a second time.

'Matthew,' he says, 'the master fondled your wife here there and everywhere, not long since. He'll get her all right, will the master.'

And I:

'No,' I says, 'if you'll excuse me, old 'un. Or if he does I'll nail you to the spot.'

So naturally the old chap makes himself scarce. And I did twenty versts on foot that day, covered a good piece of ground, and in the evening I got to the Lidino estate, to my merry master Nikitinsky. He was sitting in a room upstairs, the old man was, and he was taking three saddles to pieces: an English one, a dragoon one, and a Cossack one; and I stuck to his door like a burr, stuck there a whole hour, and all to no purpose. But then he cast his eyes my way.

'What d'you want?' he asks.

'A reckoning.'

'You've got designs on me?'

'I haven't got no designs, but I want straight out to . . .'

Here he looked away and spread out on the floor some scarlet saddlecloths. They were brighter than the Tsar's flags, those saddlecloths of his; and he stood on them, the little fellow, and strutted about.

'Freedom to the free,' he says to me, and struts about. 'I've tickled all your maternal parents, you Orthodox peasants. You can have your reckoning if you like; only don't you owe me a trifle, Matthew my friend?'

'He-he,' I answers. 'What a comical fellow you are, and that's a fact! Seems to me as it's you that owes me my pay.'

'Pay!' the master shoots out, and he knocks me down on my knees and shuffles his feet about and boxes me on the ears for all the Father, Son, and Holy Ghost's worth. 'Your pay! And have you forgotten the yoke of mine you smashed? Where's my ox-yoke?'

'I'll let you have your yoke back,' I answer my master, and turn my simple eyes upon him and kneel before him, bending lower than any earthly depth. 'I'll give you your yoke back; only don't press me with the debts, old fellow; just wait a bit.'

And what d'you think, you Stavropol boys, comrades, fellow-countrymen, my own dear brethren? The master kept me hanging on like that with my debts for five years. Five lost years I was like a lost soul, till at last the year Eighteen came along to visit me, lost soul that I was. It came along on lively stallions, on its Kabardin horses, bringing along a big train of wagons and all sorts of songs. Eh you, little year Eighteen, my sweetheart! Can it be that we shan't be walking out with you any more, my own little drop of blood, my year Eighteen? We've been free with your songs and drunk up your wine and made out your laws, and only your chroniclers are left. Eh, my sweetheart! It's not the writers that rushed about over the Kuban those days, setting the souls of generals free at a distance of one pace. And Matthew son of Rodion was lying in blood at Prikumsk at that time, and there were only five versts of the last march left to the Lidino estate. Well, I went over alone, without the detachment, and going up to the room I went quietly in. The local powers was sitting there in the room upstairs. Nikitinsky was carrying round tea and billing and cooing to them, but when he saw me his face fell, and I took off my Kuban hat to him.

'Good day,' I says to the folks. 'Accept my best regards. Receive a visitor, master; or how shall it be between us?'

'It's all going to be decent and quiet between us,' answers one of the fellows: a surveyor, I notice by his way of speaking. 'It's all going to be quiet and decent; but it looks as if you have been riding a good way, Comrade Pavlichenko, for your face is all splashed with dirt. We, the local powers, dread such looks. Why is it?'

'It's because, you cold-blooded local powers,' I answer, 'because in my looks one cheek has been burning for five years – burning in the trenches, burning on the march, burning with a woman, will go on burning till the Last Judgement. The Last Judgement,' I say, looking at Nikitinsky cheerful-like; but by this time he's got no eyes, only balls in the middle of his face, as if they had rolled those balls down into position under his forehead. And he was blinking at me with those glassy balls, also cheerful-like, but very horrible.

'Mat,' he says to me, 'we used to know one another once upon a time, and now my wife, Nadezhda Vasilyevna, has lost her reason because of all the goings on of these times. She used to be very good to you, usen't she? And you, Mat, you used to respect her more than all the others, and you don't mean to say you wouldn't like to have a look at her now that she's lost the light of reason?'

'All right,' I says, and we two go out into another room, and there he begins to touch my hands, first my right hand and then my left.

'Mat,' he says, 'are you my destiny or aren't you?'

'No,' I says, 'and cut that talk. God has left us, slaves that we are. Our destiny's no better than a turkey-cock, and our life's worth just about a copeck. So cut that talk and listen if you like to Lenin's letter.'

'A letter to me, Nikitinsky?'

'To you,' I says, and takes out my book of orders and opens it at a blank page and reads, though I can't read to save my life. 'In the name of the nation,' I read, 'and for the foundation of a nobler life in the future, I order Pavlichenko, Matthew, son of Rodion, to deprive certain people of life, according to his discretion.'

'There,' I says, 'that's Lenin's letter to you.'

And he to me: 'No! No, Mat,' he says; 'I know life has gone to pot and that blood's cheap now in the Apostolic Russian Empire, but all the same, the blood due to you you'll get, and anyway you'll forget my look in death, so wouldn't it be better if I just showed you a certain floor-board?'

'Show away,' I says. 'It might be better.'

And again he and I went through a lot of rooms and down into the wine-cellar, and there he pulled out a brick and found a casket behind the brick, and in the casket there were rings and necklaces and decorations, and a holy image done in pearls. He threw it to me and went into a sort of stupor.

'Yours,' he says, 'now you're the master of the Nikitinsky image. And now, Mat, back to your lair at Prikumsk.'

And then I took him by the body and by the throat and by the hair.

'And what am I going to do about my cheek?' I says. 'What's to be done about my cheek, kinsman?'

And then he burst out laughing, much too loud, and didn't try to free himself any more.

'You jackal's conscience,' he says, not struggling any more. 'I'm talking to you like an officer of the Russian Empire, and you blackguards were suckled by a she-wolf. Shoot me then, damned son of a bitch!'

But I wasn't going to shoot him. I didn't owe him a shot anyway, so I only dragged him upstairs into the parlour. There in the parlour was Nadezhda Vasilyevna clean off her head, with a drawn sabre in her hand, walking about and looking at herself in the glass. And when I dragged Nikitinsky into the parlour she ran and sat down in the armchair. She had a velvet crown on trimmed with feathers. She sat in the armchair very brisk and alert and saluted me with the sabre. Then I stamped on my master Nikitinsky, trampled on him for an hour or maybe more. And in that time I got to know life through and through. With shooting – I'll put it this way – with shooting you only get rid of a chap. Shooting's letting him off, and too damn easy for yourself. With shooting you'll never get at the soul, to where it is in a fellow and how it shows itself. But I don't spare myself, and I've more than once trampled an enemy for over an hour. You see, I want to get to know what life really is, what life's like down our way.

The Cemetery at Kozin

THE cemetery of a little Jewish town. Assyria and all the mysterious stagnation of the East, over those weed-grown plains of Volhynia.

Carved grey stones with inscriptions three centuries old. Crude high-reliefs hewn out in the granite. Lambs and fishes depicted above a skull, and Rabbis in fur caps – Rabbis girt round their narrow loins with leather belts. Below their eyeless faces the rippling stone line of their curly beards. To one side, beneath a lightning-shattered oak, stands the burial vault of the Rabbi Azrael, slain by the Cossacks of Bogdan Khmelnitsky. Four generations lie buried in that vault that is as lowly as a water-carrier's dwelling; and the memorial stone, all overgrown with green, sings of them with the eloquence of a Bedouin's prayer.

'Azrael son of Ananias, Jehova's mouthpiece.

'Elijah son of Azrael, brain that struggled single-handed with oblivion.

'Wolff son of Elijah, prince robbed from the Torah in his nineteenth spring.

'Judah son of Wolff, Rabbi of Cracow and Prague.

'O death, O covetous one, O greedy thief, why couldst thou not have spared us, just for once?'

Prishchepa's Vengeance

I AM on my way to Leszniów, where the Divisional Staff is quartered. My companion, as before, is Prishchepa, a young Cossack from the Kuban – a tireless ruffian who has been turned out of the Communist Party, a future rag-and-bone man, a carefree syphilitic, and a happy-go-lucky fraud. He wears a crimson Circassian coat of fine cloth, and a downy Caucasian hood is thrown back over his shoulders. On our journeys he has told me his story.

A year ago Prishchepa ran away from the Whites. In revenge, these took his parents as hostages and put them to death. Their property was seized by the neighbours. When the Whites were driven out of the Kuban, Prishchepa returned to his native settlement.

It was early morning, daybreak. The peasants' slumber sighed in the acrid stuffiness. Prishchepa hired an official cart and went about the settlement collecting his phonograph, wooden kvass-jugs, and the towels his mother had embroidered. He went out into the street in a black felt cloak, a curved dagger at his belt. The cart plodded along behind. Prishchepa went from neighbour to neighbour, leaving behind him the trail of his blood-stained footprints. In the huts where he found gear that had belonged to his mother, a pipe that had been his father's, he left old women stabbed through and through, dogs hung above the wells, icons defiled with excrement. The inhabitants of the settlement watched his progress sullenly, smoking their pipes. The young Cossacks were scattered over the steppe, keeping the score. And the score mounted up and up – and still the settlement remained silent.

When he had made an end, Prishchepa went back to his despoiled home and arranged the furniture he had taken back

94

in the places he remembered from childhood. Then he sent for vodka, and shutting himself up in the hut, he drank for two whole days and nights, singing, weeping, and hewing the furniture with his Circassian sabre.

On the third night the settlement saw smoke rise from Prishchepa's hut. Torn, scorched, staggering, the Cossack led the cow out of the shed, put his revolver in its mouth and fired. The earth smoked beneath him. A blue ring of flame flew out of the chimney and melted away, while in the stall the young bull that had been left behind bellowed piteously. The fire shone as bright as Sunday. Then Prishchepa untied his horse, leaped into the saddle, threw a lock of his hair into the flames, and vanished.

The Story of a Horse

SAVITSKY, our Divisional Commander, once took a white stallion away from Khlebnikov, Commander of the First Squadron. It was a horse of a showy appearance, but with raw lines that always seemed to me on the heavy side. In exchange for it Khlebnikov received a little black mare with a smooth trot and of quite fair breed. However, he utterly neglected the mare, thirsting only for revenge, awaiting his hour, waiting till in the end it came.

After our unsuccessful July campaign, when Savitsky was replaced and sent back to the reserve, Khlebnikov wrote to the Army Staff applying for the horse to be returned to him. The Chief of Staff wrote over his application: 'The stallion in question to be returned to its original status,' and Khlebnikov, radiant with triumph, rode a hundred versts in order to find Savitsky, who was then living in Radziwillów – a maimed little town not unlike a lady come down in the world. The dismissed Commander lived alone, and the fawning

Staff Officers ignored him. These fawning Staff Officers fished for roast chicken in the Army Commander's smiles, and basely turned their backs upon the renowned Savitsky.

Soaked in scent and resembling Peter the Great, Savitsky lived in disgrace with a Cossack woman, Pavla, whom he had lured away from a Jew in the commissariat, and with twenty thoroughbreds which we looked upon as his property.

The sun in his yard was putting forth all its might, oppressed by the blinding brilliance of its own rays. The foals in the yard were noisily sucking their dams, and the grooms, their backs damp with sweat, were sifting oats on the discoloured winnowing machines. Khlebnikov, suffering from his sense of right and wrong and driven by his thirst for vengeance, strode up to the barricaded yard.

'Is my person known to you?' he asked Savitsky, who was lying on some hay.

'I fancy I've seen you somewhere or other,' Savitsky answered, and yawned.

'Then take this Staff resolution,' said Khlebnikov firmly, 'and I must request you, comrade in the reserve, to look upon me with an official eye.'

'All right,' muttered Savitsky in a conciliatory tone.

He took the sheet of paper and began to read it, uncommonly slowly. Then he suddenly called over to him the Cossack woman, who was combing her hair in the cool under the porch.

'Pavla,' he said, 'the Lord knows you've been combing your hair ever since morning. Now what d'you say to putting on the samovar?'

The Cossack woman put aside her comb and, taking her hair into her hands, threw it back over her shoulder.

'All day long you've been going on at me, Constantine Vasilyevich,' she said, with a lazy and imperious smile, 'now one thing, now another . . .'

She went over to the Commander, bearing her bosom

on her high heels, a bosom that stirred like an animal in a bag.

'All day long you've been going on at me,' the woman repeated, beaming, and she buttoned the Commander's shirt over his chest.

'Now one thing, now another!' laughed the Commander, rising; and putting his arms round Pavla's yielding shoulders, he suddenly turned upon Khlebnikov a face drained of all life.

'I'm still alive and kicking, Khlebnikov,' he said, clasping the Cossack woman. 'My legs still walk, my horses still gallop, and my hands will get you yet, and my gun's warming against my body.'

He took out his revolver that was lying against the bare skin of his stomach and approached the Squadron Commander.

The latter turned on his heels, his spurs groaning, and went out of the yard like an orderly to whom an express message has been given. And again he rode a hundred versts to find the Chief of Staff once more – only to be rebuffed.

'Your business has been settled,' said the Chief of Staff. 'I've returned the stallion to you, and have quite enough to bother me without you.'

He refused to listen to Khlebnikov, and in the end sent the truant Commander back to his squadron. But Khlebnikov vanished for a week. During that time we were sent to camp in the Dubno forests, where we pitched our tents and lived very comfortably. Khlebnikov, I remember, returned on the Sunday morning, the twelfth. He made me give him ink and more than a ream of paper. The Cossacks planed a tree stump for him, and on it he placed his revolver and the paper and wrote till evening, covering quantities of sheets with his dirty scrawl.

'A regular Karl Marx,' remarked the squadron commissar that evening. 'Whatever are you writing, you chump?'

'Describing all sorts of thoughts in accordance with my oath,' replied Khlebnikov, and handed the commissar a declaration of his withdrawal from the Communist Party.

'The Communist Party,' read the declaration, 'was founded, as I understand it, for joy and sound justice without limit, and it ought to consider the small fry also. Now I will come to the question of the white stallion which I took from the peasants in spite of their unbelievable resistance at a time when it looked half-starved, and many of my comrades had the nerve to laugh at its looks, but I had the strength to bear all their jeers and setting my teeth for the common cause I looked after the stallion till the desired change ensued, because I am, comrades, a lover of white horses and have given them the little strength left over from the Imperialist and Civil Wars, and such stallions feel my hand, and I can feel their unspoken wants also and what they need, but the unjust black mare is not good to me, I can't feel her and I can't stand her; so that like as not things may turn out badly, and all the comrades can bear me out. And now as the Party can't give me back my very own according to the resolution, I see no way but to write this declaration with tears that are not fitting to a soldier but that will go on flowing all the same, slashing my heart, slashing my heart till it bleeds . . .'

This and a good deal besides was written in Khlebnikov's declaration, for he spent the whole day writing it, and it ran into many pages. The commissar and I struggled with it for an hour, and succeeded in making it out to the very end.

'What a fool you are,' said the commissar, tearing up the sheets. 'Come and see me after supper. We'll have a talk.'

'Don't want your talk,' answered Khlebnikov, shuddering. 'You've gone and lost me, commissar.'

He stood there shivering, his hands to his trouser seams, stood there looking about him as if considering which way to run. The commissar went right up to him, but was not cautious enough. Khlebnikov tore himself away and dashed off.

'Lost me,' he yelled wildly, and he climbed up on to the tree stump, tearing his jacket and scratching his chest.

'Kill me, Savitsky!' he cried, falling to the ground. 'Kill me straight off!'

With the help of the Cossacks we dragged him into a tent and made him tea and rolled him cigarettes. He smoked, trembling all over. Only toward evening did our Commander calm down. He said no more about his crazy declaration, but went a week later to Rovno for a medical overhaul; and since he had six wounds, he was demobilized as unfit for service.

And that was how we lost Khlebnikov. I was very upset about it, for he was a quiet fellow whose character was rather like mine. He was the only man in the squadron to possess a samovar. The days when there was a lull in the fighting we used to drink scalding tea together. We were both shaken by the same passions. Both of us looked on the world as a meadow in May – a meadow traversed by women and horses.

Konkin's Prisoner

WE was wiping out the Poles up Belaya Tserkov way. We was wiping them out and making a clean job of it, so that even the trees bent. I got a scratch in the morning, but managed to get about somehow. The day was getting on for evening, I remember, and I'd got away from the Brigade Commander with only five Cossacks of the proletariat to stick to me. All around there's hand-to-hand fighting going on, all going at one another like cats and dogs. Blood's trickling down from me and my horse. You know the sort of thing.

I and Spirka Zabuty got away together, farther away from the forest, and lo and behold – a lucky break – three hundred yards off, not more, dust what may be from a Staff, or from transport wagons. If it's Staff – all right; and if it's transport wagons – better still. The kids were going about in rags, and their shirts didn't reach down to their little bottoms.

'Zabuty,' says I to Spirka, 'you damned so-and-so, one way and another, I call upon you as the speaker – up and doing, man! That must be their Staff lighting out.'

'I don't say no,' says Spirka; 'only there's two of us and eight of them.'

'Puff away, Spirka,' I says; 'anyway, I'll go and dirty their chasubles. Come along and die for a pin and the World Revolution!'

Well, we went for them. There were eight swordsmen among 'em. Two we put out of action with our rifles. The third, I see, Spirka's gone and done in. And I takes aim at a big pot, boys, with a gold watch and chain. I got him up against a farm, all over apple trees and cherries. My big pot's mount was a regular beauty, but it was fagged. Then the Pan General drops his bridle, points his Mauser at me, and makes a hole in my leg.

'All right,' I thinks, 'I'll get you to kick your legs up all right.'

So I got busy and put two bullets in the little horse. I was sorry about the stallion. He was a little Bolshevik – a regular little Bolshevik that stallion was, all chestnut, like a copper coin, with a good brush of tail and hocks like cords. I thought to myself: I'll take it alive to Lenin. But it didn't come off: I went and did that little horse in. It plumped down all of a heap like a bride, and my big pot fell out of the saddle. He jerked to one side and turned around and made a draught in my face again. So now I've got three distinctions in action.

'Jesus,' I thinks, 'he's as like as not to go and kill me by mistake.'

So I galloped up to him, and he'd already got his sword out, and tears were running down his cheeks – white tears, real human milk.

'I'll get the Order of the Red Banner through you,' I shouts. 'Hands up, as I'm alive, Your Worship!'

'I can't, Pan,' the old fellow answers. 'You'll do me in.'

Then suddenly up comes Spirka from nowhere, all bathed in sweat and his eyes hanging from his mug by threads.

'Vasily,' he shouts to me, 'you'll never believe the amount I've finished off! As for that general with trimmings all over him, I wouldn't mind finishing him off too.'

'Go to blazes!' I says to Zabuty, losing my temper. 'The trimmings have cost me blood, I can tell you!'

And I got my mare to drive the general into a shed with hay in it or something. It was quiet in there and dark and cool.

'Pan,' I says, 'go steady in your old age. Now hands up, for the love of Mike, and we'll have a talk together.'

He puffs away with his back to the wall and wipes his forehead with his red fingers.

'I can't,' he says, 'you'll do me in. I'll only give up my sword to Budyonny.'

Go and fetch him Budyonny! That's gone and torn it! I see the old guy's had his day.

'Pan,' I shouts, crying and grinding my teeth, 'I'll give you my proletarian word that I'm myself commander-in-chief here. You needn't go looking for trimmings on me, but I've got the title all right. Here's my title: musical entertainer and drawing-room ventriloquist from the town of Nizhni – Nizhni Novgorod on the Volga River.'

And a devil in me worked me up. The general's eyes were blinking like lanterns. A red sea opened out in front of me. The offence was like putting salt in a wound, because I could see the old fellow didn't believe me. So I shut my mouth, lads, squeezed in my belly in the old way, in our way, in the

Nizhni-town way, and proved to the Pole that I was a ventriloquist.

And the old chap went quite white and clutched at his heart and sat down on the ground.

'Now d'you believe Vasily the Entertainer, Commissar of the 3rd Invincible Cavalry Brigade?'

'Commissar?' he cries.

'Commissar,' I says.

'Communist?' he cries.

'Communist,' I says.

'In my last hour,' he cries, 'as I draw my last breath, tell me, Cossack friend, are you really a Communist, or are you lying?'

'I'm a Communist all right,' I says.

Then my old fellow sits there on the ground and kisses some amulet or other and breaks his sword in two, while two lamps light up in his eyes – two lanterns over the dark steppe.

'Forgive me,' he says, 'I can't surrender to a Communist. And he shakes me by the hand. 'Forgive me,' says he. 'And kill me like a true soldier.'

This story was related to us some time ago, during a halt, and in his customary farcical manner, by Konkin, the political commissar of the N Cavalry Brigade, thrice Knight of the Order of the Red Banner.

'And what came of your talk with the general, Vasily?'

'Could anything come of it with a chap like that, full of his sense of honour? I bowed to him again, but he would stick to it, so then we took the papers that were on him, the queer old bird, and his Mauser and the saddle that's under me now. And then I noticed my strength's all ebbing away and a terrible sleepiness is descending upon me – well, and I couldn't be bothered with him any more . . .'

'So the old fellow was put out of his misery?'

''Fraid so.'

Berestechko

WE were on the march from Khotin to Berestechko, and the men were dozing in their tall saddles. A song gurgled like a brook running dry. Grotesque corpses lay upon the age-old burial mounds. Peasants in white shirts doffed their caps to us. Divisional Commander Pavlichenko's felt cloak flew like a sombre flag above the Staff. His downy Caucasian hood was thrown back over his cloak, and his curved sword hung down at his side.

We rode past the Cossack tumuli, past Bogdan Khmelnitsky's watchtower. From behind a burial stone an old fellow with a bandore crept forth and, plucking the strings, sang to us in a childish treble of the ancient glory of the Cossacks. We listened to his songs in silence; then unfurled the standards and burst into Berestechko to the sounds of a thundering march.

The inhabitants had put iron bars across their shutters, and silence, almighty silence, had ascended its small-town throne.

It so chanced that I was billeted in the house of a red-haired widow who smelt of the grief of widowhood. I washed away the traces of the march and went out into the street.

Notices were already posted up announcing that Divisional Commissar Vinogradov would lecture that evening on the second congress of the Comintern. Right under my window some Cossacks were trying to shoot an old silvery-bearded Jew for spying. The old man was uttering piercing screams and struggling to get away. Then Kudrya of the machine-gun section took hold of his head and tucked it under his arm. The Jew stopped screaming and straddled his legs. Kudrya drew out his dagger with his right hand and carefully, without splashing himself, cut the old man's throat. Then he knocked at the closed window.

'Anyone who cares may come and fetch him,' he said. 'You're free to do so.'

The Cossacks turned a corner and I went along after them, roaming through Berestechko. Jews are in the majority there, for the Russian townsfolk, tanners for the most part, are settled on the outskirts, where they live cleanly in little white houses with green shutters. Instead of vodka these Russians drink beer or mead. They grow tobacco in their little gardens and smoke it like Galician peasants out of long curved pipes. The neighbourhood of three races, active and businesslike, has awakened in them the dogged love of labour sometimes found in a Russian when he is still free from lice, drink, and despair.

In Berestechko the old order had been given an airing, but it was still firmly rooted here. Offshoots of three centuries still sprouted in Volhynia with the warm decay of ancient days. The Jews here tied with threads of gain the Russian peasant to the Polish Pan, the Czech colonist to the factory in Lodz. They were smugglers, the ablest on the frontier, and nearly always staunch defenders of their faith. Hasidism kept that superstitious population of hawkers, brokers, and tavern-keepers in stifling captivity. Boys in long garments still trod the age-long road to the Hasidic *cheder*; and, just as of yore, old women still took young brides to see the saddik with vehement prayers for fertility.

The Jews here live in spacious houses painted either white or a watery blue. The wretchedness of that architecture has centuries of tradition behind it. At the back of the house there is always a shed of two or sometimes even of three storeys. No sunshine ever penetrates them. These indescribably gloomy sheds take the place of our yards. Secret passages lead to basements and stables. In wartime the inhabitants go down into these catacombs to escape bullets and pillage. Human refuse and cow-dung accumulate here for days. Depression and horror fill the catacombs with a corrosive stench and a tainted acidity.

Berestechko reeks unredeemably even now, and a violent smell of rotten herrings emanates from all its inhabitants. The little town reeks on, awaiting a new era, and instead of human beings there go about mere faded schemata of frontier misfortunes. I wearied of them by the end of the day, and leaving the town climbed a hill and penetrated into the sacked castle of the Counts Raciborski, late owners of Berestechko.

The stilly dusk turned to blue the grass around the castle. The moon, green as a lizard, rose over the pond. From my window I could see the estate of the Counts Raciborski – meadows and hopfields, obscured by the watery ribbon of the twilight.

There used to live in that castle an insane, ninety-year-old countess, with her son whom she plagued because he had given their dying line no heir. And the peasants used to tell me that she would beat her son with a coachman's whip.

A meeting was being held in the square below. Peasants, Jews, and tanners from the outskirts had assembled there, with Vinogradov's voice above them, fired with enthusiasm, and the ringing of his spurs.

He talked about the second congress of the Comintern, while I wandered past walls where nymphs with gouged-out eyes were leading a choral dance. Then in a corner trodden by many feet I found a fragment of a letter yellow with age. In discoloured ink was written:

Berestechko, 1820. Paul, mon bien-aimé, on dit que l'empereur Napoléon est mort, est-ce vrai? Moi, je me sens bien, les couches ont été faciles, notre petit héros achève sept semaines . . .

Down below the Commissar's voice still goes on. He is passionately persuading the bewildered townsfolk and the plundered Jews.

'You are in power. Everything here is yours. No more Pans. I now proceed to the election of the Revolutionary Committee . . .'

Salt

DEAR COMRADE EDITOR,

I want to describe to you about the unconsciousness of the women who are doing us no good. I hope, when you toured the civilian fronts that you made a note of, that you didn't miss the inveterate Fastov railway station which is miles away from everywhere in some district or other, I don't know how many miles away. I was there of course and drank home-brewed beer, but only damped my whiskers as it says in the tale. There is a lot as might be said about the above-mentioned station, but as we say in our simple way, you can't go dragging the Lord's dirt around. That is why I am only going to describe to you what I saw with my own eyes.

Well it was quite a nice little night a week ago when the deserving Cavalry-Army train stopped there, all loaded with men. We were all of us burning to serve the common cause, and were bound for Berdichev. Only we noticed our train wouldn't get moving nohow. There was a hitch somewhere, and the men began to wonder what we had gone and stopped for, and started discussing among themselves. And sure enough the halt turned out to be darned important for the common cause, because the black-marketeers, our worstest enemies, what goes round trading illicitly, and among who there was also a countless force of the feminine sex, had the nerve to go and interfere with the railway authorities. They boldly took hold of the handrails, those worstest enemies did, and galloped over the iron coach-roofs and crowded and swarmed about, and the familiar salt was present in everyone's

hands, up to five poods in a bag. But the black-marketeers'
victory didn't last long.

The initiative of the men that had scrambled out of the
coaches gave the insulted railway authorities their breath
back. Only the feminine sex remained hanging around with
their sacks. Out of pity for them, the men settled some of the
women in the cars, and some of them they didn't. And in our
car too, the second platoon's, there was two girls present,
and as soon as the first bell went, up came a matronly woman
with an infant in arms and says:

'Let me come aboard, Cossack boys. What with these
stations I've had to put up with a lot all through the war with
my little baby in my arms, and now I want to go and see my
husband, but it's impossible to travel because of the railways.
Now I have deserved it, haven't I, Cossack boys?'

'My good woman,' I says to her, 'what the platoon
decides about it, that will be the way your fate will turn out.'
And turning to the platoon I expounded to them that the
matronly woman asks to go to her husband and that she
really has an infant with her, and what will be your consent –
let her aboard or no?

'Let her aboard,' cry the men; 'she won't want her husband, not when we've done with her.'

'No,' I says to the men, quite urbanely; 'all my respects,
platoon, but I am surprised to hear such coarseness from you.
Remember your own lives, platoon, and how you yourselves
were babies with your mothers, and then you will see it
don't do to talk like that.'

And the Cossacks talked among themselves, saying as how
Balmashev – that's me – had gone and growed persuasive
like, and they began to let the woman into the car, and she
climbed in thankfully, and every one of the men, sort of
boiling over with the truth of what I had said, settled her
down, saying, all competing with each other:

'Sit down in the corner, my good woman, and coddle

your baby as mothers do. Nobody will touch you in your
corner, and you will get to your husband safe and sound as
you want to, and we are reckoning on your conscience to
bring up others to take our place, because the old are getting
old and there's not many young ones about. We have seen
bad days, my good woman, on ordinary days and on emer-
gency days too, and been choked with hunger and blistered
with cold. But you sit down here, my good woman, and
don't you worry.'

And when the third bell had rung the train started off. And
the nice little night pitched its tent. And in that tent were
stars like Chinese lanterns, and the men remembered the
Kuban night and the green Kuban star. And a sort of dream-
thought flew past like a little bird. And the wheels went
rumty-tum, rumty-tum.

When the night's time was up and its guard changed and
little red drummers beat reveille on their little red drums,
the Cossacks came over to me, seeing I was sitting without
sleeping and was just about as fed up as I could be.

'Balmashev,' the Cossacks say to me, 'what are you so
terrible fed up about and sitting like that not taking a wink
of sleep?'

'My respects, men. One little request: just let me have two
words with that female citizen there.'

And shaking all over, I get up from my resting-place that
sleep had run away from like a wolf from a pack of savage
hounds, and go over to her and take the infant from her arms
and tear off the swaddling-clothes and find under them a good
pood of salt.

'That's a funny kid, comrades: one as don't ask for the
breast or wet the skirts or wake people up with its squalling!'

'Forgive me, kind Cossack lads,' the woman interrupts as
cool as a cucumber. 'It wasn't me that deceived you. It's the
trouble I'm in that did it.'

'Balmashev will forgive your trouble all right,' I answers the woman. 'It don't cost Balmashev nothing much. Balmashev sells for what he bought at. But you look at the Cossacks, my good woman, the boys that put you on a pedestal for being a mother that laboured for the republic. Look at them two girls crying at present on account of what they went through with us this night. Look at our wives in the wheat plains of the Kuban that are spending their women's strength without their husbands, and the husbands, alone too, all through dire necessity violating the girls as come into their lives. And nobody touched you, you wicked woman, though that's what would have served you right. Look at Russia crushed with misery . . .'

And she answers me back:

'I've gone and lost my salt, so I'm not afraid of telling the truth. You don't bother your heads about Russia. You just go about saving the dirty Jews Lenin and Trotsky.'

'We aren't discussing the Jews now, you noxious citizen. The Jews haven't got nothing to do with the question. By the way, I won't say nothing about Lenin, but Trotsky was the desperate son of a governor of Tambov and went over to the working classes though he himself belonged to another class. They work like niggers, Lenin and Trotsky do, to drag us on to the path of a free life; while you, abominable woman, you're more counter-revolutionary than the White General who goes about on a horse that cost a thousand and threatens us with the sharp point of his sabre. He can be seen from everywhere, that general can, and the workers are only dreaming and planning to get at him and do him in; but you incalculable citizen with your comic kids that don't ask to be fed and don't have to be potted – you can't be seen no more than a flea can, and you go biting away for all you're worth.'

And I don't mind telling you straight that I threw that female citizen down the railway embankment while the train was still going. But she, being big and broad, just sat there awhile, flapped her skirts, and started to go her vile way. And seeing that scatheless woman going along like that and Russia around her like I don't know what, and the peasant fields without an ear of corn and the outraged girls and the comrades lots of which go to the front but few return, I had a mind to jump out of the truck and put an end to my life or else put an end to hers. But the Cossacks took pity on me and said:

'Give it her with your rifle.'

So I took my faithful rifle off the wall and washed away that stain from the face of the workers' land and the republic.

And we, the men of the second platoon, swear to you, dear Comrade Editor, and to you, dear comrades in the Editor's office, that we will deal mercilessly with all the traitors that are dragging us to the dogs and want to turn everything upside down and cover Russia with nothing but corpses and dead grass.

In the name of all the men of the second platoon,

Nikita Balmashev

Soldier of the Revolution

Evening

O REGULATIONS of the Russian Communist Party! You have laid down headlong rails through the sour pastry of our Russian tales. Three bachelor hearts, full of the passions of Ryazan Jesuses, have you turned into contributors to our paper the *Red Trooper*, converted them that they may daily fill the columns of the devil-may-care paper so full already of virility and coarse humour.

Wall-eyed Galin, consumptive Slinkin, and Sychov with the gnawed-away intestines, they wander around in the sterile dust of the rear, tearing with the rebellion and fire of their leaflets through the ranks of our stout Cossack boys relieved from the front, the reserve pilferers who go by the name of Polish interpreters, the girls sent to us by the Political Section for a rest cure from Moscow.

The newspaper – dynamite fuse laid beneath the army – appears only toward nightfall. The squinting lantern of the provincial sun goes out in the sky; the darting lights of the printing press blaze uncontrollably like the passion of machinery. Then, toward nightfall, Galin steps down from the coach to shudder at the bites of his unrequited love for Irina, the washerwoman on our train.

'Last time,' said Galin, narrow-shouldered, pale and purblind, 'last time, Irina, we considered the shooting of Nicholas the Bloody by the Ekaterinburg proletariat. Now we go on to another tyrant who died the death of a dog. Peter III was strangled by Orlov, his wife's paramour, and Paul was torn to pieces by his courtiers and his own son. Nicholas the Rod poisoned himself, his son fell on March first, and his grandson died of drink. You need to know all that, Irina.'

And raising to the washerwoman a naked eye full of adoration, Galin went on ransacking the vaults of perished emperors. His rounded back was bathed in the light of the moon, stuck up on high like a pert shrew: the printing presses rapped on somewhere in the vicinity, and the wireless station shone with a pure radiance. Rubbing up against the shoulder of Vasily the cook, Irina listened to the foolish, muffled mumbling of love, while above her stars dragged through the black seaweed of the sky. The washerwoman dozed, made the sign of the Cross over her puffy lips and gaped at Galin.

Beside Irina yawned the big, heavy-jowled Vasily who, like all cooks, looks down upon humanity. Cooks have a great deal to do with the flesh of dead animals, and the greed of living ones, so that in politics they look for things that are no concern of theirs. So too Vasily. Pulling his trousers up to his nipples, he asked Galin about the civil lists of various kings, about the dowry of the Imperial daughters, and remarked with a yawn:

'It's night-time, Irina. And tomorrow's another day. So come along and squash fleas.'

They had closed the kitchen door, leaving Galin alone with the moon stuck up on high like a pert shrew. Facing the moon, on the bank of a sleeping pond, I was sitting – spectacled, with boils on my neck and bandages on my legs. With my confused poetic brains I was digesting the class-struggle when Galin approached with his gleaming walleyes.

'Galin,' I said, overwhelmed by loneliness and self-pity, 'I'm ill. It seems the end has come, and I'm so sick of being in our Cavalry Army . . .'

'You're a driveller,' replied Galin, the watch on his thin wrist showing 1.00 a.m., 'you're a driveller, and we're fated to have to put up with you drivellers. We're busy shelling and getting at the kernel for you. Not long will pass and then you'll see those cleaned kernels and take your fingers out of your nose and sing of the new life in no ordinary prose. In the meantime sit still, you driveller, and stop whimpering around us.'

He came closer to me and set right the bandages that had loosened on my suppurating wounds, and dropped his head over his pigeon-chest. Night comforted us in our miseries, a light wind fanned us like a mother's skirt, and the grass below sparkled with freshness and moisture.

The rumbling machines of our train-press gave one screech and were silent. Dawn drew a streak along the far end of the earth. The kitchen door whistled and opened very slightly. Four fat-heeled feet were thrust out into the cool, and we beheld Irina's amorous calves and Vasily's big toe with its crooked black nail.

'Vasilyok, my little cornflower,' whispered the woman in

the languishing voice of intimacy, 'leave my bed, you troubler.'

But Vasily just jerked his heel and drew closer.

'The Cavalry Army,' then said Galin to me, 'the Cavalry Army is the social focus effected by the Central Committee of our Party. The revolutionary curve has thrown into the first rank the free Cossacks still soaked in many prejudices, but the Central Committee's manœuvring will rub them down with a brush of iron.'

And Galin talked on about the political education of the First Cavalry Army. He continued for a long time in a muffled voice yet perfectly clearly. Over his walleye his eyelid twitched.

Kovel, 1920

Afonka Bida

WE were fighting at Leszniów. The wall of the enemy's cavalry kept appearing everywhere. The tightened spring of Polish strategy was unwinding with an ominous whistle. We were being hard pressed; for the first time during the whole campaign we felt on our back the devilish sharpness of flank attacks and breaks through in the rear – bites of the very same weapon that had served us so well.

The front line at Leszniów was held by infantry. The unshod, raw recruits of Volhynian peasantry were strewn along the irregularly dug ditches. This infantry was only yesterday taken from the plough in order that a reserve might be formed for the Cavalry Army. The peasants were willing enough, and fought with the utmost application. Even Budyonny's men were amazed at their snorting moujik ferocity. Their hatred for the Polish landowners was made of inconspicuous but good and solid stuff.

During the second stage of the war, when our whooping ceased to have any effect on the enemy and when cavalry attacks became impossible against their trenches, this home-made infantry might have been invaluable to us. Our want, however, got the better of us. The peasants were given one rifle among three, and cartridges that did not fit. We were obliged to abandon our idea, and send back home that genuine people's militia.

Now let us turn to the fighting at Leszniów. The foot soldiers had entrenched themselves three versts away from the little town. A stooping youth in glasses was walking about before their front lines, a sword dragging at his side. He advanced with little hopping steps, and looked dissatisfied, as if his boots were pinching him. This hetman of the peasants – elected and worshipped by them – was a Jew, a mole-eyed Jewish youth with the emaciated face and concentrated expression of a Talmudist. In action he gave proof of cautious courage and sang-froid somewhat resembling the absent-mindedness of a dreamer.

It was between two and three one spacious July day, and the rainbow web of heat shimmered in the air. Behind the hilltops glittered a holiday streak of uniforms and ribbon-tressed manes. The youth gave the signal to prepare for defence. Stumping along in their best shoes, the peasants ran to their positions and shouldered their rifles. But the alarm turned out to be false. On to the Leszniów highroad were riding Maslak's* resplendent squadrons. The horses, lean though still spirited, came along at a good pace. Magnificent standards fluttered in fiery pillars of dust above gilt staffs loaded with velvet tassels. The horsemen rode on majestically, coolly insolent. The tattered foot-soldiers crept out of their ditches and gaped at the supple grace of the steady stream.

At the head of the regiment on a bow-legged horse rode

* *Author's note:* Maslyakov, commander of the 3rd Brigade of the IV Division, an incorrigible guerrilla who soon betrayed the Soviets.

Brigade Commander Maslak, suffused with drunken blood and the putrescence of his greasy humours. His abdomen rested upon the silver-plated saddlebow like a big tomcat. Catching sight of the foot-soldiers, he grew purple with merriment and beckoned to Afonka Bida, the platoon commander we called Makhno because of his resemblance to the famous guerrilla. After they had whispered a moment together, the platoon commander turned to the First Squadron, bent down, and in a low voice ordered: 'Forward!' The Cossacks set off at a trot. Then, working their horses up into a fever of excitement, they galloped over to the trenches where the delighted foot-soldiers were feasting their eyes on the sight.

'Prepare for battle!' sang out Afonka's lugubrious voice, as though from afar.

Wheezing, coughing, and enjoying himself, Maslak rode off to one side, while the Cossacks dashed on to the attack. The poor foot-soldiers tried to flee, but too late. The Cossack's lashes were already descending upon their wretched coats. The horsemen rode around and around the field, wielding their whips with extraordinary skill.

'What are you fooling for?' I called out to Afonka.

'Fun,' he answered, fidgeting in the saddle and prying a lad out of the bushes into which he had crawled.

'For fun!' he cried, jabbing at the crazed lad.

The sport came to an end when Maslak – majestic, but mollified – waved a plump hand.

'Look out, foot-soldiers!' Afonka shouted, proudly straightening his feeble body. 'Now go and catch fleas!'

Exchanging laughs, the Cossacks reformed their ranks. Of the foot-soldiers there was no sign. Only the stooping Jew still stood in the same place, attentively and haughtily surveying the Cossacks through his spectacles.

Firing continued from the direction of Leszniów. The Poles were hemming us in. Isolated figures could be made out through field-glasses – mounted scouts galloping out of the little town and disappearing, bobbing up and down like those little dolls that insist on standing upright. Maslak drew the squadrons up in battle array along both sides of the road. The brilliant sky above us was unutterably empty, as it always is in the hour of danger. The Jew threw back his head and blew loud and mournfully on his metal whistle, and the infantry that had just received a thrashing returned to their posts. The Brigade Staff came in range of the machine-guns. We bolted headlong to the wood and began to scramble through the thicket that lay to the right of the road. Bullet-pierced boughs crackled restlessly above us. When we at last succeeded in getting through the bushes the Cossacks were no longer where they had been, but were making their way back to Brody on the Divisional Commander's orders. Only the peasants remained, snarling rare shots from their trenches, and Afonka, who had lagged behind and was now catching up with his platoon.

He rode on the very edge of the road, looking about him and sniffing the air. The firing slackened for a moment, and thinking to make the best of the lull, the Cossack set off at a gallop. At that instant his horse was shot through the neck. Afonka rode on another hundred paces, and then, in our very midst, the mount bent its forelegs and rolled over on the ground.

In a leisurely way Afonka removed his crushed leg from the stirrup, squatted down, and poked a bronzed finger into the wound. Then he straightened himself up, his eyes sadly scanning the gleaming horizon.

'Farewell, Stepan,' he said in wooden tones, stepping away from the dying animal and bowing to it from the waist. 'How shall I go back to the quiet settlement without you? What shall I do with your embroidered saddle? Farewell, Stepan!' he repeated louder, choking. Then he squeaked like a trapped mouse and broke into a howl. His gasping roars reached our ears, and we saw him bowing away without ceasing, like a woman seized with hysterics in church.

'No, I won't give in to accursed fate!' he shouted, removing his hands from his deathlike face. 'Now I'll go and butcher the bloody Poles without mercy. I'll do them in right to the heart, do them damned well in – I promise you, Stepan, in the name of my dear brethren at the settlement.'

Afonka laid his face against the wound and was silent. Riveting its deep, violet, shining eyes on its master's face, the charger listened to Afonka's gasping moans. It moved its drooping head about the ground in a gentle torpor, while two streams of blood like ruby trappings flowed down a chest faced with white muscles.

Afonka lay without stirring. Then Maslak, picking his way with his fat legs, went over to the horse, put his revolver in its ear and fired. Afonka leapt up, turning upon Maslak his pock-marked countenance.

'Collect the harness, Afonka,' said Maslak gently, 'and get along to your unit.'

From the slope we beheld Afonka wandering away to his squadron, bent beneath the weight of the saddle, his face raw and red like a chunk of meat; alone, utterly alone, in the dusty blaze of the wilderness of fields.

Late that evening I came across him again, sleeping in one of the transport wagons with his possessions – swords, jackets, and pierced gold coins – beside him. His blood-clotted head with its twisted lifeless mouth was resting as though crucified on the bend of the saddle. Next to him he had laid the harness of the dead horse, all the showy and complicated apparel of a Cossack racer – breastpieces with black tassels, supple crupper-straps studded with coloured stones, silver-plated snaffle-bridle.

Darkness came down ever denser upon us. The transport wagons wound along the Brody highroad in a never-ending file. Humble little stars slid along the Milky Way, and distant villages shone forth in the cool depths of night. Orlov the assistant squadron commander and Bitsenko with the long moustaches were sitting in the same cart as Afonka, commenting upon his sorrow.

'Brought the mount all the way from home,' said Bitsenko with the long moustaches. 'Where's he to get another like it?'

'A horse is a friend,' said Orlov.

'A horse is a father,' sighed Bitsenko; 'saves one's life time and again. Bida will be lost without his horse.'

When morning came Afonka had disappeared. The fighting at Brody began and ended, defeat gave place to transient victory, we saw a change of divisional commanders. But still there was no Afonka. Only the menacing murmurs from the countryside – traces of Afonka's savage and rapacious plundering – showed us his arduous course.

'He's hunting around for a horse,' was what the squadron said about their commander; and on those boundless evenings of our wanderings I heard many a tale of that fierce and wordless brigandage.

Men from other detachments ran across Afonka dozens of versts from our position, lying in wait for straggling Polish horsemen or scouring the woods in search of the horse-droves hidden there by peasants. He went about setting fire to villages and shooting the Polish bailiffs for concealing goods. Echoes of that ferocious and single-handed struggle reached our ears, echoes of those despairing, lone-wolf attacks upon the masses.

Yet another week went by; day after bitter day burnt from our talk the stories of Afonka's temerity, and we began to forget 'Makhno'. The rumour reached us that he had had his head staved in by Galician peasants somewhere in the woods. And the day we entered Berestechko, Emelyan Budyak of the First Squadron went to the Divisional Commander to ask for Afonka's saddle and its yellow cloth. Emelyan wanted to appear on review with a new saddle; but things fell out otherwise.

The division entered Berestechko on August the sixth. The red Cossack coat of our new Divisional Commander moved on ahead, and Lyovka, a crazy blackguard, led a mare behind him. A warlike march full of prolonged menace flew along the poor florid streets. Ancient alleys leading nowhere, a painted forest of aged and tremulous cross-beams, overran the little town, whose core, eaten away by time, breathed over us its sombre decay. The smugglers and bigots had hidden themselves in their dark, spacious huts, and only Pan Ludomirski the bell-ringer came out in his green frock-coat to meet us by the church.

We had crossed the river and made our way to the outskirts of the town. We were approaching the priest's house when Afonka came riding round a corner on a tall grey stallion.

'Greetings!' he barked, and pushing aside the men he returned to his place in the ranks.

Maslak stared out into the hueless distance and, not turning round, asked hoarsely:

'Where did you get the horse?'

'It's my own,' replied Afonka, rolling a cigarette and moistening it with a brief lick.

The Cossacks rode up one after the other to greet him. Where his left eye had been, a pink swelling gaped repulsively in his charred face.

The following morning Bida took the day off. In the church he smashed St Valentine's shrine and tried to play the organ. He wore a jacket cut out of a blue carpet with an embroidered lily in the middle of the back, and his sweaty Cossack forelock was plastered down over the gouged-out eye.

After dinner he saddled his horse and fired his rifle at the shattered windows of the Counts Raciborski. The Cossacks stood around him in a semicircle, pulling at the stallion's tail, feeling its legs, and counting its teeth.

'A fine mount,' said Orlov the assistant squadron commander.

'A well-made horse,' agreed Bitsenko with the long moustaches.

In St Valentine's Church

BERESTECHKO was occupied by our division yesterday evening. The Staff was quartered in the house of the priest Tuzinkiewicz. Disguising himself as a woman of the people, Tuzinkiewicz had fled from Berestechko before the entry of our troops. All that I know of him is that he fussed over his God for forty-five years in Berestechko and was an excellent priest. When the inhabitants want to make us realize this, they tell us that he was beloved of the Jews. It was in the time of Tuzinkiewicz that the ancient church was restored. The repairs came to an end on the third centenary of the temple. The Bishop of Zhitomir arrived for the occasion, and prelates in silk cassocks officiated before the church. They stood, portly and benign figures, like bells in the dew-drenched grass. From the neighbouring villages folk flowed in submissive streams. Peasants bent the knee and kissed hands, and in the skies that day flamed clouds such as had never before been seen: heavenly flags were flying in honour of the ancient edifice. The Bishop of Zhitomir kissed Tuzinkiewicz on the brow and called him the Father of Berestechko – *pater Berestechkae.*

I heard the story this morning at Staff Headquarters, when I was going through the report of our flank column that was reconnoitring toward Lvov, in the Radzichów district. I was reading through the papers while the snoring of orderlies behind me bore witness to our eternal homelessness. The clerks, moist for lack of sleep, copied out orders for the division, crunched cucumbers, and sneezed. It was almost midday when I had finished and was at last free. I went over to the window and saw the Berestechko church, white and mighty. It gleamed in the cool sunlight like a tower of porcelain. Noontide lightning scintillated in its shining sides, whose convex line dropped lightly down from domes of an ancient green. Rose-tinted veins smouldered in the white stone of the pediment, and at the very top were columns as slender as tapers.

I was amazed to hear the organ peal forth. Just then an old woman with loose yellow hair appeared in the doorway of the Staff quarters. She came in, hobbling like a dog with a broken paw, reeling, almost falling. Her pupils were infused with the white moisture of blindness, and were brimming with tears.

The sounds of the organ floated across to us, now slow and ponderous, now light and nimble. Their flight was laborious, and their reverberations rang on plaintively and long. The old woman wiped the tears away with her yellow hair, sat down on the floor, and began to kiss my jackboots at the knee. The organ grew still, then burst out into a guffaw in the bass. I seized the old woman by the arm and looked around. The clerks were tapping away on typewriters; the orderlies were snoring with ever increasing gusto, their sharp spurs cutting into the felt beneath the velvet upholstery of the sofas. The old woman tenderly kissed my boots, clasping them as though they were babies. I dragged her to the entrance and closed the door after us. The church rose before us dazzlingly, like scenery on a stage. The side-gates were open, and horses' skulls were lying about on the graves of Polish officers.

We hurried into the yard, went along a gloomy passage, and came out into a rectangular room adjoining the chancel.

There Sasha, a nurse of the 31st Regiment, was busy rummaging in silks that had been thrown down on the floor. The cadaverous odour of brocade and scattered flowers and aromatic decomposition rose to her quivering nostrils, tickling and poisoning them. Then some Cossacks came into the room. They burst out laughing, and seizing Sasha by the arm sent her spinning on to the mountains of stuffs and books. Sasha's body, fresh and strong-smelling as the meat of a cow that has only just been slaughtered, was laid bare; her flying skirts revealed her horsewoman's legs – shapely, cast-iron legs – and Kurdyukov the half-wit straddled her as if on horseback, shook as though in the saddle, and pretended to be satisfying his lust. She threw him off and dashed to the door, and it was only then that we passed the altar and penetrated into the church.

It was full of sunshine, full of dancing sunbeams, airy pillars, a kind of cool gaiety. How can I forget the picture painted by Apolek and hanging on the right-hand side of the chancel? There were in that picture twenty rosy Fathers rocking a ribbon-tressed cradle in which lay the chubby Infant Jesus. His toes are spread out and His body is lacquered with the hot sweat of morning. The Babe is wriggling on a back upon which fat has gathered in rolls, and the twelve Apostles in cardinals' tiaras have bent over the cradle. Their faces are so close-shaven as to be blue, and their flame-coloured mantles bulge out over their bellies. Their eyes sparkle with wisdom, determination, merriment; at the corners of their mouths hovers a little smile, and on their double chins are set fiery little warts – little warts scarlet as radishes in May.

There was in this Berestechko church quite an individual and alluring way of looking upon the mortal sufferings of the sons of men. Saints in this temple went to their deaths with all the picturesqueness of Italian singers, and the black hair of the executioners was as glossy as Holophernes' beard.

Right above the altar I beheld the sacrilegious representation of John, also from Apolek's heretical and intoxicating brush. The Baptist's beauty in that picture belonged to the reticent and equivocal type for the sake of which the concubines of kings are ready to lose their already half-lost honour and abandon their sumptuous mode of life.

At first I either did not notice the traces of destruction in the church or else they did not seem to me to be very considerable. Only St Valentine's shrine had been broken. Bits of decayed wadding lay about beneath it, and the absurd bones of the Saint looking more like the bones of a hen than anything else. And Afonka Bida was still playing the organ. He was drunk and wild and hacked to pieces, having returned only the day before with the horse he had seized from the peasants. He was stubbornly attempting to finger out a march, and someone was saying to him persuasively, in a sleepy voice, 'Drop it, Afonka. Let's go and feed.' But the Cossack would not stop, and his songs were many. Each sound was a song, and all the sounds were torn from one another. The song – its dense strain – lasted a second, then gave place to another. I listened and looked about me, and the traces of destruction did not seem to me to be very considerable. But not so thought Pan Ludomirski, bell-ringer of St Valentine's church and husband of the blind old woman.

Ludomirski emerged from somewhere or other and entered the church with even step and bowed head. The old man could not bring himself to throw a covering over the scattered relics, for a man of humble station may not finger sacred things. The bell-ringer fell upon the blue flagstones and raised his head, his blue nose rising above him like a flag above a corpse. His blue nose quivered above him; and at that instant the velvet curtain by the altar swayed and, quivering, slipped to one side. A niche was revealed, and in its blue depth, against a background of cloud-furrowed sky, ran a bearded figure in a Polish greatcoat of orange – barefooted, with torn and bleeding mouth. A hoarse cry then wrenched at our ears. The man in the orange greatcoat was being pursued by hatred and overtaken by the chase. He had put out a hand to ward off the impending blow, and blood flowed from that hand in a purple stream. A little Cossack lad who was standing beside me gave a yell, and lowering his head broke into a run; though there was indeed nothing to run from, since the figure in the niche was only that of Jesus Christ – the most extraordinary image of God I had ever seen in my life.

Pan Ludomirski's Saviour was a curly-headed Jew with a tousled beard and a low, wrinkled forehead. His sunken cheeks were painted with carmine, and above the eyes, closed in pain, arched delicate reddish eyebrows.

His mouth was torn like a horse's lip. His Polish overcoat was girdled with a costly belt, and beneath the caftan twisted little porcelain feet – painted, bare, and pierced with silver nails.

Pan Ludomirski stood in his green frock-coat beneath the statue. He raised a withered hand and cursed us. The Cossacks gaped and hung their yellow tufts. In a thundering voice the bell-ringer of St Valentine's anathematized us in the purest Latin. Then he turned his back upon us, fell on his knees, and clasped the Saviour's legs.

Returning to Staff quarters, I wrote a report to the Commander of the Division concerning the outrage done to the religious feelings of the population. An order came that the church was to be closed; and the offenders, after being investigated, were brought before a court-martial.

Berestechko, August 1920

Squadron Commander Trunov

A T midday we brought to Sokal the shot-riddled body of our Squadron Commander Trunov, who was killed this morning in action against enemy aircraft. All Trunov's wounds were in his face: his cheeks were punctured all over, and his tongue was torn away. We washed the dead man's face as best we could, so that it should appear less terrible, placed a Caucasian saddle at the head of the coffin, and dug him a grave in a place of honour, in the public gardens next to the cathedral, in the very centre of the town. Our mounted squadron, the regimental Staff and the Divisional Commissar appeared there; and at two by the Cathedral clock our decrepit old cannon fired the first shot, saluting the dead commander with all its three inches. It gave a full salute, and then we bore the coffin to the open grave. The coffin lid was up, and the pure noontide sunlight lit up the long corpse with its mouth stuffed full of broken teeth, the polished boots placed heel to heel as at drill.

'Men,' said Pugachov the regimental commander, looking at the dead man and taking his stand at the edge of the grave, 'men,' he said, trembling and straightening himself up with his arms stiff against his trouser seams, 'we are burying Paul Trunov, the world hero. We are doing Paul the last honours.' And raising to the sky eyes inflamed by lack of sleep, Pugachov shouted a speech about the dead soldiers of the First Cavalry Army and about the proud phalanx which was beating the hammer of history upon the anvil of future ages. Pugachov shouted his speech very loudly, tightly grasping the hilt of his curved Caucasian sabre and digging his torn boots with their silver spurs into the ground.

When his speech came to an end the band played the

International and the Cossacks bade farewell to Paul Trunov. The whole squadron leaped into the saddle and fired a volley in the air, and our old three-incher champed forth a second time. Then we sent three Cossacks to fetch a wreath. They dashed off, firing, at full gallop, dropping out of their saddles and performing all sorts of Cossack tricks; and returned bringing whole armfuls of red flowers. Pugachov scattered them on the coffin, and we began to move up to Trunov for the last kiss. I touched the deathly white forehead with my lips and went away into the town, into Gothic Sokal that lay in blue dust and invincible Galician mournfulness.

A big square stretched away on the left-hand side of the gardens, a square built around with ancient synagogues. Jews in long ragged garments were squabbling on that square, pulling one another about. A section of them – the Orthodox Jews – were extolling the teachings of Adassia Rabbi of Belz. For this they were being attacked by the Hasidim of moderate doctrine, the disciples of Juda Rabbi of Gussyatin. The Jews were arguing about the Cabala, making mention in their discussions of the name of Elijah, Gaon of Vilna and scourge of the Hasidim.

Forgetting the war and the volleys, the Hasidim went so far as to defame the very name of Elijah, High Priest of Vilna. And I, heavy-hearted because of Trunov, I too went pushing among them, shouting with them to ease my sorrow, till I perceived before me a Galician as lanky and cadaverous as Don Quixote.

This Galician was clothed in a white linen shirt that reached down to his heels. He was arrayed as though for his funeral or for Communion service, and he led by a rope a little tousled cow. Upon his huge body was set the nimble, tiny, pierced head of a serpent that waggled beneath a wide-brimmed hat of common straw.

The wretched little cow followed the Galician at the end

of its lead. He led it with an air of importance, his gibbet-like frame cleaving the burning brilliance of the skies.

Solemnly he crossed the square and went down a winding lane all smoky with thick and nauseating vapours. In little charred houses, in squalid kitchens, Jewish women like aged Negresses, Jewish women with excessive bosoms, were busy at work. The Galician went past them, and stopped at the end of the lane by the façade of a battered building. There, by the warped white pillars, a Gypsy blacksmith sat shoeing horses. The Gypsy was beating upon the hooves with his hammer, shaking his greasy hair, whistling and smiling. Several Cossacks were standing about him with their horses. My Galician went over to the blacksmith, silently handed him a dozen baked potatoes, and turned back without glancing at anyone. I started to follow him, but just at that moment I was stopped by one of the Cossacks who was holding his horse in readiness for shoeing. The Cossack's name was Seliverstov. He had left Makhno the guerrilla at some time or other, and was in the 33rd Cavalry Regiment.

'Lyutov,' he said, shaking me by the hand, 'you go for everybody. There's a devil in you, Lyutov. What made you go and bash Trunov about this morning?'

And in stupid, borrowed words Seliverstov shouted at me some complete nonsense about my having that morning given my Squadron Commander Trunov a hiding. Seliverstov rebuked me roundly for it, rebuked me before all the Cossacks; but there wasn't a grain of truth in his story. True, I had had a run-in with Trunov that morning because he always carried on such an interminable palaver with the prisoners. We had a run-in, it's true, but Paul is dead and there is no one to judge him on earth, and I would be the last of all to judge him. Our quarrel arose in this way:

We took today's prisoners at dawn, at Zawada station. There were ten of them, in underclothes when we took them. Clothing lay piled beside the Poles. This was just a trick of theirs to make it impossible for us to distinguish by their uniforms between the officers and the rank and file. They had thrown off their clothes, but this time Trunov made up his mind to get at the truth.

Trunov had been wounded in the head that morning. His head was bound with a rag, and blood was dripping down from it like rain off a rick.

'Officers, own up!' he repeated, and began to push the Poles about with the butt of his revolver.

Then there stepped from the crowd a thin, aged man with big, protruding bones on his back, yellow cheek-bones, and a drooping moustache.

'Finished, this war,' said the old man with incomprehensible enthusiasm in his mutilated Russian. 'All officers run away. Finished, this war . . .'

And the Pole stretched out his blue hands to the Squadron Commander.

'Five fingers, ' he said, sobbing and twisting his huge, withered hand, 'with these five fingers I brought up my family . . .'

The old man choked, swayed, burst into tears of exultation and fell on his knees before Trunov; but Trunov thrust him away with his sword.

'Your officers are damned blackguards,' said the Squadron Commander. 'Your officers have thrown their clothes down here. Well, it's all up with whoever I drop on. I'm going to make a test.'

And the Squadron Commander picked from the heap a cap with pipings and set it on the old man's head.

'Fits,' muttered Trunov, going up closer. 'Fits.' And he thrust his sword into the prisoner's throat.

The old man fell, his legs jerking. From his throat flowed a foamy coral stream. Then Andie Vosmiletov, with his shining ear-ring and round rustic neck, crept up to him. He undid the old man's buttons, shook him slightly, and began to pull the trousers off the dying man. Then he threw them over his saddle, grabbed another couple of uniforms from the heap, and rode off plying the whip. The sun came out of the clouds at that moment and impetuously surrounded Andie's horse, its lively pace, and the devil-may-care swing of its docked tail. Andie rode along the path to the wood where our transport wagons were; and the drivers stormed and whistled and made signs to Andie as though to someone deaf and dumb.

The Cossack was halfway there when Trunov suddenly fell on his knees and called after him in a raucous shout:

'Andrew!' he cried, staring at the ground. 'Andrew!' he repeated, not raising his eyes, 'our Soviet Republic is still alive. It's too early to go sharing it out in lots, so drop those rags, Andrew!'

But Vosmiletov did not even turn his head. He rode on at his amazing Cossack trot, and his little horse tossed its tail jauntily, just as if it were waving us away.

'Treachery,' then muttered Trunov, amazed. 'Treachery,' he said. He jerked his rifle to his shoulder and fired, missing in his haste. This time, however, Andrew stopped. He turned his horse about to face us, bouncing in the saddle like a peasant woman. His face grew red and angry, and he kicked his legs about.

'Just you listen to me, countryman,' he shouted, riding toward us and calming down at the sound of his own deep, powerful voice. 'I've half a mind to do you in, you damned Cossack. When you pick up a dozen Poles, you make no end of a fuss. We've picked up a hundred each and not sent for you. If you're a worker, then attend to your own job.'

And throwing the trousers and the two uniforms from the saddle, Andrew snorted and turned away from the Squadron Commander to help me make out a list of the remaining prisoners. He rubbed up against me, snorting loudly. The prisoners fled from his yells, but he pursued them and seized them in armfuls like a hunter embracing the reeds so as to get a good view of a flock of birds flying riverwards at dawn.

Dealing with the prisoners, I exhausted all the bad language I knew; but I managed somehow to take down the names of eight of them with the numbers of their units and the nature of their arms. Then I passed on to the ninth, a young lad who looked like a German athlete in a superior sort of circus – a lad with a white German chest and sidewhiskers, wearing a knitted waistcoat and soft woolly pants. He turned to me the two nipples on his high chest, threw back his sweaty fair hair, and told me his unit. Then Andie seized him by the pants and asked sternly:

'Where did you get these undies from?'

'Ma knitted them,' replied the prisoner, and swayed.

'Your ma's a regular factory,' said Andie, still peering at the things, and with his thick fingertips he touched the Pole's well-kept nails. 'Your ma's a regular factory. Guys like us never wear things like that.'

He felt the soft woolly pants again, and took the ninth prisoner by the arm to lead him off to those whose names had already been taken. At that moment I saw Trunov creeping from behind a hillock. Blood was dripping from the Squadron Commander's head like rain off a rick, and his dirty bandage had come loose and was dangling down. He crept along on his belly, holding in his hands a carbine – a powerful, lacquered carbine of Japanese make. From a distance of twenty paces Trunov sent the Polish lad's skull flying, and bits of his brains dripped over my hands. Then Trunov expelled the spent cartridges and came over to me.

'Rub one out,' he said, pointing to the list.

'I'm not going to rub out anything,' I answered. 'It looks as if Trotsky's orders weren't meant for you, Paul.'

'Rub one out,' repeated Trunov, and he thrust a black finger at the sheet of paper.

'I'm not going to rub out anything,' I shouted with all my might. 'There were ten of them, and now there's eight. The Staff won't pay any attention to you, Paul.'

'They'll pay attention to our wretched life,' Trunov answered, and moved toward me, all ragged and hoarse and smoky. Then he stopped and raised his gory head to the skies, uttering with bitter reproach: 'Buzz on, buzz on. And here another comes buzzing along.'

And the Squadron Commander pointed out to us four specks in the sky, four bombers sailing in and out of the swanlike clouds. They were planes belonging to Major Faunt Le Roy's combat squadron – big armoured planes.

'To horse!' shouted the platoon commanders, catching sight of them; and they led the squadrons off at a trot toward the forest. But Trunov did not ride off with his squadron. He stayed by the station, pressed up against the wall, silent. Andie Vosmiletov and two machine-gunners, barefooted youths in scarlet riding-breeches, stood by dithering.

'Cut away off, you boys,' said Trunov to them, and the blood began to ebb from his face. 'Here's a report from me to Pugachov.'

Upon a slip of paper torn off askew Trunov wrote in enormous peasant-letters:

'Having to die today, I consider it my duty to fire a couple of shots toward the possible bringing down of the enemy, and at the same time pass on the command to Simon Golov, platoon commander.'

He sealed the letter, sat down on the ground, and with an effort drew off his boots.

'Here, make use of them,' he said, handing over the report and the boots to the machine-gunners, 'they're new.'

'Good luck to you, commander,' muttered the machine-gunners, shifting from one foot to the other, and hesitating to go.

'Good luck to you, kids, some way or another,' replied

Trunov, and went over to the machine-guns that stood on a little mound beside the station sentry-box. There Andie Vosmiletov, the rifler of old clothes, stood waiting for him.

'Some way or another,' Trunov said to him, and started levelling a machine-gun at the enemy. 'Going to stick it with me, eh, Andie?'

'Christ!' replied Andie in a frightened voice; then he gave a soblike gasp, went white, and burst out laughing.

'Christ! My own little drop of blood.'

And he started levelling the second machine-gun at the planes.

All this time the planes were zooming ever closer over the station, busily peppering it from on high, dropping down and circling about, a pink ray of sunlight on their wings.

Meanwhile we – the fourth squadron – were in the forest. There in the forest we awaited the end of the unequal combat between Paul Trunov and the American, Major Faunt Le Roy. The Major and his three bombers showed considerable skill in the fight. They dropped to a height of three hundred metres and with their machine-guns shot up first Andie and then Trunov. None of the shots fired by our men did the Americans any harm, and they flew off to one side without spotting the squadron hidden in the forest. So, after waiting half an hour, we were able to ride out and fetch the corpses. Andie Vosmiletov's body was taken by two relatives of his in our squadron. As for Trunov, our late commander, we bore him to Gothic Sokal and buried him there in a place of honour: in one of the flowerbeds in the public gardens, in the centre of the town.

Two Ivans

DEACON AGEYEV had twice deserted from the front, and so was turned over to the Moscow regiment composed of disgraced men. The Commander-in-Chief, Sergey Sergeyevich Kamenev, reviewed this regiment at Mozhaysk before it was sent to the front.

'They're no good to me,' said the Commander-in-Chief; 'back with them to Moscow to look after the latrines.'

Somehow or other a company was got together out of these undesirables, and among them was the deacon. When he arrived at the Polish front, the deacon made out that he was deaf; and Barsutsky the Medical Officer, after spending a whole week over him, failed to break down his tenacity.

'Devil take the deaf 'un,' Barsutsky said to Soychenko the stretcher-bearer. 'Find a cart among the transport wagons. We'll send the deacon to Rovno for a proper test.'

Soychenko went along to the transport wagons and got hold of three carts. The driver of the first was Akinfiev.

'Ivan,' said Soychenko to him, 'you're going to take the deaf man to Rovno.'

'Right, I can take him,' answered Akinfiev.

'And you'll bring me back a receipt.'

'Of course,' said Akinfiev. 'And what's the cause of that there deafness of his?'

'One's own skin is dearer than somebody else's,' said Soychenko the stretcher-bearer. 'That's all there is to it. He's a malingerer; his hearing's all right.'

'Right, I can take him,' repeated Akinfiev, and followed on after the other carts.

Three carts in all assembled before the first-aid post. A sister who was being sent back to the rear was installed in the first, the second was destined for a Cossack suffering from inflammation of the kidneys, and Ivan Ageyev settled down in the third.

Having seen to everything, Soychenko called the surgeon. 'Our malingerer's gone,' he said. 'I put him in the Revolutionary Tribunal cart against a receipt.'

Barsutsky peered out of the window, saw the carts, and dashed out of the house red and hatless.

'Hey!' he shouted to Akinfiev. 'You'll kill him. The deacon must be put in another cart.'

'Where are you going to put him?' asked the Cossacks who were standing by, and they laughed. 'Our Ivan will get at him anywhere.'

Akinfiev was standing by his horses, whip in hand. He took off his cap and said politely:

'Good day, Comrade Barsutsky.'

'Good day, my friend,' replied Barsutsky. 'You know, you're the very devil! The deacon must move over.'

'I'd be interested to know,' whined the Cossack, and his upper lip quivered, crept down, and trembled over his dazzling teeth, 'I'd be interested to know if you find it right or not, at a time when the enemy's going for us hammer and tongs, when the enemy's striking below the belt, and hanging on to our legs like lead and winding about our arms like serpents – I'd like to know if you find it right to stop up one's ears in such an hour of mortal peril?'

'Listen to Ivan standing up for the commissars!' shouted Korotkov, the driver of the first cart. 'Just listen!'

'How d'you mean, standing up?' muttered Barsutsky, turning away. 'We all stand up for them. Only things have to be done according to regulations.'

'But he can hear, our deaf 'un can!' broke in Akinfiev. He rolled the whip in his fat fingers, laughed, and winked at the deacon, who was sitting in the cart, his enormous shoulders drooping and his head aquiver.

'Well, off with you, then,' shouted the surgeon in despair. 'But I hold you responsible for everything, Ivan.'

'All right, I'll be responsible,' Akinfiev said thoughtfully, and bent his head. 'Make yourself comfortable,' he said to the deacon without turning round. 'More comfortable still,' repeated the Cossack, gathering the reins in his hands.

The carts lined up and started off at a good pace along the main road. At the head drove Korotkov. Akinfiev came third, whistling a tune and waving the reins. In this way they covered about fifteen versts. But toward evening they were thrown off their course by a sudden onset of the enemy.

On that day, July 22, the Poles tore our rear to pieces by a series of swift operations. They swept down on the little town of Kozin and took many of the XI Division prisoner. The squadrons of the VI Division were thrown into the Kozin area in a counter-attack. The lightning rapidity of their manoeuvres held up the transport wagons, and the Revolutionary Tribunal carts strayed about for forty-eight hours along the seething fringe of the battle. Only on the third night were they able to get out on to the road along which the rear staffs were getting away. It was on that road that I came across them at midnight.

Numb with despair, I came upon them after the fighting round Khotin. During that fighting my horse had been killed. When I lost him I got on an ambulance-cart and picked up wounded till evening. Then all the sound men were thrown off the cart, and I was left alone beside a crumbling hovel. Night flew toward me on mettlesome horses. The whole universe resounded with vociferations from the transport wagons, and on the earth, girdled about with shrill cries, the roads fizzled out. Stars crept forth from the cool belly of night, and deserted villages blazed on the horizon. Loading my saddle on my back, I went along a churned-up field-path and stopped where it turned to make water. When I buttoned up my pants I felt splashes of something on my hand. I lit my little lantern, turned back, and saw lying on the ground the corpse of a Pole I had splattered with my urine. It was pouring out of his mouth, bubbling between his teeth, gathered in his empty eye-sockets. A notebook and fragments of Pilsudski's proclamations lay by the corpse. In the notebook were written down personal expenses, a list of the plays to be given at the Cracow theatre, the date of the birthday of a woman called Marie-Louise. With Commander-in-Chief Pilsudski's proclamations I wiped the skull of my unknown brother, and went on, bent beneath the weight of the saddle.

Just then wheels groaned somewhere near me.

'Halt!' I shouted. 'Who goes there?'

Night flew toward me on mettlesome horses, and on the horizon conflagrations wound upwards.

'Revolutionary Tribunal carts,' came a voice crushed by the obscurity.

I ran forward and collided with a wagon.

'They've killed my horse,' I cried, very loud. 'Lavrik was his name.'

I got no answer. I climbed on to the cart, put my saddle under my head, and went to sleep. I slept till dawn, warmed by the fusty hay and the body of Ivan Akinfiev, who chanced to be my bedfellow.

In the morning the Cossack woke up after me.

'It's getting on towards day, thank the Lord,' he said. He drew a revolver out from beneath a box and fired a shot above the deacon's ear. The latter was sitting just in front of us, driving. Above his enormous balding head fluttered a grey hair. Akinfiev fired again above the other ear, and stowed the revolver away in its holster.

'Good morning, Ivan,' he said to the deacon, grunting as he pulled on his boots. 'What about some grub?'

'Here, you!' I cried. 'What d'you think you're up to?'

'What I'm up to is little enough,' replied Akinfiev, getting out the food. 'It's the third day he's been trying to put it across me.'

Then Korotkov, whom I had known in the 31st Regiment, called over from the first cart and told from the beginning the whole story of the deacon. Akinfiev listened attentively, cupping his ear. Then he drew from beneath a saddle a roast ox-foot that had been lying in the hay under a covering of tow.

The deacon climbed over to us from the driver's seat, cut up the green meat with a small knife, and handed a piece to each. When breakfast was over, Akinfiev tied the ox-foot up in a bag and tucked it away in the hay.

'Ivan,' he said to Ageyev, 'let's go and drive out the devil. Got to make a halt anyhow; the horses need watering.'

He took a bottle of medicine and a Tarnovsky syringe from his pocket and handed them to the deacon. They got down from the cart and went a few yards off into a field.

'Sister,' cried Korotkov from the first cart, 'turn away your optics or Akinfiev's qualities will strike you blind.'

'A lot I care!' muttered the woman, turning away.

Akinfiev then turned his shirt up. The deacon knelt before him and did the syringing. Then he wiped the syringe with a rag and held it up to the light. Akinfiev pulled up his pants. Seizing his moment, he went behind the deacon's back and once more fired a shot just above Ageyev's ear.

'Here's to you, Ivan!' he said.

The deacon put the bottle down on the grass and rose from his knees. His light hair flew upwards.

'I shall be judged by the Supreme Judge,' he said thickly. 'It's not for you, Ivan, to sit in judgement on me.'

'Nowadays everybody judges everybody else,' interrupted the driver of the second cart, a sort of lively hump-back. 'And condemns to death – it's as simple as that.'

'Or better still,' said Ageyev, straightening himself up, 'kill me, Ivan.'

'Stop playing the fool, deacon,' said Korotkov, whom I had met before, going over to him. 'You've got to understand the sort of man you're travelling with. Any other fellow would have trussed you like a fowl and not thought twice about it, but he's just getting the truth out of you bit by bit and learning you, you unfrocked priest.'

'Or better still,' the deacon repeated obstinately, coming forward, 'kill me, Ivan.'

'It's you that'll go and kill yourself, you carrion,' replied Akinfiev, turning pale and spluttering, 'it's you that'll dig your own pit and bury yourself in it.'

He waved his arms about, tore at his collar and fell down in a fit.

'Eh, my own little drop of blood!' he cried wildly, throwing sand over his face; 'eh, you bitter little drop of blood, power of the Soviets of mine!'

'Ivan,' said Korotkov, going over to him and gently putting his hand on the other's shoulder, 'don't get all worked up, old chap. Don't worry. We must get a move on, Ivan.'

Korotkov filled his mouth with water, sprayed it over Akinfiev, and carried him to the cart. The deacon settled himself once more in the driver's seat, and we drove off.

There remained at the most another two versts to the little town of Verby. Countless transport wagons had gathered there that morning. The XI Division, the XIV, and the IV were in the town. Jews in waistcoats stood about on the doorsteps, hunching their shoulders and looking like plucked fowls. Cossacks were going from yard to yard, collecting towels and eating unripe plums. As soon as we arrived, Akinfiev snuggled into the hay and fell asleep, while I took a blanket from his cart and went to look for a shady spot. But the fields on either side of the road were sown with excrement. A bearded peasant in copper-rimmed glasses and a Tyrolean hat who was reading a newspaper in a corner caught my glance and said:

'We call ourselves human beings, and dirty the place up worse than jackals. You feel ashamed for the earth.'

And turning away he went on reading the paper through his great glasses.

I made for the wood on the left and saw the deacon coming toward me.

'Where are you off to, countryman?' Korotkov called out after him from the first cart.

'To pull myself together,' muttered the deacon, and caught at my hand and kissed it. 'You're a kind gentleman,' he whispered, grimacing, shivering, and gasping for breath. 'I would like to ask you to write to the town of Kasimov when you have a spare moment, so that my wife can shed a tear for me.'

'Are you deaf or no, father deacon?' I shouted point-blank at him.

'Pardon?' he said, 'pardon?' and bent his ear toward me.

'Are you deaf, Ageyev, or aren't you?'

'Oh yes, I'm deaf,' he said hastily. 'The day before yesterday I heard perfectly, but Comrade Akinfiev has injured my hearing with his firing. He was supposed to deliver me to Rovno, Comrade Akinfiev was, but it isn't likely he will.'

And falling on his knees the deacon crawled head foremost in between the carts, all entangled in his rumpled priest's hair. Then he rose from his knees, made his way between the carts, and went over to Korotkov. The latter poured him out some tobacco, and they rolled cigarettes and gave each other a light.

'It's safer like this,' said Korotkov, and cleared a space beside him.

The deacon sat down next to him, and they were silent.

Then Akinfiev woke up. He rolled the ox-foot out of the bag, cut the green meat with a small knife, and handed a piece to everyone. At the sight of the putrid meat I felt a sudden nausea and depression, and gave my share back.

'Good-bye, boys,' I said, 'and good luck to you.'

'Good-bye,' said Korotkov.

I took the saddle from the cart and walked away, catching as I went Ivan Akinfiev's ceaseless mutterings.

'Ivan,' he was saying to the deacon, 'you've gone and done a darned silly thing. You ought to quake in your shoes at the sound of my name, but you went and got on to my cart. You could skip about as you liked till you met me. Well now, I'm going to have sport with you, Ivan, and no mistake. You just wait and see the sport I'll have with you.'

The Story of a Horse, Continued

FOUR months ago Savitsky, our former divisional commander, took a white stallion away from Khlebnikov, commander of the First Squadron. Khlebnikov then left the army, and today Savitsky received a letter from him.

Khlebnikov to Savitsky:

'And I cannot be angry with Budyonny's army any more. I understand my sufferings in that army, and keep them in my heart purer than sacred things. And to you, Comrade Savitsky, as a world-wide hero, the labouring masses of the Vitebsk region, where I am now President of the Local Revolutionary Committee, send their proletarian cry: "On with the World Revolution!", and hope that the white stallion may carry you long years along soft paths for the good of the freedom that we all love and the fraternal Republics, in which we ought to keep a special eye on the local authorities and on district units in all that concerns public administration.'

Savitsky to Khlebnikov:

'Unchanging Comrade Khlebnikov!

'That letter you wrote me was very meritorious as regards the common cause, all the more so after your stupidity when you shut your eyes to everything save your own interests and left our Communist Party of the Bolsheviks. Our Communist Party, Comrade Khlebnikov, is an iron band of fighting men that give their blood in the first rank, and when blood flows from iron it is no joke, comrades, but a matter of win or die. It is the same thing with the common cause, whose dawn I shall not live to see, as the fighting is heavy and I have to change commanders once a fortnight. I have now been fighting for thirty days in the rearguard, covering the invincible First Cavalry Army, and I am under the active fire of the enemy's aircraft and artillery. Tardy has been killed, Lukhmannikov has been killed, Lykoshenko has been killed, Gulevoy has been killed, Trunov has been killed, and the white stallion is no longer beneath me. So that in accordance with war's change of fortune do not expect to see your beloved Divisional Commander Savitsky, Comrade Khlebnikov, but we shall meet again, to put it bluntly, in the Kingdom of Heaven, though there is a rumour going around that the old fellow up in Heaven has not got a kingdom at all, but a regular whorehouse, and clap there's plenty of on earth as it is, and so it is quite on the cards that we shall not see one another again. So good-bye, Comrade Khlebnikov.'

The Widow

THE commander of the regiment, Shevelyov, lies dying in an ambulance-cart. A woman sits at his feet. Pierced by the flashes of the bombardment, night arches over the dying man. Lyovka, the divisional commander's driver, is warming food in a pot, and his Cossack tuft dangles over the fire. The fettered horses crackle among the bushes. Lyovka is stirring

the food and saying to Shevelyov, who is lying stretched out
in the cart:

'I worked in the town of Temryuk, comrade, trick-riding,
and I was featherweight athlete too. As for women, the little
town was very dull, of course. Young chicks would notice
me, and storm the walls: "Lev Gavrilych, you won't say no
to a bite à la carte. You won't regret the time that can't be
had over again." Well, I go with one of them to an eating-
house and we order two veals and half a bottle and sit together
quietly and have a drink. Then I sees a gent coming over to
me, neatly dressed and very respectable, only I notice he has
a lot of imagination and has had one drink too many.

'"Excuse me," he says; "what may your nationality be?"

'"What are you asking about my nationality for, mister?"
I ask; "specially when I'm in the female company of a lady?"

'And he says to me:

'"What sort of an athlete d'you think you are?" he says.
"In French wrestling they knock your kind flat. Prove me
your nationality."

'Well, I wasn't about to up and hit him yet awhile.

'"Why d'you – I don't know your name," I says. "Why
d'you go causing misunderstandings that mean that one of
us has got to kick the bucket here and now or, to put it
another way, give up the ghost?" Give up the ghost,' repeats
Lyovka excitedly, stretching his arms up to the sky and surrounding himself with night as with a nimbus. The tireless
wind – the clean wind of night – sings on, fraught with
ringing, rocking souls. Stars blaze like wedding rings in the
darkness and, falling on Lyovka, are entangled in his hair and
extinguished in his tousled head.

'Lev,' Shevelyov suddenly whispers to him, his lips blue,
'come here. What gold there is – is for Sasha,' says the
wounded man, 'the rings, the harness – all for her. We lived
the best we could. I must pay her back. My clothes and linen,
the decorations I got for boundless heroism, must go to my

mother on the Terek. Send them with a letter, and say in that letter: "The Commander sends his greetings. Don't cry. The cottage is yours, old lady. Live on. If anyone gives you trouble, go to Budyonny and say: 'I'm Shevelyov's mother.'" I'll let the regiment have my charger Abramka. I'll let them have him for the peace of my soul.'

'I've understood about the charger,' mutters Lyovka, waving his arms about. 'Sasha,' he calls to the woman, 'did you hear what he said? Say it in front of him: will you give the old woman what's hers, or won't you?'

'She can go to hell for all I care,' answers Sasha, making her way through the bushes, going straight on like a blind man.

Lyovka catches up with her and seizes her by the throat.

'Will you hand over the orphan's share? Say it in front of him!'

'I will. Let go!'

Having extorted her promise, Lyovka took the pot off the fire and began to pour the broth into the dying man's rigid mouth. The cabbage soup trickled down from Shevelyov's face, and the spoon clattered against his gleaming dead teeth. And all the while the bullets sang on ever louder and more mournfully in the dense expanse of night.

'The swine are letting off their rifles,' said Lyovka.

'The aristocratic bastards,' replied Shevelyov; 'that's their machine-guns slicing us open on the right flank.'

He closed his eyes, and with the dignity of a dead body laid out on a table listened with his large waxen ears to the sounds of battle. Lyovka chewed meat beside him . . .

The loitering moon crept out from behind the clouds and lingered on Sasha's knee.

'You're warming yourselves,' murmured Shevelyov, 'while, I reckon, the XIV Division has been routed.'

The misty moon loitered about the sky like a beggar-woman. Distant firing floated through the air. The feather-grass rustled on the disturbed earth, and the stars of August fell into the grass . . .

Sasha set about changing the wounded man's bandages, and raised a little lantern over the septic wound.

'You'll be gone before morning,' she said, wiping the cold sweat from Shevelyov's body. 'You'll be gone before morning, for death's in your guts.'

At that moment there came a tremendous and reverberating crash. The four fresh brigades sent into action by the enemy's united command had fired the first shell over Busk and, tearing up our communications, had set the watershed of the Bug on fire. Fires rose obediently on the horizon, and the heavy birds of the shelling flew up out of the flames. The bush was on fire, and Lyovka went tearing through the forest in the rocking carriage that belonged to the Commander of the VI Division. He tugged at the scarlet reins and beat against the tree stumps with the lacquered wheels. The horses rearing out of their harness, Shevelyov's ambulance cart, driven carefully by Sasha, came on after him.

It was thus that they reached the skirts of the forest where the first-aid post was stationed. Lyovka unharnessed the horses and went to the Medical Officer to ask for a horsecloth. He took the road through the forest, all blocked with carts from beneath which protruded the bodies of the ambulance men, their army sheepskins gleaming in the timorous dawn. The sleeping men's boots were thrown apart; their pupils were turned up to the sky, and the black pits of their mouths were twisted.

The Medical Officer happened to have a horsecloth to spare. Lyovka returned to Shevelyov, kissed him on the forehead, and covered him from head to foot. Then Sasha came over to the cart, tying her kerchief beneath her chin and shaking the straw from her dress.

'Little Paul,' she said, 'my Jesus Christ.' And she lay sideways on the dead man, covering him with her exorbitant body.

'There's real grief!' said Lyovka. 'No one can say they didn't live well together. Now she'll have to run around the whole squadron again. Tough luck for her!'

And he drove on to Busk, where the Staff of the VI Division was quartered.

There, ten versts from the town, we were fighting the Savinkov Cossacks. The traitors were under the command of Cossack Captain Yakovlev, who had gone over to the Poles; and they fought like men.

The Divisional Commander had been with the troops for almost forty-eight hours. Not finding him in the Staff quarters, Lyovka went to his own billet, where he rubbed down the horses, dashed water over the carriage wheels, and lay down to sleep in a shed full of new-mown hay that was as incendiary as perfume. Lyovka slept his fill and then sat down to dinner. His landlady had cooked him some potatoes over which she had poured clotted milk. Lyovka was already at table when the funereal wail of trumpets and the clattering of many hoofs sounded from the street. The squadron was coming down the winding Galician street with bugles and standards. Lying on a gun-carriage was Shevelyov's body, covered with banners. Sasha rode behind the coffin on the stallion, and a Cossack song came trickling from the ranks at the rear.

The squadron made its way along the main street and turned off to the river. Then Lyovka, barefooted and capless, dashed after the retreating detachment and caught the Squadron Commander's horse by the bridle.

Neither the Divisional Commander, who had stopped at the crossroads to salute the dead commander, nor his staff heard what Lyovka said to the Squadron Commander.

'The underclothes,' the wind carried words to us in fragments, 'mother on the Terek,' we heard Lyovka's disconnected cries. Without hearing him out, the Squadron Commander jerked the bridle free and pointed at Sasha. The woman shook her head and rode on. Then Lyovka leapt up on to her saddle, grabbed her by the hair, bent her head back and smashed his fist into her face. Sasha wiped the blood away with her skirt and rode on. Lyovka dropped down from the saddle, threw back his Cossack tuft and tied a red scarf around his hips, while the wailing buglers led the squadron on to the gleaming streak of the river.

He came back to us soon afterward and shouted, his eyes shining:

'I've given it to her good and proper. "I'll send them to his mother," she says, "I'll remember myself ..." Well, remember, and don't you forget, you damned slut. You go and forget and we'll remind you again, and if you go and forget a second time – well, we'll remind you a second time too ...'

Galicia, August 1920

Zamoste

THE Divisional Commander and his Staff lay in a stubble field three versts from Zamoste. The troops were to attack the town that night. The order was that we should spend the night in Zamoste, and the Divisional Commander was awaiting reports of victory.

Rain fell. Over the flooded earth flew wind and darkness. All the stars were doused in ink-distended clouds. Our worn-out horses sighed and moved their legs restlessly in the darkness. We had nothing to give them. I tied my horse's bridle to my foot, wrapped myself in my cloak, and lay down in a waterlogged hole. The sodden ground offered me the soothing embrace of the tomb. The horse pulled at the bridle and dragged me by the foot. It discovered a patch of green and began to graze.

Then I fell asleep, and dreamed of a shed all carpeted with hay. Over the shed hummed the dusty gold of threshing. Sheaves of wheat flew about in the sky, the July sun was drawing toward evening, and the goblets of the sunset were tilted over the village. I lay stretched out on a voiceless couch, and the caress of the hay on the nape of my neck was driving me mad. Then the door of the shed opened with a whistle and a woman dressed as for a ball came over to me. She freed her breast from the black lace of her bodice and raised it to me, carefully, like a nurse proffering food. She laid her breast against mine. An aching warmth stirred in the depths of my soul, and drops of sweat – live, stirring sweat – seethed between our nipples.

'Margot,' I longed to cry out, 'the earth is dragging me like a jibbering cur by the cord of its calamities. Nevertheless I have seen you, Margot.'

I longed to shout this; but my jaws, that a sudden chill had contracted, would not come apart.

Then the woman moved away from me and fell on her knees.

'Jesus,' she said, 'receive the soul of thy departed servant.'

She placed two worn five-copeck pieces on my eyelids, and stuffed the orifice of my mouth with fragrant hay. My moaning vainly beat about inside my clamped jaws, my failing pupils turned slowly beneath the copper coins, I could not force my hands apart . . . And I awoke.

A peasant with a tousled beard was lying before me with a rifle in his hands. The sky was cleft by the black crossbar of my horse's back, and my leg was sticking in the air, caught fast in the tight noose of the bridle.

'You dropped off to sleep, countryman,' said the peasant, his sleepless nocturnal eyes smiling. 'Your horse has pulled you along for almost half a verst.'

I disentangled my leg from the strap and got up. Blood was trickling down my face, torn by the weeds of the steppe.

There, only two paces away, stretched our front line. I could see the chimneys of Zamoste, stealthy lights in the defiles of its ghetto, the watchtower with its broken lantern. The raw dawn flowed over us like waves of chloroform. Green rockets soared above the Polish camp. They shuddered in the air, scattered like roseleaves beneath the moon, and went out.

And in the stillness I could hear the far-off breath of groaning. The smoke of secret murder strayed around us.

'Someone is being killed,' I said. 'Who is it?'

'The Poles are crazed with fear,' the peasant answered. 'The Poles are killing the Jews.'

The peasant transferred his gun from his right hand to his left. His beard flapped over to one side as he looked at me affectionately and said,

'These nights on the line are long. There's no end to them. And a man sort of gets a longing to have a talk with someone else, but where's one to get someone else, I'd like to know?'

The peasant made me light a cigarette from his. 'The Jews are to blame for everything, on our side and yours. There'll be mighty few of them left after the war. How many Jews are there in the whole world?'

'Ten million,' I answered, putting the bridle on my horse.

'There'll be only two hundred thousand left,' cried the peasant, and touched my hand, afraid I would go. But I got into the saddle and galloped off to the spot where the Staff had been.

The Divisional Commander was preparing to leave. The orderlies were standing at attention before him, sleeping as they stood. Dismounted squadrons crept over the rain-soaked mounds.

'They've put our nose out of joint,' whispered the Divisional Commander, and rode off.

We followed on after him along the road to Sitanets.

More rain fell. Dead mice floated along the roads. Autumn

set its ambushes about our hearts, and trees like naked corpses set upright on their feet swayed at the crossroads.

We got to Sitanets in the morning. I was with Volkov, the Staff quartermaster. He found us a free cottage on the outskirts of the village.

'Wine,' I said to the woman. 'Wine, meat, and bread.'

The old woman was seated on the floor, feeding from her hand a calf that was hidden beneath the bed.

'Haven't got nothing,' she answered indifferently, 'and I don't remember the time I had.'

I sat down at the table, took off my revolver, and fell asleep. A quarter of an hour later I opened my eyes and saw Volkov bending over the windowsill. He was writing a letter to his fiancée.

'Honoured Valentina,' he wrote, 'do you remember me?'

I read the first line, then got my matches out of my pocket and set fire to a pile of straw on the floor. The liberated flame flared and darted toward me. The old woman lay down with her chest on the fire and put it out.

'What are you doing, Pan?' she cried, moving back in horror.

Volkov turned around, riveted empty eyes upon her, and then went on with his letter.

'I'll burn you, old 'un,' I muttered, dropping off to sleep. 'I'll burn you and your stolen calf.'

'Wait a moment,' she cried in a high voice. She ran into the entrance passage and returned with a jug of milk and some bread.

We had not eaten half she brought when shots began to rap in the yard. There were many of them, and they went on rapping a long time, tediously. We finished the milk, and Volkov went out into the yard to find out what it was all about.

'I've saddled your horse,' he said to me through the window. 'Mine's been riddled through and through. The

Poles are posting their machine-guns a hundred paces away.'

There remained only one horse for the two of us. It just managed to carry us out of Sitanets. I sat in the saddle, and Volkov hung on behind.

The transport wagons were making off, roaring and sinking in the mud. Morning oozed over us like chloroform over a hospital table.

'Are you married, Lyutov?' Volkov suddenly asked.

'My wife left me,' I answered, and dozing for a few moments dreamed I was sleeping in a bed.

Silence.

Our horse stumbled.

'The mare will be done after another couple of versts,' said Volkov, behind me.

Silence.

'We've lost the campaign,' muttered Volkov, and snored.

'Yes,' I answered.

Sokal, September 1920

Treason

COMRADE INVESTIGATOR BURDENKO,

I will reply to your question that my Party Number is 2400, delivered to Nikita Balmashev by the Party committee at Krasnodar. My life up to 1914 I will describe as domestic, doing agriculture with my parents, and from agriculture I went over to the ranks of the Imperialists to defend Citizen Pwangcarry and Ebert-Noske the hangman of the German Revolution, as went to sleep it looks like, and saw in their sleep how to help my native settlement of St Ivan in the Kuban. And so things dragged on till Comrade Lenin, along with Comrade Trotsky, turned my savage bayonet aside and showed it other predestined guts and viscera what was more worth going for. From that time on I have been carrying Number 2400 on the point of my far-seeing bayonet, and it is the limit and funny too for me to hear such a mighty queer yarn about the unheard of N. Hospital from you, Comrade Investigator Burdenko. I didn't fire at the hospital and didn't attack it, and such just couldn't be. All three of us wounded men, viz. Golovitsyn, Kustov, and me, we all of us had a blaze in the bones, but we did not go for it but only hollered in the square in hospital bathrobes in the middle of the civil population, Jews by nationality. And as for three damaged window-panes we damaged with an officer's revolver, I will tell you straight as those panes there did not answer to their purpose, them being in the storeroom where they was no use. And when Doctor Jawein saw us shooting he only laughed and sneered with a lot of smiles by the little window of his hospital, what the above-mentioned civilian Jews of the town of Kozin can all bear me out. And I will inform you that he laughed at us when us three wounded men, viz. Golovitsyn, Kustov, and me, first went along for treatment, and said to us straight off, far too rough, 'You go and have a bath, you men, and throw off your clothes and arms this very minute. I am nervous of contagion. They will go to the storeroom and no mistake.' Then, seeing a beast in front of him and no human being, Kustov put out his smashed leg and spoke up about what contagion could there be in a sharp Kuban sabre except for the enemies of our Revolution, and said he was interested about the storeroom, if there was really a Party fighter in charge of the things there or only one of the party-less masses. And then it was clear, as Doctor Jawein perceived, we could see through treason easy enough. He turned his back, and without so much as another word, but smiling a lot, sent us into a ward, and we went there limping on our broken legs and waving our mutilated arms and holding on to one another because us three are countrymen from the settlement of St Ivan, viz. Comrade Golovitsyn, Comrade Kustov, and me; we are countrymen with the same fate, and the one that got a leg torn to bits holds on to his comrade's arm, and the one that lost an arm leans on his comrade's shoulder. We went into the ward as we was told, expecting to see education going on and loyalty to the cause, but what do you think we saw when we got into the ward? We saw Red Army men, nothing but infantry without exception, sitting about on made beds playing draughts, and tall nurses of the smooth sort standing about at the windows making themselves nice to everyone.

'Done with fighting, you kids?' I exclaims to the wounded men.

'Done with fighting,' answers the wounded men, and move the draughtsmen made of bread.

'Early in the day,' I says to the wounded men. 'Your fighting is over mighty early when the enemy is creeping about only fifteen versts away from the town and when the *Red Trooper* says about our international position that it's real terrible, and that the horizon is full of clouds.' But my words bounced off the heroic infantry like sheep-dung off the regimental drum, and all that came of our talk was the sisters led us to the beds and began yarning about laying down arms as if we was already conquered! They upset Kustov proper, I can tell you, and he began tearing at his wound on his left shoulder above his loyal soldier's and proletarian heart. When they saw him taking on so, the nurses shut up, but only for a minute. Then they carried on again with their jeering, the jeering of the partyless masses, and began to urge everyone that did not mind to come and pull the clothes off us as we dozed, or make us play theatre-parts in women's clothes for educational purposes, which is not decent.

Regular sisters of mercilessness, they was. They tried giving us sleeping-powders more than once to get our clothes away, so we had to rest in turn with one eye open, and used to go to the lavatory in full uniform with revolvers, even – if you'll pardon the expression – to pee. And when we had been through all this a week and a day, we began to get wild and have visions, and in the end, when we woke up on the accursed morning of August 4, we noticed a change in us, for we was lying in bathrobes with numbers on like convicts, without arms or the clothes that our mothers, feeble old women in the Kuban, had wove. And the sun, we saw, was shining grand, and the trench infantry among which three Red Cavalrymen had been through so much was going on making fun of us, and the sisters of mercilessness also, as had bunged us up with sleeping-draughts the night before, was now wobbling their young breasts bringing us cocoa on plates with milk enough to drown in! When the fun began the infantry banged their crutches about and started a row and pinched us in the sides like we was loose women, making out that Budyonny's First Cavalry Army had also thrown in the towel. No, no, curly-headed comrades who'd stuffed their bellies so that they went off at night like machine-guns, it had not gone and thrown in the towel; but just so to speak, asking to be excused for a moment, we went all three of us out into the yard and rushed out all in a fever, with blue open wounds, to Citizen Boydermann, the President of the Local Revolutionary Committee, without which, Comrade Investigator Burdenko, that little misunderstanding as regards the shooting as like as not might not have come about, i.e. but for that President of the Local Revolutionary Committee who went and did us in. And though we have nothing definite to go on against Citizen Boydermann, yet, when we went to see him we perceived a citizen getting on in years, a Jew by nationality, sitting in a sheepskin coat at a table so heaped with papers it was awful to look at. Citizen Boydermann looks about this way and that, and it is as clear as noon that he can't make those papers out nohow, and is fed up with them, all the more so since unknown but worthy combatants go over ominous-like to Citizen Boydermann for rations, and mixed with them local workmen attempt to draw attention to the resistance in the villages hereabouts, and then up come common workmen of the Centre who wants to get married at the Local Revolutionary Committee as quick as possible and without any hanging about. So we too explained about the case of treason at the hospital, raising our voices, but Citizen Boydermann only stared at us and again looked about this way and that, sort of patting us on the back which is not official or right in government business. He did not issue us any resolution whatsoever and only said, 'Comrade combatants, if you have any respect for Soviet authority, then leave this building,' which we could not agree to leave the building, but insisted on a general account of himself and when we did not get it we went and lost our heads, and when we had lost our heads we went out into the square in front of the hospital and disarmed the militia which consisted of one chap on horseback, and destroyed with tears in our eyes three unenviable windowpanes in the above-mentioned storeroom. Doctor Jawein made a face and sneered at this inadmissible fact, and this at a time when Comrade Kustov was to die of his illness in four days!

In his short Red life Comrade Kustov was real upset about the treason that is winking at us from the window and making game of the common proletariat, but the proletariat, comrades, knows it is common and it hurts us, it does, and our souls are aflame and rend with fire the prison of the body.

I tell you, Comrade Investigator Burdenko, treason is laughing at us from the window, treason is going about the house barefoot, treason has taken off its boots so the floorboards in the burgled house don't creak.

Chesniki

THE VI Division was mustered in the wood outside the village of Chesniki, awaiting the signal to attack. But Pavlichenko, the Divisional Commander, was expecting the arrival of the Second Brigade, and did not give the signal. The Voroshilov rode up to him, pushing him in the chest with his horse's head, and said:

'We're dawdling, comrade, dawdling.'

'The Second Brigade,' replied Pavlichenko in a muffled voice, 'is riding up to the scene of operations according to your orders.'

'We're dawdling, Commander, dawdling,' said Voroshilov, tugging at his straps.

Pavlichenko took a step back.

'In the name of conscience,' he cried, twisting his raw fingers, 'in the name of conscience, stop hurrying me, Comrade Voroshilov.'

'Not hurry him!' whispered Klim Voroshilov, member of the Revolutionary War Council, and closed his eyes. He sat on his horse, his eyes half-closed. He remained silent, moving his lips. A Cossack in bast shoes and a bowler stared at him, puzzled. Like the wind, the galloping squadrons swept noisily through the wood, breaking the branches. Voroshilov combed his horse's mane with his Mauser.

'Army Commander,' he cried, turning to Budyonny, 'say a couple of words to encourage the men. There are the Poles standing on the knoll just like a picture, making fun of you.'

It was true that the Poles were visible through field-glasses. The Army Staff vaulted into the saddle, and the Cossacks began to flow up from all sides.

Ivan Akinfiev, ex-driver of the Revolutionary Tribunal, rode past us, knocking me with his stirrup.

'You at the front, Ivan?' I said to him. 'Why, you haven't any ribs!'

'Ribs be damned,' answered Akinfiev, who was sitting sideways on his horse. 'Give us a chance to hear what the fellow's talking about.'

He rode forward and bumped straight into Budyonny. The latter gave a start, and said quietly:

'Things are going badly, boys. Got to put more guts into it.'

'On to Warsaw!' shouted the Cossack in the bast shoes and bowler, rolling his eyes and slashing the air with his sword.

'On to Warsaw!' shouted Voroshilov, throwing his horse on its haunches and springing forward to the centre of the squadrons.

'Men and commanders,' he cried passionately, 'an utterly new power is struggling in Moscow, in the ancient capital. The government of workers and peasants, the first in the world, orders us, men and commanders, to attack the enemy – and beat 'em!'

'Swords – ready!' sang out Pavlichenko's voice from afar, behind the Army Commander's back, and his protruding scarlet lips glittered with foam amid the ranks. The Divisional Commander's red Cossack coat was in rags, and his fleshy face repulsive and mutilated. With the blade of his priceless sword he saluted Voroshilov.

'According to the duty imposed on me by my revolutionary oath,' said the Divisional Commander, clearing his throat and looking about him, 'I have to report to the Revolutionary War Council of the First Cavalry Army that the Second Invincible Cavalry Brigade is riding up to the scene of operations.'

'Carry on,' replied Voroshilov with a wave of his hand.

He touched the bridle, and Budyonny rode along beside him. They rode side by side, in white summer uniforms and bright silver-striped trousers, on their tall chestnut mares. Raising a shout, the men moved on after them, and pale steel gleamed in the ichor of the autumnal sun. But I heard no singleheartedness in that Cossack shout. Awaiting the attack, I went into the wood, right into the very heart of it, where our supplies were.

There lay a wounded and delirious Red Army man. And Steve Duplishchev, a quarrelsome Cossack lad, was currycombing Hurricane, a thoroughbred stallion belonging to the Divisional Commander and descended from Lyulyusha, famous for her records at Rostov. The wounded man was voluble in his reminiscences of the town of Shuya, of a certain heifer and of some flax-combing or other, while Duplishchev, drowning his plaintive mutterings, sang a song about a fat general's wife and an orderly, singing louder and louder, waving the currycomb and stroking the mount. But he was interrupted by Sasha – stout Sasha, the girl-friend of all the squadrons. She rode up to the boy and jumped to the ground.

'Shall we settle it, eh?' said Sasha.

'Push off,' answered Duplishchev, turning his back on her and plaiting ribbons in Hurricane's mane.

'You your own master, Steve?' then asked Sasha, 'or are you just a lump of clay?'

'Clear off,' repeated Steve. 'I'm my own master, all right.'

He plaited all the ribbons in the mane and suddenly called out to me in despair:

'Just look how she keeps on at me! A whole month I've had to put up with I don't know what. Can't turn around but she's there. Can't go anywhere but she's in the way. It's let her have the use of the stallion all day long. And now, the Divisional Commander's warning me every day, "There'll be lots coming to you," he says, "asking for the use of the stallion, but don't you go and let anyone have him till he's over three years old." '

'You're let out when you're over fourteen, never fear,' muttered Sasha, turning away. 'Fourteen, and you won't cause any trouble – not you – you'll just blow bubbles.'

She went over to her mare, tightened the saddle-girths, and prepared to mount.

Her spurs clashed on her shoes. Her open-work stockings were splashed with mud and spiky with hay, and her enormous breasts swung around to her back.

'I brought a rouble along,' said Sasha to no one, and placed her spurred shoe in the stirrup. 'I brought it along with me, but it seems I've got to take it away again.'

The woman took out two fifty-copeck pieces, tossed them on her palm, and hid them away again in her bosom.

'We'll settle it, eh?' said Duplishchev then, his eyes fixed on the silver, and he led up the stallion.

Sasha chose a slope in the glade and stood her mare there.

'Seems you're the only one in the world with a stallion,' she said to Steve, and led up Hurricane. 'My mare's been in the army and hasn't been covered for two years; so I thought I might as well make the most of the chance.'

Sasha managed the stallion and then led her mare off to one side.

'Well, now we've been stuffed, girl,' she whispered, and kissed her mare on the wet, piebald, equine lips from which saliva hung in slender ribbons. She rubbed up against its muzzle, then cocked an ear to the sound of clattering in the wood.

'That's the Second Brigade riding past,' she said sternly, and turned to me. 'Must get moving, Lyutych.'

'Riding past or not, cash on the nail,' cried Duplishchev, beginning to pant.

'Just you watch me pay up!' muttered Sasha, jumping on her mare.

I sped after her at a gallop. Duplishchev's hue and cry resounded behind us, together with the faint rap of a shot.

'Just look at that!' shouted the Cossack lad, dashing through the wood as fast as his legs would carry him.

The wind leaped between the boughs like a hare scared out of its senses. The Second Brigade flew between the Galician oaks, and the tranquil dust of the bombardment rose above the earth as though above a peaceful cottage. And at the Divisional Commander's signal we moved on to the attack – the unforgettable attack at Chesniki.

After the Battle

HERE is the story of my dispute with Akinfiev:

The attack at Chesniki took place on the thirty-first. The squadrons were massed in the wood near the village, and between five and six in the evening they dashed at the enemy, who were waiting for us on a height three versts away. We galloped those three versts on horses that were utterly exhausted, and galloping up the slope saw before us a deathlike wall of black uniforms and pale faces. These were Cossacks who had deserted at the very beginning of the Polish campaign and whom Cossack Captain Yakovlev had formed into a brigade. Forming his horsemen in a square, the captain waited for us with unsheathed sabre. A gold tooth gleamed in his mouth, and his black beard lay on his chest like an icon on a dead body. The enemy's machine-guns were rapping away twenty paces off, and men fell wounded in our ranks. We trampled over them and clashed with the enemy, but his square did not flinch . . . Then we fled.

That was how the Savinkov men won a fleeting victory over the VI Division. They were victorious because they did not retreat before the streaming lava of our attacking squadrons. Captain Yakovlev stood firm that day, and it was we that fled, not having reddened our swords in the wretched blood of traitors.

Five thousand men – the whole division – swept down the slopes unpursued. The enemy remained on the hill, undecided to pursue because their victory seemed unbelievable. That was how we remained alive, and were able to pour down without loss into the valley, where we were met by Vinogradov, Head of the Political Section of the VI Division. Vinogradov was whirling about on a fiery charger, sending the flying Cossacks back to fight.

'Lyutov!' he shouted, catching sight of me, 'turn the men back, or you'll pay for it!'

He struck his reeling stallion with the butt of his Mauser, yelling and calling the men together. I got away from him and rode over to Gulimov, a Kirghiz, who was streaking along not far off.

'Turn your own damn mare by the tail!' answered Gulimov, looking around. He peered stealthily about him and then fired, singeing the hair above my ear.

'Turn your own horse back!' he hissed, clutching me by the shoulder and trying to draw his sword with the other hand. But the sword had stuck fast in its sheath. The Kirghiz shivered and peered around, hugging my shoulder, and brought his eyes nearer and nearer to my face.

'Yours first,' he repeated, barely audible. 'Mine will come on after.' And he knocked me lightly on the chest with the blade of the sword that had at length yielded. The proximity of death and its stifling closeness made me feel sick. With the palm of my hand I thrust back the face of the Kirghiz, that felt as hot as a stone in the sun, and scratched him as deeply as I could. Warm blood stirred beneath my nails, tickling them. I rode away from Gulimov, panting as at the end of a long journey. My tormented friend, my horse, went at a walking pace. I rode on, not turning around, seeing nothing, till I met Vorobyov, Commander of the First Squadron. Vorobyov was searching for his quartermasters, unable to find them. We reached the village of Chesniki together, and sat down on a bench with Akinfiev, ex-driver of the Revolutionary Tribunal. Sasha, one of the nurses of the 31st Cavalry Regiment, walked past, and two commanders sat down with us on the bench, dreamily and in silence. One of them, who had been badly bruised, was shaking his head uncontrollably and blinking an eye that seemed to be rolling out of its socket. Sasha went off to notify the hospital about him and then came back to us, pulling along her mare that was dragging at the bridle and slipping in the sodden clay.

'Where have you hoisted sail for?' Vorobyov asked her. 'Sit a while with us, Sasha.'

'I'm not going to sit with you,' replied Sasha, and struck her mare on the belly. 'That I'm not.'

'Why ever not?' cried Vorobyov, laughing. 'Have you made a resolve not to have tea with men any more?'

'Not with you, anyhow,' the woman retorted, and threw the bridle from her. 'I've made up my mind never to have tea with you, Vorobyov, because I saw you today, you precious heroes, and saw your own dirty work, Commander.'

'Well, that was the time for you to fire a shot,' muttered Vorobyov.

'Fire a shot!' Sasha said in despair, and tore the hospital armlet from her sleeve. 'This is what I'm supposed to shoot with, eh?'

At that moment there came over to us the ex-driver of the Revolutionary Tribunal, Akinfiev, with whom I had an old score to settle.

'You've got nothing to shoot with, Sasha,' he said soothingly. 'Nobody's blaming you. I'm only blaming them that gets scared in the fight and don't put no cartridges in their revolvers. You went to the attack,' Akinfiev suddenly

T—F   161

shouted at me, a spasm shooting across his face, 'you went and didn't put no cartridges in. What was the reason for that?'

'Drop it, Ivan,' I said to Akinfiev, but he would not leave me alone. He came right up to me – all lopsided, epileptic, and ribless.

'The Poles go after you, and you don't go after them,' muttered the Cossack, twisting about and waggling his broken hip. 'What for?'

'The Poles go after me and I don't go after them,' I answered roughly.

'Means you're a Molokan,* one of them milk-drinkers,' whispered Akinfiev, stepping back.

'Means I'm of the Molokan Sect,' I said louder than before. 'What are you after, Ivan?'

'I want to find out if you're in your right mind,' cried Ivan, wildly triumphant. 'You're in your right mind all right, and I've got a law written down about Molokans that says they ought to be wiped out. They worship God . . .'

Collecting a crowd around him, the Cossack yelled on about Molokans without pausing for breath. I began to edge away, but he caught me up and struck me in the back with his fist.

'You didn't put no cartridges in,' Akinfiev whispered faintly into my very ear, and tried to tear my mouth with his big fingers. 'You worship God, you traitor!'

He tugged and tore at my mouth. I pushed the epileptic away and struck him in the face. Akinfiev fell sideways to the ground and began to bleed from his fall.

Then Sasha went over to him with her wobbling breasts. She threw water over Ivan and took out of his black mouth a long tooth that was swaying there like a birch by a bare highway.

'Cocks have only one thought in life – to go and tear at

* Member of a pacifist nonconformist sect.

one another,' said Sasha. 'And everything that's gone on today makes me want to go and hide my face.'

She said this sorrowfully and led the injured Akinfiev off with her. And I plodded on to the village of Chesniki, slipping in the tireless rain of Galicia.

The village was swimming and swelling, and blood-red clay was oozing from its dismal wounds. The first star glimmered above me, and fell into the clouds. Rain lashed the willows and spent itself. Evening flew up to the sky like a flock of birds, and darkness crowned me with its watery wreath. I felt my strength all ebbing away. Bent beneath the funereal garland, I continued on my way, imploring fate to grant me the simplest of proficiencies – the ability to kill my fellow-men.

Galicia, September 1920

The Song

A BAD-TEMPERED landlady fell to my lot when we were billeted in the village of Budyatichi. She was a widow, she was poor, and I knocked many a lock from her larders without finding any food.

Only guile remained. Returning home early one day before dusk, I saw the landlady closing the oven door while the oven was still warm. There was a smell of cabbage soup in the cottage, and it was just possible that there might be meat in that soup. I smelt meat in that cabbage soup of hers, and laid my revolver on the table, but the old woman was stubborn in her denials. Spasms shook her face and her black fingers. She darkened and glowered at me with fright and astonishing hatred. But nothing would have saved her. I'd have compelled her with my revolver had it not been for the intervention of Sandy Konyayev, alias Sandy the Christ.

He entered the hut with his accordion under his arm, dragging his handsome legs in boots very down at heel.

'Let's have a song,' he said, raising to me ice-blue eyes full of dreaminess. 'Let's have a song,' said Sandy. And sitting down on the bench he played some notes by way of introduction.

This meditative prelude came as though from afar. The Cossack broke off suddenly and his blue eyes filled with sadness. He turned away and, knowing full well what would give me pleasure, began a Kuban song.

'Star of the fields,' he sang, 'star of the fields above my father's house; my mother's grieving hand . . .'

I love that song. Sandy knew this, for the two of us had heard it for the first time in 1919, in the ramifications of the Don and the Kagalnitskaya settlement.

A hunter who was very active on some fish preserves there had taught us that song. Fish spawn in those waters, and birds come there in flocks. The waters teem with fish, to such an extent that they can be scooped out with ladles or simply caught by hand, and if an oar is put into the water it will stand on end, held up and carried forward by the fish. We saw this with our own eyes, and will never forget those preserves near Kagalnitskaya. All the authorities forbade hunting there, and justly so, but in 1919 heavy fighting was going on in those parts, and Yakov the hunter, who carried on his unlawful business quite openly, gave the accordion to Sandy the Christ, our squadron singer, so that we should not report him. He taught Sandy his songs, many of which were ancient melodies full of the deepest feeling. We forgave the wily hunter everything, for we needed his songs. At that time no one could see an end to the war, and Sandy alone could strew our wearisome way with resonance and tears. Bloodstained tracks marked that way of ours, and singing flew above it. So it was in the Kuban, and when we fought the Green Guerrillas. So it was in the Urals and the foothills of the Caucasus, and so it is to this day. Those songs are indispensable to us. No one can see an end to the war, and Sandy the Christ, our squadron singer, is not yet ripe for death.

So it was that evening too, when I was thwarted of my landlady's cabbage soup. Sandy calmed me down with his subdued and swaying voice.

'Star of the fields,' he sang, 'star of the fields above my father's house; my mother's grieving hand . . .'

And I listened to him, stretched out in the corner on the fusty hay. Reverie broke my bones, reverie shook the rotting hay beneath me. Through its hot downpour I could scarcely make out the old woman resting her withered cheek on her hand. Drooping her year-bitten head, she stood motionless by the wall, not stirring when Sandy came to the end of his song.

Sandy stopped playing and put the accordion aside. He gave a yawn and a laugh, as though waking from a long sleep. Then, noticing the bareness of the widow's hovel, he brushed the dirt from the bench and fetched a bucket of water.

'You see, dearie,' said the landlady to him, rubbing her back against the door and pointing at me, 'your commander there came not long ago; he shouted at me and stamped his foot and took the locks off my larders and put out his weapons to scare me. It's a sin before God to put out weapons before me, for I'm a lone woman.'

She rubbed her back against the wall again, and set about spreading a fur jacket over her son, who was snoring beneath the icon on a large bed littered with rags. He was a dumb boy with a flabby, white, swollen head and enormous feet like those of an adult. His mother wiped his nose and returned to the table.

'Missis,' said Sandy to her then, touching her on the shoulder, 'I don't mind laying myself out to be nice to you, if you like.'

But the peasant woman seemed not to have heard him.

'Never see no cabbage soup,' she said, resting her cheek against her hand. 'It's gone, my cabbage soup has. People only go and show me weapons, and when there does come along a decent chap I could have a bit of fun with, I'm so sick of everything I couldn't get no pleasure out of sinning.'

She grumbled on drearily and moved the dumb boy closer to the wall, mumbling all the while. Sandy lay down on the ragged bed beside her, and I tried to sleep, imagining dreams so as to fall asleep with pleasant thoughts in my head.

The Rabbi's Son

Do you remember Zhitomir, Vasily? Do you remember the River Teterev, Vasily, and that night when the Sabbath, the young Sabbath crept along the sunset, crushing the stars beneath her little red heel?

The slender horn of the moon bathed its darts in the dark waters of the river. Queer old Gedali, the founder of the Fourth International, led us to Rabbi Motale Bratslavsky's for evening prayers. Queer old Gedali shook the cock's feathers on his top hat in the ruddy haze of evening. The predatory eyes of lighted candles blinked in the Rabbi's room. Broad-shouldered Jews groaned dully, bent over prayerbooks, and the old buffoon of the Chernobyl saddiks jingled coppers in his frayed pocket.

Do you remember that night, Vasily? Beyond the window, horses were neighing and Cossacks shouted. The wilderness of war yawned beyond the window, and Rabbi Motale Bratslavsky prayed by the eastern wall, digging his emaciated fingers into his talith. Then the curtain of the Ark was drawn aside, and we saw in the funereal candlelight the Torah rolls sheathed in covers of purple velvet and blue silk and, bowed above the Torah, inanimate and resigned, the beautiful face of Elijah the Rabbi's son, last prince of the dynasty.

Well, only the day before yesterday, Vasily, the regiments of the XII Army opened the front at Kovel. The conqueror's bombardment thundered disdainfully over the town. Our troops faltered, and mingled in confusion. The Political Section train started crawling over the dead backbone of the fields. And a monstrous and inconceivable Russia tramped in bast shoes on either side of the coaches, like a multitude of bugs swarming in clothes. The typhus-ridden peasantry rolled before them the customary humpback of a soldier's death. They jumped up on to the steps of our train and fell back, dislodged by the butt-ends of our rifles. They snorted and scrabbled and flowed on wordlessly. And at the twelfth verst, when I had no potatoes left, I flung a pile of Trotsky's leaflets at them. But only one man among them stretched a dead and filthy hand to catch a leaflet. And I recognized Elijah, son of the Rabbi of Zhitomir. I recognized him at once, Vasily. And it was so heartrending to see a prince who had lost his pants, doubled up beneath his soldier's pack, that we defied the regulations and pulled him up into our coach. His bare knees, inefficient as an old woman's, knocked against the rusty iron of the steps. Two full-bosomed typists in sailor blouses trailed the long, shamed body of the dying man along the floor. We laid him in a corner of the editorial office, on the floor, and Cossacks in loose red trousers set straight the clothes that were dropping off him. The girls planted their bandy legs – legs of unforward females – on the floor, and stared dully at his sexual organs, the stunted, curly-covered virility of a wasted Semite. And I, who had seen him on one of my nights of roaming, began to pack in a case the scattered belongings of the Red Army man Bratslavsky.

His things were strewn about pell-mell – mandates of the propagandist and notebooks of the Jewish poet, the portraits of Lenin and Maimonides lay side by side, the knotted iron of Lenin's skull beside the dull silk of the portraits of Maimonides. A lock of woman's hair lay in a book, the Resolutions of the Party's Sixth Congress, and the margins of Communist leaflets were crowded with crooked lines of ancient Hebrew verse. They fell upon me in a mean and depressing rain – pages of the Song of Songs and revolver cartridges. The dreary rain of sunset washed the dust in my hair, and I said to the boy who was dying on a wretched mattress in the corner:

'One Friday evening four months ago, Gedali the old-clothesman took me to see your father, Rabbi Motale. But you didn't belong to the Party at that time, Bratslavsky . . .'

'I did,' the boy answered, scratching at his chest and twisting in fever, 'only I couldn't leave my mother.'

'And now, Elijah?'

'When there's a revolution on, a mother's an episode,' he whispered, less and less audibly. 'My letter came, the letter B, and the Organization sent me to the front . . .'

'And you got to Kovel, Elijah?'

'I got to Kovel!' he cried in despair. 'The kulaks opened the front to the enemy. I took over the command of a scratch regiment, but too late . . . I hadn't enough artillery . . .'

He died before we reached Rovno. He – that last of the Princes – died among his poetry, phylacteries, and coarse foot-wrappings. We buried him at some forgotten station. And I, who can scarce contain the tempests of my imagination within this age-old body of mine, I was there beside my brother when he breathed his last.

Argamak

I RESOLVED to transfer to the active forces. The Divisional Commander frowned when he heard about this.

'Why on earth go butting in there? You'll stand there gaping, and they'll counterpoint you first thing.'

But I insisted. What is more, my choice fell on the most warlike of divisions, the VI. I was attached to the Fourth Squadron of the 23rd Cavalry Regiment. The squadron was commanded by a locksmith of the Bryansk factory, Baulin, a mere boy in years. He had grown a beard to lend him authority. Ashen tufts curled beneath his chin. In his twenty-two years Baulin had never known any worry. This quality, characteristic of thousands of Baulins, formed an important element in the victory of the Revolution. Baulin was tough, of few words, stubborn, The path of his life had been laid down, and he had no doubts as to the correctness of this path. Deprivations came easy to him. He could sleep sitting up. He would sleep pressing one hand in the other, and would wake so that the passage from oblivion to wakefulness was imperceptible.

One could expect no mercy under Baulin's command. The beginning of my service was marked by a rare omen of success: I was given a horse. There were no horses, either in the reserve of mounts or in the hands of the peasants. A chance helped: the Cossack Tikhomolov took it into his head to kill a couple of captured officers. He had been ordered to take them to Brigade Staff, since the officers might have valuable information to communicate, but Tikhomolov didn't take them that far. It was first decided that the Cossack should stand trial before the Revolutionary Tribunal, but then they changed their minds. Squadron Commander Baulin thought up a punishment far more terrible than any the Tribunal could have inflicted. He deprived Tikhomolov of his stallion, Argamak by name, and sent the Cossack to the transport train.

The tortures I suffered with Argamak almost exceeded the measure of human endurance. Tikhomolov had brought the horse from his home on the River Terek. It was accustomed to the Cossack trot, to the peculiar Cossack gallop – dry, furious, abrupt. Argamak's pace was long, extended, persistent. With this devilish pace of his he would carry me away from the ranks. I would lose track of the squadron and, having no sense of direction, wander about for days looking for my unit, come within range of the enemy, spend the night in gullies, try to join up with strange regiments and be rudely rebuffed. My experience of horsemanship was limited to having served during the German War in the artillery division attached to the 15th Foot Regiment. This had for the most part meant perching on an ammunition box; occasionally we would ride in a gun team. Nowhere had I had a chance of getting used to Argamak's rough and swaying trot. Tikhomolov had left as an inheritance to his horse all the devils of his own fall. I would wobble like a sack on the stallion's long lean spine. This spine I messed up properly: sores appeared upon it, metallic flies grazed on these sores, bands of congealed black blood girdled the horse's belly. Thanks to faulty shoeing Argamak began to hitch, and his hind legs swelled up at the fetlock, developing elephantine proportions. Elsewhere Argamak grew thin. His eyes were suffused with the glare peculiar to the tortured horse, the glare of hysteria and resistance. He would not allow himself to be saddled.

'You've ruined that mount, four-eyes,' said the Platoon Commander.

In my presence the Cossacks kept silent, but behind my back they were preparing to spring, as beasts of prey prepare, in sleepy and insidious immobility. They didn't even ask me to write letters for them any more.

The Cavalry Army had gained possession of Novograd-Volynsk. In twenty-four hours we used to have to cover sixty or eighty kilometres. We were approaching Rovno. No daytime halts to speak of, and every night I had the same dream. I am dashing along on Argamak at a fast trot. By the roadside bonfires are burning, the Cossacks are cooking their food. I ride past them, and they do not raise their eyes to me. Some salute, others pay no attention: they're not concerned with me. What's the meaning of all this? Their indifference means that there is nothing special about the way I ride. I ride like everybody else, so there's no point in looking at me. I gallop on my way, and am happy. My hunger for peace and happiness was not satisfied when I was awake, and that's why I dreamed dreams.

There was no sign of Tikhomolov. He had his eye on me from somewhere on the outskirts of the march, in the unhurried files of wagons crammed with odds and ends.

The Platoon Commander once said to me:

'He keeps pestering us to know how you're making out.'

'What does it matter to him?'

'Seems it does.'

'I suppose he's got it into his head that I wronged him.'

'Didn't you, then?'

Tikhomolov's hatred reached me across forests and rivers. I could sense it with my skin, and curled up. A pair of blood-shot eyes were fastened on my path.

'Why did you make me an enemy?' I asked Baulin.

The Squadron Commander rode past, yawning.

'It's not my funeral,' he replied, not turning round. 'It's your funeral.'

Argamak's back would dry up and then open again. I would put as many as three saddlecloths under the saddle, but my seat wasn't right, and the weals failed to close. The feeling that I was sitting on an open wound made me itch all over.

One Cossack in our platoon, Bizyukov by name, came from the same part of the country as Tikhomolov. He had known the man's father there on the Terek.

'His father, you know,' Bizyukov once said to me, 'breeds horses for the hunt. A devil of a horseman, for all his fat. He'll come to the drove, and can't wait to start choosing a horse. They are led up. He stands facing a horse, straddles his legs, takes a good look. What d'you think he's up to? Just this: he swipes out with his great fist, deals one blow, and there's no more horse. "Why, Kalistrat," they say to him, "have you done the horse in?" "The way I hunt," says he, "that horse is no good to me. Not my sort of horse. When I go hunting," says he, "it's no fun." A devil of a horseman, there's no denying.'

And Argamak, left alive by Tikhomolov Senior, picked out by him, had fallen to my lot. What was I to do? I turned over in my mind plan after plan. But in the end it was the war that saved me.

The Cavalry Army attacked Rovno. The town was taken, and we spent two days in it. Next night the Poles cleared us out again. They had given battle in order to cover their retreating detachments, and the manoeuvre came off. As cover the Poles had the benefit of a hurricane, cutting rain, a heavy summer thunderstorm that upset itself over the world in torrents of black water. We vacated the town for twenty-four hours. In this fight in the dark, Dundich the Serb fell, bravest of men. Tikhomolov also fought in this battle. The Poles dashed at his wagon-train. It was a region of plains entirely lacking in cover. Tikhomolov arranged his wagons in a battle-order known to him alone. No doubt the Romans had drawn up their chariots in this way. Somehow he happened to have a machine-gun. One must suppose that he had stolen it and hidden it away just in case. With this machine-gun he warded off the attack, saved his goods and chattels, and led off the whole wagon-train with the exception of two carts, the horses of which had been shot.

'Why are you worrying the men?' they asked Baulin at Brigade Staff a few days after this battle.

'If I am, it must be because it's necessary.'

'Watch out, or you'll go too far.'

Tikhomolov was not amnestied, but we knew that he would be coming along. He came wearing galoshes on his bare feet. His fingers had been chopped about, and ribbons of black lint hung down from them, dragging after him like a cloak. Tikhomolov came to the village of Budyatichi, into the square before the Catholic church where our horses were tethered. Baulin was sitting on the steps of the church, steaming his feet in a tub. His toes were putrescent: they were pink, as iron is pink at the beginning of tempering. Tufts of youthful straw hair stuck to Baulin's forehead. The sun blazed on the bricks and tiles of the church. Bizyukov, standing next to the Squadron Commander, shoved a fag into the other's mouth and lit it. Tikhomolov, dragging his mantle of rags, went over to the horses, his galoshes squelching. Argamak stretched out his long neck and neighed toward his master, neighed in a soft squeal, like a horse in the desert. On his back the inflamed lymph twisted lacelike between the strips of torn flesh. Tikhomolov stood next to the horse. The filthy ribbons of bandage trailed unstirring on the ground.

'So it's like that?' said the Cossack, so low you could scarcely hear him.

I stepped forward.

'Let's make it up, Tikhomolov. I'm glad that you're getting the horse back. I just couldn't manage him. We'll make it up, eh?'

'It's not yet Easter, that one should go making it up,' the Platoon Commander said, rolling a cigarette behind me. His wide trousers were loosened, his shirt unbuttoned on his bronze chest, and he was resting on the steps of the church.

'Make it up with him like a good Christian,' muttered Bizyukov, Tikhomolov's countryman, who had known Kalistrat, Tikhomolov's father. 'He wants to be friends.'

I was alone among these men whose friendship I had not succeeded in gaining.

Tikhomolov stood before the horse as though thunderstruck. Argamak, breathing strongly and freely, stretched his muzzle toward him.

'So it's like that?' repeated the Cossack. Then he turned sharply to me and said point-blank: 'I'm not making it up with you.'

Scuffling his galoshes, he started to move away across the parched chalky road, sweeping with his bandages the dust of the village square. Argamak followed like a dog. The bridle swayed beneath his muzzle, his long back stretched low. Baulin was still rubbing the ironlike reddish putrescence of his feet in the tub.

'You've allotted me an enemy,' I said to him. 'And how was I to blame?'

The Squadron Commander raised his head.

'I see you,' he said. 'I see the whole of you. You're trying to live without enemies. That's all you think about, not having enemies.'

'Make peace with him,' mumbled Bizyukov, turning away.

A spot of fire was printed on Baulin's forehead. His cheek twitched.

'You know what comes of this?' he said, not controlling his breath properly. 'Boredom comes of it. Clear off, damn your eyes!'

I had to leave. I transferred to the Sixth Squadron, and there things went better. However it may have been, Argamak had taught me Tikhomolov's style of riding. Months passed, and my dream came true. The Cossacks stopped watching me and my horse.

TALES OF ODESSA

The King

WHEN the wedding ceremony was over, the Rabbi sat for a while in an armchair. Then, going outside, he viewed the tables arrayed all down the courtyard. There were so many of them that those right at the end even poked out into Hospital Street. Velvet-spread, they wound their way down the yard like so many serpents with variegated patches on their bellies, and they sang full-throatedly, those patches of velvet, orange and red.

The living-quarters had been turned into kitchens. A sultry flame beat through the soot-swathed doorways, a flame drunken and puffy-lipped. The faces of the old crones broiled in its smoky rays – old women's tremulous chins and beslobbered bosoms. Sweat with the pinkness of fresh blood, sweat as pink as the slaver of a mad dog, streamed this way and that over those mounds of exorbitant and sweetly pungent flesh. Not counting the dishwashers, three old cooks were preparing the wedding feast, and supreme over all the cooks and dishwashers reigned the octogenarian Reisl, tiny and humpbacked, as patinated with tradition as a roll of the Torah.

Before the feast began, a young man unknown to the guests made his dim and elusive way into the yard. Wanted a word with Benya Krik. Led Benya Krik unobtrusively aside.

'Listen here, King,' said the young man. 'A word in your ear. I'm from Aunt Hannah in Kostetskaya Street.'

'Right,' said Benya Krik, alias The King. 'Out with it.'

'Aunt Hannah told me to tell you that there's a new police captain down at the station.'

'Knew that much day before yesterday,' said Benya Krik. 'Go on.'

'The captain's gone and gathered the whole lot together and speechified.'

'New brooms,' said Benya Krik. 'He's planning a raid. Go on.'

'Suppose you know, King, when the raid will be.'

'It's scheduled for tomorrow.'

'For today, King.'

'Who said so, young man?'

'Aunt Hannah. You know Aunt Hannah?'

'I do. Go on.'

'The captain, I say, assembled all his men and made a speech. We must settle Benya Krik's hash, he said, seeing that where there's an emperor there's no room for a king. Today, when Krik's sister's getting married and they'll all be together, is just the day. We can nab the lot.'

'Go on.'

'Well, the cops began to worry. If we raid 'em today, they said, on a day when Krik is celebrating, he'll see red, and then blood will flow. So the captain said, Duty before everything.'

'Right. Off you go,' said the King.

'What shall I tell Aunt Hannah?'

'Tell her: Benya knows all about the raid.'

And so the young man departed. After him went three of Benya's pals. Said they'd be back in half an hour. And so they were.

Not according to their years did the wedding guests take their seats. Foolish old age is no less pitiable than timorous youth. Nor according to their wealth. Heavy purses are lined with tears.

In the place of honour sat the bride and groom. Today was their day. In the next place sat Zender Eichbaum, father-in-law of the King. Such was his right. One should know the story of Zender Eichbaum, for it is no ordinary story.

How had Benya Krik, gangster and king of gangsters, become Eichbaum's son-in-law? Become son-in-law of a man who owned sixty milk-cows, all save one? The answer lay in a raid. About a year before, Benya had written Eichbaum a letter.

'Monsieur Eichbaum,' he had written, 'have the goodness to deposit, tomorrow morning, in the entrance to No. 17 Sofievskaya Street, the sum of twenty thousand roubles. If you fail to comply with this request, something unheard of will happen to you, and you will be the talk of Odessa. Yours respectfully, Benya the King.'

Three letters, each one more to the point than the preceding, had remained unanswered. Then Benya took steps. They came in the night, nine of them, bearing long poles in their hands. The poles were wrapped about with pitch-dipped tow. Nine flaming stars flared in Eichbaum's cattle-yard. Benya beat the locks from the door of the cowshed and began to lead the cows out one by one. Each was received by a lad with a knife. He would overturn the cow with one blow of the fist and plunge his knife into her heart. On the blood-flooded ground the torches bloomed like roses of fire. Shots rang out. With these shots Benya scared away the dairymaids who had come hurrying to the cowshed. After him other bandits began firing in the air. (If you don't fire in the air you may kill someone.) And now, when the sixth cow had fallen, mooing her death-moo, at the feet of the King, into the courtyard in his underclothes galloped Eichbaum, asking:

'What good will this do you, Benya?'

'If I don't have my money, Monsieur Eichbaum, you won't have your cows. It's as simple as that.'

'Come indoors, Benya.'

And indoors they came to terms. The slaughtered cows were divided fairly between them, and Eichbaum was guaranteed the integrity of his possessions, even receiving a written pledge with affixed seal. But the wonder came later.

During the raid, on that dreadful night when cows bellowed as they were slaughtered and calves slipped and slithered in the blood of their dams, when the torch-flames danced like dark-visaged maidens and the farm-women lunged back in horror from the muzzles of amiable Brownings – on that dread night there ran out into the yard, wearing nought save her V-necked shift, Tsilya the daughter of old man Eichbaum. And the victory of the King was turned to defeat.

Two days later, without warning, Benya returned to Eichbaum all the money he had taken from him, and then one evening he paid the old man a social call. He wore an orange suit, beneath his cuff gleamed a bracelet set with diamonds. He walked into the room, bowed politely, and asked Eichbaum for his daughter's hand. The old man had a slight stroke, but recovered. He was good for another twenty years.

'Listen, Eichbaum,' said the King. 'When you die I will bury you in the First Jewish Cemetery, right by the entrance. I will raise you, Eichbaum, a monument of pink marble. I will make you an Elder of the Brody Synagogue. I will give up my own business and enter yours as a partner. Two hundred cows we will have, Eichbaum. I will kill all the other cow-keepers. No thief shall walk the street you live in. I will build you a villa where the tramline ends. Remember, Eichbaum, *you* were no Rabbi in your young days. People have forged wills, but why talk about it? And the King shall be your son-in-law – no milksop, but the King.'

And Benya Krik had his way; for he was passionate, and passion rules the universe. The newly-weds spent three months on the fat lands of Bessarabia, three months flooded with grapes, rich food, and the sweat of love's encounters. Then Benya returned to Odessa to marry off his sister Deborah, a virgin of forty summers who suffered from goitre. And now, having told the story of Zender Eichbaum, let us return to the marriage of Deborah Krik, sister of the King.

At the wedding-feast they served turkey, roast chicken,

goose, stuffed fish, fish-soup in which lakes of lemon gleamed nacreously. Over the heads of defunct geese, flowers swayed like luxuriant plumage. But does the foamy surge of the Odessa sea cast roast chicken on the shore?

All that is noblest in our smuggled goods, everything for which the land is famed from end to end, did, on that starry, that deep-blue night, its entrancing and disruptive work. Wines not from these parts warmed stomachs, made legs faint sweetly, bemused brains, evoked belches that rang out sonorous as trumpets summoning to battle. The Negro cook from the *Plutarch*, that had put in three days before from Port Said, bore unseen through the customs fat-bellied jars of Jamaica rum, oily Madeira, cigars from the plantations of Pierpont Morgan, and oranges from the environs of Jerusalem. That is what the foaming surge of the Odessa sea bears to the shore, that is what sometimes comes the way of Odessa beggars at Jewish weddings. Jamaica rum came their way at the wedding of Deborah Krik. And so, having sucked their fill like infidel swine, the Jewish beggars began to beat the ground deafeningly with their crutches. Eichbaum, his waistcoat unbuttoned, scanned with puckered eyes the tumultuous gathering, hiccuping lovingly the while. The orchestra played a fanfare. It was just like a divisional parade: a fanfare – nothing but. The gangsters, sitting in compact rows, were at first excessively embarrassed by the presence of outsiders. Later they loosened up. Lyova Rooski cracked a bottle of vodka on the head of his beloved, Monya Gunner fired a shot in the air. The rejoicings reached their pitch when, in accordance with the custom of olden times, the guests began bestowing their wedding-presents. One shammes from the synagogue after another leaped on a table and there, to the stormy wailing of the fanfare, sang out how many roubles had been presented, how many silver spoons. And now the friends of the King showed what blue blood meant, and the chivalry, not yet extinct, of the Moldavanka district. On the silver trays, with ineffably nonchalant movements of the hand, they cast golden coins, rings, and threaded coral.

Aristocrats of the Moldavanka, they were tightly encased in raspberry waistcoats. Russet jackets clasped their shoulders, and on their fleshy feet the azure leather cracked. Rising to their full height and thrusting out their bellies, they beat their palms in time with the music. With the traditional cry of 'Bitter, bitter!' they called on the married couple to kiss, and showered the bride in blossoms. And she, Deborah of forty summers, sister of Benya Krik, distorted by her illness, with her swollen crop and her eyes bulging from their orbits, sat on a pile of cushions side by side with the feeble youth, now mute with misery, whom Eichbaum's money had purchased.

The bestowal of gifts was drawing to a close, one shammes after another was growing hoarse and croaky, and the double-bass was at cross purposes with the fiddle. Over the courtyard there suddenly spread a faint smell of burning.

'Benya,' said Papa Krik, famed among his fellow-draymen as a bully, 'Benya, d'you know what I think? I think our chimney's on fire.'

'Papa,' said Benya to his inebriated parent, 'eat and drink, and don't let such trifles bother you.'

And Papa Krik took the filial advice. Drink and eat he did. But the smoke cloud grew more and more pungent. Here and there the edges of the sky were turning pink, and now there shot up, narrow as a sword blade, a tongue of flame. The guests, half rising from their seats, began to snuffle the air, and the women-folk gave little squeaks of fear. The gangsters eyed one another. And only Benya Krik, aware of nothing, was disconsolate.

'The celebration's going all to pieces,' he cried, filled with despair. 'Good friends, I beg you, eat and drink!'

But now there appeared in the courtyard the same young man who had come earlier in the evening.

'King,' he said, 'I'd like a word in your ear.'

'Out with it, then,' said the King. 'I've always a spare ear for a spare word.'

'King,' said the unknown young man, and giggled. 'It's really comical: the police station's blazing like a house on fire!'

The shopkeepers were silent. The gangsters grinned. The sexagenarian Manka, ancestress of the suburban bandits, placed two fingers in her mouth and whistled so piercingly that her neighbours jerked away in fright.

'You're not on the job, Manka,' observed Benya. 'More *sang-frwa*!'

The young man who had brought these astounding tidings was still doubled up with laughter. He was chortling like a schoolgirl.

'They came out of the station, forty of them,' he related, vigorously moving his jaws, 'all set for the raid, and they hadn't hardly gone fifty yards when the whole place was on fire. Why don't you folks drop around and watch it burn?'

But Benya forbade his guests to go and view the conflagration. He set out himself with two comrades. The station was blazing away. Policemen, their buttocks waggling, were rushing up smoky staircases and hurling boxes out of windows, while the prisoners, unguarded, were making the most of their chance. The firemen were filled with zeal, but no water flowed when the nearest tap was turned. The police captain – the broom that was to have swept clean – was standing on the opposite pavement, biting the ends of his moustache that curled into his mouth. Motionless the new broom stood there. As he passed the captain, Benya gave him a military salute.

'Good health, Your Excellency,' he said, deeply sympathetic. 'What do you say to this stroke of bad luck? A regular act of God!'

He stared hard at the burning building and slowly shook his head.

'Tut-tut-tut!'

When Benya got back home the little lamps in the court-yard were flickering out, and dawn was beginning to touch the sky. The guests had departed and the musicians were dozing, leaning their heads on their double-basses. Deborah alone was not thinking of sleep. With both hands she was urging her faint-hearted husband toward the door of their nuptial chamber, glaring at him carnivorously. Like a cat she was, that holding a mouse in her jaws tests it gently with her teeth.

1923

How It Was Done in Odessa

IT was I that began.

'Reb Arye-Leib,' I said to the old man, 'let us talk of Benya Krik. Let us talk of his thunderclap beginning and his terrible end. Three black shadows block up the paths of my imagination. Here is the one-eyed Ephraim Rook. The russet steel of his actions, can it really not bear comparison with the strength of the King? Here is Nick Pakovsky. The simple-minded fury of that man held all that was necessary for him to wield power. And did not Haim Drong know how to distinguish the brilliance of the rising star? Why then did Benya Krik alone climb to the top of the rope-ladder, while all the rest hung swaying on the lower rungs?'

Reb Arye-Leib was silent, sitting on the cemetery wall. Before us stretched the green stillness of the graves. A man who thirsts for an answer must stock himself with patience. A man possessing knowledge is suited by dignity. For this reason Reb Arye-Leib was silent, sitting on the cemetery wall. Finally he said:

Why he? Why not they, you wish to know? Then see here, forget for a while that you have spectacles on your nose and autumn in your heart. Cease playing the rowdy at your desk and stammering while others are about. Imagine for a moment that you play the rowdy in public places and stammer on paper. You are a tiger, you are a lion, you are a cat. You can spend the night with a Russian woman, and satisfy her. You are twenty-five. If rings were fastened to heaven and earth, you would grasp them and draw heaven and earth together. And your father is Mendel Krik the drayman. What does such a father think about? He thinks about drinking a good glass of vodka, of smashing somebody in the face, of his horses – and nothing more. You want to live, and he makes you die twenty times a day. What would you have done in Benya Krik's place? You would have done nothing. But *he* did something. That's why he's the King, while you thumb your nose in the privy.

He – Benya Krik – went to see Ephraim Rook, who, already in those days looking at the world out of only one eye, was already then what he is now. He said to Ephraim:

'Take me on. I want to moor to your bollard. The bollard I moor to will be the winning one.'

Rook asked him:

'Who are you, where do you come from, and what do you use for breath?'

'Give me a try, Ephraim,' replied Benya, 'and let us stop smearing gruel over a clean table.'

'Let us stop smearing gruel,' assented Rook. 'I'll give you a try.'

And the gangsters went into conference to consider the matter of Benya Krik. I wasn't at that conference, but they say that a conference was held. Chairman at that time was Lyovka Bullock.

'What goes on under his hat, under little Benya's hat?' asked the late Bullock.

And the one-eyed Rook gave his opinion:

'Benya says little, but what he says is tasty. He says little, and one would like him to say more.'

'If so,' exclaimed the late Bullock, 'then let's try him on Tartakovsky.'

'Let's try him on Tartakovsky,' resolved the conference, and all in whom conscience still had lodgings blushed when they heard this decision. Why did they blush? You will learn this if you come where I shall lead you.

We used to call Tartakovsky 'Jew-and-a-Half' or 'Nine Holdups'. 'Jew-and-a-Half' he was called because no single Jew could have had so much dash and so much cash as Tartakovsky. He was taller than the tallest cop in Odessa, and weighed more than the fattest of Jewesses. And 'Nine Hold-ups' he was called because the firm of Lyovka Bullock and Co. had made on his office not eight nor yet ten raids, but nine precisely. To the lot of Benya Krik, who was not yet the King, fell the honour of carrying out the tenth raid on Jew-and-a-Half. When Ephraim informed him accordingly, he said 'O.K.' and went out, banging the door. Why bang the door? You will learn this if you come where I shall lead you.

Tartakovsky has the soul of a murderer, but he is one of us. He originated with us. He is our blood. He is our flesh, as though one momma had born us. Half Odessa serves in his shops. And it was through his own Moldavanka lads that he suffered. Twice they held him for ransom, and once during a pogrom they buried him with a choir. The Sloboda thugs were then beating up the Jews on Bolshaya Arnautskaya. Tartakovsky escaped from them, and on Sofiyskaya met a funeral procession with a choir. He asked:

'Who's that they're burying with a choir?'

The passers-by replied that it was Tartakovsky they were

burying. The procession got to the Sloboda Cemetery. Then our chaps produced a machine-gun from the coffin and started plastering the Sloboda thugs. But Jew-and-a-Half had not forseen this. Jew-and-a-Half was scared to death. And what boss would not have been scared in his place?

The tenth raid on a man who has already once been buried was a coarse action. Benya, who was not then the King, understood this better than anyone. But he said 'O.K.' to Rook, and that day wrote Tartakovsky a letter similar to all letters of this sort:

'Highly respected Ruvim son of Joseph! Be kind enough to place, on Saturday, under the rain barrel, etc. If you refuse, as last time you refused, know that a great disappointment awaits you in your private life. Respects from the Bentzion Krik you know of.'

Tartakovsky did not play the sluggard, and replied without delay:

'Benya! If you were a half-wit I should write to you as to a half-wit. But I do not know you as such, and God forfend I ever shall! You, it is evident, want to play the child. Do you really mean you don't know that this year there is such a crop in the Argentine that there's enough to drown in, and we sitting with all our wheat and no customers? And I will tell you, hand on heart, that in my old age I am finding it tedious to swallow so bitter a piece of bread and to experience these unpleasantnesses, having worked all my life as hard as the least of draymen. And what have I from all this endless convict-labour? Ulcers, sores, troubles, and insomnia. Give up this nonsense, Benya. Your friend (much more than you suppose) Ruvim Tartakovsky.'

Jew-and-a-Half had done what he could. He had written a letter. But the letter wasn't delivered to the right address. Receiving no reply, Benya waxed wroth. Next day he turned up with four pals at Tartakovsky's office. Four youths in masks and with revolvers bowled into the office.

'Hands up!' they cried, and started waving their pistols about.

'A little more *sang-frwa*, Solomon,' observed Benya to one who was shouting louder than the rest. 'Don't make a habit of being nervous on the job.' And turning to the clerk, who was white as death and yellow as clay, he asked him:

'Is Jew-and-a-Half on the premises?'

'No, sir,' replied the clerk, one Muginstein by name. His first name was Joseph, and he was the bachelor son of Aunt Pesya the poultry-dealer on Seredinskaya Square.

'Well then, who's in charge in the old man's absence?' they started third-degreeing the wretched Muginstein.

'I am,' said the clerk, green as green grass.

'Then with God's help open up the safe!' Benya ordered, and the curtain rose on a three-act opera.

The nervous Solomon was packing cash, securities, watches, and monograms in a suitcase; the late Joseph stood before him with his hands in the air, and at that moment Benya was telling anecdotes about Jews.

'Since he's forever playing the Rothschild,' Benya was saying of Tartakovsky, 'let him burn on a slow fire. Explain this to me, Muginstein, as to a friend: if he receives, as he has, a businesslike letter from me, why shouldn't he take a five-copeck tramride and come over and see me at my place and drink a glass of vodka with my family and take pot-luck? What prevented him from opening his heart to me? "Benya," he might have said, "so on and so forth, here's my balance-sheet, gimme a coupla days to draw breath and see how things stand." What should I have replied? Pig does not see eye to eye with pig, but man with man does. Muginstein, do you catch my drift?'

'I d-do,' stuttered Muginstein, but he lied, for he hadn't the remotest idea why Jew-and-a-Half the wealthy and respected should want to take a tramride to eat a snack with the family of Mendel Krik the drayman.

And meantime misfortune lurked beneath the window like a pauper at daybreak. Misfortune broke noisily into the office. And though on this occasion it bore the shape of the Jew Savka Butsis, this misfortune was as drunk as a water-carrier.

'Ho-hoo-ho,' cried the Jew Savka, 'forgive me, Benya, I'm late.' And he started stamping his feet and waving his arms about. Then he fired, and the bullet landed in Muginstein's belly.

Are words necessary? A man was, and is no more. A harmless bachelor was living his life like a bird on a bough, and had to meet a nonsensical end. There came a Jew looking like a sailor and took a potshot not at some clay pipe or dolly but at a live man. Are words necessary?

'Let's scram,' cried Benya, and ran out last. But as he departed he managed to say to Butsis:

'I swear by my mother's grave, Savka, that you will lie next to him . . .'

Now tell me, young master, you who snip coupons on other people's shares, how would you have acted in Benya's place? You don't know how you would have acted. But he knew. That's why he's the King, while you and I are sitting on the wall of the Second Jewish Cemetery and keeping the sun off with our palms.

Aunt Pesya's unfortunate son did not die straightaway. An hour after they had got him to the hospital, Benya appeared there. He asked for the doctor in charge and the nurse to be sent out to him, and said to them, not taking his hands out of his cream pants:

'It is in my interest,' he said, 'that the patient Joseph Muginstein should recover. Let me introduce myself, just in case: Bentzion Krik. Camphor, air-cushions, a private ward – supply them with liberal hands. Otherwise every Tom, Dick and Harry of a doctor, even if he's a doctor of philosophy, will get no more than six feet of earth.'

But Muginstein died that night. And only then did Jew-and-a-Half raise a stink through all Odessa.

'Where do the police begin,' he wailed, 'and where does Benya end?'

'The police end where Benya begins,' replied sensible folk; but Tartakovsky refused to take the hint, and he lived to see the day when a red automobile with a musical-box for horn played its first march from the opera *Pagliacci* on Seredinskaya Square. In broad daylight the car flew up to the little house in which Aunt Pesya dwelt.

The automobile cast thunderbolts with its wheels, spat fumes, shone brassily, stank of petrol, and performed arias on its horn. From the car someone sprang out and passed into the kitchen, where little Aunt Pesya was throwing hysterics on the earthen floor. Jew-and-a-Half was sitting in a chair waving his hands about.

'You hooligan!' he cried, perceiving the visitor, 'you bandit, may the earth cast you forth! A fine trick you've thought up, killing live people.'

'Monsieur Tartakovsky,' Benya Krik replied quietly, 'it's forty-eight hours now that I've been weeping for the dear departed as for my own brother. But I know that you don't give a damn for my youthful tears. Shame, Monsieur Tartakovsky. In what sort of safe have you locked up your sense of shame? You had the gall to send the mother of our deceased Joseph a hundred paltry roubles. My brains shivered along with my hair when I heard this.'

Here Benya paused. He was wearing a chocolate jacket, cream pants, and raspberry boots.

'Ten thousand down,' he roared, 'ten thousand down and a pension till she dies, and may she live to a hundred and twenty. Otherwise we will depart from this residence, Monsieur Tartakovsky, and we will sit in my limousine.'

Then they used bad language at one another hammer and tongs, Jew-and-a-Half and Benya. I wasn't present at this quarrel, but those who were remember it. They compromised on five thousand in cash and fifty roubles a month.

'Aunt Pesya,' Benya said to the dishevelled old woman who was rolling on the floor, 'if you need my life you may have it, but all make mistakes, God included. A terrible mistake has been made, Aunt Pesya. But wasn't it a mistake on the part of God to settle Jews in Russia, for them to be tormented worse than in Hell? How would it hurt if the Jews lived in Switzerland, where they would be surrounded by first-class lakes, mountain air, and nothing but Frenchies? All make mistakes, God not excepted. Listen to me with all your ears, Aunt Pesya. You'll have five thousand down and fifty roubles a month till you croak. Live to a hundred and twenty if you like. Joseph shall have a Number One funeral: six horses like six lions, two carriages with flowers, the choir from the Brody Synagogue. Minkovsky in person shall sing at your deceased son's funeral.'

And the funeral was performed next morning. Ask the cemetery beggars about that funeral. Ask the shamessim from the synagogue of the dealers in kosher poultry about it, or the old women from the Second Almshouse. Odessa had never before seen such a funeral; the world will never see such a funeral. On that day the cops wore cotton gloves. In the synagogue, decked with greenstuff and wide open, the electric lights were burning. Black plumes swayed on the white horses harnessed to the hearse. A choir of sixty headed the cortège: a choir of boys, but they sang with the voice of women. The Elders of the synagogue of the dealers in kosher poultry helped Aunt Pesya along. Behind the elders walked members of the Association of Jewish Shop Assistants, and behind the Jewish Shop Assistants walked the lawyers, doctors of medicine, and certified midwives. On one side of Aunt Pesya were the women who trade in poultry on the Old Market, and on the other side, draped in orange shawls, were the honorary dairymaids from Bugayevka. They stamped their feet like gendarmes parading on a holiday. From their wide hips wafted the odours of the sea and of milk. And behind them all plodded Ruvim Tartakovsky's employees. There were a hundred of them, or two hundred, or two thousand. They wore black frock-coats with silk lapels and new shoes that squeaked like sacked sucking-pigs.

And now I will speak as the Lord God spoke on Mount Sinai from the Burning Bush. Put my words in your ears. All I saw, I saw with my own eyes, sitting here on the wall of the Second Cemetery next to Little Lisping Mose and Samson from the undertaker's. I, Arye-Leib, saw this – I, a proud Jew dwelling by the dead.

The hearse drove up to the cemetery synagogue. The coffin was placed on the steps. Aunt Pesya was trembling like a little bird. The cantor crawled out of the carriage and began the service. Sixty singers seconded him. And at this moment a red automobile flew around the turning. It played 'Laugh, clown' and drew up. People were as silent as the dead. Silent were the trees, the choir, the beggars. Four men climbed out of the red car and at a slow pace bore to the hearse a wreath of roses such as was never seen before. And when the service ended the four men inserted their steel shoulders beneath the coffin and with burning eyes and swelling breasts walked side by side with the members of the Association of Jewish Shop Assistants.

In front walked Benya Krik, whom no one as yet called the King. He was the first to approach the grave. He climbed the mound of earth and spread out his arms.

'What have you in mind, young man?' cried Kofman of the Burial Brotherhood, running over to him.

'I have it in mind to make a funeral oration,' replied Benya Krik.

And a funeral oration he made. All who wished listened to it. I listened to it; I, Arye-Leib, and Little Lisping Mose, who was sitting on the wall beside me.

'Ladies and gentlemen, and dames,' said Benya Krik. 'Ladies and gentlemen, and dames,' said he, and the sun rose above his head like an armed sentry. 'You have come to pay your last respects to a worthy labourer who perished for the sake of a copper penny. In my name, and in the name of all those not here present, I thank you. Ladies and gentlemen! What did your dear Joseph get out of life? Nothing worth mentioning. How did he spend his time? Counting other people's cash. What did he perish for? He perished for the whole of the working class. There are people already condemned to death, and there are people who have not yet begun to live. And lo and behold a bullet flying into a condemned breast pierces our Joseph, who in his whole life had seen nothing worth mentioning, and comes out on the other side. There are people who know how to drink vodka, and there are people who don't know how to drink vodka but drink it all the same. And the first lot, you see, get satisfaction from joy and from sorrow, and the second lot suffer for all those who drink vodka without knowing how to. And so, ladies and gentlemen, and dames, after we have said a prayer for our poor Joseph I will ask you to accompany to his last resting-place one unknown to you but already deceased, one Savely Butsis.'

And having finished his oration Benya Krik descended from the mound. No sound came from the people, the trees, or the cemetery beggars. Two gravediggers bore an unpainted coffin to the next grave. The cantor, stammering, finished his prayers. Benya threw in the first spadeful of soil and crossed over to Savka's grave. After him like sheep went all the lawyers, all the ladies with brooches. He made the cantor sing the full funeral service over Savka, and the sixty choirboys seconded the cantor. Savka had never dreamed of having such a funeral – take it from Arye-Leib, an old man who has seen many things.

They say that on that day Jew-and-a-Half decided to shut

up shop. I wasn't present. But that neither the cantor, nor the choir, nor the Funeral Brotherhood charged anything for the funeral, this I saw with the eyes of Arye-Leib. Arye-Leib, that's what they call me. And more than that I couldn't see, for the people, creeping quietly at first from Savka's grave, then started running as from a house on fire. They flew off in carriages, in carts and on foot. And only the four who had driven up in the red automobile also drove off in it. The musical-box played its march, the car shuddered and was gone.

'A King,' said Little Lisping Mose, looking after the car – Little Mose who does me out of the best seats on the wall.

Now you know all. You know who first uttered the word 'King'. It was Little Mose. You know why he didn't give that name to One-Eyed Rook, or to Crazy Nick. You know all. But what's the use, if you still have spectacles on your nose and autumn in your heart?

1923

The Father

EPHRAIM ROOK had once been married. That had been long ago: twenty years had passed since then. Ephraim's wife had born him a daughter and died in childbirth. Basya they called the girl. Her maternal grandmother lived in Tulchin. The old woman wasn't fond of her son-in-law, and used to say of him: 'Ephraim is a carter by trade, and he has black horses, but his soul is blacker still.'

The old woman didn't like her son-in-law, and took the newborn child to her own place. She lived twenty years with the girl, and then died. Whereupon little Basya returned to her father's. It all came about in this way:

Ephraim Rook spent Wednesday the fifth carting wheat

from the warehouses of Dreyfus and Co. to the S.S. *Caledonia* down in the harbour. Toward evening he finished his work and drove home. Rounding the corner from Prokhorovskaya Street he encountered Ivan Pyatirubel the blacksmith.

'My respects, Rook,' said Ivan Pyatirubel. 'A woman of sorts is banging on the door of your place.'

Rook drove on, and saw in his courtyard a woman of gigantic height. She had enormous hips, and cheeks of a brick-red hue.

'Dad,' said the woman in a deafening bass, 'I'm so bored all the devils in Hell are nipping me. I've been waiting for you the whole day. Grandma, you see, has died in Tulchin.'

Rook stood there on his cart goggling at his daughter.

'Don't wriggle about in front of the 'osses,' he cried in despair. 'Take a-hold of the wheeler by the bridle; you want to ruin my 'osses?'

Rook stood on his cart and waved his whip. Little Basya took the wheeler by the bridle and led the horses off to the stable. She unharnessed them, and then went off to fuss in the kitchen. The girl hung her dad's foot-wrappings on a line, scoured the sooty teapot with sand, and started warming hash in a cast-iron pot.

'Your dirt is simply unbearable, dad,' she said, and tossed through the window the sweat-soaked sheepskins that lay about on the floor. 'But I'll get rid of all this filth,' cried little Basya, and served her dad his supper.

The old man drank some vodka from an enamelled teapot and ate the hash, fragrant as a carefree childhood. Then he took his whip and went out at the gate. After him went little Basya. She had put on men's boots and an orange frock, and she wore a hat bedizened with dead birds. She settled down on the bench outside the gate. Evening sauntered past the bench, the gleaming eye of the sunset was falling into the sea beyond Peresyp, and the sky was red like a red-letter day. All the shops of Dalnitskaya had now shut, and the gangsters were driving past to Glukhaya Street, where Jo Samuelson kept his whorehouse. In lacquered carriages they drove, dressed up like birds of paradise, their jackets all colours of the rainbow. Their eyes were agoggle, each had a leg jutting out on the footboard, and each held in an outstretched arm of steel a bouquet wrapped in tissue-paper. Their lacquered jaunting cars moved at a walking-pace. In each carriage sat one gangster with a bouquet, and the drivers, protuberant on their high seats, were decked with bows like best men at weddings. Old Jewish women in bonnets lazily watched the accustomed procession flow past. They were indifferent to everything, those old Jewish women, and only the sons of the shopkeepers and shipwrights envied the kings of the Moldavanka.

Little Solomon Capon the grocer's son and Monya Gunner son of the smuggler were among those who tried to turn their eyes from the blaze of an alien glory. They both walked past Basya, swaying their hips like girls who have learned of love. They whispered together and then started moving their arms to show how they would embrace little Basya if she felt that way inclined. And blow me if little Basya didn't forthwith feel that way inclined, for she was just a simple maid from Tulchin, from that wretched little self-centred and purblind town. She weighed five poods and a few pounds over. All her life she had spent hitherto with the spiteful spawn of Podolian middlemen, itinerant book-sellers, and timber-contractors, and she had never seen people like little Sol Capon. This is why when she cast her gaze upon him she started shuffling on the ground her fat feet shod in men's boots, and said to her father:

'Dad,' she said in her voice of thunder, 'look at that little gentleman. He has tootsies just like a doll. I could strangle with kisses little tootsies like that.'

'Aha, Pan Rook,' then whispered an old Jew sitting next

to them, an old Jew called Golubchik, 'I see your child's tugging at the leash.'

'More trouble for poor me!' replied Ephraim Rook. He played with his whip awhile, went off to bed, and fell calmly asleep, for he hadn't believed what the old man said. He didn't believe the old man, and he couldn't have been wronger. Golubchik was right. Golubchik made an odd coin matchmaking on our street, nights he said prayers over wealthy stiffs, and he knew about life everything it was possible to know. Ephraim Rook was wrong; Golubchik was the one who was right.

And the fact of the matter is that from that day onward Little Basya spent all her evenings outside the gate. She would sit on the bench and sew away at her trousseau. Pregnant women would sit next to her. Mounds of linen would glide across her great straddled knees. The pregnant women, nibbling at this and that, would fill up with juice as a cow's udder fills on the pastures with the pink milk of spring, and just about this time their husbands would come home from work one after the other. The husbands of shrewish wives would squeeze out their matted beards under the tap, and then make way for humpbacked crones. The old crones would lave fat infants in troughs, slap their grandchildren on their shining buttocks, and wrap them up in worn-out skirts. And so Little Basya from Tulchin absorbed the life of our deep-bosomed mother the Moldavanka, a life crammed full of sucking infants, rags drying in the wind, and nuptial nights marked by suburban chic and soldierly indefatigability. The girl felt she wanted the same sort of life, but now she learned that the daughter of one-eyed Rook could count on no worthy mate. Then she stopped calling her father 'dad'.

'You redheaded robber,' she would call after him of an evening, 'come and gobble your supper, you redheaded robber.'

And this went on till such time as Little Basya had sewed

herself six nightgowns and six pairs of drawers with lace trimmings. Having finished the lace trimmings she started crying, her voice reedy and quite unlike her normal bawl, and said through her tears to the inflexible Rook:

'Every girl,' she said, 'every girl has her interest in life, and I alone live like a night-watchman guarding someone else's warehouse. Either do something with me or I'll make an end of myself.'

Rook heard his daughter to the end. Next day he put on a sailcloth cloak and went to visit Capon the grocer on Import Square.

Above Capon's shop gleamed a golden sign. His was the first shop on Import Square. There was a smell in it of the seven seas and of wonderful lives we know nothing of. A lad was sprinkling the cool depths of the shop with a watering-can and singing a song such as only grown-ups should sing. Little Sol, the shopkeeper's son, stood behind the counter where were displayed olives that had come from Greece, olive oil from Marseille, coffee in beans, Malaga from Lisbon, 'Philippe and Canot' brand sardines, and Cayenne pepper. Capon Senior sat in his waistcoat basking in the sun in a little glass annexe. He was eating a watermelon, a red melon with black seeds, seeds that went sideways like the sly eyes of Chinese women. Capon's belly lay on the table beneath the sun, and the sun could do nothing with it. But then the grocer saw Rook in his sailcloth cloak, and blenched.

'Good day, m'sieu Rook,' he said, and pushed back; 'Golubchik warned me that you would be looking in, and I have ready for you a pound of simply superlative tea.'

And he started chattering about a new kind of tea brought to Odessa on the Dutch steamers. Rook at first listened patiently, but then interrupted, for he was a simple man and he shunned subterfuges.

'I am a simple man and I shun subterfuges,' said Ephraim. 'I stick to my 'osses and carry on with my business. With

Little Basya I will give new underlinen and a couple of coins, and behind her I stand in person, and for who that ain't enough, let him frizzle on a slow fire.'

'Why should we frizzle?' asked Capon, the syllables galloping, and he stroked the carter's arm. 'Such words are superfluous, m'sieu Rook. After all, it is well known that in you we have a man who is capable of giving another man a helping hand, and besides that you can offend a man. And if you are not a Cracow Rabbi, well, neither did I stand beneath the wedding-crown with the niece of Moses Montefiore. But . . . but what about Madam Capon? Don't forget Madam Capon, that grandiose dame, of who God Himself doesn't know what she wants.'

'But *I* know,' Rook interrupted the shopkeeper, '*I* know that Little Sol wants Little Basya, but that Madam Capon don't want *me*.'

'That I don't,' then cried Madam Capon, who had been eavesdropping at the door, and she entered the glass annexe all ablaze and her breast heaving. 'I don't want you, Rook, any more than a man wants death. I don't want you any more than a bride wants pimples on her nose. Don't forget that our deceased grandfather was a grocer, that poor dead dad was a grocer, and that it is up to us to maintain our position.'

'You know what you can do with your position,' Rook replied to the blazing Madam Capon, and took himself home.

There Little Basya decked in her orange frock awaited him, but the old man, avoiding her gaze, spread his fur coat beneath the carts, lay down to sleep, and slept till Little Basya's powerful hand yanked him from beneath the wagons.

'You redheaded robber,' said the girl in a whisper unlike her usual whisper, 'why have I to endure your carter ways, and why are you as dumb as a tree-stump, you redheaded robber?'

'Basya,' then said Rook, 'Little Sol wants you, but Madam

Capon don't want *me*. They want someone in the grocery line.'

And straightening his fur coat the old man once more crept beneath the wagons, while Basya vanished from the yard.

All this happened of a Sabbath, a day no work is done. The purple eye of the sunset, groping over the earth, that evening lit on Rook as he snored beneath his cart. The impetuous ray fastened with flaming reproach on the sleeper and led him out to Dalnitskaya Street, dusty and gleaming like young rye in the breeze. Tartars were walking up along Dalnitskaya, Tartars and Turks with their mullahs. They were returning home from pilgrimage to Mecca, home to the Orenburg steppes and to Transcaucasia. A steamer had brought them to Odessa, and they were walking from the harbour to the inn of Mrs Lyubka Shneiveis, nicknamed Lyubka the Cossack. Inflexible striped robes stood stiffly on the Tartars, flooding the pavement with the bronze sweat of the desert. White towels were wound around their fezzes, and these distinguished such as had bowed to the dust of the prophet. Reaching the corner, the pilgrims tried to turn in at Lyubka's courtyard, but were unable to pass through because a crowd had gathered at the gate. Lyubka Shneiveis, her bag at her side, was beating a drunken peasant and pushing him out into the street. She beat his face like a tambourine with her clenched fist, and with her other hand she held the peasant so that he shouldn't slither down. Little trickles of blood crawled between the peasant's teeth and by his ear. He was pensive, and looked at Lyubka as at a stranger; then he fell on the cobbles and slumbered. Lyubka gave him a kick and returned to her shop. Her watchman Yevzel shut the gates after her and waved his hand to Ephraim Rook, who was passing.

'My respects, Rook,' he said. 'If you wish to see something of life, turn into our courtyard. There's something to laugh at.'

And the watchman led Rook to the wall where the pilgrims who had arrived the evening before were sitting. An old Turk in a green turban, an old Turk green and light as a leaf, lay on the grass. He was covered with pearly sweat, breathing with difficulty and rolling his eyes.

'Just look at that,' said Yevzel, and straightened the medal on his worn jacket. 'There's a real-life drama from the opera *The Turkish Sickness*. He's dying, the old fellow, but a doctor can't be fetched because anyone who dies on the way home from the god Mahommed is among them reckoned first in happiness and wealth. Halvash,' cried Yevzel to the dying man, and burst out laughing, 'here's a doctor come to have a look at you.'

The Turk looked at the watchman with childish fear and hatred, and turned his head away. Then Yevzel, pleased with himself, led Rook across the yard to the wine-cellar. In the cellar lamps were already burning and the orchestra was playing. Old Jews with ponderous beards were performing Jewish and Rumanian airs. Mendel Krik sat at one of the tables drinking wine from a green tumbler and relating how he had been crippled by his own sons – the elder Benya and the younger Lyovka. He yelled his tale in a hoarse and terrible voice, exhibiting his ground-down teeth and getting people to feel the wounds on his belly. Volhynian saddiks with porcelain faces stood behind his chair, listening benumbed to Mendel Krik's bragging. They were amazed at all they heard, and Rook despised them for it.

'The old braggart,' he muttered, and ordered wine.

Then Ephraim summoned the landlady, Lyubka the Cossack. She stood by the door using bad language and drinking vodka.

'Say what you've got to say,' she cried to Ephraim, and squinted in her fury.

'Madam Lyubka,' began Ephraim, seating her at his side, 'you are a wise woman, and I have come to you as my own momma. All my hope is in you, Madam Lyubka – first in God, and then in you.'

'Spit it out,' cried Lyubka. She dashed right across the cellar and then rushed back to her place.

And Rook spat it out:

'In the colonies,' he said, 'the Germans have a rich harvest of wheat, while in Constantinople groceries are dirt cheap. A pood of olives you can buy in Constantinople for three roubles, and here they are sold at thirty copecks a pound. It's a good life for grocers, Madam Lyubka. Grocers walk about with fat paunches, and if a person approached them with a delicate touch a person might be fortunate. But I work all on my own, the late Lyova Bullock is no longer with us, there's nowhere I can turn for help, and so I'm all by myself, like God in His Heaven.'

'Benya Krik,' then said Lyubka. 'You tried him on Tartakovsky. In what way does Benya Krik not meet your measure?'

'Benya Krik!' repeated the flabbergasted Rook. 'He's a bachelor, ain't he now?'

'A bachelor,' said Lyubka. 'Splice him with Basya, give him some dough, make something of him.'

'Benya Krik,' repeated the old man like an echo, a far-off echo. 'I hadn't thought of *him*.'

He stood up, muttering and stuttering. Lyubka rushed on ahead and Ephraim plodded along behind. They went out into the yard and climbed to the first floor. There, on the first floor, lived the girls that Lyubka kept for callers.

'Our bridegroom's taking a tumble with Kate,' said Lyubka to Rook. 'Wait for me in the corridor.' And she went into the end room, where Benya Krik was in bed with the girl named Kate.

'That's enough slobbering,' the landlady said to the young man. 'First you must get fixed up with a steady job, and then you can do your slobbering. Ephraim Rook is looking for you. He's after a fellow to work for him, and can't find one.'

And she told him all she knew about Little Basya and the affairs of the one-eyed Rook.

'I'll think it over,' Benya replied, covering Kate's bare legs with the sheet. 'I'll think it over. The old man can wait.'

'Wait for him,' Lyubka said to Ephraim, who had remained in the corridor. 'Wait for him; he's thinking it over.'

The landlady gave Ephraim a chair, and he plunged into measureless expectancy. He waited patiently, like a peasant in a government office. Beyond the wall Kate moaned, beyond the wall Kate choked with laughter. The old man snoozed for two hours at her locked door, two hours and maybe more. Evening had long since turned to night, the sky had grown black, and its milky ways were filled with gold, glitter, and coolness. Lyubka's wine-cellar was closed now, drunkards lay strewn about the yard like pieces of broken-down furniture, and the old mullah in the green turban died toward midnight. Then music came from the sea: French horns and trumpets from the English ships. Music came from the sea and then fell silent, but Kate, the whole-hogging Kate, was still heating up for Benya Krik her many-coloured, Russian, and rubicund paradise. She moaned beyond the wall and shouted with laughter. Old Ephraim sat motionless at her door; he waited till one in the morning, and then knocked.

'Man,' he said, 'are you making a joke of me?'

Then Benya at long last opened the door of Kate's room.

'M'sieu Rook,' he said, embarrassed, radiant, and covering himself with a sheet, 'when we are young we look on women as wares, but all they are is straw that burns away at nothing at all.'

And having dressed he straightened out Kate's bed, beat up her pillows, and went out into the street with the old man. As they strolled they came to the Russian cemetery, and there by the cemetery was a meeting of the minds of Benya Krik and one-eyed Rook the superannuated gangster. They agreed that Little Basya should bring her husband a dowry of three thousand roubles, two full-blooded horses, and a pearl neck-lace. They also agreed that Capon would have to pay two thousand roubles to Benya, Basya's betrothed. He was guilty of family pride, was Capon of Import Square. He had grown rich on Constantinople olives, he had shown no mercy for Basya's first love, and for this reason Benya Krik resolved to make it his business to collect from him two thousand roubles.

'I'll make it my business, pop,' he said to his future father-in-law. 'With God's help we will show all grocers where they get off.'

This was said at dawn, when the night had already passed. And here begins another story, the story of the fall of the House of Capon, the tale of its slow ruination, of arson, and of shots fired in the night. And all this – the fate of the over-weening Capon and the fate of the virginal Basya – was settled on that night when her father and her abruptly be-trothed strolled past the Russian cemetery. Lads were then dragging lasses behind the fences, and kisses re-echoed above the tombstones.

1924

Lyubka the Cossack

IN the Moldavanka district, on the corner of Dalnitskaya and Balkovskaya, there stands the house of Lyubka Shneiveis. In her house there is a wine-cellar, an inn, an oat-shop, and a dovecot for a hundred pairs of Kryukov and Nikolayev pigeons. These establishments, together with Section No. 46 of the Odessa quarries, belong to Lyubka Shneiveis, known as Lyubka the Cossack, and only the dovecot is the property of her watchman Yevzel, a retired soldier with a medal. On Sundays Yevzel makes his way to the bird-market and sells pigeons to government officials from the town and urchins from the neighbourhood. Apart from the watchman there also dwell in Lyubka's yard one Pesya-Mindl, cook and procuress, and Tsudechkis the manager, a little Jew resembling with his puny build and wretched little beard our Moldavanka Rabbi Ben-Zkharya. I know a lot of stories about Tsudechkis. The first of them is the story of how he got the job of manager at the inn of Lyubka, nicknamed the Cossack.

Some ten years ago Tsudechkis negotiated the sale to a landowner of a threshing-machine worked by a horse that walked round and round, and that evening he took the land-owner to Lyubka's to wet the deal. His client wore long dangling moustaches and went about in patent-leather shoes. Pesya-Mindl dished him up gefüllte fish for his supper, and later on a very good-looking young woman named Anastasia. The landowner spent the night at the inn, and next morning Yevzel the watchman roused Tsudechkis, who had curled up in a ball on the threshold of Lyubka's room.

'Look now,' said Yevzel, 'you were bragging yesterday evening how the landowner had bought a threshing-machine through your good offices, so note the fact that after he had spent the night here he skipped at dawn like the last of so-and-sos. Now stump up two roubles for a dish of delicatessen and four roubles more for the other dish. You're a smart one, for sure!'

But Tsudechkis refused to fork out, so Yevzel pushed him into Lyubka's room and turned the key.

'See now,' said the watchman, 'you will stay right here, and later Lyubka will come home from the quarry, and then, with God's help, she'll knock the living daylight out of you. Amen.'

'You galley-slave,' Tsudechkis retorted to the old soldier, and started looking around the scene of his incarceration.

'You don't know a thing, you galley-slave, except about pigeons. But I still believe in God, Who will lead me out from here as He has led all Jews out – first from Egypt, and then from the wilderness.'

There was a lot more the little broker wanted to say to Yevzel, but the old soldier pocketed the key and went off clumping his boots. Then Tsudechkis continued his inspection and saw sitting by the window Pesya-Mindl, the procuress, who was reading a book called *Miracles and the Heart of Baal-Shem*. She was conning the gilt-edged Hasidic book and rocking a wooden cradle with her foot. In the cradle lay Lyubka's son, Little Dave, squalling.

'I see there's a fine state of affairs on this Sakhalin Island,' said Tsudechkis to Pesya-Mindl. 'Here's a child lying and yelling its little guts out enough to make you weep, and you, you great fat thing, sit like a boulder in a forest and can't ease him with the breast.'

'*You* ease him with the breast,' retorted Pesya-Mindl, not raising her eyes from the book, 'provided he'll take it from you, you old twister – the breast, I mean. For see, he's a big boy now, as big as a Rooski-boy, and all he wants is his momma's milk, and his momma is careering around her old quarries, drinking tea with Jews at the Bear tavern, buying smuggled goods at the harbour, and thinking as much about her son as about last year's snow.'

'Yes,' the little broker then said to himself, 'you're in the hands of Pharoah, my old Tsudechkis.' And he went over to the eastern wall, mumbled the whole of the morning prayer with appendices, and then took the weeping child in his arms. Little Dave looked at him in amazement and waggled his little raspberry legs bathed in infant sweat, and the old man started walking about the room and, swaying like a saddik at prayer, singing a song that went on and on.

'Ah-ah-ah,' he sang, 'other little boys shall have pinches, but our little Dave shall have cakes, so that by day and by night he'll go straight off to sleep when he wakes. Ah-ah-ah, other little boys shall have punches . . .'

Tsudechkis showed Lyubka's little son a tiny fist covered with grey hairs, and went on repeating the business about pinches and punches till such time as the child fell asleep and the sun had reached the zenith in the gleaming sky. It climbed to the middle of the sky and hung there quivering like a fly overcome by the heat. Wild peasants from Nerubaysk and Tatarka who had put up at Lyubka's inn crawled under their wagons and there fell into a wild and loud-echoing slumber. A drunken apprentice staggered to the gate and, casting his plane one way and his saw the other, collapsed on the ground, collapsed and started snoring in a world filled with golden flies and the blue lightning-flashes of July. Not far from him wrinkled German colonists who had brought Lyubka wine from the Bessarabian border had settled down in the shade. They lit their pipes, and the smoke-rings from their bent stems began to grope their way through the silvery bristles on elderly and unshaven cheeks. The sun lolled from the sky like the pink tongue of a thirsty dog, a gigantic sea rolled its surf upon far-away Peresyp, and the masts of distant vessels swayed on the emerald waters of Odessa Bay. Day sat in a gaily-painted coracle, day sailed on toward evening. It was only between four and five that Lyubka returned from town. She rode up on a little roan nag with a large belly and an overgrown mane. A lad with fat legs and wearing a print shirt opened the gate to her, Yevzel took her horse's bridle, and then Tsudechkis cried to Lyubka from his prison:

'My respects to you, Madam Shneiveis, and a very good day. Now you've ridden off for three years on business and left me at the mercy of a famished babe in arms.'

'Whisht, you scarecrow,' Lyubka replied to the old man, and climbed down from the saddle. 'Who's that opening his big mouth in my window?'

'It is Tsudechkis, the smart old man,' the old soldier with

the medal informed his mistress, and he started telling her the whole business of the landowner. But he didn't reach the end of his tale, for the broker, interrupting him, started squealing with all his might:

'What imperence!' he wailed, and hurled his skullcap on the floor. 'What imperence, throwing somebody else's child into one's arms and gallivanting off for three years. Come on, give him the tit.'

'I'll give *you* something you don't expect, you man of business,' muttered Lyubka, sailing up the stairs. She entered the bedroom and pulled her breast from her dusty blouse.

The child strained toward her, bit at her monstrous nipple, but achieved no milk. A vein swelled on the mother's forehead, and Tsudechkis said to her, shaking his skullcap:

'You want to grab everything for yourself, you greedy Lyubka. You drag the whole world to yourself, as children drag the tablecloth with all its crumbs. You want the first wheat and the first grapes, you want to bake white loaves where the sun is hottest, but your little child, a child like a little star, has to mope milkless.'

'How can you expect milk,' cried the woman, squeezing her breast, 'how can you expect milk when the *Plutarch* put in this day and I've covered fifteen versts in the broiling heat? And you, you old Jew, instead of your song and dance, would do better to fork out the six roubles.'

But again Tsudechkis refused to pay up. He loosened his sleeve, bared his arm, and shoved his thin and grimy elbow into Lyubka's mouth.

'Choke, you jailbird,' he said, and spat in the corner.

Lyubka held the alien elbow in her mouth for a while and then took it out again. She locked the door behind her and went into the yard. There awaited her Mr Trottyburn, a man like a pillar of russet meat. Mr Trottyburn was Chief Engineer on the *Plutarch*. He had brought two sailors with him to Lyubka's. One of the sailors was an Englishman, the

other a Malay, and the three of them dragged into the yard
a heavy box of contraband from Port Said. They dropped it
on the ground, and out of the box tumbled cigars mixed up
in Japanese silk. A crowd of peasant women flocked around
the box, and two visiting gypsies, swaying, jangling their
bangles, started to sidle near.

'Be off, you starvelings,' Lyubka cried at them, and led
the sailors to the shade beneath the acacia. There they sat
down at table. Yevzel served them vodka, and Mr Trottyburn
spread out his wares. Out of his bale he took cigars and fine
silks, cocaine and files, unbonded tobacco from the State of
Virginia, and dark wine from the Island of Chios. Each ware
had its own price, each figure they drank down with Bessarabian wine that smelt of sun and bugs. Dusk scuttled across
the yard, dusk flowed like an evening wave on a wide river,
and the drunken Malay, full of wonder, touched Lyubka's
breast with his finger. Touched it with one finger, then with
all his fingers in turn.

His tender yellow eyes hung suspended above the table
like paper lamps in a Chinese alley. He started singing a
scarcely audible song, and fell to the ground when Lyubka
pushed him with her fist.

'There's a cultured fellow for you,' Lyubka said to Mr
Trottyburn. 'He'll cause my last drop of milk to dry up, that
Malay will, and there's that Jew has already chewed me up
along of my milk.'

And she pointed to Tsudechkis, who was standing in the
window washing his socks. The little lamp smoked in the
room behind him, and he poked his head out of the window,
sensing that he was being talked about, and shouted despairingly.

'Save me, folks!' he cried, and waved his arms.

'Whisht, you scarecrow!' shouted Lyubka, roaring with
laughter. 'Put one of them socks in it!'

She threw a stone at the old man, and missed. Then the

woman grasped an empty wine-bottle. But Mr Trottyburn, the Chief Engineer, took the bottle from her, aimed carefully, and sent it flying through the open window.

'Miss Lyubka,' said the Chief Engineer, standing up and gathering his drunken legs together, 'many worthy folk come to me for goods, that they do, Miss Lyubka, but I don't let anyone have them, neither Mr Kuninzon, nor Mr Bat, nor Mr Kupchik, nor nobody except you, because a talk with you is a nice way to pass the time of day.'

And having established himself on legs that had threatened to play him false, he took his men by the shoulders, one an Englishman and the other a Malay, and went dancing with them across a yard that had now grown chilly. Men from the *Plutarch*, they danced in a profoundly thoughtful silence. An orange star that had slid to the very brim of the horizon gazed wide-eyed at them. Then they pocketed their money, linked arms, and went out into the street, swaying as a gimbal-lamp sways in a ship. From the street they could see the sea, the black waters of Odessa Bay, toy flags on submerged masts and penetrating lights lit in spacious wombs. Lyubka saw her dancing guests to the crossing; then, alone in the empty street, she laughed at her thoughts and returned home. The sleepy lad in the print shirt locked the gate behind her. Yevzel handed his mistress the day's takings, and she made her way up to bed. There Pesya-Mindl, the procuress, was already snoozing, and Tsudechkis was rocking the oak cradle with his bare toes.

'How you have tortured me, you unconscionable Lyubka,' said he, and took the child from its cradle. 'Now you learn from me, you odious mother . . .'

He placed a fine-toothed comb against Lyubka's breast and laid the child by her in the bed. The child struggled toward its mother, pricked itself on the comb, and started to cry. Then the old man pushed a nursing bottle at him, but Little Dave spurned the bottle.

'What magic are you working on me, you old rascal?' mumbled Lyubka as she fell asleep.

'Be silent, you odious mother!' cried Tsudechkis. 'Be silent and learn, devil take you!'

The child again pricked itself on the comb; then took the bottle with fumbling hands and started to suck.

'There you are,' said Tsudechkis, and laughed. 'I've weaned your child for you. Learn from me, devil take you!'

Little Dave lay in the cradle, sucking the bottle and blowing blissful bubbles. Lyubka woke up, opened her eyes, and closed them again. She had seen her son, and the moon breaking in at her window, a moon that skipped through black clouds like a stray calf.

'Very well,' Lyubka said, 'open the door for Tsudechkis, Pesya-Mindl, and let him look in tomorrow for a pound of American tobacco.'

And next day Tsudechkis looked in for his pound of unbonded tobacco from the State of Virginia. He received it, and a quarter-pound of tea into the bargain. And a week later, when I called on Yevzel to purchase some pigeons, I saw the new manager in Lyubka's yard. He was tiny, like our Rabbi Ben-Zkharya. The new manager was Tsudechkis. He stayed in the job some fifteen years, and during this time I heard many a tale about him. And if I am able I will tell them all one after the other, for they are very entertaining tales.

1924

STORIES

The Sin of Jesus

ARINA was a servant at the hotel. She lived next to the main staircase, while Seryoga, the janitor's helper, lived over the back stairs. Between them there was shame. On Palm Sunday Arina gave Seryoga a present – twins. Water flows, stars shine, a man lusts, and soon Arina was big again, her sixth month was rolling by – they're slippery, a woman's months. And now Seryoga must go into the army. There's a mess for you!

So Arina goes and says: 'No sense, Seryoga. There's no sense in my waiting for you. For four years we'll be parted, and in four years, whichever way you look at it, I'll be sure to bring two or three more into this world. It's like walking around with your skirt turned up, working at the hotel. Whoever stops here, he's your master, let him be a Jew, let him be anybody at all. By the time you come home, my insides will be no good any more. I'll be a used-up woman, no match for you.'

'That's so,' Seryoga nodded.

'There's many that want me. Trofimych the contractor – but he's no gentleman. And Isai Abramych, the warden of Nikolo-Svyatsky Church, a feeble old man, but anyway I'm sick to the stomach of your murderous strength. I tell you this now, and I say it like I would at confession, I've got the wind plain knocked out of me. I'll spill my load in three months, then I'll take the baby to the orphanage and marry the old man.'

When Seryoga heard this, he took off his belt and beat her like a hero, right on the belly.

'Look out there,' Arina says to him, 'go soft on the belly. It's your stuffing, no one else's.'

There was no end to the beating, no end to the man's tears and the woman's blood, but that is neither here nor there.

Then the woman came to Jesus Christ.

'So on and so forth,' she says, 'Lord Jesus, I am the woman from the Hotel Madrid and Louvre, the one on Tverskaya Street. Working at the hotel, it's just like going around with your skirt up. Just let a man stop there, and he's your lord and master, let him be a Jew, let him be anyone at all. There is another slave of yours walking the earth, the janitor's helper, Seryoga. Last year on Palm Sunday I bore him twins.'

And so she described it all to the Lord.

'And what if Seryoga were not to go into the army after all?' the Saviour suggested.

'Try and get away with it – not with the policeman around. He'll drag him off as sure as daylight.'

'Oh yes, the policeman,' the Lord bowed His head, 'I never thought of him. Then perhaps you ought to live in purity for a while?'

'For four years?' the woman cried. 'To hear you talk, all people should deny their animal nature. That's just your old ways all over again. And where will the increase come from? No, you'd better give me some sensible advice.'

The Lord's cheeks turned scarlet, the woman's words had touched a tender spot. But He said nothing. You cannot kiss your own ear – even God knows that.

'I'll tell you what, God's servant, glorious sinner, maiden Arina,' the Lord proclaimed in all His glory, 'I have a little angel here in heaven, hanging around uselessly. His name is Alfred. Lately he's got out of hand altogether, keeps crying and nagging all the time: "What have you done to me, Lord? Why do you turn me into an angel in my twentieth year, and me a hale young fellow?" So I'll give you Alfred the angel as a husband for four years. He'll be your prayer, he'll be your protection, and he'll be your solace. And as for offspring, you've nothing to worry about – you can't bear a duckling from him, let alone a baby, for there's a lot of fun in him, but no seriousness.'

'That's just what I need,' the maid Arina wept gratefully. 'Their seriousness takes me to the doorstep of the grave three times every two years.'

'You'll have a sweet respite, God's child Arina. May your prayer be light as a song. Amen.'

And so it was decided. Alfred was brought in – a frail young fellow, delicate, two wings fluttering behind his pale-blue shoulders, rippling with rosy light like two doves playing in heaven. Arina threw her hefty arms about him, weeping out of tenderness, out of her woman's soft heart.

'Alfred, my soul, my consolation, my bridegroom . . .'

In parting, the Lord gave her strict instructions to take off the angel's wings every night before he went to bed. His wings were attached to hinges, like a door, and every night she was to take them off and wrap them in a clean sheet, because they were brittle, his wings, and could snap as he tossed in bed – for what were they made of but the sighs of babes, no more than that.

For the last time the Lord blessed the union, while the choir of bishops, called in for the occasion, rendered thunderous praises. No food was served, not a crumb – that wasn't the style in heaven – and then Arina and Alfred, their arms about each other, ran down a silken ladder, straight back to earth. They came to Petrovka, the street where nothing but the best is sold. The woman would do right by her Alfred, for he, if one might say so, not only lacked socks but was altogether as natural as when his mother bore him. And she bought him patent-leather half-boots, checked jersey trousers, a fine hunting jacket, and an electric-blue waistcoat.

'The rest,' she says, 'we'll find at home.'

That day Arina begged off from work. Seryoga came and raised a fuss, but she did not even come out to him, only said from behind her locked door:

'Sergey Nifantyich, I am at present a-washing my feet and beg you to retire without further noise.'

He went away without a word – the angel's power was already beginning to manifest itself!

In the evening Arina set out a supper fit for a merchant – the woman had devilish vanity! A half-pint of vodka, wine on the side, a Danube herring with potatoes, a samovar of tea. When Alfred had partaken of all these earthly blessings, he keeled over in a dead sleep. Quick as a wink, Arina lifted off his wings from the hinges, packed them away, and carried him to bed in her arms.

There it lies, the snowy wonder on the eiderdown pillows of her tattered, sinful bed, sending forth a heavenly radiance: moon-silver shafts of light pass and repass, alternate with red ones, float across the floor, sway over his shining feet. Arina weeps and rejoices, sings and prays. Arina, thou hast been granted a happiness unheard of on this battered earth. Blessed art thou among women!

They had drunk the vodka to the last drop, and now it took effect. As soon as they fell asleep, she went and rolled over on top of Alfred with her hot, six-months-big belly. Not enough for her to sleep with an angel, not enough that nobody beside her spat at the wall, snored and snorted – that wasn't enough for the clumsy, ravening slut. No, she had to warm her belly too, her burning belly big with Seryoga's lust. And so she smothered him in her fuddled sleep, smothered him like a week-old babe in the midst of her rejoicing, crushed him under her bloated weight, and he gave up the ghost, and his wings, wrapped in her sheet, wept pale tears.

Dawn came – and all the trees bowed low to the ground. In distant northern forests each fir-tree turned into a priest, each fir-tree bent its knees in silent worship.

Once more the woman stands before the Lord's throne. She is broad in the shoulders, mighty, the young corpse drooping in her huge red arms.

'Behold, Lord . . .'

But here the gentle heart of Jesus could endure no more, and He cursed the woman in His anger:

'As it is on earth, so shall it be with you, Arina, from this day on.'

'How is it then, Lord?' the woman replied in a scarcely audible voice. 'Was it I who made my body heavy, was it I that brewed vodka on earth, was it I that created a woman's soul, stupid and lonely?'

'I don't wish to be bothered with you,' exclaimed the Lord Jesus. 'You've smothered my angel, you filthy scum.'

And Arina was thrown back to earth on a putrid wind, straight down to Tverskaya Street, to the Hotel Madrid and Louvre, where she was doomed to spend her days. And once there, the sky was the limit. Seryoga was carousing, drinking away his last days, seeing as he was a recruit. The contractor Trofimych, just come from Kolomna, took one look at Arina, hefty and red-cheeked: 'Oh, you cute little belly,' he said, and so on and so forth.

Isai Abramych, the old codger, heard about this cute little belly, and he was right there too, wheezing toothlessly:

'I cannot wed you lawfully,' he said, 'after all that happened. However, I can lie with you the same as anyone.'

The old man ought to have been lying in cold mother earth instead of thinking of such things; but no, he too must take his turn at spitting into her soul. It was as though they had all slipped the chain – kitchen-boys, merchants, foreigners. A fellow in trade – he likes to have his fun.

And that is the end of my tale.

Before she was laid up, for three months had rolled by in the meantime, Arina went out into the back-yard, behind the janitor's rooms, raised her monstrous belly to the silken sky, and said stupidly:

'See, Lord, what a belly! They hammer at it like peas falling in a colander. And what sense there's in it I just can't see. But I've had enough.'

With His tears Jesus laved Arina when He heard these words. The Saviour fell on His knees before her.

'Forgive me, little Arina. Forgive your sinful God for all He has done to you . . .'

But Arina shook her head and would not listen.

'There's no forgiveness for you, Jesus Christ,' she said. 'No forgiveness, and never will be.'

1922

The Story of My Dovecot

To M. GORKY

WHEN I was a kid I longed for a dovecot. Never in all my life have I wanted a thing more. But not till I was nine did father promise the wherewithal to buy the wood to make one and three pairs of pigeons to stock it with. It was then 1904, and I was studying for the entrance exam to the preparatory class of the secondary school at Nikolayev in the Province of Kherson, where my people were at that time living. This province of course no longer exists, and our town has been incorporated in the Odessa Region.

I was only nine, and I was scared stiff of the exams. In both subjects, Russian language and arithmetic, I couldn't afford to get less than top marks. At our secondary school the *numerus clausus* was stiff: a mere five per cent. So that out of forty boys only two that were Jews could get into the preparatory class. The teachers used to put cunning questions to Jewish boys; no one else was asked such devilish questions. So when father promised to buy the pigeons he demanded top marks with distinction in both subjects. He absolutely tortured me to death. I fell into a state of permanent daydream, into an endless, despairing, childish reverie. I went to the exam deep in this dream, and nevertheless did better than everybody else.

I had a knack for book-learning. Even though they asked cunning questions, the teachers could not rob me of my intelligence and my avid memory. I was good at learning, and got top marks in both subjects. But then everything went wrong. Khariton Efrussi, the corn-dealer who exported wheat to Marseille, slipped someone a 500-rouble bribe. My mark was changed from A to A minus, and Efrussi Junior went to the secondary school instead of me. Father took it very badly. From the time I was six he had been cramming me with every scrap of learning he could, and that A minus drove him to despair. He wanted to beat Efrussi up, or at least bribe two longshoremen to beat Efrussi up, but mother talked him out of the idea, and I started studying for the second exam the following year, the one for the lowest class. Behind my back my people got the teacher to take me in one year through the preparatory and first-year course simultaneously, and conscious of the family's despair I got three whole books by heart. These were Smirnovsky's *Russian Grammar*, Yevtushevsky's *Problems*, and Putsykovich's *Manual of Early Russian History*. Children no longer cram from these books, but I learned them by heart line upon line, and the following year in the Russian exam Karavayev gave me an unrivalled A plus.

This Karavayev was a red-faced, irritable fellow, a graduate of Moscow University. He was hardly more than thirty. Crimson glowed in his manly cheeks as it does in the cheeks of peasant children. A wart sat perched on one cheek, and from it there sprouted a tuft of ash-coloured cat's whiskers. At the exam, besides Karavayev, there was the Assistant Curator Pyatnitsky, who was reckoned a big noise in the school and throughout the province. When the Assistant Curator asked me about Peter the Great, a feeling of complete oblivion came over me, an awareness that the end was near:

an abyss seemed to yawn before me, an arid abyss lined with exultation and despair.

About Peter the Great I knew things by heart from Putsy-kovich's book and Pushkin's verses. Sobbing, I recited these verses, while the faces before me suddenly turned upside down, were shuffled as a pack of cards is shuffled. This card-shuffling went on, and meanwhile, shivering, jerking my back straight, galloping headlong, I was shouting Pushkin's stanzas at the top of my voice. On and on I yelled them, and no one broke into my crazy mouthings. Through a crimson blind-ness, through the sense of absolute freedom that had filled me, I was aware of nothing but Pyatnitsky's old face with its silver-touched beard bent toward me. He didn't interrupt me, and merely said to Karavayev, who was rejoicing for my sake and Pushkin's:

'What a people,' the old man whispered, 'those little Jews of yours! There's a devil in them!'

And when at last I could shout no more, he said:

'Very well, run along, my little friend.'

I went out from the classroom into the corridor, and there, leaning against a wall that needed a coat of whitewash, I began to awake from my trance. About me Russian boys were playing, the school bell hung not far away above the stairs, the caretaker was snoozing on a chair with a broken seat. I looked at the caretaker, and gradually woke up. Boys were creeping toward me from all sides. They wanted to give me a jab, or perhaps just have a game, but Pyatnitsky suddenly loomed up in the corridor. As he passed me he halted for a moment, the frock-coat flowing down his back in a slow heavy wave. I discerned embarrassment in that large, fleshy, upper-class back, and got closer to the old man.

'Children,' he said to the boys, 'don't touch this lad.' And he laid a fat hand tenderly on my shoulder.

'My little friend,' he went on, turning me toward him, 'tell your father that you are admitted to the first class.'

On his chest a great star flashed, and decorations jingled in his lapel. His great black uniformed body started to move away on its stiff legs. Hemmed in by the shadowy walls, moving between them as a barge moves through a deep canal, it disappeared in the doorway of the headmaster's study. The little servingman took in a tray of tea, clinking solemnly, and I ran home to the shop.

In the shop a peasant customer, tortured by doubt, sat scratching himself. When he saw me my father stopped trying to help the peasant make up his mind, and without a moment's hesitation believed everything I had to say. Calling to the assistant to start shutting up shop, he dashed out into Cathedral Street to buy me a school cap with a badge on it. My poor mother had her work cut out getting me away from the crazy fellow. She was pale at that moment; she was experiencing destiny. She kept smoothing me, and pushing me away as though she hated me. She said there was always a notice in the paper about those who had been admitted to the school, and that God would punish us, and that folk would laugh at us if we bought a school cap too soon. My mother was pale; she was experiencing destiny through my eyes. She looked at me with bitter compassion as one might look at a little cripple boy, because she alone knew what a family ours was for misfortunes.

All the men in our family were trusting by nature, and quick to ill-considered actions. We were unlucky in everything we undertook. My grandfather had been a rabbi somewhere in the Belaya Tserkov region. He had been thrown out for blasphemy, and for another forty years he lived noisily and sparsely, teaching foreign languages. In his eightieth year he started going off his head. My Uncle Leo, my father's brother, had studied at the Talmudic Academy in Volozhin. In 1892 he ran away to avoid doing military service, eloping with the daughter of someone serving in the commissariat in the Kiev military district. Uncle Leo took this woman to

California, to Los Angeles, and there he abandoned her, and died in a house of ill-fame among Negroes and Malays. After his death the American police sent us a heritage from Los Angeles, a large trunk bound with brown iron hoops. In this trunk there were dumbbells, locks of women's hair, uncle's talith, horsewhips with gilt handles, scented tea in boxes trimmed with imitation pearls. Of all the family there remained only crazy Uncle Simon-Wolf, who lived in Odessa, my father, and I. But my father had faith in people, and he used to put them off with the transports of first love. People could not forgive him for this, and used to play him false. So my father believed that his life was guided by an evil fate, an inexplicable being that pursued him, a being in every respect unlike him. And so I alone of all our family was left to my mother. Like all Jews I was short, weakly, and had headaches from studying. My mother saw all this. She had never been dazzled by her husband's pauper pride, by his incomprehensible belief that our family would one day be richer and more powerful than all others on earth. She desired no success for us, was scared of buying a school jacket too soon, and all she would consent to was that I should have my photo taken.

On 20 September 1905 a list of those admitted to the first class was hung up at the school. In the list my name figured too. All our kith and kin kept going to look at this paper, and even Shoyl, my grand-uncle, went along. I loved that boastful old man, for he sold fish at the market. His fat hands were moist, covered with fish-scales, and smelt of worlds chill and beautiful. Shoyl also differed from ordinary folk in the lying stories he used to tell about the Polish Rising of 1861. Years ago Shoyl had been a tavern-keeper at Skvira. He had seen Nicholas I's soldiers shooting Count Godlevski and other Polish insurgents. But perhaps he hadn't. *Now* I know that Shoyl was just an old ignoramus and a simple-minded liar, but his cock-and-bull stories I have never forgotten: they were good stories. Well now, even silly old Shoyl went along to the school to read the list with my name on it, and that evening he danced and pranced at our pauper ball.

My father got up the ball to celebrate my success, and asked all his pals – grain-dealers, real-estate brokers, and the travelling salesmen who sold agricultural machinery in our parts. These salesmen would sell a machine to anyone. Peasants and land-owners went in fear of them: you couldn't break loose without buying something or other. Of all Jews, salesmen are the widest-awake and the jolliest. At our party they sang Hasidic songs consisting of three words only but which took an awful long time to sing, songs performed with endless comical intonations. The beauty of these intonations may only be recognized by those who have had the good fortune to spend Passover with the Hasidim or who have visited their noisy Volhynian synagogues. Besides the salesmen, old Lieberman, who had taught me the Torah and ancient Hebrew honoured us with his presence. In our circle he was known as Monsieur Lieberman. He drank more Bessarabian wine than he should have. The ends of the traditional silk tassels poked out from beneath his waistcoat, and in ancient Hebrew he proposed my health. In this toast the old man congratulated my parents and said that I had vanquished all my foes in single combat: I had vanquished the Russian boys with their fat cheeks, and I had vanquished the sons of our own vulgar parvenus. So too in ancient times David King of Judah had overcome Goliath, and just as I had triumphed over Goliath, so too would our people by the strength of their intellect conquer the foes who had encircled us and were thirsting for our blood. Monsieur Lieberman started to weep as he said this, drank more wine as he wept, and shouted '*Vivat!*' The guests formed a circle and danced an old-fashioned quadrille with him in the middle, just as at a wedding in a little Jewish town. Everyone was happy at our ball. Even mother took a sip of vodka, though she neither liked the stuff nor understood how anyone else could – because of this she considered all Russians cracked, and just couldn't imagine how women managed with Russian husbands.

But our happy days came later. For mother they came when of a morning, before I set off for school, she would start making me sandwiches; when we went shopping to buy my school things – pencil-box, money-box, satchel, new books in cardboard bindings, and exercise-books in shiny covers. No one in the world has a keener feeling for new things than children have. Children shudder at the smell of newness as a dog does when it scents a hare, experiencing the madness which later, when we grow up, is called inspiration. And mother acquired this pure and childish sense of the ownership of new things. It took us a whole month to get used to the pencil-box, to the morning twilight as I drank my tea on the corner of the large, brightly-lit table and packed my books in my satchel. It took us a month to grow accustomed to our happiness, and it was only after the first half-term that I remembered about the pigeons.

I had everything ready for them: one rouble fifty and a dovecot made from a box by Grandfather Shoyl as we called him. The dovecot was painted brown. It had nests for twelve pairs of pigeons, carved strips on the roof, and a special grating that I had devised to facilitate the capture of strange birds. All was in readiness. On Sunday, October 20, I set out for the bird market, but unexpected obstacles arose in my path.

The events I am relating, that is to say my admission to the first class at the secondary school, occurred in the autumn of 1905. The Emperor Nicholas was then bestowing a constitution on the Russian people. Orators in shabby overcoats were clambering on to tall kerbstones and haranguing the people. At night shots had been heard in the streets, and so mother didn't want me to go to the bird market. From early morning on October 20 the boys next door were flying a kite right by the police station, and our water-carrier, abandoning all his buckets, was walking about the streets with a red face and brilliantined hair. Then we saw baker Kalistov's sons drag a leather vaulting-horse out into the street and start doing gym in the middle of the roadway. No one tried to stop them: Semernikov the policeman even kept inciting them to jump higher. Semernikov was girt with a silk belt his wife had made him, and his boots had been polished that day as they had never been polished before. Out of his customary uniform, the policeman frightened my mother more than anything else. Because of him she didn't want me to go out, but I sneaked out by the back way and ran to the bird market, which in our town was behind the station.

At the bird market Ivan Nikodimych, the pigeon-fancier, sat in his customary place. Apart from pigeons, he had rabbits for sale too, and a peacock. The peacock, spreading its tail, sat on a perch moving a passionless head from side to side. To its paw was tied a twisted cord, and the other end of the cord was caught beneath one leg of Ivan Nikodimych's wicker-chair. The moment I got there I bought from the old man a pair of cherry-coloured pigeons with luscious tousled tails, and a pair of crowned pigeons, and put them away in a bag on my chest under my shirt. After these purchases I had only forty copecks left, and for this price the old man was not prepared to let me have a male and female pigeon of the Kryukov breed. What I liked about Kryukov pigeons was their short, knobbly, good-natured beaks. Forty copecks was the proper price, but the fancier insisted on haggling, averting from me a yellow face scorched by the unsociable passions of bird-snarers. At the end of our bargaining, seeing that there were no other customers, Ivan Nikodimych beckoned me closer. All went as I wished, and all went badly.

Toward twelve o'clock, or perhaps a bit later, a man in felt boots passed across the square. He was stepping lightly on swollen feet, and in his worn-out face lively eyes glittered.

'Ivan Nikodimych,' he said as he walked past the bird-fancier, 'pack up your gear. In town the Jerusalem aristocrats are being granted a constitution. On Fish Street Grandfather Babel has been constitutioned to death.'

He said this and walked lightly on between the cages like a barefoot ploughman walking along the edge of a field.

'They shouldn't,' murmured Ivan Nikodimych in his wake. 'They shouldn't!' he cried more sternly. He started collecting his rabbits and his peacock, and shoved the Kryukov pigeons at me for forty copecks. I hid them in my bosom and watched the people running away from the bird market. The peacock on Ivan Nikodimych's shoulder was last of all to depart. It sat there like the sun in a raw autumnal sky; it sat as July sits on a pink riverbank, a white-hot July in the long cool grass. No one was left in the market, and not far off shots were rattling. Then I ran to the station, cut across a square that had gone topsy-turvy, and flew down an empty lane of trampled yellow earth. At the end of the lane, in a little wheeled arm-chair, sat the legless Makarenko, who rode about town in his wheel-chair selling cigarettes from a tray. The boys in our street used to buy smokes from him, children loved him, I dashed toward him down the lane.

'Makarenko,' I gasped, panting from my run, and I stroked the legless one's shoulder, 'have you seen Shoyl?'

The cripple did not reply. A light seemed to be shining through his coarse face built up of red fat, clenched fists, chunks of iron. He was fidgeting on his chair in his excitement, while his wife Kate, presenting a wadded behind, was sorting out some things scattered on the ground.

'How far have you counted?' asked the legless man, and moved his whole bulk away from the woman, as though aware in advance that her answer would be unbearable.

'Fourteen pairs of leggings,' said Kate, still bending over, 'six undersheets. Now I'm a-counting the bonnets.'

'Bonnets!' cried Makarenko, with a choking sound like

a sob; 'it's clear, Catherine, that God has picked on me, that I must answer for all. People are carting off whole rolls of cloth, people have everything they should, and we're stuck with bonnets.'

And indeed a woman with a beautiful burning face ran past us down the lane. She was clutching an armful of fezzes in one arm and a piece of cloth in the other, and in a voice of joyful despair she was yelling for her children, who had strayed. A silk dress and a blue blouse fluttered after her as she flew, and she paid no attention to Makarenko, who was rolling his chair in pursuit of her. The legless man couldn't catch up. His wheels clattered as he turned the handles for all he was worth.

'Little lady,' he cried in a deafening voice, 'where did you get that striped stuff?'

But the woman with the fluttering dress was gone. Round the corner to meet her leaped a rickety cart in which a peasant lad stood upright.

'Where've they all run to?' asked the lad, raising a red rein above the nags jerking in their collars.

'Everybody's on Cathedral Street,' said Makarenko pleadingly, 'everybody's there, sonny. Anything you happen to pick up, bring it along to me. I'll give you a good price.'

The lad bent down over the front of the cart and whipped up his piebald nags. Tossing their filthy croups like calves, the horses shot off at a gallop. The yellow lane was once more yellow and empty. Then the legless man turned his quenched eyes upon me.

'God's picked on me, I reckon,' he said lifelessly; 'I'm a son of man, I reckon.'

And he stretched a hand spotted with leprosy toward me.

'What's that you've got in your sack?' he demanded, and took the bag that had been warming my heart.

With his fat hand the cripple fumbled among the tumbler pigeons and dragged to light a cherry-coloured she-bird. Jerking back its feet, the bird lay still on his palm.

'Pigeons,' said Makarenko, and squeaking his wheels he rode right up to me. 'Damned pigeons,' he repeated, and struck me on the cheek.

He dealt me a flying blow with the hand that was clutching the bird. Kate's wadded back seemed to turn upside down, and I fell to the ground in my new overcoat.

'Their spawn must be wiped out,' said Kate, straightening up over the bonnets. 'I can't a-bear their spawn, nor their stinking menfolk.'

She said more things about our spawn, but I heard nothing of it. I lay on the ground, and the guts of the crushed bird trickled down from my temple. They flowed down my cheek, winding this way and that, splashing, blinding me. The tender pigeon-guts slid down over my forehead, and I closed my solitary unstopped-up eye so as not to see the world that spread out before me. This world was tiny, and it was awful. A stone lay just before my eyes, a little stone so chipped as to resemble the face of an old woman with a large jaw. A piece of string lay not far away, and a bunch of feathers that still breathed. My world was tiny, and it was awful. I closed my eyes so as not to see it, and pressed myself tight into the ground that lay beneath me in soothing dumbness. This trampled earth in no way resembled real life, waiting for exams in real life. Somewhere far away Woe rode across it on a great steed, but the noise of the hoofbeats grew weaker and died away, and silence, the bitter silence that sometimes overwhelms children in their sorrow, suddenly deleted the boundary between my body and the earth that was moving nowhither. The earth smelled of raw depths, of the tomb, of flowers. I smelled its smell and started crying, unafraid. I was walking along an unknown street set on either side with white boxes, walking in a get-up of bloodstained feathers, alone between the pavements swept clean as on Sunday, weeping bitterly, fully and happily as I never wept again in all my life. Wires that had grown white hummed above my head, a watchdog trotted on in front, in the lane on one side a young peasant in a waistcoat was smashing a window-frame in the house of Khariton Efrussi. He was smashing it with a wooden mallet, striking out with his whole body. Sighing, he smiled all around with the amiable grin of drunkenness, sweat, and spiritual power. The whole street was filled with a splitting, a snapping, the song of flying wood. The peasant's whole existence consisted in bending over, sweating, shouting queer words in some unknown, non-Russian language. He shouted the words and sang, shot out his blue eyes; till in the street there appeared a procession bearing the Cross and moving from the Municipal Building. Old men bore aloft the portrait of the neatly-combed Tsar, banners with grave-yard saints swayed above their heads, inflamed old women flew on in front. Seeing the procession, the peasant pressed his mallet to his chest and dashed off in pursuit of the banners, while I, waiting till the tail-end of the procession had passed, made my furtive way home. The house was empty. Its white doors were open, the grass by the dovecot had been trampled down. Only Kuzma was still in the yard. Kuzma the yardman was sitting in the shed laying out the dead Shoyl.

'The wind bears you about like an evil wood-chip,' said the old man when he saw me. 'You've been away ages. And now look what they've done to granddad.'

Kuzma wheezed, turned away from me, and started pulling a fish out of a rent in grandfather's trousers. Two pike perch had been stuck into grandfather: one into the rent in his trousers, the other into his mouth. And while grandfather was dead, one of the fish was still alive, and struggling.

'They've done grandfather in, but nobody else,' said Kuzma, tossing the fish to the cat. 'He cursed them all good and proper, a wonderful damning and blasting it was. You might fetch a couple of pennies to put on his eyes.'

But then, at ten years of age, I didn't know what need the dead had of pennies.

'Kuzma,' I whispered, 'save us.'

And I went over to the yardman, hugged his crooked old back with its one shoulder higher than the other, and over this back I saw grandfather. Shoyl lay in the sawdust, his chest squashed in, his beard twisted upwards, battered shoes on his bare feet. His feet, thrown wide apart, were dirty, lilac-coloured, dead. Kuzma was fussing over him. He tied the dead man's jaws and kept glancing over the body to see what else he could do. He fussed as though over a newly-purchased garment, and only cooled down when he had given the dead man's beard a good combing.

'He cursed the lot of 'em right and left,' he said, smiling, and cast a loving look over the corpse. 'If Tartars had crossed his path he'd have sent them packing, but Russians came, and their women with them, Rooski women. Russians just can't bring themselves to forgive, I know what Rooskis are.'

The yardman spread some more sawdust beneath the body, threw off his carpenter's apron, and took me by the hand.

'Let's go to father,' he mumbled, squeezing my hand tighter and tighter. 'Your father has been searching for you since morning, sure as fate you was dead.'

And so with Kuzma I went to the house of the tax-inspector, where my parents, escaping the pogrom, had sought refuge.

1925

First Love

WHEN I was ten years old I fell in love with a woman called Galina. Her surname was Rubtsov. Her husband, an officer, went off to the Russo-Japanese War and returned in October, 1905. He brought a great many trunks back with him. These trunks, which weighed nearly half a ton, contained Chinese souvenirs such as screens and costly weapons. Kuzma the yardman used to tell us that Rubtsov had bought all these things with money he had embezzled while serving in the engineer corps of the Manchurian Army. Other people said so too. The Rubtsovs were happy, so it was hard for people not to gossip about them. Their house adjoined our place, and their glass veranda jutted out over our premises, but father didn't make a fuss about it. The elder Rubtsov, who was a tax-inspector, had a reputation in our town for being a fair-minded man: he was friendly with Jews. When the officer, the old man's son, returned from the war, we could see how well he and his wife got on together.

Galina would hold her husband's hand all day long. She stared at him incessantly; she had not seen him for a year and a half. But her gaze frightened me, and I would turn away and shiver, glimpsing that obscure and shameful side of human existence. I longed to fall into a strange sleep, to forget about this life that surpassed all my fancies. Galina would glide through the rooms with her braid hanging down her back, wearing elegant red shoes and a Chinese robe. Under the lace of her deep-cut slip one could see the swelling of her white breasts squeezed downward, and the depression between them. On her robe were embroidered pink silk dragons, birds, trees with hollows in their trunks.

The whole day long she sauntered about with a meaningless smile on her moist lips, brushing against the trunks that had not yet been unpacked and the ladders for doing physical exercises strewn about the floor. Galina would bruise herself, pull her robe above her knee, and say to her husband: 'Kiss baby better.' The officer would bend his long legs in their narrow dragoon's trousers, in their smooth, taut leather boots with spurs, and crawling across the littered floor on his knees, smile and kiss the bruised flesh, just where a little bulge rose above the garter.

I saw those kisses from my window, and they caused me

agony. Unbounded fantasies tormented me – but what's the use of talking about it? The love and the jealousy of a ten-year-old boy are in every way the same as the love and jealousy of a grown-up. I stopped going near the window and avoided Galina for two weeks, and then an event brought us together.

It was the pogrom against the Jews that broke out in 1905 in Nikolayev and other towns where Jews were permitted to live. A mob of hired murderers plundered my father's shop and killed Grandfather Shoyl. All this happened when I was out. That sad morning I had bought some pigeons from Ivan Nikodimych the fancier. For five of my ten years I had dreamed with my whole soul about pigeons. But when I finally bought them, Makarenko the cripple smashed them against my temples. Then Kuzma found me and took me to the Rubtsovs'. On their gate a cross had been chalked. Nobody molested them, and they hid my parents in their house. Kuzma led me to the glass veranda. My mother and Galina were there in the green rotunda.

'Now we must wash,' Galina said. 'We must wash, my little rabbi. Our face is covered with feathers, and the feathers are bloody.'

She put her arms around me and led me along a hallway full of pungent odours. My head leaned against her hip, her hip that moved and breathed. We went into the kitchen, and Galina put my head under the tap. A goose was frying on the tiled stove, glowing pots and pans hung on the wall, and next to them, in the cook's corner, was Tsar Nicholas decorated with paper flowers. Galina washed off the last smear of pigeon sticking to my cheek. 'You'll look like a bridegroom now, my sweet boy,' she said, kissing my mouth with her full lips and turning away.

'Your dad has troubles, you see,' she suddenly whispered. 'He roams the streets all day long with nothing to do. Fetch your dad home.'

I saw through the window the empty street under the vast sky, and my redheaded father walking along in the roadway. He walked bareheaded, his soft red hair fluttering, his paper dickey askew and fastened to the wrong button. Vlasov, a drunken workman dressed in a soldier's wadded rags, was stubbornly pursuing him.

'Babel,' Vlasov was saying in a hoarse, emotional voice, 'we don't need freedom so that the Jews can corner all the business. Shine a light in the working-man's life, for his toil, for his great burdens. That's what you should do, my friend. D'you hear?'

The workman was begging my father for something, grabbing at his arm. Flashes of pure drunken inspiration and a gloomy sleepiness appeared in his face interchangeably. 'We should live like the Molokan Sect,' he mumbled, swaying on his weak legs. 'We should live like the Molokans, but without that old God of the Old Believers. Only Jews get anything from him, nobody else.'

Vlasov yelled in wild desperation against the God of the Old Believers who took pity only on the Jews. Vlasov wailed, stumbled, and tried to catch up with his Unknown God, but at that moment a Cossack patrol rode by, barring his way. An officer with stripes on his trousers and a parade belt of silver rode in front of the patrol, a tall peaked cap set stiffly on his head. The officer rode slowly, not looking right or left. He rode as though through a mountain pass, where one can only look ahead.

'Captain,' my father mumbled when the Cossacks came abreast of him; 'captain,' my father said, grasping his head in his hands and kneeling in the mud.

'Do what I can,' the officer answered, still looking straight ahead, and raising his hand in its lemon-coloured chamois glove to the peak of his cap.

Right in front of them, at the corner of Fish Street, the mob was looting and smashing up our shop, throwing out into the street boxes filled with nails, machines, and my new photo in school uniform.

'Look,' my father said, still on his knees, 'they are destroying everything dear to me. Captain, why is it?'

The officer murmured something, and again put the lemon glove to his cap. He touched the reins, but his horse did not move. My father crawled in front of the horse on his knees, rubbing up against its short, kindly, tousled legs.

'At your service,' the officer said, tugged at the reins, and rode off, the Cossacks following. They sat passionless on their high saddles, riding through their imaginary mountain pass and disappearing into Cathedral Street.

Galina again gently pushed me to the window.

'Fetch father home,' she said. 'He hasn't had anything to eat since morning.'

I leaned out of the window.

My father turned when he heard my voice.

'My little son,' he stuttered with immeasurable tenderness.

He and I went on to the Rubtsovs' veranda where my mother was lying in the green rotunda. Near her couch dumbbells and gymnastic apparatus were scattered.

'That cursed money,' my mother cried at us. 'You gave up everything for it. Human life, the children, our wretched little bit of happiness. Cursed money!' she cried out in a hoarse voice quite unlike her real voice. She jerked on the couch and fell silent.

And then in the stillness my hiccups were heard. I was standing by the wall with my cap pulled down over my forehead, and I couldn't stop hiccuping.

'You shouldn't do that, my sweet boy,' Galina said with her disdainful smile, flipping me with her stiff robe. She went to the window in her red shoes and began to hang Chinese curtains on the weird cornice. Her bare arms were drowned in silk, and her braid was alive, swinging down over her hip. Enchanted, I stared at her.

I was a bookish boy, and I looked at her as at a distant scene glaringly limelighted. Then I imagined that I was Miron, son of the coalman who had his shop on our corner. I imagined myself to be a member of the Jewish Defence Corps. Like Miron, I am wearing torn shoes tied together with string, and on my shoulder a useless rifle hangs by a green cord. I am kneeling by a wooden fence shooting at the murderers. Behind the fence an empty lot stretches, heaps of dusty coal lie there. The antiquated rifle shoots badly. The murderers have beards and white teeth, they approach stealthily. I have a proud feeling of imminent death, and in the skies, in the world's blueness, I see Galina. I see a loophole cut in the wall of a gigantic house built of myriads of bricks. This purple house weighs heavily on the valley where the grey earth is loosely stamped. In the highest loophole stands Galina. From the loophole, out of reach, she smiles mockingly. Her husband, the officer, half-dressed, stands behind her kissing her neck.

Trying to halt my hiccups, I imagined all this so that I might love Galina with a bitterer, warmer, more hopeless love, or perhaps because for a ten-year-old boy the measure of sorrow was too great. O foolish fancies that helped me forget the death of the pigeons, and Shoyl's death!

Maybe I would have forgotten those murderers if Kuzma had not come to the veranda with Aba, the repulsive Jew.

It was dusk when they came. On the veranda a poor bent lamp was burning. Its flame blinked, flickering companion of unhappiness.

'I put the shroud on Grandfather,' Kuzma said as he entered. 'He's a treat to look at now, lying there. And I've brought the sexton along. Let him gab a bit over the dead.'

Kuzma pointed to Aba the shammes.

'Let him whine awhile,' the yardman said amiably. 'If the sexton gets his belly filled, he'll pester God all night long.'

Kuzma was standing on the threshold, his friendly broken

nose twisted in all directions, and he wanted to tell us with as much feeling as he could how he had bound the dead man's chin. But my father interrupted old Kuzma.

'Please, Reb Aba,' my father said, 'pray for the deceased. I will pay you.'

'But I'm scared you won't pay,' answered Aba in his tedious voice, and he placed his bearded, squeamish face on the tablecloth. 'I'm afraid you'll take my rouble and go off with it to the Argentine, to Buenos Aires. You'll start a wholesale business with my rouble . . . a wholesale business,' said Aba, champing his disdainful lips and dragging the newspaper across the table to him. In the paper a story was printed about the Tsar's manifesto of October 17, about the proclamation of freedom.

'Citizens of free Russia,' Aba read syllable by syllable, chewing a mouthful of his beard, 'citizens of free Russia, greetings on this blessed Sunday . . .'

The old shammes held the swaying paper sideways. He read drowsily in his singsong voice, strangely accentuating the unfamiliar Russian words. Aba's accent resembled the confused mumblings of a Negro who has just come to a Russian port from his native land. It made even my mother laugh.

'I am committing a sin,' she exclaimed, leaning forward from her rotunda. 'I am laughing, Aba. You'd better tell me how you're getting on, you and your family.'

'Ask me something else,' growled Aba, not easing the grip of his teeth on his beard, and he went on reading the paper.

'Ask him something else,' said my father, echoing Aba's words, and he stepped to the centre of the room. His eyes, smiling at us through his tears, suddenly turned in their sockets and focused on a point we could not see.

'*Oy*, Shoyl,' my father said in a level, lying voice that was on the verge of bursting, '*oy*, Shoyl, you dear man . . .'

We saw that he would be shouting any moment, but mother forestalled us.

'Manus,' she cried, her hair dishevelled in an instant; and she started tearing at her husband's breast. 'See how sick our boy is! Can't you hear how he's hiccuping? Why can't you, Manus?'

My father stopped.

'Rachel,' he said timidly, 'I can't tell you how sad I am for Shoyl.'

He went to the kitchen and came back with a glass of water.

'Drink, little play-actor,' said Aba, coming over to me. 'Drink the water. It will help you as a censer helps a dead man.'

He was right: the water did not help me. My hiccups increased. A howl escaped from my breast. A swelling, pleasant to touch, rose on my throat. It breathed, expanded, spread on my throat and bulged over my collar. Inside the swelling bubbled my torn and gasping breath, bubbling like water on the boil. And when toward night I was no longer the lop-eared lad I had been all my life, but a writhing mass, my mother covered herself with a shawl and, grown taller and shapelier, approached the paralysed Galina.

'Dear Galina,' said my mother in a strong, ringing voice, 'how we are disturbing you and your whole family! I am so ashamed, dear Galina.'

Her cheeks burning, mother pushed Galina toward the door. Then she hurried back to me and stuffed my mouth with her shawl to muffle my groans.

'Try to stand it,' she whispered. 'Try to stand it for mother's sake.'

But even had it been possible to stand I should not have tried to do so, for I no longer felt any shame.

So began my illness. I was then ten years old. Next morning they took me to the doctor's. The pogrom continued, but we were not interfered with. The doctor, a fat man, diagnosed nervous trouble.

He told us to go to Odessa as soon as possible to consult

experts, and to wait there for the warm weather and the sea-bathing.

And so we did. A few days later I went with mother to Odessa, to Grandfather Leivi-Itzkhok's and Uncle Simon's. We went by the morning steamer, and already by noon the brown waters of the Bug had given place to the heavy green swell of the sea. Life at crazy Grandfather Leivi-Itzkhok's opened out before me, and I said good-bye for ever to Nikolayev, where ten years of my childhood had passed. And now, remembering those sorrowful years, I find in them the beginning of the ills that torment me, the cause of my early fading.

1925

The End of St Hypatius

YESTERDAY I was up at the monastery of St Hypatius, where Father Hilary, last of the resident monks, showed me over the home of the Romanov boyars.

Here in 1613 came the people of Moscow to beg Michael Fyodorovich Romanov to accept the throne of Muscovy.

I saw the trampled corner where the nun Martha, mother of the Tsar, used to say her prayers; her gloomy bedchamber and the lookout tower whence she watched the wolf-hunts in the forests of Kostroma.

Hilary and I passed over the little old snow-buried draw-bridges, scared away the crows that nested in the boyars' chamber, and came out to a church of indescribable beauty.

Crowned with a wreath of snow, painted with crimson and azure, it rose against the smoky northern sky like a peasant woman's many-coloured kerchief embroidered with Russian flowers.

The lines of its unpretentious cupolas were chaste, its little blue outbuildings were pot-bellied, and the patterned window-frames shone in the sun with a superflous brilliance.

In this deserted church I came on the iron gates presented by Ivan the Terrible, and walked around viewing the ancient icons, the whole of the crypt, the decay of a holiness that knew no mercy.

The Saints, naked demoniac peasants with rotted thighs, writhed on the dilapidated walls, and next to them was a painting of a Russian Mother-of-God: a thin peasant woman with knees ajar and dangling breasts that seemed like so many useless green arms.

The ancient icons wrapped my carefree heart in the chill of their deathly passions: I barely escaped them, those sepulchral saints.

Their god lay in the church, ossified, clean as a body already bathed at home but left without burial.

Alone, Father Hilary wandered among his corpses. He had a game left leg, was liable to fall into a doze, kept scratching his filthy beard, and soon bored me stiff.

Then I threw open the gates of Ivan the Terrible and ran beneath the black vaulting out on to the little square, and there the Volga flashed at me, ice-fettered.

The smoke of Kostroma rose, forcing its way through the snowdrifts. Peasants clad in a yellow halo of sharp frost were carting flour on sledges, and the cart-horses drove their iron hooves into the ice.

The russet cart-horses, draped with hoarfrost and steam, breathed noisily on the river. The pink lightning-flashes of the North flew about among the pines, and crowds, anonymous crowds, were crawling up the icy slopes.

An incendiary wind blew upon them from the Volga. A multitude of peasant women tumbled into snowdrifts, but still climbed higher and higher, advancing on the monastery with the shrill whistle of besieging columns.

Loud female laughter thundered above the hill, tea-urn

tubes and washtubs drove up the slope, the skates of urchins groaned on the bends.

Old old women were dragging a burden up the tall hill, the hill of Saint Hypatius. Infants slept in old women's toboggans, and white nanny-goats were led on leashes by old women.

'Devils,' I cried, viewing them, and retreated before the unheard-of incursion, 'I suppose you're here to see Martha the Nun, to beg for her son Michael as Tsar?'

'Devil take you!' a peasant woman answered me, and stepped forward from the ranks. 'Why do you trifle with us on the road? Would you have us bear you brats?'

And packing herself in her sled she drove it spanking on to the monastery courtyard, almost knocking the distraught Father Hilary off his pins. Into the cradle of the Tsars of Muscovy she drove her washtubs, her geese, her hornless phonograph. And having given her name as Savicheva, demanded that apartment No. 19 in the episcopal quarters should be assigned to her.

And to my amazement she was allotted this apartment, and after her all the rest were given quarters.

And it was now explained that the Union of Textile Workers had vacated, in a block that had burnt down, forty dwellings for workers of the Kostroma United Flax Manufactory, and that today they were moving into the monastery.

Father Hilary stood by the gate, counting all the nanny-goats and other immigrants. Then he invited me to tea, and silently placed on the table cups he had stolen in the courtyard when the gear of the Romanov boyars was being taken to the museum.

From these cups we drank tea till the sweat came, while the bare legs of peasant women tramped past me on the window-sills as they washed the panes in their new quarters.

Then as though at a word of command smoke billowed

from every stovepipe. A cock that hadn't been introduced flew up on to the tomb of Father Sionius the Abbot and there gave voice. Someone's accordion, having yearned its way through the preliminary twiddles, launched itself on a heart-melting melody, and an old crone we hadn't seen before and wearing a peasant overcoat poked her head into Father Hilary's cell and asked for the loan of a pinch of salt for the cabbage soup.

Evening had fallen when the overcoated crone looked in. Crimson clouds billowed above the Volga, the thermometer on the wall outside registered forty degrees of frost, gigantic bonfires flared up and died down on the river, and still a lad who refused to be beaten was stubbornly trying to clamber up the frozen ladder to the crossbar above the gate, clambering there in order to hang up a little lamp and a signboard on which were inscribed the multitudinous letters U.S.S.R. and R.S.F.S.R., with the emblem of the Textile Union, and the sickle and hammer, and a picture of a woman standing at a loom from which rays shot in all directions.

1925

With Old Man Makhno

THE previous night six Makhno boys had raped the servant-maid. Learning of this in the morning, I thought I would see how the woman looked after her sixfold ravishing. I found her in the kitchen, where bent over a tub she was washing clothes. She was a fat wench with blooming cheeks. Only unhurried existence on the fruitful Ukrainian soil can imbue a Jewess with such bovine juices, lend her face such a suety sheen. The girl's legs, fat, brick-red, swollen like globes, gave off a sickly-sweet smell like fresh-sliced meat. And it seemed to me that of yesterday's virginity there remained only the cheeks, more than usually inflamed, and the eyes, thrust downward.

Apart from the servant-maid, in the kitchen there also sat the urchin Kikin, runner for the Staff of Old Man Makhno. He had the reputation at H.Q. of being a simpleton, and he didn't think twice of walking on his hands at the most unsuitable moments. More than once I had found him at the looking-glass. Sticking out his leg in its torn trouser, he would be winking at himself, slapping himself on his bare boyish belly, singing battle songs, and cutting grimaces of triumph that made even him roar with laughter. The lad's imagination was unusually vivid. Today I once more found him busy at a special job of work; he was sticking strips of gilt paper on to a German helmet.

'How many did you take on yesterday, Rukhlya?' he asked as, screwing up his eyes, he surveyed his decorated helmet.

The girl said nothing.

'You took on six,' the boy went on, 'and there are women as can take on as many as twenty. Our lads kept going and going at one housewife in Krapivno till they themselves was all in. Still, I reckon she was a bit plumper than you.'

'Fetch some water,' said the girl.

Kikin brought a pail of water from the courtyard. Then, scuffling his bare feet, he went over to the glass, pulled the helmet with its golden trailers over his head, and attentively examined his reflection. The view in the glass absorbed him. Poking his fingers into his nostrils, the boy avidly watched how the shape of his nose changed under the pressure from inside.

'I'm quitting my job,' he remarked, turning to the Jewish girl. 'Mum's the word, Rukhlya. Stetsenko is taking me into his squadron. There at least you get equipment, a position you can be proud of. And I shall have real soldiers as comrades, a change from the crowd here. Yesterday, when they had grabbed you, and I was holding you by the head, I said to Matvey Vasilyich, "Look here, Matvey Vasilyich," I said, "now the fourth one is having a go, and all I do is hold on to the head. You've had two goes, Matvey Vasilyich, but as I'm only a lad and not in your unit everyone thinks he can put upon me." I dare say you yourself heard what he replied, Rukhlya: "You, young Kikin," he said, "aren't going to be put upon by anyone; just let all the orderlies have a go, and then it'll be your turn." So they did say I could have a go. It was when they was already dragging you into the wood, Matvey Vasilyich says to me, "Go on, Kikin, if you feel like it." – "No thanks, Matvey Vasilyich," I said, "not after Vasya's been, and regret it all my life."'

Kikin snorted angrily and was silent. He lay down on the floor and fixed his gaze on somewhere far away; bare-footed, lengthy, aggrieved, with his bare belly and the gleaming helmet set on his strawlike hair.

'People go around saying all sorts of fine things about the Makhno crowd, about what stout lads they are,' he said morosely; 'but knock around with them for a while and you'll soon find that each has a heart of stone.'

The Jewish girl raised her blood-suffused face from the tub, glanced at the boy, and went out of the kitchen with the awkward gait of a cavalryman when he puts his numbed legs on the ground after a long ride. Remaining alone, the boy cast a dispirited gaze around the kitchen, sighed, pressed his palms to the floor, threw his legs in the air and, his protruding heels rigid, started walking quickly about on his hands.

1923

You Were Too Trusting, Captain

THE S.S. *Halifax* had put in at the port of Odessa. It had come from London to load Russian wheat.

On the twenty-seventh of January, the day of Lenin's funeral, the coloured members of the crew – three Chinese, two Negroes, and one Malay – asked the captain to come on deck. In the town, orchestras were thundering and a blizzard was blowing.

'Captain O'Nearn,' said the Negroes, 'there's no loading to do today. Let us go ashore till evening.'

'Stay where ye are,' replied O'Nearn. 'There's a strong gale blowing and it's blowing stronger, the *Beaconsfield* is stuck in the ice by Sanzheyka, the barometer reading ought to be blue-pencilled. In such weather the crew's place is on board. Stay where you are.'

And having said this, Captain O'Nearn went along to see the second mate. He and the second mate cracked jokes together, smoked cigars, and kept pointing at the town, where in unrestrained grief the blizzard wept and brass bands wailed.

The two Negroes and the three Chinese slouched aimless about the deck. They blew on their numbed palms, stamped their rubber boots, and kept looking in at the half-open door of the captain's cabin. Thence out into the fifty m.p.h. gale flowed the velvet of divans that had been warmed up by brandy and fine tobacco-smoke.

'Bos'n!' cried O'Nearn, seeing the sailors. 'The deck is no ruddy seaside resort. Send those men packing to the hold.'

'Aye aye, sir,' replied the bos'n, a pillar of red flesh overgrown with red hair. 'Aye aye, sir.' And he took the dishevelled Malay by the scruff of his neck. He pushed him toward the seaward side of the ship and chucked him out on to the rope ladder. The Malay scrambled down and ran off across the ice. The three Chinese and the two Negroes fled after him.

'Have you sent the men packing to the hold?' asked the captain, sitting in the cabin warmed up with brandy and fine tobacco-smoke.

'That I have, sir,' replied the bos'n, that pillar of red flesh, and he stood by the bulwarks like a sentinel in a storm.

The wind was blowing from the sea – fifty miles per hour like fifty shells discharged by the frozen batteries of the sea. White snow raged above the icefloes. And across the petrified waves there sped frantically toward the shore, to where the boats moored, five hunched-up commas, five little coloured freaks with charred faces and billowing jackets. Scraping their hands, they scrambled ashore up the ice-covered piles, ran through the harbour and flew into the town that shuddered in the wind.

A detachment of stevedores with black banners was marching into the square, to the place where Lenin's statue was to be raised. The two Negroes and the Chinese took their stand beside the stevedores. Panting for breath, they shook hands with all sorts of people and rejoiced with the rejoicing of escaped convicts.

At that moment on the Red Square in Moscow Lenin's body was being lowered into the crypt. Down our way, in Odessa, hooters wailed, the blizzard blew, and the crowd marched along in mustered rows. And only on the S.S. *Halifax* the impenetrable bos'n stood by the bulwarks like a sentinel in a storm. Beneath his ambiguous protection Captain O'Nearn drank brandy in his smoke-filled cabin.

He relied on the bos'n, did Captain O'Nearn. Captain O'Nearn had been too trusting.

1924

Karl-Yankel

WHEN I was a kid Jonah Brutman had a blacksmith's shop at Peresyp. There gathered horse-dealers, draymen, butchers from the city slaughterhouses. The blacksmith's shop was near the Balta Station. If you chose it as an observation post you could easily intercept peasants carting oats and Bessarabian wine to the city. Jonah was an easily-scared little man, but he had a palate for wine. In him dwelt the soul of an Odessa Jew.

In my time he had three sons at home. The father reached up to their waists. It was on the beach at Peresyp that for the first time I pondered the potency of the powers that dwell secretly in Nature. Three well-fed bitterns with crimson shoulders and feet like spades, the sons used to carry their skinny little father down to the water just like an infant in arms. Yet he and none other begat them, no doubt about it. The blacksmith's wife went to the synagogue twice a week, on Friday evening and Saturday morning. The synagogue was of the Hasidic persuasion, and there at Passover they used to dance themselves silly, just like dervishes. Jonah's wife used to pay tribute to the emissaries sent out through the provinces of the South by the saddiks of Galicia. The blacksmith did not interfere in his wife's relations with God. After work he used to go off to a wine-cellar near the slaughterhouses and there, sucking in the cheap pink wine, he would listen meekly to what was being talked of – politics or fat-stock prices.

In strength and build the sons took after their mother. Two of them, when they grew up, went off and joined the partisans. The eldest was killed at Voznesensk. The second Brutman boy, Simon, went over to Primakov and joined the Red Cossacks. He was chosen commander of a Cossack regiment. From him and from a few other small-town lads grew that unexpected breed of Jews, the tough fighting-men, raiders, and partisans.

The third son inherited the blacksmith's calling. He is now working at the Gen plough-factory in the old town. He has never married or begotten anyone.

Simon's children moved about with his division. The old woman needed a grandson whom she might tell about Baal-Shem, and she expected a grandson from her youngest daughter Polina. Alone of all the family, the girl had taken after little old Jonah. She was easy to scare, short of sight, tender of skin, and she had lots of suitors. Polina chose Ovsey Belotserkovsky – we could never understand why. Even more amazing was the news that the young people were leading a very happy married life. A woman's household is her own affair; outsiders don't see how the pots get broken. In this case the breaker of pots was Ovsey Belotserkovsky. A year after the wedding he sued his mother-in-law, Brana Brutman. Taking advantage of Ovsey's absence on an official mission somewhere, and of the fact that Polina had gone to hospital with mastitis, the old woman kidnapped her newborn grandson, carried him off to the little foreskin-clipper Naftula Gerchik, and there, in the presence of ten ruins, ten ancient and poverty-stricken old men, assiduous attenders at the Hasidic synagogue, the ceremony of circumcision was performed upon the infant.

All this Ovsey Belotserkovsky learned when he got back. Ovsey had his name down for admission to the Party. He decided to have a word with Bychach, the secretary of the Party organization in the Imports and Exports Office.

'You have been morally defiled,' Bychach told him. 'You can't leave the matter as it is.'

The Odessa Prosecutor's Office determined to hold a public trial at the Petrovsky Factory. The little snipper Naftula

Gerchik and the sixty-two-year old Brana Brutman found themselves in the dock.

In Odessa Naftula was just as much a part of the town as the Duc de Richelieu's statue. Often he would pass our windows on Dalnitskaya carrying the worn and greasy midwife's bag in which he kept his simple appliances. Now he would pull from it a little knife, now a bottle of vodka and a piece of gingerbread. He would sniff the gingerbread before drinking, and when he had drunk he would start moaning prayers. He was redheaded, Naftula was, like the first redheaded man on earth. When he was doing his snipping he didn't drain the blood off through a little glass tube but sucked it away with his splayed lips, and his tangled beard got all blood-smeared. When he went out to the assembled guests he would be tipsy, his bear-eyes shining with merriment. Redheaded, like the first redheaded man on earth, he would nasally intone a blessing over the wine. With one hand he would tip the vodka into the hirsute, crooked and fire-breathing pit of his mouth; in his other would be a plate. On it lay the little knife crimson with infant gore, and a piece of lint. When he was collecting his fee, Naftula would present this plate to all the guests, bump about among the women-folk, roll on them, grab them by the bosoms, and yell so that the whole street could hear.

'Fat mommas,' the old man would yell, his coral eyes gleaming, 'bud little boys for Naftula, thresh wheat on your bellies, do your best for Naftula. Bud little boys, you fat mommas.'

The husbands would cast coins on his plate; the wives would wipe the blood from his beard with napkins. The courtyards of Glukhaya and Hospital Streets knew no lack of children: they seethed with them like river mouths with fish-roe. Naftula used to toddle about with his little bag just like a tax-collector. But Prosecutor Orlov put an end to his wanderings.

The Prosecutor thundered from the dais, endeavouring to prove that the little surgeon was the servant of a cult.

'Do you believe in God?' he asked Naftula.

'Let him believe in God who has won two hundred thousand,' returned the old man.

'Were you not surprised by the arrival of Citizeness Brutman at a late hour, in the rain, with a newborn child in her arms?'

'I am surprised,' replied Naftula, 'when a human being does something in an inhuman way; but when he just plays the fool, then I am not surprised.'

These answers did not satisfy the Prosecutor. The question of the little glass tube cropped up. The Prosecutor tried to prove that by sucking the blood with his lips the accused was exposing children to the risk of infection. Naftula's head, the clotted little walnut of his head, was now bobbing somewhere in the region of the floor. He was sighing, closing his eyes, and wiping his caved-in mouth with his little fist.

'What are you mumbling, Citizen Gerchik?' the President of the court asked him.

Naftula fastened his extinguished gaze on Prosecutor Orlov.

'The late Monsieur Zusman,' he said, sighing, 'your late poppa, had a head on him such as you wouldn't find anywhere else in all the world. And, glory to God, he had no apoplexy when thirty years ago he summoned me to your circumcision. And now we see that you have grown up to be a big man in the Soviet land, and that Naftula didn't take with him, along of that little bit of nothing at all, anything that could later have been of service to you.'

He blinked his bear-eyes, shook his little red walnut, and fell silent. He was answered by big guns of mirth, thundering salvoes of laughter. Orlov, born Zusman, waving his arms, was shouting something that the cannonade made it impossible to hear. He was demanding that it should go on record that . . . Sandy Svetlov, the columnist of the *Odessa News*, sent him a note from the Press-box: 'Don't be a goat, Simon, ran the note, 'slay him with irony, it's only what's funny that's fatal. Yours, Sandy.'

The courtroom was hushed when the witness Belotserkovsky was called in. The witness repeated his written testimony. He was a lengthy individual in riding-breeches and cavalry boots. According to Ovsey, the Tiraspol and Balta district Party committees had shown him perfect collaboration in the work of collecting quotas of oil cake. In the midst of the work he had received a telegram announcing the birth of a son. On consulting the chairman of the Balta committee, he had decided, in order not to interrupt the work, to limit himself to a telegram of congratulation, and had not reached home till two weeks later. Throughout the region sixty-four thousand poods of oil cake in all had been collected. At his apartment, aside from the female witness Kharchenko, a neighbour, he had found no one. His wife had been taken to hospital, and the witness Kharchenko, as she rocked the child's cradle, which is an outmoded custom, was singing a lullaby. Knowing that the witness Kharchenko was addicted to drink, he had not considered it necessary to take in the words she was singing, but he was surprised to observe that she was calling the infant Yankel, whereas he had given instructions that his son was to be named Karl, in honour of our teacher Karl Marx. Upon unswaddling the child he had been confronted with the evidence of his misfortune.

The Prosecutor had a few questions. The Defence stated that it had no questions. The court usher led in the witness Polina Belotserkovsky. Staggering, she went to the bar. The bluish spasm of recent maternity twisted her face, on her forehead were drops of sweat. She cast a glance at the little blacksmith, dressed up with a bow and new boots as for a holiday; at the bronzed and grey-whiskered face of her mother. The witness did not reply when asked what she knew about the matter under consideration. She said that her father had been a poor man, had worked for forty years at the smithy by the Balta railway. Her mother had borne six children: three of them were dead, one was a Red Army commander, another was working at the Gen factory.

'My mother is very devout, as all can see. She always suffered from the knowledge that her children were not believers, and could not bear the thought that her grand-children would not grow up to be Jews. You must take into account the sort of family my mother was brought up in. You all know the little town of Medzhibozh. The women there still wear wigs . . .'

'Tell us, witness,' a sharp voice interrupted her, and Polina was silent. The sweat-drops on her forehead turned red, just as though the blood was oozing through her skin. 'Tell us, witness,' repeated a voice that belonged to the former advocate Samuel Lining.

If the Sanhedrin existed in our days, Lining would be at its head. But there is no Sanhedrin, and Lining, who learned to read Russian at the age of twenty-five, had in his fourth decade begun to write appeals to the Senate in no way differing from Talmudic treatises.

The old man had slept through the whole case. His jacket was covered with tobacco-ash. He woke up at the sight of Polina Belotserkovsky.

'Tell us, witness,' clashed the fishlike row of blue teeth always on the verge of falling out; 'did you know of your husband's resolve to call the child Karl?'

'I did.'

'What name did your mother have him given?'

'Yankel.'

'And you, witness, what did you call your son?'

'I called him "sweety-pie".'

'What was your motive in calling him "sweety-pie".'

'I call all children "sweety-pie".'

'Let us continue,' said Lining. His teeth fell out. He caught them with his lower lip and thrust them back between his jaws. 'Let us continue. On the evening when the child was abducted to the abode of the accused Gerchik, you were not at home: you were in hospital. Is that correct?'

'I was in hospital.'

'At what hospital were you being treated?'

'On Nezhin Street, by Doctor Drizo.'

'Under treatment by Doctor Drizo?'

'Yes.'

'You are quite sure of that?'

'Why shouldn't I be?'

'I have a document to submit to the court,' Lining's lifeless face loomed above the table. 'From this document the court will perceive that at the period in question Doctor Drizo was attending the Pediatric Congress at Kharkov.'

The Prosecutor raised no objection to admitting the document.

'Let us continue,' said Lining, rattling his teeth. The witness leaned the full weight of her body against the bar; her whisper was scarcely audible.

'Perhaps it wasn't Doctor Drizo,' she said, lying on the bar. 'I can't remember everything. I'm worn out . . .'

Lining poked in his yellow beard with a pencil, rubbed his stooping back against the bench and jiggled his false teeth.

When requested to present her Health Insurance card, the witness averred that she had mislaid it.

'Let us continue,' said the old man.

Polina passed her hand over her forehead. Her husband was sitting on the edge of a bench away from the other witnesses. He was sitting as straight as a poker, his long legs in their cavalry boots gathered beneath him. The sun fell on his face, crammed with the crossbars of petty and cross-grained bones.

'I'll find the card,' whispered Polina, and her hands slithered from the bar.

At that moment an infant's yells rang out. Next door a child was weeping and groaning.

'What are you thinking of, Polina?' cried the old woman in a hoarse voice. 'The child's not been fed since morn, the child's yelling its poor little guts out.'

The Red Army men woke with a start and grabbed their rifles. Polina slipped lower and lower, her head jerked back and lay on the floor. Her arms flew up, threshed the air, and subsided.

'Recess,' cried the President.

Uproar exploded in court. The green hollows in his cheeks gleaming, Belotserkovsky stepped cranelike toward his wife.

'Feed the child!' people were shouting from the back rows, making megaphones of their hands.

'They'll do that,' replied a female voice from afar. 'No need of your help!'

'The girl's in it, you mark my words,' observed a working-man sitting next to me. 'Knows a lot more than she'll tell.'

'Family life, brother,' said his neighbour. 'Nocturnal goings on, dark goings on. At night they tie things up that you can't disentangle by day.'

The sun was shooting oblique rays through the courtroom. The crowd threshed about, breathing fire and sweat. Using my elbows, I made my way out into the corridor. The door of the clubroom was ajar; thence came the groanings and champings of Karl-Yankel. In the clubroom hung a picture of Lenin, the one in which he is speaking from the armoured car on the square at the Finland Station. The picture was surrounded by diagrams in colour produced at the Petrovsky Factory. Along the wall there were flags, and rifles in wooden stands. A working-woman who looked like a Kirghiz, her head bent, was feeding Karl-Yankel. He was a chubby little fellow of five months old, in knitted bootees and with a white tuft on his head. Sucked fast to the Kirghiz woman, he was rumbling, beating his nurse on the breast with his little clenched fist.

'The fuss he's making!' said the Kirghiz woman. 'Not everyone would be willing to give him suck.'

In the room there was also a wench of about seventeen in a red kerchief and with great knobbly cheeks like fir-cones. She was busy rubbing Karl-Yankel's sanitary diaper dry.

'He'll be a military man,' said the girl. 'Just listen how he's yelling!'

The Kirghiz woman, pulling gently, drew her nipple from Kark-Yankel's mouth. The child started growling, and in despair jerked back his head with its white tuft. The woman uncovered her other breast and presented it to the little boy. He looked at the nipple with dull little eyes, and something gleamed in them. The Kirghiz woman gazed down at Karl-Yankel, squinting a dark eye.

'Why should he be a military man?' she asked, straightening the child's bonnet. 'He'll be an airman, you'll see, and fly about beneath the sky.'

In the courtroom the case had been resumed.

Battle was now being waged between the Prosecutor and the experts, who had insisted on reaching an evasive conclusion. The Social Plaintiff, half rising in his seat, was banging the desk with his fist. I could also see the first rows of the public: Galician saddiks with their beaver caps on their knees. They had made the journey to be present where, it said in the Warsaw papers, the Jewish religion was on trial. The faces of the Rabbis sitting in the front rows hung motionless in the dusty brown sunshine.

'Down with 'em!' cried a Young Communist who had forced his way right to the dais.

The battle flamed up more fiercely.

Karl-Yankel, fastening senseless eyes upon me, sucked away at the Kirghiz woman's breast.

From the window flew the straight streets trodden by my

childhood and youth: Pushkin Street stretching itself along to the station, Little Arnautskaya jutting out into the park by the sea.

I had grown up on these streets, and now it was Karl-Yankel's turn. But they hadn't fought for me as now they were fighting for him: few were those to whom I had been of any concern.

'It's not possible,' I whispered to myself, 'it's not possible that you won't be happy, Karl-Yankel. It's not possible that you won't be happier than I.'

In the Basement

I WAS an untruthful little boy. It was because of my reading: my imagination was always working overtime. I read during lessons, during recess, on my way home, at night under the table, hidden by the hanging tablecloth. My nose buried in a book, I let slide everything that really mattered, such as playing truant in the harbour, learning the art of billiards in the coffee-houses on Greek Street, going swimming at Langeron. I had no pals. Who would have wanted to waste his time with a boy like me?

One day I noticed that Mark Borgman, our top student, had got hold of a book on Spinoza. He had just read it, and simply had to tell the other boys about the Spanish Inquisition. What he told them was just a mumble of long words: there was no poetry in what he said. I couldn't help butting in. I told those willing to listen to me about old Amsterdam, the twilight of the ghetto, the philosophers who cut diamonds. To what I had read I added much of my own. I just had to. My imagination heightened the drama, altered the endings, made the beginnings more mysteriously involved. The death of Spinoza, his free and lonely death, appeared to me like a battle. The Sanhedrin was trying to make the dying man repent, but he wouldn't. I worked in Rubens. It seemed to me that Rubens was standing by Spinoza's deathbed taking a mask of the dead man's face.

My schoolmates listened mouths agape to the fantastic tale I told with so much brio, and dispersed unwillingly when the bell went. In the next recess Borgman came over to me and took me by the arm, and we started strolling about together. Soon we had come to terms. Borgman wasn't bad as top students go. To his powerful mind, secondary-school wisdom seemed mere scribbles in the margin of the real book, and this book he sought avidly. Twelve-year-old ninnies as we were, we could tell that an unusual, a learned life awaited Borgman. He didn't even do his lessons, but just listened to them. This sober, self-controlled boy became attached to me because of the way I had of garbling every possible thing, things that couldn't have been simpler.

That year we moved up to the third class. My report-card consisted chiefly of the remark 'poor'. I was such a queer, fanciful lad that after much thought the teachers decided not to mark me 'very poor', and so I moved up with the rest. At the beginning of the summer Borgman invited me to the family villa outside Odessa. His father was manager of the Russian Bank for Foreign Trade. He was one of the men who were turning Odessa into a Marseille or a Naples. The leaven of the old-time Odessa trader worked in him; he was one of those sceptical, amiable rakes. Borgman Senior didn't speak Russian if he could help it, preferring to express himself in the coarse and fragmentary language of Liverpool captains. When the Italian Opera visited our city in April, a dinner for the members of the company was arranged at Borgman's house. The obese banker, last of the Odessa traders, started a two-months' affair with the large-bosomed prima donna. She departed with memories that did not burden her conscience, and a necklace chosen with taste and not too expensive.

In the Basement

The old man was Argentine consul and president of the stock-exchange committee. It was to his house I was invited. My Aunt Bobka announced this in a loud voice to the whole courtyard. She dressed me up as best she could, and I took the little steam tram to the sixteenth Great Fountain stop. The villa stood on a low red bluff right by the shore. On the bluff a flower garden was laid out, with fuchsias and clipped globes of thuja.

I came of a poverty-stricken and ramshackle family, and the set-up at the Borgman villa shook me. In verdure-hidden walks wicker-chairs gleamed whitely. The dining-table was a mass of flowers, the windows had green frames outside. Before the house a low wooden colonnade stood spaciously.

Toward evening the bank manager came home. After dinner he placed a wicker-chair right on the edge of the bluff overlooking the moving plain of the sea, tucked up his legs in their white trousers, lit a cigar, and started reading the *Manchester Guardian*. The guests, ladies from Odessa, started a poker game on the veranda. On the corner of the table a slender tea-urn with ivory handles hissed and bubbled.

Card addicts and sweet-tooths, untidy female fops with secret vices, scented lingerie, and enormous thighs, the women snapped their black fans and staked gold coins. Through the fence of wild vine the sun reached at them, its fiery disc enormous. Bronze gleams lent weight to the women's black hair. Drops of the sunset sparkled in diamonds – diamonds disposed in every possible place: in the profundities of splayed bosoms, in painted ears, on puffy bluish she-animal fingers.

Evening fell. A bat whispered past. Blacker than before, the sea rolled up on to the red rocks. My twelve-year-old heart swelled with the joy and lightness of other people's wealth. My friend and I walked arm in arm up and down a distant and secluded path. Borgman was telling me that he was going to be an aircraft engineer. It was rumoured that his father was to be sent to represent the Russian Bank for Foreign Trade in London. Mark would be able to study in England.

In our house, Aunt Bobka's house, such things were never talked of. I had nothing to give in return for all this measureless magnificence. So I told Mark that though everything at our place was quite different, grandfather Leivi-Itzkhok and my uncle had travelled all around the world and had thousands of adventures. I narrated these adventures one after the other. All awareness of the possible abandoned me; I took Uncle Simon-Wolf through the Russo-Turkish War, to Alexandria, to Egypt.

Night towered in the poplars, stars lay heavy on the bowed leaves. Waving my hands, I talked on and on. The fingers of the future aircraft-engineer shuddered in mine. Struggling awake from his trance, he promised to come and see me on the following Sunday, and hoarding this promise I took the little steam tram home, to Aunt Bobka's.

All the week following my visit I kept picturing myself as a bank manager. I did deals with Singapore and Port Said running into millions. I bought a yacht and made solitary voyages. On Saturday it was time to wake from my dreams. Next day young Borgman was coming, and nothing I had told him about really existed. What did exist was different, and much more surprising than anything I had invented, but at the age of twelve I had no idea how things stood with me and reality. Grandfather Leivi-Itzkhok, the rabbi expelled from his little town for forging Count Branicki's signature on bills of exchange, was reckoned crazy by the neighbours and all the urchins of the locality. My Uncle Simon I just couldn't stick on account of his loud-mouthed eccentricity, his crazy fits of enthusiasm, the way he shouted and bullied. Aunt Bobka was the only sensible one. But Aunt Bobka was proud of my friendship with a bank manager's son. She felt that this meant the beginning of a brilliant career, and she baked apple strudel with jam and poppy-seed tarts for the guest. The whole heart of our tribe, a heart so inured to stubborn resistance, was cooked into those tarts. Grandfather, with his battered top-hat and the old boots on his swollen feet, we stowed away with our neighbours the Apelkhots, after I had begged him not to show his face till our visitor had left. Uncle Simon was also arranged for: he went off with his broker friends to drink tea at the Bear tavern. At this place of refreshment they used to lace their tea with vodka, so one could rely on Uncle taking his time. Here it is necessary to observe that the family I spring from was not like other Jewish families. We had drunkards amongst us, and some of us had gone in for seducing the daughters of generals and abandoning them before reaching the frontier. Grandfather, as I have said, had done a bit of forging in his day, and had composed blackmailing letters for women who had been thrown over.

To make sure that Uncle Simon would stay away the whole day, I gave him three roubles I had saved up. Three roubles take a deal of spending. Uncle would be back late, and the bank manager's son would never learn that the tale of my uncle's strength and magnanimity was untrue from beginning to end. Though to tell the truth, if you go by the heart, it wasn't all that untrue; but it must be admitted that one's first sight of the filthy, loud-mouthed fellow did nothing to corroborate this transcendent truth.

On Sunday morning Aunt Bobka decked herself in a brown frock. Her kindly fat bosom lay all over the place. She put on a kerchief with black print blossoms, the kerchief they put on in the synagogue at Atonement and Rosh Hashana. On the table she set pies, jam, and cracknels. Then she started to wait. We lived in a basement; Borgman raised his brows as he passed along the hump-backed floor of the corridor. I showed him the alarm-clock made by grandfather down to the last screw. A lamp was fitted to the clock, and when the clock marked the half-hour or the hour the lamp was lit up.

I also showed him the barrel of boot-polish. The recipe for this polish had been invented by Leivi-Itzkhok, and he would reveal the secret to no living soul. Then Borgman and I read a few pages of grandfather's manuscript. It was written in Hebrew on square yellow sheets of paper as large as maps. The manuscript was entitled 'The Headless Man', and in it were described all the neighbours he had had in his seventy years, first at Skvira and Belaya Tserkov and later on at Odessa. Gravediggers, cantors, Jewish drunkards, cooks at circumcisions, and the quacks who performed the ritual operation – such were Leivi-Itzkhok's heroes. They were all as mad as hatters, tongue-tied, with lumpy noses, pimples on their bald pates, and backsides askew.

While we were reading, Aunt Bobka appeared in her brown dress. She floated in surrounded by her great bosom and bearing a tea-urn on a tray. I performed the introductions. Aunt Bobka said 'Pleased to meet you,' thrust out her stiff, sweaty fingers, and scuffled both feet. Everything was going better than one could have hoped. The Apelkhots kept grandfather safely tucked away. I pulled out his treasures one after the other: grammars in all languages, sixty-six volumes of the Talmud. Mark was dazzled by the barrel of polish, by the ingenious alarm clock and the mountain of Talmud: things that were not to be seen in any other house in town.

We had two glasses of tea each with the strudel, then Aunt Bobka, nodding her head and retreating backward, disappeared. I grew light of heart, struck a pose, and started reciting poetry. Never in my life have I loved anything more than the lines I then started spouting. Antony, bending over Caesar's corpse, addresses the Roman crowd:

> *Friends, Romans, countrymen, lend me your ears;*
> *I come to bury Caesar, not to praise him.*

So Antony begins his stuff. I choked with excitement and pressed my hands to my breast.

He was my friend, faithful and just to me;
But Brutus says he was ambitious;
And Brutus is an honourable man.
He hath brought many captives home to Rome,
Whose ransoms did the general coffers fill.
Did this in Caesar seem ambitious?
When that the poor have cried, Caesar hath wept;
Ambition should be made of sterner stuff.
Yet Brutus says he was ambitious;
And Brutus is an honourable man.
You all did see that on the Lupercal
I thrice presented him a kingly crown,
Which he did thrice refuse. Was this ambition?
Yet Brutus says he was ambitious;
And sure he is an honourable man.

Before my eyes, in the vapours of the universe, the face of Brutus hung. It grew whiter than chalk. The Roman people moved muttering upon me. I raised my hand, and Borgman's eyes obediently followed it. My clenched fist trembled, I raised my hand – and through the window saw Uncle Simon crossing the courtyard accompanied by Leikakh the broker. They were staggering beneath the weight of a clothes-hanger made of antlers and a red trunk with fittings shaped like lions' jaws. Through the window Aunt Bobka also saw them. Forgetting about our visitor, she dashed into the room and seized me in her trembling arms.

'My precious, he's been buying furniture again!'

Borgman started to get up, neat in his school uniform, and bowed uncertainly to Aunt Bobka. The door was being assaulted. In the corridor there was the stamping of boots, the noise of the trunk being shunted. The voices of Uncle Simon and the red-haired Leikakh thundered deafeningly. They had been drinking.

'Bobka,' shouted Uncle Simon, 'guess how much I paid for these horns!'

He was blaring like a trumpet, but there was uncertainty in his voice. Even though he was drunk, he knew how we hated the red-haired Leikakh, who instigated all his purchases and inundated us with ridiculous bits of furniture that we didn't want.

Aunt Bobka said nothing. Leikakh hissed something at Uncle Simon. To drown his serpentine susurration, to deaden my dismay, I cried with the voice of Antony:

> But yesterday the word of Caesar might
> Have stood against the world. Now lies he there,
> And none so poor to do him reverence.
> O masters! If I were dispos'd to stir
> Your hearts and minds to mutiny and rage,
> I should do Brutus wrong, and Cassius wrong,
> Who, you all know, are honourable men.

At this point there was a dull thud. It was Aunt Bobka falling to the floor, felled by a blow from her husband. She must have made some cutting remark about horns. The curtain had risen on the daily performance. Uncle Simon's brazen voice caulked all the cracks in the universe.

'You drag the glue out of me,' cried my uncle in a voice of thunder, 'drag the glue from my entrails to stuff up your dog-mouths. I've been unsouled by toil. I've nothing left to work with: no hands, no legs. A millstone you have hung around my neck, from my neck a millstone is suspended . . .'

Cursing me and Aunt Bobka with Hebrew curses, he promised us that our eyes would trickle out, that our children would rot in the womb, that we'd be unable to give each another decent burial and that we would be dragged by the hair to a mass grave.

Little Borgman rose from his chair. He was pale, and kept looking furtively around. He couldn't understand the twists and turns of Hebrew blasphemy, but with Russian oaths he was familiar, and Uncle Simon didn't disdain them either. The bank-manager's son crumpled his little peaked cap in his hands. I saw him double as I strove to outshout all the evil in the world. My death-agony despair and the death of the already dead Caesar coalesced: I was dead, and I was shouting. A throaty croak rose from the depths of my being:

> *If you have tears, prepare to shed them now.*
> *You all do know this mantle. I remember*
> *The first time ever Caesar put it on.*
> *'Twas on a summer's evening in his tent.*
> *That day he overcame the Nervii.*
> *Look, in this place ran Cassius' dagger through.*
> *See what a rent the envious Casca made.*
> *Through this the well-beloved Brutus stabb'd;*
> *And as he pluck'd his cursed steel away,*
> *Mark how the blood of Caesar follow'd it. . . .*

Nothing could out-shout Uncle Simon. Sitting on the floor, Aunt Bobka was sobbing and blowing her nose. The imperturbable Leikakh was shoving the trunk around behind the partition. And now my crazy grandfather was filled with the desire to lend a hand. He tore himself from the clutches of the Apelkhots, crept over to our window, and started scraping away on his fiddle, no doubt so that people passing the house should not be able to hear Uncle Simon's bad language. Borgman looked through the window – it was at street level – and he started back in horror: he had beheld my poor grandfather twisting his blue and ossified mouth. On the old man's head was his bent top-hat. He wore a long black padded cloak with bone buttons, and his elephantine feet bulged from the inevitable torn boots. His tobacco-stained beard hung in tatters, swaying in the window. Mark took to his heels.

'It's quite all right,' he mumbled as he made his escape. 'Quite all right, really . . .'

His little uniform and his cap with the turned-up edges flashed across the yard.

When Mark had gone I grew calmer. I was waiting for evening. When grandfather, having covered his square sheet of paper with Hebrew squiggles (he was describing the Apelkhots, with whom thanks to me he had spent the day), had lain down on his truckle-bed and was asleep, I made my way into the corridor. There the floor was earthen. I moved through the darkness, barefooted, in my long patched shirt. Through chinks in the boards cobblestones shot blades of light. In the corner, as ever, stood the water-barrel. Into it I lowered myself. The water sliced me in two. I plunged my head in, lost my breath, and surfaced again. From a shelf the cat looked down at me sleepily. Once more I stuck it, longer this time. The water gurgled round me, my groans were swallowed in it. I opened my eyes and saw on the bottom of the barrel the swollen sail of my shirt and two feet pressed against one another. Again my forces failed me, again I surfaced. By the barrel stood grandfather, wearing a woman's jacket. His sole tooth shone greenly.

'Grandson,' he said, pronouncing the word with scornful distinctness, 'grandson, I am going to take a dose of castor oil, so as to have something to lay on your grave.'

I gave a wild shriek and splooshed down into the water. Grandfather's infirm hand drew me forth again. Then for the first time that day I shed tears. And the world of tears was so huge, so beautiful, that everything save tears vanished from my eyes.

I came to myself in bed, wrapped in blankets. Grandfather was stalking about the room whistling. Fat Aunt Bobka was warming my hands on her bosom.

'How he trembles, our blessed ninny!' said Aunt Bobka. 'Where can the child find the strength to tremble so?'

Grandfather tugged at his beard, gave a whistle and stalked off again. On the other side of the wall Uncle Simon snored agonizingly. Battler by day, he never woke up nights.

1930

Awakening

ALL the folk in our circle – brokers, shopkeepers, clerks in banks and steamship offices – used to have their children taught music. Our fathers, seeing no other escape from their lot, had thought up a lottery, building it on the bones of little children. Odessa more than other towns was seized by the craze. And in fact, in the course of ten years or so our town supplied the concert platforms of the world with infant prodigies. From Odessa came Mischa Elman, Zimbalist, Gabrilowitsch. Odessa witnessed the first steps of Jascha Heifetz.

When a lad was four or five, his mother took the puny creature to Zagursky's. Mr Zagursky ran a factory of infant prodigies, a factory of Jewish dwarfs in lace collars and patent-leather pumps. He hunted them out in the slums of the Moldavanka, in the evil-smelling courtyards of the Old Market. Mr Zagursky charted the first course, then the children were shipped off to Professor Auer in St Petersburg. A wonderful harmony dwelt in the souls of those wizened creatures with their swollen blue hands. They became famous virtuosi. My father decided that I should emulate them. Though I had, as a matter of fact, passed the age-limit set for infant prodigies, being now in my fourteenth year, my shortness and lack of strength made it possible to pass me off as an eight-year-old. Herein lay father's hope.

I was taken to Zagursky's. Out of respect for my grandfather, Mr Zagursky agreed to take me on at the cut rate of a rouble a lesson. My grandfather Leivi-Itzkhok was the laughing-stock of the town, and its chief adornment. He used to walk about the streets in a top hat and old boots, dissipating doubt in the darkest of cases. He would be asked what a Gobelin was, why the Jacobins betrayed Robespierre, how you made artificial silk, what a Caesarean section was. And my grandfather could answer these questions. Out of respect for his learning and craziness, Mr Zagursky only charged us a rouble a lesson. And he had the devil of a time with me, fearing my grandfather, for with me there was nothing to be done. The sounds dripped from my fiddle like iron filings, causing even me excruciating agony, but father wouldn't give in. At home there was no talk save of Mischa Elman, exempted by the Tsar himself from military service. Zimbalist, father would have us know, had been presented to the King of England and had played at Buckingham Palace. The parents of Gabrilowitsch had bought two houses in St Petersburg. Infant prodigies brought wealth to their parents, but though my father could have reconciled himself to poverty, fame he must have.

'It's not possible,' people feeding at his expense would insinuate, 'it's just not possible that the grandson of such a grandfather . . .'

But what went on in my head was quite different. Scraping my way through the violin exercises, I would have books by Turgenev or Dumas on my music-stand. Page after page I devoured as I deedled away. In the daytime I would relate impossible happenings to the kids next door; at night I would commit them to paper. In our family, composition was a hereditary occupation. Grandfather Leivi-Itzkhok, who went cracked as he grew old, spent his whole life writing a tale entitled 'The Headless Man'. I took after him.

Three times a week, laden with violin-case and music, I made my reluctant way to Zagursky's place on Witte (formerly Dvoryanskaya) Street. There Jewish girls aflame with hysteria sat along the wall awaiting their turn, pressing to their feeble knees violins exceeding in dimensions the exalted persons they were to play to at Buckingham Palace.

The door of the sanctum would open, and from Mr Zagursky's study there would stagger, big-headed, freckled children with necks as thin as flower-stalks and an epileptic flush on their cheeks. The door would bang to, swallowing up the next dwarf. Behind the wall, straining his throat, the teacher sang and waved his baton. He had ginger curls and frail legs, and sported a big bow-tie. Manager of a monstrous lottery, he populated the Moldavanka and the dark culs-de-sac of the Old Market with the ghosts of pizzicato and cantilena. Afterward old Professor Auer lent these strains a diabolical brilliance.

In this crew I was quite out of place. Though like them in my dwarfishness, in the voice of my forbears I perceived inspiration of another sort.

The first step was difficult. One day I left home laden like a beast of burden with violin-case, violin, music, and twelve roubles in cash – payment for a month's tuition. I was going along Nezhin Street; to get to Zagursky's I should have turned into Dvoryanskaya, but instead of that I went up Tiraspolskaya and found myself at the harbour. The allotted time flew past in the part of the port where ships went after quarantine. So began my liberation. Zagursky's saw me no more: affairs of greater moment occupied my thoughts. My pal Nemanov and I got into the habit of slipping aboard the S.S. *Kensington* to see an old salt named Trottyburn. Nemanov was a year younger than I. From the age of eight onward he had been doing the most ingenious business deals you can imagine. He had a wonderful head for that kind of thing, and later on amply fulfilled his youthful promise. Now he is a New York millionaire, director of General Motors, a company no less powerful than Ford. Nemanov took me along with him because I silently obeyed all his orders. He used to buy pipes smuggled in by Mr Trottyburn. They were made in Lincoln by the old sailor's brother.

'Gen'lemen,' Mr Trottyburn would say to us, 'take my word, the pets must be made with your own hands. Smoking a factory-made pipe – might as well shove an enema in your mouth. D'you know who Benvenuto Cellini was? He was a grand lad. My brother in Lincoln could tell you about him. Live and let live is my brother's motto. He's got it into his head that you just has to make the pets with your own hands, and not with no one else's. And who are we to say him no, gen'lemen?'

Nemanov used to sell Trottyburn's pipes to bank managers, foreign consuls, well-to-do Greeks. He made a hundred per cent on them.

The pipes of the Lincolnshire master breathed poetry. In each one of them thought was invested, a drop of eternity. A little yellow eye gleamed in their mouthpieces, and their cases were lined with satin. I tried to picture the life in Old England of Matthew Trottyburn, the last master-pipemaker, who refused to swim with the tide.

'We can't but agree, gen'lemen, that the pets has to be made with your own hands.'

The heavy waves by the sea wall swept me farther and farther away from our house, impregnated with the smell of leeks and Jewish destiny. From the harbour I migrated to the other side of the breakwater. There on a scrap of sandspit dwelt the boys from Primorskaya Street. Trouserless from morn till eve, they dived under wherries, sneaked coconuts for dinner, and awaited the time when boats would arrive from Kherson and Kamenka laden with watermelons, which melons it would be possible to break open against moorings.

To learn to swim was my dream. I was ashamed to confess to those bronzed lads that, born in Odessa, I had not seen the sea till I was ten, and at fourteen didn't know how to swim.

How slow was my acquisition of the things one needs to

know! In my childhood, chained to the Gemara, I had led
the life of a sage. When I grew up I started climbing trees.

But swimming proved beyond me. The hydrophobia of
my ancestors – Spanish rabbis and Frankfurt money-changers
– dragged me to the bottom. The waves refused to support
me. I would struggle to the shore pumped full of salt water
and feeling as though I had been flayed, and return to where
my fiddle and music lay. I was fettered to the instruments of
my torture, and dragged them about with me. The struggle
of rabbis versus Neptune continued till such time as the local
water-god took pity on me. This was Yefim Nikitich Smolich, proof-reader of the *Odessa News*. In his athletic breast
there dwelt compassion for Jewish children, and he was the
god of a rabble of rickety starvelings. He used to collect them
from the bug-infested joints on the Moldavanka, take them
down to the sea, bury them in the sand, do gym with them,
dive with them, teach them songs. Roasting in the perpen-
dicular sunrays, he would tell them tales about fishermen and
wild beasts. To grown-ups Nikitich would explain that he
was a natural philosopher. The Jewish kids used to roar with
laughter at his tales, squealing and snuggling up to him like
so many puppies. The sun would sprinkle them with creeping
freckles, freckles of the same colour as lizards.

Silently, out of the corner of his eye, the old man had been
watching my duel with the waves. Seeing that the thing was
hopeless, that I should simply never learn to swim, he included
me among the permanent occupants of his heart. That cheerful heart of his was with us there all the time; it never went
careering off anywhere else, never knew covetousness, and
never grew disturbed. With his sunburned shoulders, his
superannuated gladiator's head, his bronzed and slightly
bandy legs, he would lie among us on the other side of the
mole, lord and master of those melon-sprinkled, paraffin-
stained waters. I came to love that man, with the love that
only a lad suffering from hysteria and headaches can feel for

a real man. I was always at his side, always trying to be of service to him.

He said to me:

'Don't you get all worked up. You just strengthen your nerves. The swimming will come of itself. How d'you mean, the water won't hold you? Why shouldn't it hold you?'

Seeing how drawn I was to him, Nikitich made an exception of me alone of all his disciples. He invited me to visit the clean and spacious attic where he lived in an ambience of straw mats, showed me his dogs, his hedgehog, his tortoise, and his pigeons. In return for this wealth I showed him a tragedy I had written the day before.

'I was sure you did a bit of scribbling,' said Nikitich. 'You've the look. You're looking in *that* direction all the time; no eyes for anywhere else.'

He read my writings, shrugged a shoulder, passed a hand through his stiff grey curls, paced up and down the attic.

'One must suppose,' he said slowly, pausing after each word, 'one must suppose that there's a spark of the divine fire in you.'

We went out into the street. The old man halted, struck the pavement with his stick, and fastened his gaze upon me.

'Now what is it you lack? Youth's no matter – it'll pass with the years. What you lack is a feeling for nature.'

He pointed with his stick, at a tree with a reddish trunk and a low crown.

'What's that tree?'

I didn't know.

'What's growing on that bush?'

I didn't know this either. We walked together across the little square on the Alexandrovsky Prospect. The old man kept poking his stick at trees; he would seize me by the shoulder when a bird flew past, and he made me listen to the various kinds of singing.

'What bird is that singing?'

I knew none of the answers. The names of trees and birds, their division into species, where birds fly away to, on which side the sun rises, when the dew falls thickest – all these things were unknown to me.

'And you dare to write! A man who doesn't live in nature, as a stone does or an animal, will never in all his life write two worthwhile lines. Your landscapes are like descriptions of stage props. In heaven's name, what have your parents been thinking of for fourteen years?'

What *had* they been thinking of? Of protested bills of exchange, of Mischa Elman's mansions, I didn't say anything to Nikitich about that, but just kept mum.

At home, over dinner, I couldn't touch my food. It just wouldn't go down.

'A feeling for nature,' I thought to myself. 'Goodness, why did that never enter my head? Where am I to find someone who will tell me about the way birds sing and what trees are called? What do *I* know about such things? I might perhaps recognize lilac, at any rate when it's in bloom. Lilac and acacia – there are acacias along De Ribas and Greek Streets.'

At dinner father told a new story about Jascha Heifetz. Just before he got to Robinat's he had met Mendelssohn, Jascha's uncle. It appeared that the lad was getting eight hundred roubles a performance. Just work out how much that comes to at fifteen concerts a month!

I did, and the answer was twelve thousand a month. Multiplying and carrying four in my head, I glanced out of the window. Across the cement courtyard, his cloak swaying in the breeze, his ginger curls poking out from under his soft hat, leaning on his cane, Mr Zagursky, my music teacher, was advancing. It must be admitted he had taken his time in spotting my truancy. More than three months had elapsed since the day when my violin had grounded on the sand by the breakwater.

Mr Zagursky was approaching the main entrance. I dashed

to the back door, but the day before it had been nailed up for fear of burglars. Then I locked myself in the privy. In half an hour the whole family had assembled outside the door. The women were weeping. Aunt Bobka, exploding with sobs, was rubbing her fat shoulder against the door. Father was silent. Finally he started speaking, quietly and distinctly as he had never before spoken in his life.

'I am an officer,' said my father. 'I own real estate. I go hunting. Peasants pay me rent. I have entered my son in the Cadet Corps. I have no need to worry about my son.'

He was silent again. The women were sniffing. Then a terrible blow descended on the privy door. My father was hurling his whole body against it, stepping back and then throwing himself forward.

'I am an officer,' he kept wailing. 'I go hunting. I'll kill him. This is the end.'

The hook sprang from the door, but there was still a bolt hanging on to a single nail. The women were rolling about on the floor, grasping father by the legs. Crazy, he was trying to break loose. Father's mother came over, alerted by the hubbub.

'My child,' she said to him in Hebrew, 'our grief is great. It has no bounds. Only blood was lacking in our house. I do not wish to see blood in our house.'

Father gave a groan. I heard his footsteps retreating. The bolt still hung by its last nail.

I sat it out in my fortress till nightfall. When all had gone to bed, Aunt Bobka took me to grandmother's. We had a long way to go. The moonlight congealed on bushes unknown to me, on trees that had no name. Some anonymous bird emitted a whistle and was extinguished, perhaps by sleep. What bird was it? What was it called? Does dew fall in the evening? Where is the constellation of the Great Bear? On what side does the sun rise?

We were going along Post-Office Street. Aunt Bobka held me firmly by the hand so that I shouldn't run away. She was right to. I was thinking of running away.

1930

The S.S. Cow-Wheat

IN the summer of 1917 Sergev Vasilyevich Malyshev, who later became chairman of the Nizhni Novogorod Fair Committee, organized the first produce expedition in our country. With Lenin's approval he loaded several trains with the things that peasants need, and set off for the Volga region in search of grain in exchange.

I found myself on the bookkeeping staff of this expedition. As our scene of action we had selected the Novo-Nikolayev district of the Province of Samara. According to the calculations of those who ought to know, this district could, if properly worked, provide enough food for the whole Moscow region.

Not far from Saratov, at the river station of Uvek, the goods were loaded on to a barge, the hold of which had been converted into a self-contained department store. Between the concave ribs of the floating warehouse we nailed up portraits of Lenin and Marx, surrounding them with ears of corn. We laid out on shelves cotton goods, scythes, nails, leather, nor were accordions and balalaikas lacking.

At the same place, Uvek, we were reinforced by a tug, the *Ivan Tupitsyn*, named after a Volga merchant once a big noise in those parts. The 'staff' – Malyshev with his assistants and cashiers – took up their quarters on the steamboats, and the soldiers to guard us and the clerks to sell our goods were billeted on the barge, under lean-tos.

Loading took a week. Then one morning in July the *Ivan*

Tupitsyn, emitting fat gusts of smoke, towed us up the Volga to Baronsk. The Germans had known this place as Katarinen-stadt; it was now the capital of the region of the Volga Germans, a beautiful region inhabited by manly folk sparing of words.

The steppe near Baronsk is covered with heavy golden wheat such as you find only in Canada; it is a land abounding in sunflowers and oily clouds of black earth. From St Petersburg, licked by a granite fire, we had moved to a Russian, and hence more improbable, California. In our California a pound of grain cost sixty copecks, and not ten roubles as in the North. We flung ourselves on the bread with a ferocity now impossible to describe, our dog-teeth sharpened by hunger plunging into the cobwebby pulp. For two weeks after our arrival we were drunk with a blissful indigestion. The blood that now started coursing through our veins had, it seemed to me, the taste and colour of raspberry jam.

Malyshev had calculated correctly: there was a ready sale. From all parts of the steppe slow streams of peasant carts made their way to the riverbank. The sun slid over the croups of well-fed horses, it gilded the tops of wheaten hills. Wagons like thousands of dots slithered down to the Volga. By the horses strode giants in woollen jerseys, descendants of the Dutch farmers settled in the Volga regions in Catherine's day. Their faces were as they had been in Saardam and Harlem. Beneath the patriarchal moss of their eyebrows, in the network of leathery wrinkles, shone drops of faded turquoise. Tobacco-smoke melted into the blue lightning-flashes above the steppe. The colonists climbed slowly up the ladder on to the barge; their wooden clogs clattered like bells tolling firmness and tranquillity. The wares were chosen by old women in starched bonnets and long brown cloaks, and then borne ashore to the wagons. Home-grown painters had scattered armfuls of wild flowers and pink bull-snouts along the sides of these carts; their outsides were usually painted a deep blue, and in the blue glowed waxen apples and plums touched by a sunray.

Customers arrived on camels from distant parts. The beasts settled down on the riverbank, streaking the horizon with their collapsing humps. Our trading used to end toward evening. We would shut up shop; the disabled soldiers of the guard and the salesmen pulled off their clothes and sprang from the sides of the barge into a Volga aflame with the sunset. Over the distant steppe stretched red waves of wheat, and in the sky the walls of the sunset caved in. The bathing of the workers in the Produce Expedition to the Province of Samara, as we were officially called, presented an unusual spectacle. The cripples sent muddy pink fountains shooting from the water. These men of the guard were one-legged, or were short an arm or an eye, and they used to link up in twos so as to swim. Two men, equipped between them with one pair of legs, would beat the water with their stumps, and whirlpools of muddy water would swirl between their bodies. Growling and snorting, the cripples would roll out on to the bank; bubbling over, they would shake their docked limbs at the coursing heavens, sprinkle themselves with sand and wrestle, kneading one another's truncated extremities. After bathing we used to go off to supper at Karl Biedermeyer's inn. This supper crowned our days. Two wenches with blood-red hands, Augusta and Anna, would serve us chops – russet cobblestones drowned in streams of steaming butter and piled high with hayricks of roast potatoes. To flavour this mountainous rural food they added leek and garlic, and they placed before us jars of sour gherkins. Through the little round windows set high up near the ceiling the smoke of the sunset drifted from the market-place. The gherkins steamed in the crimson vapours, smelling of the seashore. We swallowed our meat down with cider. Inhabitants of Peski and Okhta, denizens of Petersburg suburbs iced over with yellow urine, each evening we had the feeling of conquerors. The little windows cut in walls blackened by the smoke of centuries resembled port-holes. Through them shone a little courtyard divinely clean, a German courtyard with rosebushes and wistaria and the violet abyss of the open stable. Old women in cloaks were knitting Gulliver his stockings by the porches. Herds were returning from the pastures. Augusta and Anna would settle down by the cows on milking-stools; iridescent bovine eyes glimmered in the dusk. One felt there was not, and never had been, any war on earth. And yet the front of the Ural Cossacks lay twenty versts from Baronsk. Karl Biedermeyer didn't dream that the civil war was moving toward his home.

Through the night I would return to our quarters in the hold with Seletsky, another of the office staff. On the road he would strike up a song, and heads in nightcaps would emerge from lancet windows. The moonlight flowed down red canals of tiles; the muffled barking of dogs rose above the Russian Saardam. Augusta and Anna, petrified, listened to Seletsky's singing. His bass voice bore us along to the steppe, to the Gothic enclosure of wheat-barns. Crossbars of moonlight trembled on the river, the darkness was almost weightless as it shifted over to the sand by the shore, in a torn net shining worms contorted themselves.

The strength of Seletsky's voice was quite unnatural. A great chap well over six feet tall, he was one of the race of provincial Chaliapins, of whom to our good fortune great numbers are scattered about the Russian land. He had the same sort of face as Chaliapin, a cross between the face of a Scotch coachman and that of a magnate of Catherine the Great's time. Unlike his divine prototype, he was rather slow on the uptake; but his voice, spreading out limitless and fatal, filled the soul with the sweetness of self-destruction and gypsy oblivion. He preferred convict songs to Italian arias. It was from Seletsky that I heard for the first time Grechaninov's 'Death'. Dread, implacable, passion-drenched, it soared through the night above the dark waters:

> *She'll not forget; she will come with caresses;*
> *She will embrace, with a love that is endless,*
> *Laying her bride's wreath upon her dark tresses!*

In its transient integument called man, the song flows on like the waters of eternity, washing all away, giving birth to all.

The front was twenty versts away. Having linked up with Major Voženílek's Czech battalion, the Ural Cossacks were attempting to drive the scattered Red detachments from Nikolayevsk. Farther to the North, from Samara, the troops of the Committee of Members of the Constituent Assembly were advancing. Our dispersed and untrained units regrouped on the left bank. Muravyov had just betrayed us; Vatsetis had been appointed Soviet Commander-in-Chief.

Weapons used to be brought up to the front from Saratov. Once or perhaps twice a week the pink-and-white steamer *Cow-Wheat* tied up at the Baronsk landing-stage, bringing rifles and shells. The deck would be a litter of boxes with skulls stencilled on them, and with the word 'fatal' under the skulls.

The ship was commanded by Korostelyov, an emaciated man with drooping flaxen hair. Korostelyov was an Old Believer, a man with an unsettled soul, a born vagrant. He had sailed the White Sea before the mast, tramped the length and breadth of Russia, spent time serving a sentence in prison and doing penance in a monastery.

On our way back from Biedermeyer's we always used to drop in on Korostelyov if the lights of the *Cow-Wheat* were visible at the landing-stage. One night, having drawn level with the wheat-barns, with that magic line of blue and brown castles, we saw a torch floating high in the sky. Seletsky and I were returning in the softened and passionate condition produced by this unusual part of the country, by youth, the night, the melting rings of fire on the river.

Noiseless, the Volga rolled past. No lights were to be seen on the *Cow-Wheat*, and the hulk of the vessel lay dark, like a dead thing; only the torch flared smokily at the masthead. Seletsky was singing, his pale face thrown back. He went singing down to the water's edge, and then broke off. We climbed up on to the unguarded landing-stage. On the deck, boxes and gun wheels lay about. I pushed the door of the captain's cabin, and it swung open. On the drink-splashed table a tin lamp without a glass was burning; the metal wick-holder was melting. The windows had been nailed up with humpbacked boards. From the petrol-cans lying about under the table came a sulphurous waft of home-distilled spirits. Korostelyov in a canvas shirt was sitting on the floor among green trails of vomit. His monkish clotted hair stood out around his face. He was staring up from the floor at his commissar, Larson the Latvian, who had propped before him a copy of *Pravda* in a yellow cardboard cover and was reading by the light of the deliquescent kerosene bonfire.

'That's the sort of chap you are,' said Korostelyov from the floor. 'Go on with what you were saying. Torture us if you want to.'

'Why should *I* talk?' retorted Larson, turning his back and barricading himself with his cardboard. 'It'll be better if I listen to *you*.'

On the velvet divan, dangling his legs, sat a red-haired peasant.

'Lisha,' said Korostelyov to the peasant, 'some vodka.'

'All gone,' replied Lisha, 'and no place to get any more.'

Larson pushed his cardboard aside and suddenly started guffawing, just as though he were tapping out a rapid drum-roll.

'Mother Russia needs a drink,' said the Latvian with his queer accent. 'The Russian soul has finally felt the urge, but there's not a drop to be got hereabouts. What's the point of calling it the Volga?'

Korostelyov's neck, meagre as a child's, stuck out; his legs in their canvas trousers shot apart across the floor. A pitiful amazement was reflected in his eyes; then they started shining.

'Torture us,' he said almost inaudibly, stretching out his neck; 'torture us, Karl.'

Lisha placed his chubby hands together and looked sideways at the Latvian.

'Blow me if he ain't putting the Volga in the wrong now! No, comrade, don't you wrong our Volga, don't you defame it. You know the way our song goes: "Mother Volga, queen of rivers . . ."'

Seletsky and I were still standing by the door. I kept thinking of beating a retreat.

'Now I simply cannot understand,' said Larson, addressing us but clearly continuing an argument, 'perhaps the comrades will explain to me how it comes to pass that reinforced concrete is worse than birches and aspens, and airships worse than Kaluga dung.'

Lisha twisted his head in its padded collar. His legs did not reach to the floor. His chubby fingers pressed to his belly, he was plaiting an invisible net.

'What do you know about Kaluga, friend?' he asked soothingly. 'In Kaluga, I'll tell you, there live famous folk – splendid folk, if you want to know.'

'Some vodka,' ordered Korostelyov from the floor. Larson threw back his porcine head and guffawed sharply.

'Muddling along,' he murmured, pulling the newspaper toward him. 'Somehow or other we'll manage, I don't think!'

Tempestuous sweat stood out on his brow, oily streams of fire swam in the *plica Polonica* of his colourless hair.

'Some damned way or other,' he snorted with laughter again; 'let's hope for the best.'

Korostelyov scrabbled about with his fingers. Sweeping

out in front with his arms, he started crawling forward, dragging behind him a skeleton in a canvas shirt.

'You mustn't torture Russia, Karl,' he whispered when he had crawled over to the Latvian. He shot his little clenched fist out at the other's face and started pummelling it, squeaking.

The Latvian gazed reproachfully at us all over glasses that had slipped down his nose. Then he dug his fingers into the silken river of Korostelyov's hair and squashed the man's face to the floor. He raised it and again let it drop.

'Take that,' said Larson jerkily, and tossed the bony body aside. 'There's more where that came from.'

Korostelyov, supporting himself on his hands, rose doglike above the floor. Blood was flowing from his nostrils, his eyes were squinting. They wavered about, then he jerked himself up and plunged under the table, howling.

'Russia,' he muttered under the table, and started throwing a fit. 'Russia . . .'

The shovels of his bare feet dug in and out. Only one word, uttered with a groaning whistle, could be made out in his screeching.

'Russia,' he wailed, stretching out his hands and thrashing about with his feet.

The red-haired Lisha sat on the velvet divan.

'They started about noon,' he said to me and Seletsky, 'squabbling about Russia, pitying Russia . . .'

'Vodka,' said Korostelyov firmly from beneath the table. He crawled out and staggered to his feet, his blood-drenched hair falling over his cheek.

'How about that vodka, Lisha?'

'The vodka, friend, is at Voznesenskoye, forty versts off – forty versts by water, fifty versts by land, whichever you like. There's a temple there now, there must be home-brew. Do what they may, the Germans can't put a stop to it.'

Korostelyov turned around and went out on his straight stork-legs.

'We be Kaluga-folk, we be.' Larson cried suddenly.

'No respect for Kaluga,' sighed Lisha, 'do what you will. But I, now, I've been there, in Kaluga. Decent folk dwell there, famous folk . . .'

Outside an order was shouted, the anchor rattled as it was drawn up. Lisha's eyebrows rose.

'Are we bound for Voznesenskoye by any chance?'

Larson started laughing, his head thrown back. I ran out of the cabin. Barefooted, Korostelyov stood on the little captain's-bridge, brazen moonlight upon his gashed face. The gangway fell away to the shore. Sailors circled about, winding up moorings.

'Captain,' Seletsky cried from somewhere above, 'let us two at any rate go ashore. This is no concern of ours.'

The engines exploded into a disjointed thumping. The paddle-wheel dug into the water. A rotten plank on the landing-stage splintered softly. The *Cow-Wheat* rolled its nose about.

'Off we go,' said Lisha, emerging from the cabin. 'All aboard for Voznesenskoye and home-brew.'

Untwisting its paddle, the *Cow-Wheat* was gaining speed. The engines worked up an oily clank, a rustle, a whistle, a wind. We flew through the darkness, cutting corners, kicking aside beacons, spar buoys, and red lights. The water foamed beneath the paddles, flying backward like a bird's gilded wing. The moon plunged through black whirlpools. 'The fairway of the Volga is tortuous,' I remembered a phrase from a schoolbook; 'it abounds in shoals . . .' Korostelyov shuffled to and fro on the bridge, blue skin clung gleaming to his cheekbones.

'Full steam ahead,' he said into the speaking-tube.

'Aye aye, sir,' came a muffled voice from the unseen.

'A bit more speed.'

Silence from below.

'We shall blow up,' stated the voice, after a pause.

The torch was torn from the masthead and slithered over a convulsed wave. The steamer tilted, the shudder of an explosion passed through the hull. We were flying through the murk, headlong. On shore a rocket soared, and shots from a three-inch gun struck us. A shell whistled through the masts. The cook's boy, who was lugging a tea-urn up on deck, raised his head. The tea-urn slipped from his hands, clumped down the stairway, burst, and a gleaming stream shot down the grimy steps. The cook's boy grinned, crouched down on the steps, and went to sleep. From his mouth came the deathly smell of home-brew. Below, amid oily cylinders, the stokers, bare to the waist, were yelling, waving their arms about, rolling on the floor, their distorted faces reflected in the pearly gleam of the shafts. The crew of the *Cow-Wheat* was drunk. Alone the helmsman stood firm at his wheel. He turned, perceiving me.

'Jew,' said the helmsman to me, 'what will come of the children?'

'What children?'

'The children are getting no schooling,' said the helmsman, spinning his wheel. 'The children will all turn out thieves.'

He brought his blue leaden cheekbones close to me and ground his teeth. His jaws grated like millstones; you felt his teeth were being ground to sand.

'I'll bite you to death.'

I edged back from him. Lisha was passing along the deck.

'What will become of us, Lisha?'

'He'll get us there, I reckon,' said the red-haired peasant, and sat down on a bench to rest his legs.

He was put ashore at Voznesenskoye. We found no temple there, no lights, no merry-go-round. The sloping shore was dark, covered up with low sky. Lisha sank into the darkness. When he had been away for more than an hour he suddenly loomed up at the water's edge laden with petrol-cans. With him was a pock-marked peasant-woman, shapely as a horse.

A child's blouse, much too small for her, dragged her breasts together. Some sort of dwarf in a sharp-pointed padded hat and tiny shoes, his mouth wide open, stood by her, watching us as we loaded.

'Plum brandy,' said Lisha, placing the cans on the table. 'The plummiest of home-brew going.'

And then our spectral ship set out on its wild return journey. We approached Baronsk toward daybreak. The river stretched limitless, water trickled down from the bank leaving a trail of dark satiny shadow. A pink ray pierced the mist that hung on scraps of bushes. The windowless painted walls of the barns, their slender spires, turned slowly and began to float toward us. We steamed up to Baronsk amid peals of song. Seletsky had cleared his throat with a bottle of the plummiest home-brew going, and was in fine voice. He worked in a bit of everything: Mussorgsky's flea, Mephistopheles' laughter, the demented miller's aria that goes 'I am no miller, a raven am I . . .'

Barefooted, Korostelyov lay bent over the edge of the bridge. His head with its closed eyelids swayed, his gashed face was thrown up to the sky, and a vague childish smile wandered over it. He came to as we were reducing speed.

'Alyosha,' said Korostelyov into the speaking tube, 'full steam ahead.'

And we drove at full speed into the landing-stage. The plank we had crushed on leaving flew to pieces. The engines were stopped just in time.

'You see, he brought us back,' said Lisha, appearing at my side. 'And you, friend, worried all the time.'

Ashore some of Chapayev's machine-gun carts were already drawn up. Rainbow stripes darkened and grew cool on the bank just abandoned by the water. By the landing-stage lay cartridge-boxes thrown down on previous arrivals. On one of the boxes, in an unbelted shirt and a tall Caucasian fur cap, sat Makeyev, commander of one of Chapayev's detachments. Korostelyov went over to him, his arms spread wide.

'I've played the fool again, Tino,' he said with his childish smile. 'Used up all the fuel . . .'

Makeyev sat sideways on the box, tufts of his fur cap hung around the browless yellow arches of his eyes, a Mauser with an unpainted butt lay on his knees. He fired without turning around, and missed.

'Well now!' babbled Korostelyov, radiant. 'Fancy losing your temper like that!' He spread his skinny arms still wider. 'I'm really surprised!'

Makeyev sprang up, spun around, and discharged all the bullets from the Mauser. The shots rapped hurriedly. Korostelyov wanted to say something more, but couldn't manage it. He gave a sigh and fell on his knees. He sank toward the felloes, the wheels of the machine-gun carts. His face flew to pieces, and milky strips of skull fastened on the felloes. Makeyev, bending down, was jerking the last jammed bullet from the chamber.

'They've had their fun,' he said, surveying the Red Army men and all the rest of us who had crowded together by the gangway.

Lisha, bobbing down, trotted past with a horse blanket in his arms and threw it over Korostelyov, who lay there lengthy as a felled tree. Occasional shots rang out on the steamer: running about the deck, the Chapayev boys were arresting the crew. By the rail the peasant woman, her palm to her pock-marked face, was looking with screwed-up, unseeing eyes at the shore.

'You too,' Makeyev said to her, 'I'll teach you to waste fuel.'

One by one the sailors were led ashore. Behind the barns they were met by the Germans who had come sprinkling from their houses. Karl Biedermeyer stood among his compatriots. War had reached his threshold.

That day we had a lot of work to do. The large village of Friedenthal came for wares. A chain of camels lay down by the water. In the distance, on the colourless tin of the horizon, windmills turned.

By dinnertime we had poured Friedenthal grain into the barge. Toward evening Malyshev sent for me. He was washing on the deck of the *Tupitsyn*. A disabled soldier with a pinned-up sleeve was pouring water over him from a pitcher. Malyshev snorted, grunted, put his cheeks under the stream. Drying himself with a towel, he said to his assistant, obviously continuing a conversation already begun:

'Quite right. It's all very well to be a fine fellow three times over, to have spent time in hermitages, to have sailed the White Sea, to be a desperate chap generally; but please don't waste fuel . . .'

Malyshev and I went into the cabin. There I stacked data around myself and started taking down a telegram to Ilyich:

'Moscow. The Kremlin. Lenin.'

In the telegram we reported the dispatch to the proletariat of St Petersburg and Moscow of the first trainloads of wheat: two trains with twenty thousand poods of grain in each.

1920–1928

Guy de Maupassant

IN the winter of 1916 I found myself in St Petersburg with a forged passport and not a cent to my name. Alexey Kazantsev, a teacher of Russian literature, took me into his house.

He lived on a yellow, frozen, evil-smelling street in the Peski district. The miserable salary he received was padded out a bit by doing translations from the Spanish. Blasco Ibáñez was just becoming famous at that time.

Kazantsev had never so much as passed through Spain,

but his love for that country filled his whole being. He knew every castle, every garden, and every river in Spain. There were many other people huddling around Kazantsev, all of them, like myself, flung out of the round of ordinary life. We were half-starved. From time to time the yellow press would publish, in the smallest print, unimportant news-items we had written.

I spent my mornings hanging around the morgues and police stations.

Kazantsev was happier than any of us, for he had a country of his own – Spain.

In November I was given the chance to become a clerk at the Obukhov Mills. It was a rather good position, and would have exempted me from military service.

I refused to become a clerk.

Even in those days, when I was twenty years old, I had told myself: better starve, go to jail, or become a tramp than spend ten hours every day behind a desk in an office.

There was nothing particularly laudable in my resolve, but I have never broken it and I never will. The wisdom of my ancestors was firmly lodged in my head: we are born to enjoy our work, our fights, and our love; we are born for that and for nothing else.

Listening to my bragging, Kazantsev ruffled the short yellow fluff on the top of his head. The horror in his stare was mixed with admiration.

At Christmas-time we had luck. Bendersky the lawyer, who owned a publishing house called 'Halcyon', decided to publish a new edition of Maupassant's works. His wife Raïsa tried her hand at the translation, but nothing came of her lofty ambition.

Kazantsev, who was known as a translator of Spanish, had been asked whether he could recommend someone to assist Raïsa Mikhaylovna. He told them of me.

The next day, in someone else's coat, I made my way to

the Bendersky's. They lived at the corner of the Nevsky and the Moyka, in a house of Finland granite adorned with pink columns, crenellations, and coats-of-arms worked in stone.

Bankers without a history and catapulted out of nowhere, converted Jews who had grown rich selling materials to the army, they put up these pretentious mansions in St Petersburg before the war.

There was a red carpet on the stairs. On the landings, upon their hind legs, stood plush bears. Crystal lamps burned in their open mouths.

The Benderskys lived on the second floor. A high-breasted maid with a white cap on her head opened the door. She led me into a drawing-room decorated in the old Slav style. Blue paintings by Roerich depicting prehistoric stones and monsters hung on the walls. On stands in the corners stood ancestral icons.

The high-breasted maid moved smoothly and majestically. She had an excellent figure, was near-sighted and rather haughty. In her open grey eyes one saw a petrified lewdness. She moved slowly. I thought: when she makes love she must move with unheard-of agility. The brocade portiere over the doorway suddenly swayed, and a black-haired woman with pink eyes and a wide bosom entered the room. It was easy to recognize in Raïsa Bendersky one of those charming Jewesses who have come to us from Kiev and Poltava, from the opulent steppe-towns full of chestnut trees and acacias. The money made by their clever husbands is transformed by these women into a pink layer of fat on the belly, the back of the neck and the well-rounded shoulders. Their subtle sleepy smiles drive officers from the local garrisons crazy.

'Maupassant,' Raïsa said to me, 'is the only passion of my life.'

Trying to keep the swaying of her great hips under control, she left the room and returned with a translation of *Miss*

Harriet. In her translation not even a trace was left of Maupassant's free-flowing sentences with their fragrance of passion. Raïsa Bendersky took pains to write correctly and precisely, and all that resulted was something loose and lifeless, the way Jews wrote Russian in the old days.

I took the manuscript with me, and in Kazantsev's attic, among my sleeping friends, spent the night cutting my way through the tangled undergrowth of her prose. It was not such dull work as it might seem. A phrase is born into the world both good and bad at the same time. The secret lies in a slight, an almost invisible twist. The lever should rest in your hand, getting warm, and you can only turn it once, not twice.

Next morning I took back the corrected manuscript. Raïsa wasn't lying when she told me that Maupassant was her sole passion. She sat motionless, her hands clasped, as I read it to her. Her satin hands drooped to the floor, her forehead paled, and the lace between her constricted breasts danced and heaved.

'How did you do it?'

I began to speak of style, of the army of words, of the army in which all kinds of weapons may come into play. No iron can stab the heart with such force as a full stop put just at the right place. She listened with her head down and her painted lips half open. In her hair, pressed smooth, divided by a parting and looking like patent leather, shone a dark gleam. Her legs in tight-fitting stockings, with their strong soft calves, were planted wide apart on the carpet.

The maid, glancing to the side with her petrified wanton eyes, brought in breakfast on a tray.

The glassy rays of the Petersburg sun lay on the pale and uneven carpet. Twenty-nine volumes of Maupassant stood on the shelf above the desk. The sun with its fingers of melting dissolution touched the morocco backs of the books – the magnificent grave of a human heart.

Coffee was served in blue cups, and we started translating *Idyl*. Everyone remembers the story of the youthful, hungry carpenter who sucked the breast of the stout nursing-mother to relieve her of the milk with which she was overladen. It happened in a train going from Nice to Marseille, at noon on a very hot day, in the land of roses, the birthplace of roses, where beds of flowers flow down to the seashore.

I left the Benderskys with a twenty-five rouble advance. That night our crowd at Peski got as drunk as a flock of drugged geese. Between drinks we spooned up the best caviare, and then changed over to liver sausage. Half-soused, I began to berate Tolstoy.

'He turned yellow, your Count; he was afraid. His religion was all fear. He was frightened by the cold, by old age, by death; and he made himself a warm coat out of his faith.'

'Go on, go on,' Kazantsev urged, swaying his birdlike head.

We fell asleep on the floor beside our beds. I dreamed of Katya, a forty-year-old washerwoman who lived a floor below us. We went to her every morning for our hot water. I had never seen her face distinctly, but in my dream we did god-awful things together. We almost destroyed each other with kisses. The very next morning I couldn't restrain myself from going to her for hot water.

I saw a wan woman, a shawl across her chest, with ash-grey hair and labour-worn, withered hands.

From then on I took my breakfast at the Benderskys' every day. A new stove, herrings, and chocolate appeared in our attic. Twice Raïsa took me out in her carriage for drives to the islands. I couldn't prevent myself from telling her all about my childhood. To my amazement the story turned out to be quite sordid. From under her moleskin cowl her gleaming, frightened eyes stared at me. The rusty fringe of her eyelashes quivered with pity.

I met Raïsa's husband, a yellow-faced Jew with a bald skull

and a flat, powerful body that seemed always poised obliquely, ready for flight.

There were rumours about his being close to Rasputin. The enormous profits he made from war supplies drove him almost crazy, giving him the expression of a person with a fixed hallucination. His eyes never remained still: it seemed that reality was lost to him for ever. Raïsa was embarrassed whenever she had to introduce him to new acquaintances. Because of my youth I noticed this a full week later than I should have.

After the New Year Raïsa's two sisters arrived from Kiev. One day I took along the manuscript of *L'Aveu* and, not finding Raïsa at home, returned that evening. They were at dinner. Silvery, neighing laughter and excited male voices came from the dining-room. In rich houses without tradition dinners are always noisy. It was a Jewish noise, rolling and tripping and ending up on a melodious, singsong note. Raïsa came out to me in evening dress, her back bare. Her feet stepped awkwardly in wavering patent-leather slippers.

'I'm drunk, darling,' she said, and held out her arms, loaded with chains of platinum and emerald stars.

Her body swayed like a snake's dancing to music. She tossed her marcelled hair about, and suddenly, with a tinkle of rings, slumped into a chair with ancient Russian carvings. Scars glowed on her powdered back.

Women's laughter again came from the dining-room. Raïsa's sisters, with delicate moustaches and as full-bosomed and round-bodied as Raïsa herself, entered the room. Their busts jutted out and their black hair fluttered. Both of them had their own Benderskys for husbands. The room was filled with disjointed, chaotic feminine merriment, the hilarity of ripe women. The husbands wrapped the sisters in their sealskins and Orenburg shawls and shod them in black boots. Beneath the snowy visors of their shawls only painted glowing cheeks, marble noses, and eyes with their myopic Jewish glitter could be seen. After making some more happy noise they left for the theatre, where Chaliapin was singing *Judith*.

'I want to work,' Raïsa lisped, stretching her bare arms to me; 'we've skipped a whole week.'

She brought a bottle and two glasses from the dining-room. Her breasts swung free beneath the sacklike gown, the nipples rose beneath the clinging silk.

'It's very valuable,' said Raïsa, pouring out the wine. 'Muscatel '83. My husband will kill me when he finds out.'

I had never drunk Muscatel '83, and tossed off three glasses one after the other without thinking. They carried me swiftly away into alleys where an orange flame danced and sounds of music could be heard.

'I'm drunk, darling. What are we doing today?'

'Today it's *L'Aveu*. "The Confession", then. The sun is the hero of this story, *le soleil de France*. Molten drops of it pattering on the red-haired Céleste changed into freckles. The sun's direct rays and wine and apple-cider burnished the face of the coachman Polyte. Twice a week Céleste drove into town to sell cream, eggs, and chickens. She gave Polyte ten sous for herself and four for her basket. And every time Polyte would wink at the red-haired Céleste and ask: "When are we going to have some fun, *ma belle?*" – "What do you mean, Monsieur Polyte?" Jogging up and down on the box, the coachman explained: "To have some fun means . . . why, what the hell, to have some fun! A lad with a lass; no music necessary . . ."

"'I do not care for such jokes, Monsieur Polyte," replied Céleste, moving further away the skirts that hung over her mighty calves in red stockings.

'But that devil Polyte kept right on guffawing and coughing: "Ah, but one day we shall have our bit of fun, *ma belle*," while tears of delight rolled down a face the colour of brick-red wine and blood.'

I downed another glass of the rare muscatel. Raïsa touched

glasses with me. The maid with the stony eyes crossed the room and disappeared.

'*Ce diable de Polyte* . . . In the course of two years Céleste had paid him forty-eight francs; that is, two francs short of fifty! At the end of the second year, when they were alone in the carriage, Polyte, who had had some cider before setting out, asked her his usual question: "What about having some fun today, Mamselle Céleste?" And she replied, lowering her eyes: "I am at your disposal, Monsieur Polyte."'

Raïsa flung herself down on the table, laughing. '*Ce diable de Polyte* . . .'

'A white spavined mare was harnessed to the carriage. The white hack, its lips pink with age, went forward at a walking-pace. The gay sun of France poured down on the ancient coach, screened from the world by a weatherbeaten hood. A lad with a lass; no music necessary . . .'

Raïsa held out a glass to me. It was the fifth.

'*Mon vieux*, to Maupassant!'

'And what about having some fun today, *ma belle*?'

I reached over to Raïsa and kissed her on the lips. They quivered and swelled.

'You're funny,' she mumbled through her teeth, recoiling.

She pressed herself against the wall, stretching out her bare arms. Spots began to glow on her arms and shoulders. Of all the gods ever put on the crucifix, this was the most ravishing.

'Be so kind as to sit down, Monsieur Polyte.'

She pointed to an oblique blue armchair done in Slavonic style. Its back was constructed of carved interlacing bands with colourful pendants. I groped my way to it, stumbling as I went.

Night had blocked the path of my famished youth with a bottle of Muscatel '83 and twenty-nine books, twenty-nine bombs stuffed with pity, genius, and passion. I sprang up, knocking over the chair and banging against the shelf. The twenty-nine volumes crashed to the floor, their pages flew open, they fell on their edges . . . and the white mare of my fate went on at a walking-pace.

'You are funny,' moaned Raïsa.

I left the granite house on the Moyka between eleven and twelve, before the sisters and the husband returned from the theatre. I was sober and could have walked a chalk-line, but it was pleasanter to stagger, so I swayed from side to side, singing in a language I had just invented. Through the tunnels of the streets bounded by lines of street-lights the steamy fog billowed. Monsters roared behind the boiling walls. The roads amputated the legs of those walking on them.

Kazantsev was asleep when I got home. He slept sitting up, his thin legs extended in their felt boots. The canary fluff rose on his head. He had fallen asleep by the stove bending over a volume of *Don Quixote*, the edition of 1624. On the title-page of the book was a dedication to the Duc de Broglie. I got into bed quietly, so as not to wake Kazantsev; moved the lamp close to me and began to read a book by Edouard Maynial on Guy de Maupassant's life and work.

Kazantsev's lips moved; his head kept keeling over.

That night I learned from Edouard Maynial that Maupassant was born in 1850, the child of a Normandy gentleman and Laure Lepoitevin, Flaubert's cousin. He was twenty-five when he was first attacked by congenital syphilis. His productivity and *joie de vivre* withstood the onsets of the disease. At first he suffered from headaches and fits of hypochondria. Then the spectra of blindness arose before him. His sight weakened. He became suspicious of everyone, unsociable, and pettily quarrelsome. He struggled furiously, dashed about the Mediterranean in a yacht, fled to Tunis, Morocco, Central Africa . . . and wrote ceaselessly. He attained fame, and at forty years of age cut his throat; lost a great deal of blood, yet lived through it. He was then put away in a madhouse. There he crawled about on his hands and knees, devouring his own excrement. The last line in his hospital report read: *Monsieur de Maupassant va s'animaliser.* He died at the age of forty-two, his mother surviving him.

I read the book to the end and got out of bed. The fog came close to the window, the world was hidden from me. My heart contracted as the foreboding of some essential truth touched me with light fingers.

Oil

... LOTS of news, as ever. Shabsovich has been awarded a prize for his work at the refinery; he now walks about got up foreign style, and his chief has been promoted. Hearing of the new appointment, everyone saw the light: the lad had grown up. On account of this I have stopped going around with him. 'Having grown up,' the lad feels he knows a truth that is concealed from us ordinary mortals, and has become so 100-per cent and orthodox (ortho*box*, as Kharchenko says) that you can't budge him an inch. When we ran into one another a couple of days ago he asked me why I didn't acknowledge his greeting. I replied: 'Who is one supposed to be greeting, him or Soviet power?' He got it, wriggled, said 'Ring me up some time ...' His better half immediately sniffed this out. Yesterday the phone went: 'Claudia my dear, we now have excellent connexions; if you need anything in the way of lingerie ...' I replied that I hoped to see the World Revolution in on my own clothes-ration.'

And now about me. You must know that I am office-head of the Oil Syndicate. Hints were thrown out some time ago, but I kept turning the job down. My reasons: no gift for office work, and besides, I wanted to enrol at the Industrial Academy. The question came before the bureau four times;

I had to agree in the end, and now I'm not sorry. From where I am I get a clear picture of the whole set-up; I've managed to get a thing or two done, organized an expedition to our part of Sakhalin Island, put some zip into the prospecting; I take a lot of interest in the Oil Institute. Zinaida is with me. She is well, having a baby soon, been through a lot. She didn't tell her Max Alexandrovich (Max and Moritz, I call him) about her pregnancy till it was fairly far gone, in the fourth month. He pretended to be thrilled to death, planted an icy kiss on Zinaida's brow and then let it be known that he was on the threshold of a great scientific discovery, that his thoughts were far removed from ordinary existence, that it was impossible to imagine anyone more unsuited to family life than he, Max Alexandrovich Sholomovich; but, of course, he wouldn't hesitate a moment to give up everything, and so on and so forth. Zinaida, being a woman of the twentieth century, shed a few tears, but didn't give way. She couldn't sleep all night, kept tossing and turning. At the crack of dawn, her hair anyhow, looking terrible, in an old skirt, she dashed off to Max's institute, begged him to forget what she had said the day before; she would get rid of the child, but would never forgive people for what had happened. All this is going on in the corridor of the Institute, people all over the place. Max and Moritz blushes and blenches, mumbles:

'We must get together some time and talk it over . . .'

Zinaida didn't finish listening, flew to me and declared:

'I shan't go to work tomorrow!'

I blew up, didn't consider it necessary to control myself, and gave her a proper telling-off. Just think, the girl's in her thirties, no beauty by any means, any ordinary decent fellow wouldn't look at her twice, and here this Max and Moritz turns up (and it wasn't so much in *her* he was interested as in her foreignness, her aristocratic forebears), and gets her pregnant. Very well, hang on, then, and give it a chance to grow; Jewish half-castes often turn out fine, as we know –

just look at the specimen Anya produced – and when should one bear children if not now, when the abdominal muscles are working and one can still give the breast? To everything the same answer: 'I can't bear my child to have no father'; i.e. a hang-over from the nineteenth century, papa the general will emerge from his study with an icon and curse her (or is it without an icon? – I don't know how they did the cursing in those days); the maids will cart the infant off to the Foundling Home or into the country to a fostermother.

'Fiddlesticks, Zina!' I say to her, 'other days, other ways. We'll manage without Max and Moritz.'

I hadn't finished saying my say when I was called to a meeting. At that time the question of Victor Andreyevich was very much in the air. And now we were faced by the Central Committee's decision that, instead of the former version of the Five-Year Plan, oil-extraction in 1932 should be brought up to forty million tons. The materials were handed over to the planners, i.e. to Victor Andreyevich, to be worked up. He shuts himself up in his office, then calls me in and shows me a letter he has written. Addressed to the Presidium of the Supreme Economic Council. Contents: I divest myself of responsibility for the planning department. I regard the figure of forty million tons as so much eyewash. It is proposed to get more than a third from unprospected regions, which means counting chickens not merely before they're hatched but even before they're laid. Furthermore, from the three cracking-plants at work today we are, according to the new proposal, jumping to a hundred and twenty in the last year of the Plan. And this with a deficit of metal and the fact that we've still not acquired the cracking process. The letter ended: Like all mortals, I am all for high rates of production, but my sense of duty, etc., etc. I read the letter. He asks:

'Shall I send it or not?'

I say:

'Victor Andreyevich, I just can't accept your reasons or your whole attitude, but I don't consider myself entitled to advise anyone to keep his views dark.'

So he sent the letter off. The Supreme Economic Council went up in the air. A meeting was called. Bagrinovsky came from the Council. On the wall they put up a map of the Soviet Union showing the new oil wells, the run-through plants, the pipes for crude and refined oil; as Bagrinovsky said:

'A country with a new blood-circulation.'

At the meeting young engineers of the 'omnivorous' variety demanded that Victor Andreyevich should be forced to his knees. I made a speech lasting forty-five minutes. 'Not doubting the knowledge and goodwill of Professor Klossovsky and even bowing before them, we reject the fetichism of the figures of which he is captive.' That's the idea I was defending.

'Let us reject the multiplication table as a guide to statesmanship. Merely on the figures, was it possible to say that we should fulfil the Five-Year Plan as far as crude oil was concerned in two and a half years? Was it possible, just going by the figures, to say that from 1931 onward we should increase our exports ninefold and reach second place after the United States?'

Muradyan spoke after me, criticizing the proposed lie of the Caspian-Moscow pipeline. Victor Andreyevich was silently taking notes. On his cheeks an elderly pinkness; you could see the veins blushing. I felt sorry for him, didn't stay to the end and went off to my own quarters. Zinaida was still sitting in the study, her hands clasped.

'Are you going to have the child,' I asked, 'or aren't you?'

She looks without seeing, her head waggles. She speaks, and there is no sound in her words.

'There are two of us, Claudia,' she says, 'I and my grief, which has been stuck on my back like a hump. And how quickly one forgets everything: already I can't remember how people live without unhappiness.'

She says this, her nose poking out even more than usual and quite red, her peasant cheekbones (aristocrats have cheekbones like that, you know) jutting out all over the place. Max and Moritz, I think to myself, wouldn't be all that enthusiastic if he saw you like this. I lost my temper, hustled her into the kitchen, and made her peel potatoes.

Don't laugh. If you come, I'll make you peel potatoes too. Such a short time-limit has been set for planning the Orsky Factory that the design-room and the draughtsmen are busy day and night. For dinner Vasilisa does them potatoes and herring, makes them an omelette – and at it again. So Zinaida goes into the kitchen. A moment later I hear a cry. I rush in: Zinaida's on the floor; no pulse, eyes showing the whites. We had an awful time with her, Victor Andreyevich, Vasilisa, and I. We sent for the doctor. She came to in the night, touched my hand – you know the way Zina is, her terrific tenderness. I could see that she had been through hell during those hours, and it might start all over again. There was no time to be lost.

'Zina,' I say to her, 'we'll ring up Rose Mikhaylovna.' (She continues to be our court-consultant in such matters.) 'Ring her up and tell her that you've changed your mind, that you won't be coming to see her after all. Shall I ring her up?'

She made a sign meaning: Yes, go and ring her up. On the sofa next to her sat Victor Andreyevich, feeling her pulse non-stop. I went out, and on the way I heard him say:

'I am sixty-five, Zina. On the ground my shadow is growing weaker and weaker. I am a learned, elderly fellow, and God' (we must keep dragging God in!) 'has so arranged things that the last five years of my life have coincided with this ... this ... you know, the Five-Year Plan. Now till the day I die I shall have no time to draw breath, to think of myself. And if of an evening a daughter didn't come and pat me on the shoulder, if sons didn't write me letters, I should be more melancholy that I can say. Have the child, Zina, and Claudia Pavlovna and I will treat it as our own.'

The old man mumbles on. I ring up Rose Mikhaylovna and say that you see, my sweet Rose Mikhaylovna, Zina promised to come tomorrow, but she's changed her mind. A buoyant voice in return:

'That's champion, her changing her mind; perfectly wizard!'

Our court-lady is always the same: a pink silk blouse, an English skirt, well curled, showers, physical jerks, admirers.

We took Zina home. I tucked her up warmly in bed and made some tea. We slept together – shed a few tears, remembered things best forgotten, talked everything over, you know, mingling our tears, and finally went to sleep. My 'demon' was sitting quietly at work, translating a technical book from the German. You wouldn't recognize the 'demon' any more, Dasha; he's drawn in his horns, gone all hunched up, quieted down completely. It rather worries me. All day he slaves away at the State Plan, and all the evening he's doing his translations.

'Zina's having her baby,' I tell him. 'What shall we call the boy?' (It definitely won't be a girl.) We decided on Ivan; far too many Georges and Leonids about. He will probably be a rather horrid little boy with sharp teeth, enough teeth for sixty. We've produced enough petrol for him; he'll be driving his girl-friends to Yalta or Batum; we have to make do with the Sparrow Hills. Good-bye, Dasha. The 'demon' is writing separately. How are things with you?

Claudia

P.S. I'm scribbling this at work. A tremendous racket overhead, the plaster flaking from the ceiling. It appears our building is still firm on its pins; to the original four stories we're adding four more. Moscow is all torn to bits; nothing but trenches, tubes, and bricks all over the place, trainlines entangled, an elephant's trunk is tossing imported machinery about, they are ramming and rattling, there's a smell of tar, smoke billowing just like a house on fire. Yesterday I saw a young fellow on Varvarskaya Square, his red close-shaven head shining, no belt to his jacket, sandals on his bare feet. The two of us were hopping from one bit of dry land to another, from hillock to hillock, clambering out of holes and falling in again.

'This is what it's like now the battle's started,' he said to me. 'There's a regular front in Moscow now, miss; a real battlefield.'

He had a kind mug, and was smiling like a child. I can still picture him.

Dante Street

FROM five to ten the groans of love used to send our hotel, the Hôtel Danton, soaring through the air. Experts were at work in the bedrooms. Arriving in France convinced that the nation had gone to the dogs, I was not a little surprised by these labours of love. In our country a woman is not brought to such white heat; far from it. My neighbour, Jean Biénal, once said to me:

'*Mon vieux*, in the thousand years of our history we have created woman, cooking, and literature. No one can deny us those achievements.'

In the matter of getting to know about France, Jean Biénal, dealer in second-hand cars, did more for me than the books I read and the towns I visited. At our first meeting he asked me about my restaurant, my café, the brothel I went to. My replies horrified him.

'*On va refaire votre vie.*'

And so we did. We started dining at the place opposite the *Halles aux vins* where cattle-dealers and wine-merchants took their meals. Country wenches in flapping slippers would serve us lobsters in red sauce, roast hare stuffed with garlic and truffles, wine unobtainable elsewhere. Biénal did the ordering, and I did the paying; but I only paid what the French pay. It wasn't cheap, but it was the proper price. And I paid the same price at the brothel near the Gare Saint-Lazare patronized by a number of senators. It cost Biénal more trouble to introduce me to the inmates of this house than if I had wanted to attend a sitting of parliament when a ministry was being thrown out. We used to finish the evening at the Porte Maillot in a café where boxing-match promoters and racing motorists forgather. My mentor belonged to the half of the nation that deals in motor cars; the other half exchanges them. He was an agent for Renault and did business with Balkan countries, those most ambiguous of countries, and above all with Rumanian men of affairs, those dirtiest of men of affairs. In his free time Biénal would teach me the art of buying a second-hand car. For this purpose, according to him, it was necessary to make one's way to the Riviera toward the tail-end of the season, when the English were dispersing, abandoning in garages cars that had seen only two or three months' service. Biénal himself used to ride about in a battered Renault which he drove as a Samoyed drives a dog-team. On Sundays we used to cover in this jolting conveyance the 120 kilometres to Rouen to eat duck which they there roast in its own gore. We would be accompanied by Germaine, who sold gloves in an establishment on the rue Royale. Her and Biénal's days were Wednesday and Sunday. She would arrive at five o'clock. A moment later their room would resound with growls, the thud of falling bodies, cries of fright; and then the woman's tender death-agony would begin:

'Oh, Jean . . .'

I used to calculate to myself: Well, now Germaine has gone in, she has closed the door behind her, they have exchanged kisses, the girl has taken her hat and gloves off and put them on the table; and according to my calculations they had no time left. No time to undress in. Without having uttered a single word they would be bouncing about in their sheets like a couple of hares. Having groaned awhile, they would shriek with laughter and prattle of their affairs. I knew about this all that a neighbour can know who lives on the other side of a board partition. Germaine had differences with Monsieur Henriche, the manager of the gloveshop. Her parents lived at Tours, and she used to go and stay with them. One Saturday she bought herself a fur boa, another Saturday she saw *La Bohème* at the Opera. Monsieur Henriche made his saleswomen wear severe tailor-mades. Monsieur Henriche had given an English finish to Germaine; she was now one of those flat-bosomed business-women, brisk, tightly curled, painted with flaming brown paint; but her rounded ankle, her low rapid laughter, the gaze of her keen and flashing eyes, and that death-agony groan (*oh, Jean!*) – all this was Biénal's preserve.

Through the smoky gold of the Parisian evening Germaine's strong slender body surged along before us. Laughing, she would throw back her head and press her nimble pink fingers to her breast. The cockles of my heart used to warm at those hours. There is no solitude more deadly than solitude in Paris.

For all those who come from afar this town is a form of exile, and it used to occur to me that our need for Germaine was greater than Biénal's. With this thought in my mind I travelled south to Marseille.

After a month in Marseille I returned to Paris. I waited for Wednesday, to hear Germaine's voice.

Wednesday passed, and no one disturbed the silence behind

the wall. Biénal had changed his day. On Thursday I heard a woman's voice at the customary five o'clock. Biénal gave his visitor time to take off her hat and gloves. Germaine had changed her day, and she had also changed her voice. No longer was there a jerky, pleading *oh, Jean* . . . and then silence, the menacing silence of someone else's happiness. Now this was replaced by a hoarse domestic bustle, by guttural exclamations. The new Germaine grated her teeth, plumped down on the couch, and in the intervals held forth in a thick drawling voice. She said nothing of Monsieur Henriche, and having growled till seven prepared to depart. I half-opened the door to get a glimpse of her, and saw coming along the corridor a mulatto with a cockscomb of horsehair and large, protuberant, and sagging breasts. The mulatto, shuffling her feet in their worn and heelless slippers, passed along the corridor. I knocked on Biénal's door. He was sprawled on the bed in his shirt-sleeves; crumpled, grey, wearing socks threadbare with washing.

'*Mon vieux*, have you pensioned Germaine off?'

'*Cette femme est folle*,' he replied, and started to hunch up. 'The simple fact that on earth there is winter and summer, beginning and end, that after winter comes summer and contrariwise – all this does not concern Mademoiselle Germaine. Such things are not for her. She piles a burden on your back and insists that you should bear it . . . but where to? No one knows save Mademoiselle Germaine.'

Biénal sat up on the bed, his trousers bagged around his skinny legs, the pale skin on his head glimmered through the matted hair, the triangle of his moustache quivered. Some Mâcon at four francs a litre put my friend to rights. Over dessert he shrugged his shoulders and said, replying to his own thoughts:

'Besides eternal love there are on earth also Rumanians, bills of exchange, bankrupts, broken-down motor-cars. *Oh, j'en ai plein le dos* . . .'

Over a glass of cognac at the Café de Paris he cheered up. We were sitting on the terrace beneath the white awning. Wide stripes lay across it. Mingled with the electric stars, crowds flowed along the pavement. Opposite us there stopped a car that stretched this way and that like a mine shaft, and from it emerged an Englishman and a woman in a sable mantelet. She swept past us in a warm cloud of perfume and fur, unnaturally elongated, with a little shining porcelain head. On seeing her, Biénal jerked forward, put out his leg in its shabby trousering and gave a wink as one winks at girls from the rue de la Gaîté. The woman smiled with the corner of her carmined mouth, nodded her tightly bound pink head almost imperceptibly and, swaying and dragging her serpentine body, disappeared. After her, crackling, strode the unbending Englishman.

'*Ah, canaille!*' said Biénal after them. 'A couple of years ago she was satisfied with an *apéritif.*'

We parted late. On the Saturday I had arranged with myself to go to Germaine's place, invite her to the theatre, go with her to Chartres if she felt inclined; but it so happened that I saw them – Biénal and his erstwhile girl-friend – earlier than that. On the evening of the following day the police occupied the entrances to the Hôtel Danton, and their blue cloaks swung wide in our vestibule. They let me pass on ascertaining that I was one of Mme Truffeau's lodgers. I found gendarmes at my threshold. The door to Biénal's room was ajar. Biénal lay on the floor in a pool of blood, his eyes glazed and half-closed. The stamp of death in the streets was growing cold on him. He had had his throat cut, had my friend Biénal; well and truly cut. Germaine in her tailor-made and a little hat crushed in at the sides was sitting at the table. Greeting me she bent her head, and with her head the feather on her little hat bowed too.

All this occurred at six in the evening, at the hour of love; in each room there was a woman. Before departing – half-dressed, with stockings to their thighs like medieval pages – they were hastily piling on the rouge and sketching their mouths in red. Doors were open; men in unlaced shoes had been lined up in the corridor. In the room occupied by the wrinkled Italian racing-cyclist a barefooted little girl was weeping into a pillow. I made my way down to warn Mme Truffeau; the girl's mother sold newspapers in the rue Saint-Michel. In the little office the old women from our street, the rue Dante, had already gathered: greengrocers and janitresses, vendors of roast chestnuts and hot potatoes; mounds of wry and goitrous flesh, bewhiskered, stertorous of breath, with wall-eyes and purple blotches.

'*Voilà qui n'est pas gai,*' I said as I went in. '*Quel malheur!*'

'*C'est l'amour, monsieur. Elle l'aimait . . .*'

From beneath the lace Mme Truffeau's bosom bulged; her elephantine legs bestrode the room, her eyes flashed.

'*L'amore,*' said like an echo behind her Signora Rocca, keeper of a restaurant on Dante Street. '*Iddio castiga coloro che non conoscono l'amore . . .*'

The old crones had bunched up and were all muttering together. A variolous flame set their cheeks on fire, their eyes were starting from the sockets.

'*L'amour,*' repeated Mme Truffeau, advancing upon me, '*c'est une grosse affaire, l'amour.*'

The shepherd's horn of the ambulance sounded in the street. Accustomed hands bore the murdered man down the stairs. He had become a mere number, had my friend Biénal; he had lost his name in the tide-run of Paris. Signora Rocca went over to the window and inspected the corpse. She was pregnant, her belly protruding menacingly; silk lay on her straddled hips; the sun slid over her yellow, puffy face and soft yellow hair.

'*Iddio,*' affirmed Signora Rocca, '*tu non perdoni coloro che non amano.*'

Darkness was falling on the worn network of the Latin

Quarter; the squat crowds scuttled into its crevices, a burning breath of garlic wafted from its courtyards. Dusk covered the house of Mme Truffeau, its Gothic façade with two windows, the remnants of turrets and volutes, ivy that had turned to stone.

Here dwelt Danton a century and a half ago. From his window he had seen the Conciergerie, the bridges cast lightly across the Seine, the array of blind-eyed hovels pressed close to the river; the same breath had risen to him. Jostled by the wind, the rusty trusses and the inn-signs creaked.

The End of the Old Folks' Home

DURING the famine no one lived better in Odessa than the inmates of the poorhouse by the Second Jewish Cemetery. At some time or other Kofman the cloth-merchant had erected the poorhouse next to the cemetery wall in memory of his wife Isabella. This propinquity caused a lot of amusement at the Café Franconi, but Kofman proved right. After the Revolution the old men and women sheltering next door to the cemetery were able to monopolize the jobs of grave-diggers, cantors, women who washed corpses. Furthermore, they went into business with an oak coffin with a pall and silver tassels, hiring it out to folk in need.

At that time timber was not to be had in Odessa for love or money, and the coffin for hire did not stand idle. The deceased lay in the oak box the allotted time in his home and at the service; but into the grave he was lowered in his shroud. This was in accordance with a forgotten Jewish law.

The sages taught that it was not fitting to hinder the worms from uniting with the carrion, for it was unclean. 'From the earth thou camest, and to the earth thou shalt return.'

Because this ancient law had been revived, the old folk

received on top of their rations an addition such as no one dreamed of in those years. Of an evening they caroused in Zalman Krivoruchka's wine-cellar, and they sold their neighbours the scraps left over from their feasts.

Their well-being was not disturbed until the rising occurred in the German colonies. In the battle the Germans killed Hersch Lugovoy, commander of the garrison, and he was buried with full honours. The troops arrived at the cemetery with brass bands, field kitchens, and machine-guns on carts. By the open grave speeches were made and oaths pledged.

'Comrade Hersch,' cried Lyonka Broitman the Divisional Commander, straining himself, 'Comrade Hersch entered the Russian Social-Democratic Workers' Party of Bolsheviks in 1911, where he carried on propaganda work and acted as liaison agent. Comrade Hersch suffered repressive measures together with Sonya Yonavskaya, Ivan Sokolov, and Monoszon in 1913 in the town of Nikolayev.'

Arye-Leib, elder of the poorhouse, stood ready with his mates. Lyonka had barely concluded his farewell words when the old men began turning the coffin on its side so as to roll out the flag-covered corpse. Lyonka gave Arye-Leib a quiet poke with his spur.

'Move off,' he said, 'move farther away. Hersch was a faithful servant of the Republic.'

Before the eyes of the petrified old men Lugovoy was interred together with the oak coffin, the tassels, and the black pall, on which shields of David and a verse from an ancient Hebrew prayer for the dead were worked in silver.

'We are dead men,' said Arye-Leib to his mates after the funeral, 'we are in the hands of Pharaoh.'

And he dashed off to Broidin, the man in charge of the cemetery, with the request that timber should be issued for the construction of a new coffin and cloth to make a pall. Broidin promised to do what he could, and did nothing. His plans did not include enriching old men. In the office he said:

'It's for the municipal workers out of a job that my heart aches, not for those old speculators.'

Broidin promised all, and did nothing. At Zalman Krivoruchka's wine-cellar Talmudic curses showered on his head, and on the heads of the members of the Union of Municipal Workers. The old men cursed the marrow in the bones of Broidin and the members of the Union, the fresh seed in their wives' wombs, wishing each a different variety of paralysis and ulcer.

Their income was reduced. The ration now consisted of a blue broth in which fishbones floated. As second course there was pearl-barley gruel with not a drop of grease in it.

An old man of Odessa can eat any sort of broth, whatever it may have been brewed from, if only laurel leaf, garlic, and pepper have been included. But in the blue broth there was none of these things.

The Isabella Kofman Poorhouse shared the common fate. The fury of the famished aged rose, and fell again on the head of a person who least of all expected it. This person was none other than Dr Judith Shmaiser, who had come to the poorhouse to give smallpox injections.

The Provincial Executive Committee had published an order making inoculation for smallpox compulsory. Judith Shmaiser laid out her instruments on the table and lit her alcohol lamp. Outside the windows rose the emerald walls of the bushes in the cemetery. The little blue tongue of flame mingled with the lightning-flashes of June.

Nearest of all to Judith stood Meyer Endless, a thin old man, morosely watching her preparations.

'Just a little prick,' said Judith, and swung her tweezers. She started pulling from the enveloping rags the light-blue whipcord of his arm.

The old man jerked his arm back.

'There's nothing to prick.'

'It won't hurt,' cried Judith, 'it's not painful in the soft part.'

'I haven't no soft part,' said Meyer Endless. 'There ain't nothing to prick.'

He was seconded by a dull sobbing from the corner of the room. It was Doba-Leah, the former cook at circumcisions, who was sobbing. Meyer twisted his decayed cheeks.

'Life is a dungheap,' he mumbled, 'the world a brothel, and people a lot of crooks.'

The pince-nez on Judith's little nose swayed, her bosom bulged from her starched gown. She opened her mouth to explain the benefits of inoculation for smallpox, but she was halted by Arye-Leib, the elder of the poorhouse.

'Young lady,' said Arye-Leib, 'we were born by a mother just as you were. This woman, our mother, bore us that we should live, not that we should be tortured. She wished that we should live well, and she was right, as a mother can be. A man who lacks what Broidin lets him have, that man is unworthy of the stuff that went to his making. Your object, young lady, consists in inoculating smallpox, and you, with God's help, inoculate it. Our object consists in living our lives to the end, and not torturing it to the end; and we are not fulfilling that aim.'

Doba-Leah, a bewhiskered old woman with the face of a lion, on hearing these words started sobbing louder still. She sobbed in a bass voice.

'Life is a dungheap,' repeated Meyer Endless, 'and people a lot of crooks.'

The paralysed Simon-Wolf seized the steering-rod of his little carriage, and squealing and turning out his palms moved toward the door. His skullcap slipped from his swollen raspberry-coloured head.

After Simon-Wolf, snarling and grimacing, all thirty old men and women swooped out on to the main avenue. They brandished their crutches, yelling like hungry donkeys.

Seeing them, the watchman slammed the cemetery gates shut. The gravediggers raised their spades with earth and grass roots sticking to them, and stood thunderstruck.

At the uproar the bearded Broidin emerged, in his leather leggings and cycling-cap and docktailed jacket.

'Profiteer,' Simon-Wolf shouted at him, 'there's no place to prick us ... there's no flesh on our arms.'

Doba-Leah showed her teeth and growled. She started to steer the paralytic's carriage belligerently at Broidin. Arye-Leib began, as always, with allegories and parables that crept up from afar and toward an aim that not all could perceive.

He began with the parable of the Rabbi Hosea, who gave his property to his children, his heart to his wife, his fear to God, his taxes to Caesar, and kept for himself only a place beneath the olive tree where the sun as it set shone longer than anywhere else. From the Rabbi Hosea, Arye-Leib passed on to the subject of boards for a new coffin and the question of rations.

Broidin planted his legs in their leggings wide apart and listened, not raising his eyes. The brown barricade of his beard lay motionless on his new jacket; it seemed he was immersed in sad and placid thoughts.

'You will forgive me, Arye-Leib,' sighed Broidin, addressing the cemetery sage, 'you will forgive me if I say, Arye-Leib, that I cannot but see those who know what they are doing just as you know what you are doing.'

Here Broidin raised his eyes. In a trice they had filled with the white water of fury. The quivering hillocks of his pupils fastened on the old folk.

'Arye-Leib,' said Broidin in his powerful voice, 'read the telegrams from the Tartar Republic, where great quantities of Tartars seem to have lost their senses. Read the appeals of the toiling Petersburg proletariat who are waiting, hungry, by their lathes.'

'*I* have no time to wait,' Arye-Leib interrupted the overseer. 'I haven't any spare time.'

'There are people,' thundered Broidin, not listening, 'there are people who live worse than you, and there are thousands upon thousands of people who live worse than the people who live worse than you. You are sowing unpleasantness, Arye-Leib, and you will reap wind in the belly. You will be dead men, all of you, if I turn away from you. You will die if I go my way and you yours. You, Arye-Leib, will die. You, Simon-Wolf, will die; and you, Meyer Endless. But before you die, tell me – I am interested in the answer – have we by any chance got Soviet power, or haven't we? If we haven't, and I am mistaken, then take me along to Mr Berzon on the corner of De Ribas and Yekaterininskaya, where I worked all the years of my life as a waistcoat-maker. Tell me that I am mistaken, Arye-Leib.'

And the cemetery overseer went right up to the cripples. His quivering pupils dangled at them. They swept over the petrified and groaning herd like the beams of a searchlight, like tongues of flame. Broidin's leggings crackled, sweat seethed on his ploughed-up face. He stepped closer and closer to Arye-Leib and demanded an answer to the question whether or not he had been mistaken in thinking that Soviet power had already been installed.

Arye-Leib was silent. This silence might have been his ruin, had the barefooted Theo Stepun not appeared in his sailor shirt at the end of the avenue.

Theo had at some time or other been blown up by a shell near Rostov; he was convalescing in a hut next to the cemetery, carried a police whistle on an orange lanyard and a revolver that had lost its holster.

Theo was drunk. His forehead was revetted with stony curls. Beneath the curls a face with high cheekbones twisted spastically. He went over to where faded wreaths lay about Lugovoy's tomb.

'Where were you, Lugovoy,' Theo asked the dead man, 'when I was storming Rostov?'

The sailor ground his teeth, blew on his police whistle, and pulled the revolver from his belt. Its burnished muzzle flashed.

'Tsars have been knocked off their perches,' cried Theo, 'there are no more tsars. Let 'em lie uncoffined.'

The sailor squeezed his revolver. His breast was bare. On it the word 'Riva' was tattooed, and a dragon whose head curved toward Theo's nipple.

The gravediggers crowded around him with their spades raised. The women who washed corpses emerged from their cubbyholes and prepared to yell in unison with Doba-Leah. Wailing waves beat against the closed cemetery gates.

Relatives who had brought their late lamented on wheelbarrows demanded admittance. Paupers banged their crutches against the railings.

'Off their perches they've been knocked,' cried the sailor, and fired at the sky.

People came hopping and skipping along the avenue. Broidin was slowly going pallid. He raised his hand, agreed to all the poorhouse demanded, and turning soldier-fashion went off to his office. At the same moment the gates swung open. The relatives of the dead, pushing their little carts before them, trundled jauntily along the paths. Above the ready-dug tombs self-styled cantors sang '*El moley rachamim*' in piercing falsettos. That evening the victory was celebrated at Krivoruchka's, and Theo was stood three quarts of Bessarabian wine.

'*Hevel havolim*,' said Arye-Leib, touching glasses with the sailor, 'you're a pearl of a man, the sort it's possible to get on with . . . *Vehakol hevel*.'

The landlady, Krivoruchka's wife, was rinsing glasses behind the partition.

'If a Russian happens to have a good character,' observed

Madam Krivoruchka, 'then it's an absolute pleasure to meet him.'

Theo was helped outside between one and two in the morning.

'*Hevel havolim*,' he mumbled the ruinous and incomprehensible words as he wavered along Stepovaya Street, '*vehakol hevel* . . .'

Next day the old people at the poorhouse were given four lumps of sugar apiece and some meat to make borsch. In the evening they were taken to the theatre for a show got up by Social Security: *Carmen*. For the first time in their lives the old crocks and cripples saw the gilt tiers of the Odessa theatre, the velvet of its partitions, the oily gleam of its lustres. In the intervals they were given liver-sausage sandwiches.

Then they were taken back to the cemetery on an army lorry. Thundering and exploding, it forged its way through the silent streets. The old people fell asleep, their bellies bulging. They belched in their sleep, and satiety made them tremble like dogs that have run overmuch.

Next morning Arye-Leib rose from his slumbers before the others. He turned to the East to pray, and saw a notice pinned on the door. On the paper Broidin announced that the poorhouse was being closed for repairs, and that all the inmates must that day appear at the provincial Social Security department to register for such work as they were capable of.

The sun sailed over the top of the green cemetery grove. Arye-Leib raised his fingers to his eyes; a tear oozed from the quenched hollows.

The chestnut avenue gleamed its way toward the mortuary. The chestnuts were in bloom, and the trees bore tall white flowers along on their spread paws. A woman no one had seen before, in a shawl that caught her breasts tight, was busy in the mortuary. There everything had been done up fresh: the walls had been decorated with fir trees, the tables scoured. The woman was washing a dead infant. Nimbly she turned it from side to side, and the water flowed in a diamond stream down the hollow little spotted back.

Broidin in his leggings was sitting on the steps of the mortuary, looking like a man at rest. He took off his cap and wiped his forehead with a yellow handkerchief.

'I told Comrade Andreychik so at the Union,' sang the unknown woman's voice, 'we don't try to wriggle out of work. Let them argue our case at Yekaterinoslav. Yeka-terinoslav knows all about the work we does.'

'Make yourself at home, Comrade Blyuma; make yourself at home,' said Broidin peaceably, stowing his yellow hand-kerchief away in his pocket. 'I'm easy to get on with. Easy to get on with,' he repeated, and turned his sparkling eyes on Arye-Leib, who had dragged himself to the mortuary steps, 'just see that you don't cross me . . .'

Broidin had not finished his allocution when a jaunting-car drawn by a tall black horse pulled up at the gates and the manager of communal property in an open-necked shirt started to get out. Broidin helped him down and led him to the cemetery.

The quondam tailor's apprentice showed his superior officer around a hundred years of Odessa history asleep beneath the granite flagstones. He pointed out the monuments and vaults of the wheat exporters, ships' brokers, and business men who had built the Russian Marseille where once had stood the village of Hadjibey. They lay there facing the gates, Ash-kenazis, Hessens, and Efrussis, glossily finished misers, philo-sophical roisterers, creators of wealth and of Odessa anecdotes. There they lay beneath the monuments of pink marble and labradorite, secured by chains of chestnuts and acacias from the plebs pressed up against the walls.

'When they were alive they didn't let others have a decent life,' said Broidin, and banged a monument with his boot, 'and when they were dead they didn't let others have a decent death.'

Growing enthusiastic, he told the manager of communal property about his programme for redesigning the cemetery, his plan of campaign against the Burial Brotherhood.

'And *they* must be moved out,' said the manager, pointing to the paupers crowding at the gate.

'It's being done,' replied Broidin, 'little by little everything's being taken care of.'

'Well, keep at it,' said Mayorov the manager. 'You have things well under control, I see.'

His boot on the footboard of the jaunting-car, he remembered Theo.

'Who might that queer character happen to be?'

'A fellow who was too near a shell when it went off,' said Broidin, lowering his eyes, 'tends to get a bit out of hand in consequence. But now things have been explained to him he's full of apologies.'

'Head screwed on the right way,' said Mayorov, and drove off.

The tall horse bore him and the manager of the department of public welfare townwards. On their way they passed the old folk who had been evicted from the poorhouse. Limping, bowed beneath their bundles, they plodded along in silence. Bluff Red Army men were keeping them in line. The little carts of paralytics squeaked; the whistle of asthma, a humble gurgling issued from the breasts of retired cantors, jesters at weddings, cooks at circumcisions, and ancient shop-assistants.

The sun stood high in the sky, and its rays scorched the rags trailing along the road. Their path lay along a cheerless, parched, and stony highway, past huts of rammed clay, past stone-cluttered fields, past houses torn open by shells, past the Plague Mound. An unspeakably sorrowful road once led from the cemetery to Odessa.

1920–1929

Through the Fanlight

THERE'S a woman I knew – a Madam Kebchik. In her day, Madam Kebchik will assure you, she would never accept less than five roubles – not for anything in the world. Now in her apartment she had a family set-up, and in the apartment there were two girls – Marusya and Tamara. Marusya had more customers than Tamara.

One window of the girls' room looked on the street; the other – a fanlight just under the ceiling – had a view of the bathroom. I realized this, and said to Fanny Kebchik (her father's name was Joseph):

'Of an evening you'll put a ladder up to the little window in the bathroom. I'm going up the ladder to take a peek at Marusya when she's at home. Five roubles: is it a deal?'

Fanny said, What a spoilt fellow you are!, and we shook on it. Nowadays she didn't often get five roubles a time. When Marusya had guests I used to make the most of the little window. Everything was going along fine when one day I had a stupid accident.

There I was, standing on the ladder. As luck would have it, Marusya hadn't switched the light off. This time the caller was an agreeable, easily pleased, cheerful sort of chap with a long moustache of the innocent variety. He took his things off just as though he was in his own bedroom. He undid his collar, took a look in the glass, found a pimple under his moustache, gave it a thorough examination and squeezed it out with his hanky. He pulled off a boot and gave it the once-over too: anything wrong with the soles?

They kissed, got undressed, and smoked a cigarette apiece. I was just going to climb down again. And at that moment I felt the ladder slipping and swaying beneath me. I clutched at the window-frame, and my fist went through the glass. The ladder fell with a clatter. There I was, hanging right up at the ceiling. The apartment was in an uproar. In rushed Fanny, Tamara, and an official I'd never seen before in the uniform of the Finance Ministry. They helped me down; I was in a pitiful state. Into the bathroom came Marusya and her visitor – a lanky fellow he was. The girl looked at me closely, went all stiff, and said in quiet amazement:

'The beast! Oh, what a beast!'

She fell silent, looked around at us all with unseeing eyes, went over to the lanky individual, and for some reason or other kissed his hand, shedding a tear or two. Weeping, kissing his hand, she said:

'How sweet you are; goodness, how sweet!'

The lanky chap stood there looking a regular fool. My heart was pumping. I drove my nails into my palms and went off to Fanny's room.

A few minutes later Marusya knew all. All was known, and all forgotten. But what I was wondering is: Why was she kissing him?

'Madam Kebchik,' I said, 'put the ladder up for one last go. Ten roubles.'

'Not merely up the ladder, but up the pole!' said Madam, and we struck a bargain.

And there I was standing once more at the fanlight looking into the room, and what did I see? Marusya had wound her slim arms around her visitor. She was kissing him with long kisses, and tears were flowing from her eyes.

'Sweetheart,' she whispered, 'goodness, how sweet!' And gave herself with the passion of one in love. And her expression said that there was only one person to protect her in all the world: the lanky bloke.

And the lanky bloke wallowed in businesslike bliss.

1924

The Kiss

WITH a view to reorganizing our cadres, the General Staff sent us to Budyachi early in August. This place had been occupied by the Poles at the beginning of the war, and then retaken by our forces. The brigade entered the village at dawn. When I got there at noon the best billets had already been allotted, and all that was left for me was the school-master's house. In a low-ceilinged room, among tubs with fruit-bearing lemon trees, an old paralysed man sat in an armchair. On his head he wore a Tyrolean bonnet, and his white beard reached to his chest, which was sprinkled with tobacco ash. His eyes twitched, and he was stammering some sort of prayer.

When I had washed I went to H.Q. and didn't come back till after midnight. My orderly, Michael Surovtsev, a shrewd Orenburg Cossack, reported that besides the paralysed old man the household consisted of the schoolmaster's daughter, Elizabeth Tomilin, and the daughter's son, called Michael like my orderly and five years old. The young woman was the widow of an officer killed in the World War. She seemed respectable enough, but according to Surovtsev's information was quite prepared to be nice to a decent fellow.

'That can be fixed for you,' he said in conclusion, and made his way to the kitchen, whence the clatter of dishes soon reached me. The schoolmaster's daughter was helping him at his job. As they prepared the meal Surovtsev told her of my bravery, of how I had killed two Polish officers in single combat, adding that I was well considered by the Soviet higher-ups. The girl replied in a voice full of reserve. 'Where do you sleep?' asked Surovtsev as he left the kitchen. 'Bed down near him; we're live men, you know.' Then he brought in an enormous panful of fried eggs and put it on the table.

'She's biting,' he informed me as he settled down to eat. 'But she won't say nothing definite.'

At that moment we heard muffled rumours and scraping noises, a lumbering and surreptitious bustle. We hadn't had time to finish our fried eggs when through the house there tramped a procession of old men on crutches and old women with their heads tied up in rags. Little Michael's bed was transferred to the dining-room and placed in the shade of the lemon trees near grandfather's armchair. Our infirm hosts, determined to defend Elizabeth's honour, crouched against one another like a flock of ewes in a thunderstorm. They barricaded the door and played cards all night, scarcely daring to announce the stakes and trembling at the slightest noise. Tormented and muddled, I could not get to sleep on the other side of that door, and feverishly awaited the dawn.

Next morning, meeting the girl in the corridor, I hastened to inform her:

'You must know that I have a law degree, and am reckoned a highbrow.'

She stood before me numb with fright, her arms dangling, her slim body moulded by an old-fashioned dress. Her blue eyes, in which tears shone, widened as she fastened an unwavering gaze upon me.

Two days later we were friends.

The schoolmaster's family – decent, feeble folk they were – lived in boundless fear and ignorance. The Polish authorities had persuaded them that Russia, like Rome in its day, had gone down in flames and barbarism. A childlike and timid joy filled them when I started talking about the theatre, art, Lenin; about Moscow, where the future was beating on the door. Of an evening we were joined by a general or two, Bolsheviks of twenty-five, bearded and unkempt. We would smoke Muscovite cigarettes, eat meals that Elizabeth cooked

us from army rations, sing student songs. Leaning forward
in his armchair, the paralytic would listen avidly to us, and the
Tyrolean bonnet trembled in time with our songs. All the
time the old man was living in a vague hope, spontaneous
and violent. In order not to cloud his happiness, he tried to
tone down our bloodthirsty bravado, the loud-mouthed
simplicity that in those days we brought to the solution of
all world problems.

After the victory – so the family council decided – the
Tomilins would settle in Moscow. We would get a celebrated
professor to cure the old man, Elizabeth would study at the
University, and Michael would go to school. The future
seemed ours for the asking, the war like an impetuous pro-
logue to happiness, and happiness the hallmark of our character. All that remained to be defined were the details, and we
used to discuss them for nights on end, nights when the
candle-end was reflected in the opaque glass of the vodka-
bottle. Elizabeth, radiant, was our wordless audience. I had
never met so fanatical, emancipated and timid a creature.

Sometimes, in an old wagonette requisitioned in the Kuban,
the cunning Surovtsev would drive us to the hill where the
abandoned chateau of the Princess Gonsiorowski shone in the
flames of the setting sun. Thin, but tall and racy, the horses
ran cheerfully, obeying the red reins. An ear-ring swung carefree in Surovtsev's ear, and presently round towers rose above
a moat spread with a cloth of golden flowers. Against the sky
the tumbled walls traced a long curve swollen with crimson
blood; dog-roses hid the recesses, and a blue step, all that
remained of a staircase once trodden by the kings of Poland,
gleamed amid the brambles. Sitting on this step one evening,
I drew Elizabeth's face toward me and kissed her. She slowly
freed herself, stood up, and leaned against the wall, holding
on to it with both hands. Motionless she stood there, a mote-
specked sunbeam playing around her head. Then she shuddered, and raised her head as though to listen to a far-off

sound. Her fingers loosened themselves from the wall, and she started to run with swift and stumbling steps. I called to her, but there was no reply.

Down below, stretched out in the wagonette, Surovtsev was sleeping, his scarlet face shining in the sun.

That night, when all the household was asleep, I crept to Elizabeth's room. She was reading, holding the book at arm's length; and her hand on the table seemed inanimate. At my footsteps she rose from her chair.

'No,' she said, fixing her gaze on me. 'No, no, my darling.' And putting her long bare arms around my neck she kissed me with a silent, with an ever more violent, with an unending kiss. The ringing of the phone in the next room tore us apart. H.Q. was calling me.

'We are leaving,' came over the line. 'You are to report to the commander immediately.'

I ran hatless, sorting my papers on the way. Horses were being led out of stables; riders galloped past, yelling. The commander of the brigade, adjusting his cloak, informed us that the Poles had just pierced our lines in the region of Liublany. We had been ordered to effect a flanking movement, and the two regiments were to set out in an hour's time.

The old man had woken up, and was watching me uneasily through the leaves of the lemon-trees.

'Promise me that you'll come back,' he kept saying, and his head waggled.

Elizabeth, a fur coat thrown over her nightdress, came out on to the porch to say good-bye to us. In the darkness an unseen squadron of horses galloped madly past.

On the edge of the fields I turned around: leaning down to Michael she was buttoning his smock, and the flame of the lamp standing on the windowsill flowed over her gentle, bony nape.

After a forced march of one hundred kilometres we linked

up with the XIV Mounted Division, and withdrew fighting. We would sleep in the saddle. At the halts, dead with sleep, we would roll down on the ground, and the horses, tugging at the bridle, would drag us sleeping through the harvested fields. It was the beginning of autumn; the little noiseless Galician rains poured their waters down on us. Crouching one against the other, we were a silent and dishevelled crew. We wandered at random, described circles, plunging into the bag held by the Poles and struggling out again. We had lost all sense of time.

As I was settling down for the night in the church at Tochenko it didn't even occur to me that we were only ten kilometres from Budyachi. It was Surovtsev who came and reminded me.

'If only the horses wasn't fagged out, we could pop over,' he said with a smile.

'Out of the question,' I said. 'In the night our absence would be spotted.'

But we went all the same. Before leaving we hung on our saddles a present or two: a fur cloak, a live kid fifteen days old, a sugar-loaf.

The way led through a forest of wet trees shaken by the wind; a steely star wandered through the oak-leaves. In less than an hour we had reached the village. It was half burnt down, choked with lorries white with flour-dust, with gun-carriages and broken shafts.

Without dismounting I rapped on the familiar window; a white cloud passed across the bedroom. Elizabeth ran out on to the porch wearing the same old nightdress with its tired lace.

She took my hand in her warm palm and led me into the house. In the large room men's shirts were drying on the ravished lemon trees. Unknown men were sleeping in camp-beds lined up as in a hospital, exhibiting dirty feet, mouths fixed in a grimace. They were crying out hoarsely in their sleep, and their breathing, avid and noisy, filled the room.

The house was occupied by our Spoils Commission. The Tomilins had to make do with a single room.

'When will you take us away from here?' asked Elizabeth, holding my hand.

The old man, now awake, was waggling his head. Little Michael, pressing the kid to his chest, was laughing a happy, silent laugh. Surovtsev, who impressed him by his height, searched with a morose air in the pockets of his wide Cossack trousers, bringing to light spurs, coins with holes in the middle, a whistle fastened to a thick yellow lanyard.

In this house occupied by the Spoils Commission it was impossible to be alone. We had to seek refuge, Elizabeth and I, in the wooden shack where potatoes and bee-keeping equipment were stacked for the winter. Here, in this shack, I learned the full peril of the path we had first trodden when we kissed at the castle of the Princess Gonsiorowski.

Not long before dawn Surovtsev knocked on the door.

'When will you take us away?' breathed Elizabeth, turning her gaze aside.

I made no reply, and set out for the house to say good-bye to the old man.

Surovtsev barred my path.

'No time for that. Come on, get mounted.'

He pushed me into the street and led my horse up.

Elizabeth was still holding my hand, which had suddenly grown chill.

The horses, which had had a rest during the night, bore us off at a trot. A flaming sun was rising amid the black weft of the oaks. My whole being was filled with the triumphant joy of morning.

In the forest we came out on to a clearing. I let go the bridle, turned my head, and cried to Surovtsev:

'I could have stayed a while longer. You got us up too early.'

'You mustn't think that,' he replied, pushing the damp, gleaming branches aside. 'It was because of the old fellow; I might even have come earlier. He talked on and on, and got into quite a state. Suddenly damned if he didn't fall over sideways. I jumped over to him, and what did I see? Dead, he was, the old fellow . . . handed in his checks.'

We emerged from the forest and found ourselves in a ploughed field where no paths led. Surovtsev straightened up in the saddle, looked right and left, gave a whistle, sniffed for the right direction and breathed it in with the air; then he leaned forward and shot off at a gallop.

We got there just in time. The men of the squadron were beginning to stir. The sun was shining, announcing a hot day. A few hours later our brigade crossed the old frontier of the Kingdom of Poland.

Line and Colour

I MET Alexander Fyodorovich Kerensky for the first time on 20 December 1916 in the dining-room of the Olila Sanatorium.

We were introduced to one another by Zatzareny, the lawyer from Turkestan. All that I knew of Zatzareny was that he had had himself circumcised at the age of forty. The Grand Duke Nicholas Constantinovich, off his head, in disgrace and exiled to Tashkent, had made much of his friendship with the lawyer. This Grand Duke used to walk about the streets of Tashkent with his buttons undone. He had a Caucasian woman as wife; used to burn candles before the portrait of Voltaire as though it were an icon, and had arranged for an immense stretch of the Amur-Darya to be dried up. Zatzareny was his friend.

We were at the Olila, then. Ten kilometres away we could see the great blue lights of Helsingfors. O Helsingfors, dream of my heart! And thou, azure sky, dripping with light above the esplanade and losing thyself in the infinite!

So we were at the Olila. In vases flowers from the north were dying. Elk-horns blurred the sombre ceiling. The dining-room smelled of pine-trees, of the Countess Tyszkiewicz's fresh shoulders, and of the English officers' silk underwear.

At the table Kerensky was seated next to a converted Jew from the Police Department, an extremely polished individual. On his right Nikkelsen the Norwegian, owner of a whaler; close at hand the Countess Tyszkiewicz, beautiful as Marie Antoinette. When he had eaten three cakes, Kerensky rose and took me by the arm, and we went for a walk in the forest. *Fröken* Kirsti swept past us on skis.

'Who was that?' asked Alexander Fyodorovich.

'Nikkelsen's daughter Kirsti,' I told him. 'Good-looking, isn't she?'

Then old Johann drove past on his sledge.

'Who was that?'

'Old Johann,' I said. 'He carts fruit and brandy to Helsingfors. Is it possible you don't know Johann the sledge-driver?'

'I know everyone here,' replied Kerensky, 'but I can't distinguish one from t'other.'

'You're short-sighted, eh?'

'Quite so.'

'Alexander Fyodorovich, you ought to wear glasses.'

'Never!'

Then, bubbling over like a mere boy, I said to him:

'Just think: you're not merely blind, you're practically dead! Line, that divine trait, mistress of the world, eternally escapes you. Here we are, you and I, walking about in this magic garden, this Finnish forest that almost baffles description. All our lives we shall never see anything more beautiful.

And you can't see the pink edges of the frozen waterfall, over there by the stream! You are blind to the Japanese chiselling of the weeping willow leaning over the waterfall. The red trunks of the pines are covered by snow in which a thousand sparks are gleaming. The snow, shapeless when it fell, has draped itself along the branches, lying on their surfaces that undulate like a line drawn by Leonardo. In the snow flaming clouds are reflected. And think what you'd have to say about *Fröken* Kirsti's silk stockings; about the line of her leg, that lovely line! I beseech you, Alexander Fyodorovich, buy a pair of glasses!'

'My child,' he replied, 'don't waste your time. Forty copecks for spectacles are the only forty copecks I've no wish to squander. I don't need your line, vulgar as truth is vulgar. You live your life as though you were a teacher of trigonometry, while I for my part live in a world of miracles, even when I'm only at Klyazma. What do I need to see *Fröken* Kirsti's freckles for, if even when I can scarcely make her out I can see in her all I wish to see? What do I need Finnish clouds for, when above my head I see a moving ocean? What do I need line for, when I have colour? To me the whole universe is a gigantic theatre, and I am the only member of the audience who hasn't glued opera glasses to his eyes. The orchestra is playing the overture to the third act; the stage is far away, just as in a dream; my heart swells with ecstasy. I see Juliet's purple velvet, Romeo's lilac silk, and not a single false beard. And you want me to blind myself with forty-copeck spectacles!'

That evening I left for Helsingfors. O Helsingfors, refuge of my dreams!

Six months later I saw Alexander Fyodorovich once more; it was June 1917, and he was now supreme god of our armies and arbiter of our destinies.

That day the Troitsky bridge had been dismantled. The workers of the Putilov Factory were marching on the Arsenal.

Trams lay like dead horses in the streets. A rally had been called at the House of the People, and there Alexander Fyodorovich made a speech about Russia – Russia, mystic mother and spouse. The animal passion of the crowd stifled him. Could he, the only member of the audience without opera glasses, see how their hackles were rising? I do not know. But after him Trotsky climbed to the speaker's tribune, twisted his mouth, and in an implacable voice began:

'Comrades!'

Di Grasso

A TALE OF ODESSA

I WAS fourteen, and of the undauntable fellowship of dealers in theatre tickets. My boss was a tricky customer with a permanently screwed-up eye and enormous silky handlebars; Nick Schwarz was his name. I came under his sway in that unhappy year when the Italian Opera flopped in Odessa. Taking a lead from the critics on the local paper, our impresario decided not to import Anselmi and Tito Ruffo as guest artistes but to make do with a good stock company. For this he was sorely punished; he went bankrupt, and we with him. We were promised Chaliapin to straighten out our affairs, but Chaliapin wanted three thousand a performance; so instead we had the Sicilian tragedian Di Grasso with his troupe. They arrived at the hotel in peasant carts crammed with children, cats, cages in which Italian birds hopped and skipped. Casting an eye over this gypsy crew, Nick Schwarz opined:

'Children, this stuff won't sell.'

When he had settled in, the tragedian made his way to the market with a bag. In the evening he arrived at the theatre with another bag. Hardly fifty people had turned up.

We tried selling tickets at half-price, but there were no takers.

That evening they staged a Sicilian folk-drama, a tale as commonplace as the change from night to day and vice versa. The daughter of a rich peasant pledges her troth to a shepherd. She is faithful to him till one day there drives out from the city a young slicker in a velvet waistcoat. Passing the time of day with the new arrival, the maiden giggled in all the wrong places and fell silent when she shouldn't have. As he listened to them, the shepherd twisted his head this way and that like a startled bird. During the whole of the first act he kept flattening himself against walls, dashing off somewhere, his pants flapping, and on his return gazing wildly about.

'This stuff stinks,' said Nick Schwarz in the intermission. 'Only place it might go down is some dump like Kremen-chug.'

The intermission was designed to give the maiden time to grow ripe for betrayal. In the second act we just couldn't recognize her: she behaved insufferably, her thoughts were clearly elsewhere, and she lost no time in handing the shep-herd back his ring. Thereupon he led her over to a poverty-stricken but brightly painted image of the Holy Virgin, and said in his Sicilian patois:

'Signora,' said he in a low voice, turning away, 'the Holy Virgin desires you to give me a hearing. To Giovanni, the fellow from the city, the Holy Virgin will grant as many women as he can cope with; but I need none save you. The Virgin Mary, our stainless intercessor, will tell you exactly the same thing if you ask Her.'

The maiden stood with her back to the painted wooden image. As she listened she kept impatiently tapping her foot.

In the third act Giovanni, the city slicker, met his fate. He was having a shave at the village barber's, his powerful male legs thrust out all over the front of the stage. Beneath the

Sicilian sun the pleats in his waistcoat gleamed. The scene represented a village fair. In a far corner stood the shepherd; silent he stood there amid the carefree crowd. First he hung his head; then he raised it, and beneath the weight of his attentive and burning gaze Giovanni started stirring and fidgeting in his barber-chair, till pushing the barber aside he leaped to his feet. In a voice shaking with passion he demanded that the policeman should remove from the village square all persons of a gloomy and suspicious aspect. The shepherd – the part was played by Di Grasso himself – stood there lost in thought; then he gave a smile, soared into the air, sailed across the stage, plunged down on Giovanni's shoulders, and having bitten through the latter's throat, began, growling and squinting, to suck blood from the wound. Giovanni collapsed, and the curtain, falling noiselessly and full of menace, hid from us killed and killer. Waiting for no more, we dashed to the box office in Theatre Lane, which was to open next day, Nick Schwarz beating the rest by a short neck. Came the dawn, and with it the *Odessa News* informed the few people who had been at the theatre that they had seen the most remarkable actor of the century.

On this visit Di Grasso played *King Lear*, *Othello*, *Civil Death*, Turgenev's *The Parasite*, confirming with every word and every gesture that there is more justice in outbursts of noble passion than in all the joyless rules that run the world.

Tickets for these shows were snapped up at five times face value. Scouting round for ticket-traders, would-be purchasers found them at the inn, yelling their heads off, purple, vomiting a harmless sacrilege.

A pink and dusty sultriness was injected into Theatre Lane. Shopkeepers in felt slippers bore green bottles of wine and barrels of olives out on to the pavement. In tubs outside the shops macaroni seethed in foaming water, and the steam from it melted in the distant skies. Old women in men's boots dealt in seashells and souvenirs, pursuing hesitant purchasers with loud cries. Moneyed Jews with beards parted down the middle and combed to either side would drive up to the Northern Hotel and tap discreetly on the doors of fat women with raven hair and little moustaches, Di Grasso's actresses. All were happy in Theatre Lane; all, that is, save for one person. I was that person. In those days catastrophe was approaching me: at any moment my father might miss the watch I had taken without his permission and pawned to Nick Schwarz. Having had the gold turnip long enough to get used to it, and being a man who replaced tea as his morning drink by Bessarabian wine, Nick Schwarz, even with his money back, could still not bring himself to return the watch to me. Such was his character. And my father's character differed in no wise from his. Hemmed in by these two characters, I sorrowfully watched other people enjoying themselves. Nothing remained for me but to run away to Constantinople. I had made all the arrangements with the second engineer of the S.S. *Duke of Kent*, but before embarking on the deep I decided to say good-bye to Di Grasso. For the last time he was playing the shepherd who is swung aloft by an incomprehensible power. In the audience were all the Italian colony, with the bald but shapely consul at their head. There were fidgety Greeks and bearded externs with their gaze fastened fanatically upon some point invisible to all other mortals; there was the long-armed Utochkin. Nick Schwarz had even brought his missis, in a violet shawl with a fringe; a woman with all the makings of a grenadier she was, stretching right out to the steppes, and with a sleepy little crumpled face at the far end. When the curtain fell this face was drenched in tears.

'Now you see what love means,' she said to Nick as they were leaving the theatre.

Stomping ponderously, Madam Schwarz moved along Langeron Street; tears rolled from her fishlike eyes, and the shawl with the fringe shuddered on her obese shoulders.

Dragging her mannish soles, rocking her head, she reckoned up, in a voice that made the street re-echo, the women who got on well with their husbands.

'"Ducky" they're called by their husbands; "sweety-pie" they're called . . .'

The cowed Nick walked along by his wife, quietly blowing on his silky moustaches. From force of habit I followed on behind, sobbing. During a momentary pause Madam Schwarz heard my sobs and turned around.

'See here,' she said to her husband, her fish-eyes agoggle, 'may I not die a beautiful death if you don't give the boy his watch back!'

Nick froze, mouth agape; then came to and, giving me a vicious pinch, thrust the watch at me sideways.

'What can I expect of him,' the coarse and tear-muffled voice of Madam Schwarz wailed disconsolately as it moved off into the distance, 'what can I expect but beastliness today and beastliness tomorrow? I ask you, how long is a woman supposed to put up with it?'

They reached the corner and turned into Pushkin Street. I stood there clutching the watch, alone; and suddenly, with a distinctness such as I had never before experienced, I saw the columns of the Municipal Building soaring up into the heights, the gas-lit foliage of the boulevard, Pushkin's bronze head touched by the dim gleam of the moon; saw for the first time the things surrounding me as they really were: frozen in silence and ineffably beautiful.

MORE ABOUT PENGUINS
AND PELICANS

For further information about books available from Penguins please write to Dept EP, Penguin Books Ltd, Harmondsworth, Middlesex UB7 0DA.

In the U.S.A.: For a complete list of books available from Penguins in the United States write to Dept CS, Penguin Books, 625 Madison Avenue, New York, New York 10022.

In Canada: For a complete list of books available from Penguins in Canada write to Penguin Books Canada Ltd, 2801 John Street, Markham, Ontario L3R 1B4

In Australia: For a complete list of books available from Penguins in Australia write to the Marketing Department, Penguin Books Australia Ltd, P.O. Box 257, Ringwood, Victoria 3134.

In New Zealand: For a complete list of books available from Penguins in New Zealand write to the Marketing Department, Penguin Books (N.Z.) Ltd, P.O. Box 4019, Auckland 10.